Kentucky
CHANCES

Kentucky
CHANCES

Three Brothers
Find Romance
Far from Home

Cathy Marie
HAKE

Kelly Eileen
HAKE

BARBOUR
PUBLISHING

Last Chance © 2005 by Cathy Marie Hake
Chance Adventure © 2005 by Kelly Eileen Hake
Chance of a Lifetime © 2005 by Kelly Eileen Hake

ISBN 978-1-59789-366-4

Cover image by Stephen Simpson/Getty Images

All scripture quotations are taken from the King James Version of the Bible.

This book is a work of fiction. Names, characters, places, and incidents are either products of the author's imagination or used fictitiously. Any similarity to actual people, organizations, and/or events is purely coincidental.

The herbs mentioned in this piece were carefully researched and authentic to the era. Some have since been found to be questionable or even dangerous. In no way does the author advocate the use of any herb, medication, or curative without checking first with your medical doctor.

Published by Barbour Publishing, Inc., P.O. Box 719, Uhrichsville, Ohio 44683, www.barbourbooks.com

Our mission is to publish and distribute inspirational products offering exceptional value and biblical encouragement to the masses.

ecpa Member of the
Evangelical Christian
Publishers Association

Printed in the United States of America.

Last Chance

by Cathy Marie Hake

Chapter 1

Salt Lick Holler, Kentucky, June 1872

I cain't have it. No, I cain't." Silk Trevor stood on the rickety porch of her shack and hung on to either side of the doorsill like a crawdad with juicy bait in both pincers. "You go on ahead and leave my kin here."

Lovejoy Spencer set down her battered canvas valise and carefully unhinged the troublesome brass clasp. She'd expected Silk to kick up a fuss. The strap securing her dulcimer to her back slashed taut across her bosom as she crouched, but the real tightness in her chest came from thinking the whole arrangement might fall apart if Silk didn't cooperate. Drawing a jar from the valise, Lovejoy whispered, "Lord, have mercy and let this work."

After rising and taking a step closer, she held out her offering. "Blackberry jam, Miz Silk—my special recipe. I reckon it'll take away a wee bit of the bitterness of the day. Each time you spread a dab on that delicious bread of yourn, you cain think on how you've sent yore nieces off to a better life."

Silk's tears miraculously stopped. Her eyes narrowed. "You think a half-pint's all the both of them are worth?"

"All the gold in heaven wouldn't begin to buy such fine young gals," Lovejoy responded without hesitation. "Fact is, I'm not buying them. Jesus ransomed their souls from Lucifer."

"Glory be!" Silk let go of the doorjamb and lifted her hands in praise.

"And there's not a body in all of Salt Lick Holler who doesn't know you've done right by Eunice and Lois. The MacPhersons from up at Hawk's Fall remembered them and honored your family by sending a bridal offer."

Tempy stepped up and nodded. "My sister's right, Miz Silk. Why, everyone here in Salt Lick and folks clear up at Hawk's Fall are all going to ponder on what a wondrous thing you did, rearing Eunice and Lois so the MacPhersons kept pining after them even after moving clear across the country."

It took considerable effort for Lovejoy to keep from flashing her baby sister a smile. At eighteen, Tempy was smart as a whip. If she tried, the girl could likely charm a snake into a knot. From the way Silk perked up, Lovejoy knew her sister had hit the right note.

She chimed in, "Abner MacPherson set all of Salt Lick into a dither when he rode over from Hawk's Fall to deliver the greenbacks. His boys have been sending money home regular-like and still had enough to buy not one, but three train tickets. Bucks like them could snap up any woman, but they picked your nieces."

"Now it's a fact, they did," Silk granted.

"That's sayin' plenty," Lovejoy continued. "They're bright young women, and you've always done what's best for them."

Silk let out a woebegone sigh. "You truly aim to go along, Lovejoy Spencer? I don't want my girls out in that wild world on their own."

"I give you my word. I'll travel the whole way. They'll be married right and tight to good men who'll provide well for them."

Silk nodded. "I reckon that's the best a body could hope for." The minute she plodded out of the doorway, Eunice and Lois hustled out with a trunk betwixt themselves. Pa didn't get down from the buckboard to help, but no one really expected him to. Lovejoy and Tempy helped hoist the trunk onto the wagon bed; then hugs, kisses, and the blackberry jam were traded. They all piled on, and Pa drove them to the pass.

Not a yard went by that Lovejoy didn't study with a mixture of sadness and joy. Spring brought a bounty of healing yarbs. As a healer, Lovejoy knew a wealth of uses for each plant. Smelly as they were, the wild leeks they called ramps could cure many a complaint. Coltsfoot, teaberry, burdock—each belonged in her healing arsenal. Gathering as much as she could of those and dozens upon dozens of other plants in these last few weeks, Lovejoy hoped she'd stored up enough for when she returned.

And she would return to the raw beauty of Kentucky. But she'd be leaving her beloved baby sister clear off in Californy. *'Tis a good life a-waitin' her. I'll dwell on that thought.*

The train wasn't supposed to stop at the pass. Then again, once a week Pa just happened to be sitting there waiting. He'd hand up jugs of moonshine, empty jugs got passed back down, and he'd leave with a smile and a pocketful of cash money.

Last week he'd arranged for the girls to ride clear across these United States to San Francisco, then for the stage ride to Reliable where the MacPhersons lived. He'd groused at the cost as if he'd paid for the tickets himself. When Lovejoy announced she was going as a chaperone, he flatly refused to pay for her.

She'd not given in, though.

Her baby sister was about to be a bride. So were Eunice and Lois. The MacPherson brothers had written a letter asking the three gals to come out and do them the honor of becoming their wives. Truth was, Lovejoy determined to go along regardless of the cost. These young gals weren't going to marry up with the MacPhersons unless the men passed her muster.

She'd been bound in a marriage that brought nothing but misery. Long as she drew breath, she refused to let Tempy—or any gal—get roped into matrimony if all it would become was a noose.

Being a widow woman of the ripe age of four-and-twenty, Lovejoy didn't answer to any man. Added to that, she owned a small place and was a trained granny-woman. Folks came to her for all sorts of other healing, too. Chickens, cheese, a bottle of molasses—her patients paid however and whatever they could afford. Hardscrabble as they lived, it amounted to precious little. That being the case, the notion that Tempy, Eunice, and Lois might have a better life out in Californy made Lovejoy pry up the floorboard and pull out the precious stash of coins she kept in a coffee can for a rainy day.

Stooped with age, Widow Hendricks reckoned she'd be able to fill in for a season as the healer—seein' as that season would be warm and dry. With the dear Lord providing enough money for Lovejoy to make the trip and someone to tend the folks back home, she felt certain it was His will for her to go.

When Pa realized he'd not stop her, he'd gone off and gotten roostered on his own 'shine. Years ago, Lovejoy had Tempy move in with her, and Pa had a habit of showing up at suppertime more often than not. His other daughters—married and up to their hips in young'uns—never had a place for him at their tables. Lovejoy's only rule was that she wouldn't open her door to him if he was drunk. He'd shown up that night reeking of the devil's brew and making wild threats. If anything, that only strengthened her resolve. Lovejoy wanted her sister away from this.

Now at the pass, Pa jerked the trunk and satchels off the wagon—more out of the need to reach his moonshine than to be a gentleman. He lined up the jugs and helped himself to a stiff belt of who-hit-John from the flask he habitually carried. "You oughtn't tag along," he said to Lovejoy.

Her stomach roiled when she caught a whiff of his fetid breath. She dug in her heels. "Mama put Tempy under my wing back on the day she was born."

"Your ma woulda done better to give me sons 'stead of a passel of girls." He took another swig.

"I know you loved her in your own way, Pa. God rest her soul, Mama loved you back." Mama had turned a blind eye to Pa's still because it was the only way they could put food on the table. By the time Lovejoy was sixteen, Pa married her off to Vern Spencer. Jug-bit men did foolish things, and both Pa and Vern did their share of drinking. Lovejoy still believed Pa was a good man when he wasn't drinking; just two days after Vern took her to wife, she knew she couldn't say the same for him. The four years of marriage that followed felt like forty.

The metal rail by Lovejoy's toe started to vibrate. "Train'll be here in a minute."

Pa nodded. The train always moved slowly through the winding hills and hollers, so stopping wasn't all that difficult. Once it came to a standstill, he held the gals back. "First things first." He took care of his illegal business transaction, then let them board the train. He wiped a tear from his weathered cheek after he gave Tempy a bear hug and lifted her onto the train steps. Lovejoy stepped forward, stood on tiptoe, and gave him a kiss, too.

"You really goin' through with this foolish plan of yourn?" he whispered gruffly.

"I've gotta, Pa."

"Then go." He crammed real paper money into her hand and shoved her onto the train.

Chance Ranch, Reliable, California

"Pretty as a princess," Daniel Chance recited as he pulled his comb through little Polly's hair. "Your mama was pretty as can be. Hair as soft and light as a moonbeam."

"Just like mine," his daughter said gleefully.

Polly never tired of hearing about her mama, and Dan wanted his daughters to grow up knowing what an extraordinary woman she'd been. It was part of their morning ritual, and it gave Daniel an opportunity to cherish his memories and pass them along. Just after the birth of their second daughter, Hannah passed on and took most of his heart with her. What little was left, he devoted entirely to his daughters.

Daniel continued to comb the waves left by her nighttime braids. One of his sisters-in-law would plait Polly's hair after breakfast. His big hands were made for chopping wood and branding cattle—not for braiding cornsilk-fine hair on a wiggly four-year-old.

"Mama in heben." Two-year-old Ginny Mae curled her toes on the cold floor and leaned into him for warmth.

"Yes. Mama's in heaven." Dan strove to keep his tone even. "Polly, go get your shoes and socks. Bring Ginny's, too."

Polly scampered through the "hall" to the adjoining cabin. The Chance brothers had connected the two cabins so Daniel would have sufficient space. He'd refused to move out of the little cabin he and his beloved Hannah shared, but it grew far too cramped with the girls' bed. They didn't have enough room to turn around without tripping over something or bumping into each other. The girls' cabin boasted a loft and a bit more room, but more important, it had a potbellied stove so it stayed warmer.

Daniel pulled Ginny Mae onto his lap and warmed her tiny feet in his hands. "Piggy, Daddy!"

"This little piggy went to market. . . ."

Polly came back carrying Ginny's shoes and one sock and wearing her own shoes on the wrong feet. "Sissy gots only one sock, Daddy. I can't find the other one."

Daniel grimaced. Ginny had had an accident last evening, and he'd intended to wash out the wet sock. Somehow he'd gotten distracted. "She'll wear one today."

Polly fidgeted as he slipped the sock and first shoe on her sister. Suddenly, she pointed at Ginny Mae's feet and sing-songed, "Diddle, diddle dumplin', my son John, went to bed with his trousers on."

"I a girl," Ginny protested. "I no wear tr'srs."

"One shoe off and one shoe on," Polly sang louder.

"She has both shoes on now." Daniel stood and set her down. He took a moment to make his bed—not because he thought it important, but if he didn't, Miriam, Alisa, or Delilah would do it. He didn't want his sisters-in-law doing more on his behalf. They already did his laundry, stitched his girls' sweet little dresses, and minded his daughters. Much as he hated being beholden to them, he had no choice.

Besides, making the bed killed a few more minutes. He didn't like showing up to breakfast until it was on the table. Though he didn't begrudge his brothers their happy marriages, it hurt something fierce to stand by and watch them and their wives radiating early morning contentment. To their credit, they'd not pushed him to remarry, and they put up with his curt ways. Dan did his best to shield his daughters from his grief, but it took everything he had to do just that. Fortunately, the girls' aunts and uncles stepped in and doted on them to help fill in the empty spaces in their young hearts and lives. As soon as he wolfed down his breakfast and kissed his daughters, he could escape for the day. No matter how hard the work, though, he never managed to escape the soul-deep emptiness that plagued him since Hannah went to the hereafter.

$\infty\sim\sim\infty$

"No need to waste good cash money on hiring a ride," Lovejoy Spencer said to her charges. "We'll walk. It's only seven miles or so."

"But we have our belongings!"

Lovejoy gave Eunice a pat. "I know you're a tad weary. Think on how each step's a-takin' you closer to your intended. That ought to make the load light."

Lois elbowed her sister. "She don't know how much you stuffed in your half of the trunk."

"We need to get directions." Tempy gawked up and down the busy street.

"Easy as fallin' off a log. Never seen so many folks in one place." Lovejoy looked about Reliable and silently compared it to Salt Lick Holler. White's Mercantile looked pert near as fancy as any big city store, and though it was Wednesday, the men all wore their Sunday-go-to-meetin' best.

It would take more than fancy duds to win Lovejoy's approval, though. She was far more concerned with whether the MacPhersons would be steady men and cherish the gals. "We'll get started right quick. I ken yore all eager to meet yore men."

Eunice quavered, "I brought every last thing I own."

Lovejoy smiled at her. "No shame in you bringing along your treasures to turn the house into a home. Now that I think on it, your trunk's right heavy. Mayhap the storekeeper'll know of someone headin' our way."

"It occurs to me, as many strapping men as there are hereabouts"—Lois flashed a smile and waved at a pair of men by the saloon's hitching post—"if things don't work out with the MacPhersons, I'll still be able to find me a husband."

"Last thing you need is a man who likes his likker." Lovejoy scowled at the men, but to her dismay, they weren't discouraged. They ambled across the road and doffed their hats.

"Good day, ladies." The smooth talker flashed them a smile that would do any snake oil salesman proud. "What a wonder it is to find such a bevy of beauties here in our fair town."

"Nice of you to swap howdies with us, but we're here to meet up with the MacPhersons." Lovejoy stepped forward and sensed Tempy at her side. Between the two of them, they shoved Eunice and Lois behind them. They'd perfected this move by now after five days of travel.

"The MacPhersons?" One of the men hooked his thumbs in his suspenders and craned his neck so he could catch a better view of Lois and Eunice's flame-haired beauty. "My, my. We didn't put much store in their boasts that they had brides coming."

Tempy bristled. "Mike MacPherson's no flannel-mouthed liar!"

"Don't get your back up, miss. He was just making conversation." The first one flashed Tempy that same smile again.

Lovejoy took exception to how he spoke to her sister. Before she could say a thing, the other tacked on, "It's always a pleasure to have available women arrive."

Lovejoy pressed her hand to her bosom and used the other hand to shove Tempy behind herself with the others. "Sir, I'll have you know these are not 'available women.' They're ladies, and they're already bespoken."

"Least they're not getting snapped up by the Chance brothers this time," another man said as he moseyed up.

"We're due at the MacPhersons'." Lovejoy scanned the rapidly growing semicircle of men.

Several men volunteered to take them, but they all seemed too willing. Lovejoy was about to announce they'd walk when a woman came out of the mercantile. She called, "Todd Dorsey's at the blacksmith's. He's the MacPhersons' nearest neighbor. I've sent my husband to fetch Mr. Dorsey. You gals come on in here to wait."

"Much obliged, ma'am." Lovejoy shepherded the girls to safety and knew she'd met an ally when the woman blocked the mercantile door.

"You men get back to your own business. I won't have you pestering these women." She shut the door and turned. "I'm Reba White."

Lovejoy introduced her charges and repeated, "Much obliged to you, ma'am. That was quite a pack of curly wolves."

"I promised the MacPhersons and Chances that I'd keep an eye out for you." Reba grinned. "They didn't have to ask. I can't tell you how delighted I am to have a few more good, God-fearing women moving to Reliable."

They didn't have to wait long at the mercantile. Good thing, that. Tempy and Eunice started mooning over every last wondrous, new-fangled thing in the place. Lois satisfied herself by standing at the specialty display case, choosing her favorite wedding band from the three shown there alongside fancy gold pocket watches. Mr. Dorsey loaded the trunk and their satchels on the wagon, and then they all clambered aboard.

About a mile down the road, Mr. Dorsey cleared his throat. "If you all don't mind me stopping off at my place, I can drive you the rest of the way tomorrow."

"It's a mighty fine offer, but we're expected." Tempy smoothed her skirts. "Helping us out even partway was right neighborly of you."

Awhile later, as they stood on the dusty road and waved good-bye to Mr. Dorsey, Lois said, "He's got mean, beady eyes. I didn't trust him a lick. Good thing you said we wouldn't go home with him!"

"Mrs. White back at the store spoke highly of him." Lovejoy looked at the other fork in the road. "Best we jump to what lies ahead rather than waste time judging what's past."

Another mile down the road, Eunice set down her end of the trunk and wailed, "I cain't do this. It's too heavy."

Dust swirled as Lois dropped her end and plopped down on the trunk. "She's right." Her brow puckered. "If'n the MacPhersons are expectin' us, why didn't they fetch us?"

"I told the truth. They are expecting us. I just didn't say when." Tempy fanned herself.

"Men cain't very well stop everything and go to town each day—leastways, not hardworking ones." Lovejoy stared at the trunk. "This is a genuine opportunity. We'll show them you're just as tireless."

❦

"There!" Lovejoy stood back about half an hour later and surveyed their creation. They'd lashed hickory broomsticks to the ends of the trunk with a length of clothesline rope. "Why, it's just like how they carried the ark of the covenant in the Old Testament."

"I hope it looked better than this," Lois muttered.

Lovejoy started to laugh. "Sure and enough, it did. After all, our rods are sideways."

"Hope the cherubims don't take offense." Tempy giggled. She pointed to the satchels and valises piled atop the trunk. "The angels' wings are supposed to meet over the ark. That baggage looks more like gargoyles."

"What're gargles?" Eunice scratched her elbow.

"Gargoyles are funny-looking stone critters on old, old churches," Tempy explained patiently.

Lovejoy felt a spurt of pleasure at her sister's book learning. Tempy was better educated than any other woman in Salt Lick. That wasn't saying much, but at moments like this, when Tempy shared her knowledge, Lovejoy knew the sacrifices she'd made on her baby sister's behalf were worth it all.

"So gargoyles are sorta like those dog-ugly wooden owls Otis Nye keeps a-carvin' and setting up on his barn?"

"I never thought of them that way, but you got the drift of it." Tempy looked at Lovejoy. "Reckon we ought to pick this up and step lively."

Each of them took hold of the hickory broom handles and hefted. "Let's sing so we step in time," Lovejoy suggested. She thought for a moment then started in, "We're marching to Zion, beautiful, beautiful Zion. . . ."

The sun had set, and she'd begun to worry that they'd made the wrong decision about which fork to take a mile ago when she spied a group of buildings ahead. "Pony up, gals. The chimney's smokin', and yonder's your future."

The tempo of the hymn and their footsteps picked up. Just as they drew even with the first building, a huge bear of a man stepped from the shadow and blocked their path. "This isn't Zion, so you can just turn around and march the other way."

Chapter 2

The short, brown-haired gal closest to him laughed.

Daniel glowered at her.

"Now there speaks a man in sore want of his supper." Merriment rang in her voice. Even in the twilight, her hazel eyes sparkled. As she spoke, she somehow managed to ease something into his hand. A stick.

"If you tell us where to go, we'll be happy to put together something that'll fill your belly."

The stick was attached to an odd affair and carried considerable weight. How a scrap of a woman managed to carry it was beyond him, but Daniel refused to be sidetracked. "Ma'am, I already told you where to go—turn around and march the other way. You'd best be quick about it. It's going dark."

"He's 'bout as friendly as a riled porcupine."

"I'm fixin' to tell my intended to turn him loose and let him find labor elsewhere."

The spunky one up front cut in, "Gals, be charitable. He's probably worked long and hard today." She tried to take the stick back from him.

Daniel refused to let go.

"You cain turn loose now, mister. I brung hale gals. They mebbe tired, but you'll see they don't quail at totin' a fair load."

"Daniel!" Gideon called from a ways off. "Who are you talking to?"

In the slim minutes since he'd met the troop of women, the sky had darkened significantly. Daniel hated admitting defeat, but he couldn't send four defenseless women into the night. "Don't know who they are."

"That other feller don't sound like he's from back home," one of the redheads in the back whispered.

"I'm Lovejoy Spencer, mister. These gals are under my wing. I'm to deliver them to the MacPhersons." She stared up into his eyes and tacked on, "And I'm figurin' we shoulda veered t'other direction back at the road's bend."

"Give me this." He tugged her out of the way and hefted the entire load onto his back. "Gideon, the mail-order brides got turned around. I'm walking them over to the MacPhersons'."

"Way too late for that. Ladies, come on in. The women are setting supper on the table."

"We don't want to be a bother."

Daniel snorted. "Miss Spencer, it's the nature of women to do just that."

15

"Pardon Daniel. He's always surly. I'm Gideon Chance."

To Daniel's relief, his brother assumed half the burden. *How were those scrawny little women hauling this?* "We can take this on over to the barn and—"

"The main house," Gideon interrupted. "Ladies, you'd do well to follow along behind us." He raised his voice and called to his wife, "Miriam!"

Daniel didn't move. He squinted at Lovejoy and the woman standing by her side. "The bows and quivers aren't going inside."

"Bows and—oh! 'Tisn't that a'tall. Mine is a dulcimer, and Tempy's toting a mandolin."

"Wonderful," Gideon said as he started walking so Dan had to move to keep from dumping the trunk. "Perhaps you could grace us with a tune or two after supper."

Once they got inside the main house, Dan set down his end of the trunk and turned to get a better look at the women. Miriam and Delilah were making a big fuss over them. The redheads and the one with a mandolin across her back all jostled about the washstand. Lovejoy knelt on the floor on the far side of the table. She had her head tilted to the side and an arm about Polly's shoulders, while gently dabbing at his daughter's runny nose.

"Polly. Ginny Mae." He clapped his hands. "Come to Daddy."

Lovejoy released Polly and nimbly gained her feet. "The Lord shorely blessed you with such lassies, Mr. Chance."

He nodded curtly.

"There are only three MacPhersons; I'm countin' four women." Bryce bit his lip and stared at the gals.

"I'm a widow woman. Came 'long to be sure the girls would be happy. Then I'm a-goin' back home. I'm Lovejoy Spencer. This here's my baby sister, Temperance." She then gestured toward the two gals whose hair matched the color of a terra-cotta flowerpot. "Eunice and Lois are our neighbors from back home."

Gideon introduced the Chance clan. These gals from the backwoods would probably remember how to tell apart Miriam, Delilah, and Alisa because they were respectively blond, black haired, and in the motherly way. Daniel figured it was an exercise in futility when it came to the strangers recalling his brothers' names.

"You've met Daniel," Gideon yammered on. "Paul is Delilah's husband. Titus is married to Alisa. Logan and Bryce are the young ones."

While folks exchanged pleasantries and carried food to the matched pair of tables, Daniel got waylaid by Ginny Mae for a few minutes. Both of his daughters acted a mite cranky, but with all the hoopla, he wasn't too surprised.

Logan elbowed his way to the table and sat between the redheaded sisters. "Parson Abe preached about Eunice and Lois a few months back. They were in the Bible, you know."

Alisa passed the corn to Lovejoy. "I've never heard of anyone bearing your name before."

Lovejoy hitched her shoulder. "Ma named us girls all after the fruits of the Spirit. After me, she decided she'd best slow down and limit herself to one apiece, 'cept she skipped over longsuffering because 'twas a vicious mean handle to slap on a dab of a babe."

"You have a sister named Gentleness?" Alisa couldn't mask her surprise.

"Yes'm," Temperance answered. "Call her Nessie. Goodness—well, since we couldn't right well have us two Nessies, we call her Goody."

"Peace died of the whooping cough," Eunice said.

Chiming right in, Lois said, "And then their Ma skipped over using Meekness and gave Tempy her name 'cuz she was a-prayin' her man would stop brewing moonshine."

The room suddenly went silent. Ginny coughed, Daniel patted her on the back, then Tempy acted as if nothing had been said amiss. "Lovejoy's a healer back home. If comfort were one of the fruits of the spirit, Mama should have given that name to Lovejoy."

Dan didn't care much about the conversation. He had other things on his mind, but from what he saw, Comfort would have been an apt name for the young widow sitting beside him. She'd been soothing Polly from the minute she arrived. Once he shoveled in his own meal and managed to get Ginny Mae to have a few slurps of soup, he begged off any further social obligation and took the girls back to their cabin.

❦

"Ain't niver seen a place so extraordinary as this here ranch," Lois said as they got ready for bed.

"I'm liable to pinch myself black and blue," her sister said. "Do you imagine our beaux will have such a fine spread?"

"They haven't been here long enough." Tempy's voice sounded muffled as she squirmed into her flannel nightdress.

"It's not just what they have right now; you have to imagine what a place you'll be able to carve out with your men as your years unfold," Lovejoy said as she plaited her hair.

"I cain scarce believe this." Lois climbed into a bed and scooted over to make room for her sister. "Above-the-ground beds—and just two of us in each!"

"Cain you fathom it—this whole cabin is just for them two younger boys. They each got a bed to themselves." Eunice crept in by Lois and thumped the pillow. "I'm thinkin' we could match 'em up with Uncle Asa's girls."

"Hold your horses." Lovejoy looked at her three charges. "Nothing's for certain yet—not for any of you. 'Til I'm positive those MacPherson boys are good husband material, no one's hot footin' it to the altar. Worldly goods don't count for much when a woman's heart is achin' from being hitched to a bad 'un."

"Don't worry for me, Lovey." Tempy buttoned her gown. "Whilst you tended Mike's mama in her last days, I got to know him. A better man I'll never find. Not a doubt tarries in my mind 'bout him and me being happy together."

"We recollect Obadiah and Hezekiah from when they come to buy their hound." Lois yawned. "They stayed to supper."

"The hounds stayed, or the men?" Tempy teased.

They all laughed. Tempy gave Lovejoy a hug and whispered, "Don't worry, Sis. It won't be like you and Vern."

Lovejoy's breath caught. She gave her sister a big squeeze and pulled away. She didn't discuss her marriage. Ever. "Guess I'd best blow out the lantern. Say your prayers and sleep well."

Exhausted from travel and toting that trunk, the others fell asleep almost at once. Lovejoy couldn't—not after having heard Vern's name. The memory of the children he fathered with two other women haunted her even years after he'd died. *Lord above, when will his betrayal stop hurtin'?*

⤜⤏⤛⤏⤜

Before morning broke, Lovejoy slipped out of bed. She dressed and tucked a knife in her leather sheath before grabbing a gunnysack and shimmying out the door. Purply blue with a mere glimmer of fading moonlight, the sky held the moisture of dew and the squawks of scrappy jaybirds. She took a deep breath of crisp air then let it out and set to walking.

"'Morning, Lord. Thou hast outdone Thyself here. Cain't say as I expected it. Home was beautiful, but here—well, it just seems more green than gritty."

She took out her knife and started to identify plants and harvest leaves, bark, and roots. Back inside that dandy little cabin, her healin' satchel held some of the things she used most often, but it would be wise to start Tempy off with a supply of her own. More important, those wee lassies in the cabin next door coughed during the night. They'd been on the fractious side at supper last evening, too. Might as well put together a few things for this household while she was at it.

She hoped and prayed the Chances were right about the MacPhersons. They all spoke well of the bachelors 'round the table last night. Why, if Obie, Hezzy, and Mike turned out half as favorable as they sounded, her charges were trading up to a far better life than they would have had back in Salt Lick Holler.

Fine folks, these Chances. They'd make for good neighbors. The three married brothers and their wives billed and cooed like turtledoves when they didn't think a body was a-watching, and the two youngest lads were right cute saplings. Too bad about that widow man Daniel. He's got hisself two darlin' little daughters, but he's grouchier than an early-woke springtime bear.

⤜⤏⤛⤏⤜

Daniel tossed off the blanket and sat on the edge of his bed. His stomach growled. The last thing he wanted was to go to breakfast, because those women would be there. His brothers and their wives never expected him to make much conversation—especially first thing in the morning. Their uninvited guests wouldn't know better.

Those three young hillbilly women chattered nineteen to the dozen last night. At least Lovejoy Spencer hadn't bothered him much. Instead, she'd held Polly on her lap and gently coaxed her to get through supper. He'd done his best to stay civil through the meal, and he'd done fairly well to his way of thinking. Coming back to the house right after eating was supposed to be an escape. He didn't feel like getting trapped into conversation, and the girls needed to go to bed. Nonetheless, he'd heard the music from the house and known the bitter tang of loneliness.

Coughs sounded from his daughters' cabin. They were both out of sorts last night. He wouldn't be surprised if they caught colds. Taking them on over to Miriam and asking her for some elixir would be wise.

He stood, stretched, and yanked on his clothes. His first inclination was to pad over in his bare feet, but since he'd take the girls to the main house, he might as well lace on his boots. Both socks on and the first boot laced, he couldn't stand it anymore. His baby girls were starting to sound downright croupy. Dan opened the door to the "hallway" and felt a flare of relief that the doors existed. Normally, he left them wide open so he could hear the girls, but he'd shut them last night to keep the stove's precious heat from escaping.

Five quick, lopsided strides to the girls. Diddle, diddle dumplin', my son John. . . How did that go? He forgot what Polly said next, but "one shoe off and one shoe on" rang in his mind. She'd be tickled at seeing him like this. Might make her perk up.

Polly's clear, high voice carried through the door, "Ginny, put your hand on your mouth when you cough. Do it like this."

Dan grinned as he opened the door. Polly was a bossy little bit of goods, but she did a nice job of trying to teach her sister things. His smile faded immediately.

"What are you doing here?"

Chapter 3

Lovejoy Spencer stood by the dresser with clippings that amounted to half the forest piled all over the top of the oak piece. Swirling a pie tin over the glass chimney of a kerosene lantern, she said matter-of-factly, "Your lassies are a-barking. Figured they could use an elixir to soothe their throats and loosen up the phlegm."

"Miriam keeps medicaments at the main house."

"I imagine she does. Problem is, the few a body cain get from the mercantile that actually are healthful pack a far too powerful kick for wee ones. Most of 'em are worthless and are little more than likker."

She hadn't said a thing he could disagree with. As she spoke, she rotated her wrist in such a way as to keep the liquid in the pie pan whirlpooling. A surprisingly pleasant aroma emanated from the affair. Even so, that didn't prove that she had any idea of what she was doing.

"The wrong plant can cause harm. I don't want my daughters to—"

"Right you are. But I've had me plenty of training and experience. I'm a granny-woman. I don't mean to sound puffed up, but I do have a knack with yarbs and such."

Yarbs? That did it. Daniel decided he wasn't going to trust his precious children to this backwoods woman.

"Neither of them's runnin' a fever, so I didn't add in willow bark. You've got gracious plenty out there, but seein' as how it's bitter, I'm just as glad not to add it in."

Everyone knows willow bark works for fevers and tastes bitter. It's going to take far more than that to convince me—

"But God be praised, it bein' summer, elderberries are ripe. I clumb up and got a wee bit of honeycomb, and out in your verra own garden, I found a hip on your dog rose. Fancy that, will ya? Don't normally find them till autumn's on the way. God provides, I say. We'll have your girls feelin' tiptop by the time they sit down to breakfast."

"I'll have Miriam give them what they need."

Just then, Ginny Mae let out a brace of coughs.

Lovejoy looked down at her with compassion, but Daniel refused to let his heart soften. His babies' safety rated far above this strange woman's feelings. "Come here, Ginny."

She poked out her bottom lip. "I want juice."

To his surprise, Lovejoy petted Ginny's hair a single stroke then gave her a gentle nudge. "Honor your father. Obey him. He loves you."

He lifted Ginny and tried to ignore how Lovejoy blew out the lantern and put down the pie tin. Wordlessly, she swiped all the leaves, berries, and twigs into a burlap bag. He hadn't meant to hurt her feelings, but she shouldn't have stuck her nose in where she wasn't invited.

"Daddy, the lady fried Sissy's socks on the stove."

A flush of embarrassment heated his neck. He'd forgotten to wash that sock again last night. Here it was, clean, dry, and fresh smelling on his daughter's leg. Her little shoes were tied, and the girls' bed was made up smart as a one-buck hotel's with the blankets all snug, then the sheet folded fancylike to peep over the top with something on each pillow to finish the effect.

"We'd better get on over to breakfast." He snagged Polly as she scampered past.

"I wanna take my mouse."

"Mouse?" He looked about. Vermin did manage to get in on occasion, but borrowing Delilah's Shortstack always worked. For being a little gimpy, that cat still knew her job and took it seriously.

"Miss Lovejoy made my mouse." Polly wiggled from his grasp. "See?" She pulled the little decoration off the pillow and galloped back over. A scrap of light brown cloth in her hand was knotted and twisted to form a creditable-looking mouse.

"I gots babies in a blanket, Daddy." Ginny pointed to the blue scrap on her pillow.

A draft swept across the room, then the door shut. Daniel stared at the far wall. Lovejoy Spencer had tried to do nice things for his girls, but he'd just put an end to that by rejecting her efforts. He didn't want her to be prying into his business or inviting herself.

⌒◟∼◞⌒

Tryin' to do right ain't the same as doin' right. Widow Hendricks's words echoed in Lovejoy's mind as she stashed her gathering bag into the cabin. She'd wanted to help, but she'd overstepped. Daniel Chance was a good father, and he protected his daughters. Stumbling into a stranger first thing in the morning was good cause for him to be wary. Too bad, though. The lassies needed something for their coughs.

Tempy lifted her head from the pillow. "You trying to beat the rooster on coaxing the sun up?"

"There's no time like dawn to take a bit of a walk. It's good for the soul to spend time appreciatin' what God made and gave. You gals hop to. Don't take too long sprucin' up, because these folks could be chasing me for the rooster's job." She left them and headed for the main house, sure she could lend a hand there.

Miriam answered her knock. "Good morning."

Before Lovejoy could respond, the door on the nearest cabin banged open.

Delilah dashed out and around the corner.

"What was that all about?" Miriam wondered aloud.

"Don't rightly know." Lovejoy held a suspicion, but it wasn't for her to voice such a thing.

Miriam's brows furrowed. "I wonder. . . ." Her voice dropped to a mere whisper. "You'd be able to tell, wouldn't you? Eunice said you're a midwife."

Lovejoy avoided the topic. "Menfolk are gonna be hungry. I'm happy to holp make breakfast." She walked into the house, went over to the stove, and stoked it. Her first order of business was to start two big pots of coffee while Miriam began to mix up a batch of biscuits.

Bryce toted in a big basket of eggs.

"Now looky there! You must have plenty of fine layin' hens to have so many eggs."

"Got us five dozen," he declared proudly.

"And he's named every last one," Logan tacked on as he brought in a brimming milk can. Daniel and the girls followed in right after him.

Lovejoy started cracking eggs into a big, green-striped earthenware bowl. "You men eat one egg or two at breakfast?"

"Four apiece, ma'am."

Shocked at his answer, she smashed the egg on the bowl's rim and felt the goo rush out over her fingers. "Four?"

"Well, the gals don't eat that much," Logan mused.

"Miriam?" Gideon sauntered out of the bedroom with a baby on his shoulder. "Caleb's got a rash."

Lovejoy wiped her hands on a dishcloth. "What kind of rash?"

"He's prone to diaper rash."

She tugged the baby from Gideon and cuddled him. "I'll be happy to scorch some flour. Got any zinc?"

"Zinc?"

"If we add it to the flour, it makes the rash heal faster." Titus scooted past Daniel and headed to a wooden box on top of the pie safe. "I don't know about zinc. I'm just hoping we've got Barne's Remedy in here."

"I have some in my satchel if you don't." Lovejoy held baby Caleb in one arm and started cracking more eggs. These men looked hungry, and Miriam was the only one here who seemed to have any idea as to what needed to be done to get a meal on the table. "Your belly givin' you fits?"

"Not mine. Alisa's."

"She oughtn't have Barne's. It's got rye malt. If the rye is harvested moist, it cain have ergot that'll put her into early labor. I'll make her soda biscuits and ginger tea."

Gideon poured himself a mug of coffee. "I wish we would have known that for Miriam."

Miriam nodded. "My first few months with Caleb were rough."

Tempy, Lois, and Eunice arrived. They jumped right in and helped set the table, make gravy, and scramble eggs. Freed up, Lovejoy got water to boiling for tea. She turned as Delilah came in. No one seemed to mind the gimpy, brown-spotted white kitten that dodged at her hem.

Lovejoy took one look at how pale Delilah was and suggested, "How 'bout you having a sit-down?"

"That's a good idea," Miriam chimed in as she led Delilah to a chair in the corner. "Lovejoy, why don't you bring Caleb over to her?"

Lovejoy caught Miriam's wink.

"I don't know what got into me," Delilah said vaguely as Lovejoy approached.

Lovejoy tucked Caleb into her arms and murmured under her breath, "Green as you are, I'd venture you got a baby into you."

Delilah gave her a flummoxed look. "I thought it must be something I ate."

"Alisa's belly's tipsy today, too." Miriam smiled at her sister-in-law and tacked on, "But everyone ate the same meal last night."

"No one else is sick," Delilah said. Her eyes widened, and her face flushed. She looked around the bustling room.

Miriam whispered, "Want to step outside with Lovejoy for a minute? I'll keep the men busy in here."

Delilah nodded. As soon as they were on the front porch, she whispered, "I can scarce believe. . . . Could I ask you a few questions?"

"You go on ahead."

It wasn't but a few moments later that Delilah let out a weak laugh. "I'd better get out a needle and thread. Paul's going to pop every button off his shirt. We've only been married six weeks."

Paul exited the house and shut the door. Concern lined his face, and he wrapped his arm around his wife's shoulders. "You okay, sweetheart?"

Lovejoy swiped Caleb and walked back inside. Some moments were meant just for two. A quick glance as she shut the door showed Paul enveloping Delilah in a hug and smiling like a coon in a henhouse. *If Mike treats Tempy half this good, Lord, I'll be eternally thankful.*

❧

During breakfast, Polly and Ginny Mae's coughs left Daniel frowning. The only thing Miriam had that the kids could safely take was horehound, and that hadn't helped one bit. Lovejoy knew the right stuff for Caleb's rash, had nixed letting Alisa use Barne's Remedy, and got both Alisa and Delilah's stomachs settled enough that neither gal looked quite so green.

"Those young'uns of yourn have a case of the barks, don't they?" one of the redheaded gals across the table asked.

"Lovejoy's good with yarbs and such," the other redhead said. "She could fix you up right quick with something."

One last look at Polly made his resolve crumble. Daniel cleared his throat. "Mrs. Spencer brewed something for them earlier, but it was too hot."

"It smelled pretty." Polly's eyes lit up at the realization that she might get some.

"Would you mind if I fetched it now?" Lovejoy asked the question without the smallest hint of gloating.

Daniel nodded.

A few minutes later she reappeared with a pale pinkish liquid in the bottom of a canning jar. Each girl drank her share, then the healer reached into the pocket of her apron and handed Daniel a tube.

He broke out in a cold sweat. "Nitroglycerin?"

Chapter 4

No need to get riled. It's the cough elixir. That there's enough for each of your lassies to have another dose."

"This glass vial—"

"Oh, they don't use 'em for the nitroglycerin anymore. Onc't that man invented his dynomite, the mine stopped using blast juice. Asa Pleasant back home said he knew a company that had a heap of these glass tubes. He got me two crates, and they're right useful."

"You emptied them?" Titus asked the question, but he'd stolen the words out of Daniel's mouth.

She looked at him like he'd taken leave of his senses. "They wasn't never used. I got 'em afore they ever held a drop of anything."

Miriam patted Lovejoy's arm. "You'll have to forgive them. The Chance men are protective."

"Ma'am, seems to me you're blessed as cain be to have such a fine passel of men as kin."

"Speaking of kin. . ." Paul covered Delilah's hand. "We suspect the family's due to see another addition."

"Already?" Bryce blurted out.

Daniel left the table and headed straight for the barn. Five years ago he and Hannah had made that announcement. It had been one of the best days of his life. The day they'd revealed they'd be blessed with a second child was just as sweet. *What kind of brother am I? Paul's thrilled, and I'm slinking away, licking my wounds.* But it hurt—seeing the wedded bliss his brothers enjoyed when he'd been robbed of his beloved wife.

Let them all celebrate. I'll hitch up the wagon and take those strange women to the MacPhersons. The horse snorted, and Daniel let out a rueful laugh. "Just what I was thinking."

As neighbors went, the MacPhersons were solid men. Honest. Hardworking. But odd! The hillbilly gals back in the house would be good matches for them.

It took little time to hitch the buckboard and lead the horse out to the yard. Daniel went to Bryce and Logan's cabin. They'd slept out in the barn last night so the women could have warm beds. Knowing he shouldn't barge in, he knocked. When no one answered, he tentatively pushed open the door.

The compact cabin hadn't looked this tidy since Logan and Bryce first moved in. Miriam, Alisa, and Delilah didn't brave it. Logan and Bryce set out their laundry on wash day and picked it up at the main house that evening. Bone tired as those backwoods women had been, they'd come in and swept the logs from roof to floor, dusted the surfaces, and made the beds. Instead of the normal jumble of items on the floor, his brothers' stray clothes, a harness, and the razor strop now hung neatly on hooks and pegs.

Daniel hefted the women's trunk, carried it out, and dropped it onto the buckboard with a satisfying thump. Satchels and a valise went on his next trip. Wanting to be sure he'd gotten everything they brought, Daniel went back to check. He almost missed the gunnysack. It barely peeped out from beneath Bryce's bed. One quick tug, and the bulging sack Mrs. Spencer had when she'd been in his daughter's cabin slid right out. Fragrances rose from it—pine, flowers, leaves—almost like a bouquet.

Hannah loved flowers.

"Mr. Chance."

He wheeled around and stared at Lovejoy.

She smiled. "The peace out here's extry sweet after all the mornin' ruckus, ain't it? 'Tis a blessing to have a big, loving family, but the noise cain be a bit much. 'Tis my habit to rise up of a mornin' and have some time to myself."

He nodded. Odd how she seemed to share that quirk of his.

"I come to tell you, when you give the lasses the elixir, they need to drink more water."

"Fine. I'll see to it."

She didn't fill the momentary silence with inane chatter. Instead, she stepped forward to claim the gunnysack. He shook his head in a silent refusal. It wasn't heavy, but he wasn't about to have a woman carry something.

"Thankee for loading up the wagon. My charges are eager to go meet their intendeds."

Intendeds. The word seemed so ungainly. Awkward. Not that charges was any better. The word lilted off her tongue as if she were some old governess doting over toddlers instead of a vibrant young woman.

Her smile faltered. "It's been nigh unto a year since I seen the MacPhersons. They had plenty to commend them back then."

She hadn't posed him the question, but Daniel answered it the best he knew how. "They're good to my girls."

Those few words drained the tension out of her jaw and shoulders. She beamed at him. "No one could deny what wondrous fine daughters you got."

He hefted the gunnysack over his shoulder. "What do I owe you?"

Lovejoy shook her head. "Nary a thing. You and your kin put us up for the night and practically killed the fatted calf for those feasts."

"You exaggerate."

Lovejoy's steady gaze held his. "If'n your family always eats like that, mister, this must be the promised land."

He hadn't paid much attention to what they'd eaten. Then, too, he hadn't paid much attention to this woman. Last night had been dark, and this morning he'd been worried about his daughters. Daniel took a closer look at Lovejoy. Had she been gaunt, he'd have spotted it right off, but now that he studied her, little things took on new significance. Her high cheekbones were a tad too prominent, her dress a mite baggy. She had narrow shoulders and delicate wrists. What he'd taken for being a slightly built woman was really someone who'd known lean times. It bothered him to think she'd gone hungry.

"Could be your lassies were croupy from the night fog; but if'n they don't shake their cough, you let me know. I'll fix 'em up more of that elixir."

"Lovejoy!" someone called.

"Here!" She turned in the open doorway, and Daniel caught a glimpse of just how narrow her waist was. Women often cinched themselves in for vanity's sake, but he knew Lovejoy owed her shape to a shortage of food. He wanted to haul her back into the house and feed her a big platter of steak and eggs.

Oblivious to his consternation, she headed toward the buckboard. Delilah's kitten, Shortstack, crossed her path, and Lovejoy scooped her up and absently stroked her. "Just look how blessed we are, girls. Mr. Chance hitched his wagon and loaded our goods so's you cain go see your grooms."

"Daddy, I wanna go see brooms, too."

He fought back his scowl. "No, Ginny."

"She's not coughing anymore," one of the redheads said. "Lovejoy's elixir worked in a trice."

"Mayhap you cain come callin' after we've settled in," Lovejoy said. She leaned down and tapped Ginny Mae's nose. "But for today, best you listen to your pa and stay put. Here. This little kitty's a-wantin' a sweet lass like you to pet her."

Twice now Lovejoy had reinforced his authority. For all her strange ways, she had a level head on her shoulders. Odd as she was, he admitted she displayed a pleasant blend of kindness and common sense. *Another man*, he told himself, *might find her likable.*

Eager to meet the MacPhersons, the women scrambled into the buckboard without a bit of help. With his brothers there, it would have been natural enough for the women to be assisted. *They're barely civilized*, Daniel thought.

Daniel drove toward the MacPherson ranch, not knowing what lay ahead. He and his brothers had been on their spread for nine years; the MacPhersons had arrived in the dead of winter just this year. From experience he knew it took about five years to firmly establish a spread. Sven Gilder had tried to make a go of that sector and failed after two years, so the MacPhersons didn't need a barn raising. They'd shown up, gotten the land, and tended their own business.

Sven slept in his barn. Are the MacPherson men doing the same? We offered to help them knock together a cabin, and they refused. Daniel tried to ignore the mail-order brides' excited chatter. *Maybe the MacPhersons would have a tent. Plenty of folks lived in a tent for a year or so. Even with it being summer, these scrawny women'll freeze at night.*

Fencing. Every rancher worth his salt kept his fences in good repair. From the looks of things, the MacPhersons were doing a fair job of that. No cattle in sight yet, but they might be in a different pasture. Ground here would sustain a sizable herd.

"I wondered if the plants would be different from back home," Lovejoy said from beside him. "Plenty of what I'm spying is familiar."

Daniel shrugged.

"Rich soil. Looky there at how much it supports. The garden your women-folk tend near burst through the fence, it was so bountiful. Do the MacPhersons have much of a garden put in?"

He shrugged again. Daniel had more than enough to tend without sticking his nose in on other men's business. The MacPhersons showed up for worship and lent a hand to others. They'd not been here but a week before they picked up the bad habit many other men in the region displayed of "dropping by" at mealtime.

"We brung seeds, didn't we, Lois?"

"Gracious plenty. We'll set to gardening straight off, Eunice. I reckon with this much property, the men ain't had much time to plant beans and such."

Daniel followed a bend in the road and sucked in a sharp breath. Lovejoy did the same.

His stomach lurched. He'd hoped things would be better than this.

～～～

"Lord be praised." The words spilled out of Lovejoy.

"That barn's twice as big as the Peasleys'." Tempy's voice held nothing short of awe.

Eunice started laughing like a loon. "Good thing I filled the trunk with all my stuff. Look at the house!"

"Yoo-hoo! Anybody ta home?" Lois cupped her hands over her mouth and repeated, "Yoo-hoo!"

A cabin just like the one they'd slept in last night sat not far from the barn. Lovejoy nodded approvingly. "Square-built."

"It's got glass winders," Eunice squealed.

"Whoa." Daniel halted the buckboard as Mike MacPherson came out of the house. "These women belong to you?"

Mike let out a hoot and dashed toward the wagon. "They're here!"

Tempy half-dove into his arms. He swung her 'round and 'round, and Lovejoy hoped with all her heart her sister had fallen into the keeping of the man God wanted for her.

"Temperance Spencer," Mike declared as he set her on her feet, "you are a sight for sore eyes!"

"Temperance Linden," she corrected. "Lovejoy's a widow woman."

He hugged her again. "Soon as I get the parson, it'll be Temperance MacPherson."

Daniel had hopped out of the buckboard and swept Lovejoy down to earth. "Thankee," she stammered. She couldn't recall anyone helping her in or out of anything—ever.

Ignoring her, he pivoted and assisted Eunice and Lois out of the wagon. "I have their belongings here."

Mike pulled away from Temperance. An unrepentant grin split his face. "We'll tote them inside."

Lovejoy held up a hand. "Hold it there. These gals move in; you MacPherson bucks move out."

"Wouldn't have it otherwise." Mike grabbed the satchels and valise. "Y'all come on inside and make yourself to home."

The girls flocked around him and squealed delightedly as they stepped inside the cabin. Lovejoy lagged back. She walked alongside Daniel, who toted the trunk as if it didn't weigh more than a fistful of cattails. "Thankee, Daniel Chance. We're grateful for all you done."

He grunted, entered the cabin, and plunked the trunk against a wall. Squinting as he straightened up, he judged, "Cabin's well-chinked."

"Where are—" Lois began.

"Obadiah and Hezekiah?" Eunice chimed in.

"Obie's in the far pasture. Hezzy took a mind to go a-huntin'. Come suppertime, they'll find their way back home."

Seeing the disappointment on the girls' faces, Lovejoy rubbed her hands together. "Now if that's not perfect, I don't know what is. You gals cain surprise your men with the best meal they've et in ages."

Lois burst into tears. "Oh my—a real stove!"

"I left my gatherin' bag back on your wagon," Lovejoy told Daniel when he headed toward the door. The man had a fair stride, but Lovejoy never minded stretching her legs for a brisk walk. She marched right alongside him toward the buckboard. "Isn't it wondrous?"

"What?"

"The MacPherson land. Soil's vital 'stead of worked to death." They came to a halt, and she finished her thought. "Lots of promise in these here acres."

Daniel stared just over her shoulder in silence, as if he needed to come to terms with something important.

She surveyed the property and smiled. "I re█████this place is just one stripe short of the rainbow."

Steady and smooth as could be, he cinched his hands around her waist, pulled her close, and lifted.

Chapter 5

T he missing stripe is on that skunk waddling up behind you."
As if his actions hadn't been enough to startle her, Daniel's words took Lovejoy by complete surprise. He carefully set her in the back of the buckboard and speedily joined her there.

"Poor little polecat. Must be a mama, worryin' over her kit if she's out scroungin' food in the daytime." Lovejoy opened her gathering bag and pulled berries free from the twigs. By tossing the berries in an arc, she managed to coax the skunk into meandering in the other direction.

"Little?" Daniel gawked at her. "It was big as a barn cat!"

"Gotta admire a mama who loves her young'uns." She wiped her palm on her skirt and nodded to herself as she nimbly slipped off the back of the buckboard. "A papa, too. Clear as water, you hold your daughters dear. 'Member to let me know if'n they need more cough elixir, and thankee again for carryin' us all here."

Daniel tipped his hat, climbed from the bed of the buckboard onto the seat, and headed back toward home. If he stayed here talking to that crazy woman, she might start making sense.

Back home he halted the buckboard in the yard and went to the main house to check in on his girls. Dressed in the little gingham aprons Alisa had made them for Christmas, they were "helping" Miriam make corn bread. Miriam glanced up at him. "Lovejoy's medicine worked. I'll have to find out what she put in it." She lifted the bowl and let Polly scrape the last of the batter into the pan. "Bryce is in the barn. Something's wrong with Raven."

Satisfied his girls were fine, Daniel strode to the barn. Of all the Chance brothers, Bryce had a gift when it came to dealing with animals. Most often he'd take care of things without asking for help or an opinion. Raven was Titus's mare, though. He put plenty of store in that horse, and Dan decided to see if his help was needed.

Bryce sat in a corner of the stall wrapping one of the mare's forelegs. "She's started nodding up."

"I didn't notice her favoring her leg."

"Neither did Titus." Bryce shrugged. "Nodding up means a foreleg. When a horse nods down, it's a rear leg. I felt her, and she's got a hot spot. We caught it early, and I mudded her. She ought to fare well."

Daniel studied the sleek black mare. Bryce wasn't a braggart in the least. Daniel shifted his weight. "You've a way with animals. If you're of a mind, I'll bring up a family vote in favor of sending you to vet school."

Bryce shook his head. "It'd be a waste of money. I have the hands and the instinct, but I don't have the brains. I wouldn't mind apprenticing for a season to pick up more knowledge, but in the long run, I'm content where I am."

Late that night Daniel tugged the covers back over his precious little girls, walked through the "hallway" into his cabin, and sighed. Hannah's quilt topped his lonely bed. All around him life continued. His brothers had married and were having children. Lovejoy Spencer was undoubtedly playing matchmaker with her charges and the MacPhersons.

Bryce's words echoed back: *I'm content where I am.*

Well, I'm not. My little girls don't have a mother. Daniel wanted to grow old with Hannah, but all he had was the gnawing emptiness left by her death. *God, how could You do this to me?*

Heavenly Father, thank Ye for all Thou hast done for me. Lovejoy tumbled into the pallet and snuggled beneath the quilt. Going to sleep wasn't easy. The day rated as being one of the most exciting of her life.

After Daniel left, she and the girls had set to work. They'd spruced up the cabin, weeded what little garden existed, planted a summer crop with the seeds they brought, and fixed supper.

"You gals may as well talk out loud 'stead of whisperin'," she said.

Eunice and Lois giggled guiltily. Lois said, "They couldn't tell us apart."

Tempy snorted, "You couldn't tell them apart, either."

"Well, we only saw them once when they come to buy a hound," Eunice said.

"And they'd only seen you that once," Lovejoy pointed out with a laugh.

"We didn't ask them to marry up, though," Eunice staunchly insisted.

"You've got a point there. I 'spect it'll take a few days for you to iron out who makes your heart sing."

"Oh, I don't need no time a-tall." Eunice sighed. "Ain't no man in the world for me 'cept Obie. He's got the cutest smile, and he loved my squirrel stew."

Lovejoy and Tempy exchanged a look across the pillow they shared and burst out laughing. "That was Hezzy!"

"Yeah. Obie's the one who et five of my biscuits." Lois ruined the solid tone of her assertion by tacking on a tentative, "Right?" When everyone else started giggling again, she said plaintively, "Well, they're both big and have beards!"

"Yes, you're right," Lovejoy sang out. "But Hezzy has a mustache, and Obie doesn't."

"Coulda just said so and saved us all this trouble," Eunice grumbled.

Lovejoy didn't want the girls to go to bed embarrassed, so she decided to give them cause to feel better. "Cain you jist imagine the men out in the barn? They're probably tryin' to figure out how to tell Eunice and Lois apart."

"And they have it real tough." Tempy snorted with glee. "After all, neither of them have mustaches!"

Two days later Lovejoy stretched to pick a few more flowering stems. "Now take a look here, Tempy. Yarrow. 'Tis good for wounds. Widow Hendricks called it 'Nosebleed' 'cuz a few of these tiny leaves in your nose stop a bleed."

"Lovejoy, I'm sure this is important, but you're staying here for a while. There'll be time enough for me to learn it." Tempy gave her a pleading. "Can't we do this some other day? I wanted to go riding with Mike."

"I'm trying to keep the two of you apart," Lovejoy confessed. "I don't want you to mistake a spring fancy for enduring love. A bit of distance lets the heart be wise."

"I already traveled the distance, and my mind's made up."

Lovejoy rested her hands on her hips. "Let's suppose you're right. Jist for the sake of laying the whole feast out on the table, let's see what all you're dishin' up. I grant you and Mike are a right fair match when it comes to smarts. He's got a sound head on his shoulders, and the two of you'll throw off a passel of young'uns that're clever as raccoons."

"Then what's the holdup?"

"What's his favorite vegetable? Does he rise up early of a mornin' in a fine mood? When money's tight and you both need shoes, who's gonna stay in the old ones?"

"We can learn those things as time passes."

Lovejoy shook her head. "Once you speak your vows before the parson, it's a done deal. If you wake up a month or year later and decide that man with his head on the pillow beside you makes you want to pack your bag and run away, you cain't. You're stuck. Best to be sure the table's solid afore you put your cookin' on it."

"Lovey, you know I've never been one to leap 'lest I looked first—"

"And I aim to make sure you're not changin' that habit this time," Lovejoy interrupted. "Anybody cain put on a fine show for a few days. It's when time moves on and wears off the polish that you see what you got for every day."

"I met Mike back in Hawk's Fall. I saw how gentle he acted with his ma when she was dying. It near tore him up, watching her go, but he knelt at her side. His pa's getting cash money from the sons, and since Mike's the only one who can write, I know he's behind it. That's plenty enough for me."

"We've always been honest to the roots, Tempy. I don't want that a-changin' 'twixt us. Truth be told, I wouldn't have brung you out here if'n I didn't think God was pointin' this way."

"Then—"

"Now you simmer down and let me speak my piece." She gave her sister a stern look. "When you marry up, you don't jist git the man, you take on his kith and kin. Obie and Hezzy aren't the sharpest knives in the kitchen. They're bigger and stronger. If'n they've got tempers, 'tis best we determine that now."

"The two of them are as dangerous as Asa Pleasant's new kid goat." Tempy's eyes lit with humor. "And they eat just about as much!"

"Supposin' you tied the knot and had to sit down to supper with them three men. Could you put up with livin' in Eunice and Lois's apron pockets? There's but one cabin."

"I reckon Mike's seen the Chance spread and knows they give their brides a house of their own. He'd not want me to have less."

"You're doing a lot of plannin' and hopin' and wishin', Temperance Linden."

"I've also been doin' a fair bit of praying."

"Are you asking God's will, or are you too busy tellin' Him yourn?" Her sister blushed, and Lovejoy knew her question hit a tender spot. She didn't belabor the issue. Gathering more yarrow, she said, "Even if things are sunny 'twixt you and Mike, you cain't verra well get hitched so quick. Obie and Hezzy would start pressurin' Lois and Eunice, and the four of them ain't even sure who likes whom yet."

"At least they've decided who is who."

Lovejoy winked. "As Mama used to say, 'Wonders never cease!' "

Tempy picked up a sunny, young dandelion, blew the dust from it, then ate the flower. "The only reason I'm not fighting you about waiting to marry Mike is because once I wed, you'll go back home. I can't imagine you not being in hollering distance."

Her sister's words made Lovejoy's steps falter. She exhaled slowly. "They'll need me back home; you won't. 'Tis the way of things. When you was born, Mama gave you to me. God gives us folks to love, but He never promises how long we'll have 'em. You're a growed woman, Temperance. I love havin' you 'neath my wing, but you're starting to test your own wings. Time's comin' soon when you'll want to fly and have your own nest."

"I'll always have room in my nest for you, Sis. Just like I'll take on Mike's kin, he'll take on mine. You know you're welcome."

Lovejoy laced hands with her sister and walked along the meadow. " 'Member when we memorized that passage from Ecclesiastes? It's been running through my mind. 'To every thing there is a season, and a time to every purpose under the heaven. . . .' "

" 'A time to be born, and a time to die,' " Tempy said. " 'A time to plant, and a time to pluck up that which is planted.' " She reached over with her other hand and tugged at Lovejoy's gathering bag. "I think that verse is for you. You catch babes and dispatch the old'uns to heaven. You garden and gather."

Lovejoy blinked back her tears. "Time's a-comin', my baby sis. Time's a-comin' for you to love and for me to leave and go home to Salt Lick Holler. I know it in my heart. So long as you're wed to a man who'll cherish you, I'll thank the Lord and leave you in His hands."

"Whose? God's or Mike's?"

"Sweetheart, Mike has Jesus in his heart. If he's in God's hands, and you're in Mike's, then you'll be in God's keeping as well."

Chapter 6

With the weather being nice, folks of Reliable were showing up for church each Sunday, same as they had since Miriam arrived. Dragging benches out into the barnyard for the service didn't take much time. Daniel helped—not because he wanted to attend, but because Hannah would have wanted him to rear their daughters that way.

"What are the two of you fiddling with?" he called to Titus and Paul.

Titus must not have heard him because he kept whistling—until he banged his thumb with a hammer and let out a yelp.

Dan posed the question again. Paul picked up the hammer and pounded in a nail as he explained, "It's too hot out here for our wives. We're setting up a canopy."

"Could have told me," he grumbled. "My girls could use some shade so they don't freckle."

Logan overheard that comment and hooted. "You're fretting over your daughters' ladylike complexions? Oh, brother. Just wait till—"

"Just you wait till you have daughters," Gideon interrupted.

Dan cleared his throat. "While we're at it, we probably ought to put up shade for the MacPhersons' brides."

"Actually. . ." Titus scowled at his banged-up thumb as he spoke. "I've been thinking we need to have a real church building."

"You thinking of saving souls," Dan asked, "or saving your fingers?"

"He might not have any fingers left if he helps build the church." Gideon chuckled.

"We could donate half an acre over where the road forks between here and the MacPhersons," Paul suggested. "In fact, if we made an announcement today at church, we could have one built so they'd be wed in a church."

Daniel scowled. "Forget that nonsense. If they're following through with that cockamamie plan Delilah cooked up and marrying those girls on a whim and a letter, they'll need houses, not a chapel."

"Delilah's plan was brilliant." Paul stopped hammering and looked mad enough to spit nails.

"The only reason you're saying that is because it kept them from courting her." Daniel stared straight back.

Tension crackled for a moment, then Paul grinned. "So you figured that out, did you?"

"Even Bryce figured it out," Logan said as he nudged a bench to rest parallel to the others.

"What're the conditions at their place?" Gideon folded his arms across his chest.

"Single cabin 'bout the size of Daniel's. Those men hammered a big, old bent serving spoon to the door as the handle." He winced at the memory. "Lovejoy shoved the men out to the barn. Those four gals are sleeping on pallets on the floor."

"So they do have spoons," Logan deadpanned. "Even if they don't know how to use them."

Daniel grimaced at the memory of Polly innocently suggesting the Mac-Phersons use silverware to eat when they'd slurped stew directly from their bowls. "Before we go off half-cocked and plan cabin raisings, let's see if the women are willing to stay there."

Miriam had come out to place the Bible on the table they used as a pulpit. "They'll stay. Obie, Hezzy, and Mike are good men, and they'll be protective and solid providers."

"That's dim praise. There should be more to marriage than feeling safe and full."

"Daniel, after you left the breakfast table the day they were here, Lois started crying when we offered her a second flapjack." Miriam's voice quavered. "To a woman who's lived in want, the promise of a home and a full stomach must sound like heaven."

"The promised land." He looked at his sister-in-law and cleared his throat. "Lovejoy said this place was like the promised land."

Conversation came to a halt as neighbors started to arrive for worship. It wasn't long before the MacPhersons arrived. Daniel stood rooted to the ground in utter amazement.

"Their hair—it's sandy-colored, not brown," Logan whispered.

The MacPherson brothers' clean hair was just part of the shock. The hillbilly women had come and done the impossible: The MacPhersons were duded up and looked downright decent. Freshly bathed, hair clean and trimmed, rowdy beards clipped and disciplined, and white shirts crisply ironed. A man could have himself a real belly laugh at the henpecked transformation if the MacPhersons weren't positively beaming with delight.

"Yoo-hoo! Miriam! Delilah!" Lovejoy scrambled down from the wagon and hastened up. "Where's our Alisa? She still peaked?"

"She's inside braiding the girls' hair."

"And your lassies, Dan'l Chance—are they chipper?"

"Fair to middlin'." From the look in her eyes, she'd wanted an honest answer instead of a polite "just fine." Daniel surprised himself by continuing the conversation. "I've kept them sipping plenty of water like you suggested."

"Good. Good." She bobbed her head. "It takes young'uns time to shake a cough." Lovejoy tugged on his sleeve.

"What?"

She drew another of her nitroglycerin tubes from a pocket and handed it to him. "I fixed up a fresh batch of elixir last night. Thought you ought to have it on hand just in case they need it someday. Mike tells me you cain read jist fine, so I pasted a label on it."

He held the tube and nodded. "Obliged."

She flashed a bright smile at him. Then her eyes popped open wide. "Well, imagine that!"

"What?"

"Reba White brung a saloon gal to worship! I'll go on over and welcome her."

Daniel choked and held her back. "That's Reba's daughter, Priscilla. She came back from a fancy young ladies' academy gussied up like that."

"Oh my. Thangs are different here. Back home in Salt Lick Holler, rouge and false yeller curls like that—well, it don't matter. God looks on the heart." She waved and called out, "As I live and breathe, Reba White! How wonderful 'tis to see you again."

Daniel stood off to the side as folks got settled for the service. His brothers managed to slap together a decent sunshade for all the women. Just as the hymns started up, he walked the girls over to sit at the women's feet. Lois and Eunice promptly pulled his girls onto their laps.

The MacPhersons must have told them to bring their instruments, because Lovejoy played her dulcimer and Tempy accompanied on her mandolin. Titus played his guitar. All in all, it made for some of the best-sounding music they'd ever had.

Once Titus finished leading the hymns, Mike stood up and hollered, "Fellers, that pretty one in the green dress what just played the mandolin's mine. Y'all cain listen and look, but that's it, 'cuz she's spoken for."

"That ain't much of an introduction," Marv Wall called.

Mike nodded. "Her name's Temperance Linden for now, but she'll be Tempy MacPherson soon as I get the parson here."

Obie rose, patted Hezzy on the shoulder, and said, "Other two are ourn."

"Which two? There're three left," someone called.

"The purty ones." Hezzy boasted. "Lois and Eunice come from back in Salt Lick Holler to marry up with us."

Daniel's eyes narrowed as he sought Lovejoy's face. Hezzy meant to compliment the other two, but in his backhanded, clumsy way, he'd just announced Lovejoy was plain. Only Dan caught a glimpse of her face as she sat down and turned to swipe Ginny Mae from Lois—and Lovejoy didn't look the least bit put out. She was smilin' to beat the band.

Maybe she just hides her hurt.

That thought stopped him cold. He couldn't remember the last time he'd thought about someone else's feelings. Well, that didn't matter. The important thing was, this conversation shouldn't disintegrate further and cause Lovejoy any more upset, so he stood and announced, "These gals deserve homes of their own. How's midweek looking for you men?"

⟡⟡⟡

"If'n Hezzy didn't already have claim of me, I'd marry up with Daniel Chance at the drop of a hat," Eunice claimed as they rode back home. "Imagine him a-standin' there, rustlin' up holp for us to have cabins!"

Lovejoy gave Hezzy a piercing look. "So you've proposed?"

"Yes'm, I shore 'nuff did. Whilst Eunice helped me hitch up the wagon this mornin', I told her I was ready to get hitched myself. Eunice and me—we'll step together right fine."

As proposals went, it wasn't the most romantic thing Lovejoy had ever heard. Then again it was much better than Vern Spencer's shoving sugar and a length of copper tubing at Pa, then yanking her by the wrist and declaring, "Yore mine now."

Tempy nestled closer to Mike. "My man took me out to look at the North Star last night. Said he'd be constant as that star if I'd but wed him."

Her sister had already shared that sweet news with her, but Lovejoy knew Eunice and Lois were hearing it for the first time. Mike shot her a grin. He'd sought Lovejoy's permission for that walk, and he was prouder than a rooster with two tails.

"Don't you go looking to me to ask for your hand right now." Obie glared at Lois from the wagon seat. "A man's supposed to pick the time and place, and I'm not gonna have my plans all ruint."

As it turned out, Obie's plan unfolded at the lunch table when Lois found the ring she'd been mooning over at the mercantile. Obie managed to stick it in her mashed potatoes while Hezzy distracted her. "Reba tole me you liked that one the best."

Lois wound her arms around Obie. "I like you the best!"

"Hold yer horses there." Lovejoy set the bowl of peas down on the table with a loud thump. Several jumped out and rolled across the warped surface. "When we set out on this venture, I had a firm understanding—no weddings till I was satisfied the matches would last a lifetime. The sap might be running, but that's something y'all are gonna have to suffer. I don't want no spoonin' or sparkin' betwixt you. These boys cleaned up right fine and boast plenty of fertile ground and a decent herd." The girls all nodded emphatically. Lovejoy turned to the men. "These gals are hardworking, decent, God-fearin' women. There'll be years and years ahead for them to be your wives and bear your young'uns."

"Yeah, but—"

"No yabbuts." Lovejoy gave Hezzy a withering look. "A woman makes for a better wife if she's got memories stored up of how her man courted her. On cold nights when the babes are sick and the money's tight, a gal needs to harken back to her sweetheart days when her man promised her he'd stand by her side through thick and thin."

Lovejoy knocked her knuckles on the table. "I'm holding you all accountable. In six weeks, if'n you're all still moon-eyed, we'll have a dandy wedding. Till then, hand holdin' and maybe a kiss on the cheek's all yore 'lowed. Plenty wants doin' 'round here that'll keep you busy. You men, I want you fillin' the smokehouse."

"What smokehouse?" Obie muttered.

"The one we're going to build," Mike promptly said.

Lovejoy nodded. "That's the spirit. Onc't the new cabins are up, these gals are each gonna take one and get finicky as any broody hen does on her first nest. Gonna fix up a home you men'll each be proud to own."

"I'm already proud of this'un." Hezzy's brows furrowed as he licked honey off his knife.

"Rightly so," Tempy said. She looked at Mike. "Are Hezzy and Eunice keepin' this one, or do you reckon on buildin' three new ones so this'll be the extry one what serves as the family kitchen?"

"I get a new cabin, don't I, Hezzy?"

Hezzy wore the look of a man going under for the third time. "If that's what you want, Eunice."

Eunice beamed at him.

Lovejoy clapped her hands. "Now looky there. That's what I'm a-talkin' 'bout. Hezzy, years from now, Eunice is gonna recollect the time you promised her a home of her verra own."

Hezzy looked doubtful. "For true?"

"Oh, yes." Eunice gave him a starry-eyed smile. "I stitched a sampler with mornin' glories and made the purdiest geese in flight quilt you ever seen. I brung everything I could. We'll have us the grandest house of anyone in Reliable."

Tempy glanced at Mike then shamefacedly dipped her head. "I only had a few things to tote along here. Mostly, I'll fill our home with love."

"Darlin', that's all your man wants or needs."

Lovejoy took a serving of peas and relaxed a little. *Lord, things are turnin' out better than I dared hope. Please let this all work out.*

Mike turned to his brothers. "What say I take Tempy and go to town tomorrow? We'll buy up the glass for everyone to get windows for their cabins."

"Glass winders?" Eunice squealed.

"We need to bring down more trees," Hezzy decided. "Pick up another saw, will ya?"

"Sure. Since we're havin' neighbors by, we'll need to stock up on vittles." Mike nodded toward the door. The men got up, walked out, yammered in a knot for a few minutes, then came back in. Mike looked at Tempy. "Best we make a list of what we need after supper."

"We cain make do with what's on hand," Lois said.

"Shore cain." Eunice nodded. "I'm a fair hand at tyin' lairs for hares and such, and you got beans aplenty."

"I'll go gathering with my sister." Tempy patted her. "Lovejoy knows what's good to eat, and we'll have greens—"

"I cain't do it," Obie said mournfully as he looked at his brothers. "I jist cain't."

Chapter 7

Hezzy's face went red, and he started chewing on his lip.

Lovejoy felt a bolt of panic. Everything had been going so well. Too well. If the men were going to back out, now was the time. But Lois looked ready to keel over from shock.

Hezzy shook his head. "I cain't do it, neither."

Eunice let out a wail.

"Wait! Wait! Eunice, I aim to marry up and give you that house. It's something else."

Obie snatched Lois's hand. "Same here, lambkins. I'd niver let you go. It's jist that we been keepin' a secret." He looked to Mike.

Any relief Lovejoy had felt over their immediate proclamations of love washed away at the sickening fact that they'd kept a secret. Vern's secrets never failed to tear her apart.

Mike shrugged. "I'm more than glad to tell 'em." He folded his hand over Tempy's. "We ain't rich, but we're far from havin' the wolf at the door. Halfway 'cross the country, we ran outta money. We worked at a mine."

"Mike knows all 'bout 'splosives. He made hisself good money—sorta." Obie's features twisted.

"The mine wasn't doing well. They couldn't make payroll, and men walked off. I was the only one left who knew blasting. The owner promised me a cut if I stayed on and we struck gold." Mike shrugged. "A week later, boom! We hit a real sweet vein."

"Gold?" Lois and Eunice gasped.

Tempy grabbed his wrist with her free hand. "Mike—you coulda got yourself blowed up!"

"Hezzy said the same thing. Soon as word got out that we made a strike, the other blasters came back."

Obie slid his arm around Lois. "We decided to take the money and get outta there. Came here."

"You didn't tell the girls because you didn't want brides who came for money," Lovejoy said quietly.

"Yes'm. We had us a pact not to tell 'em till after the parson tied the knot, but it's too hard seein' them fret." Obie squeezed Lois. "No brass or tin ring for my bride."

Mike cleared his throat. "We're not rich. Fact is, we spent most of what we had on this land and livestock." He lifted Tempy's hand and kissed the back of her fingers. "But you won't never go hungry or cold."

Lovejoy got up from the table, went outside, and walked down past the barn. There, in the shadows of the barn, she wept with relief.

❧

"Kisses, Daddy."

Daniel scooped up his daughters and gave them each a loud smooch. "Be good for your aunts while I'm gone."

" 'Kay, Daddy," they said in unison.

"Take this with you." Alisa tucked one last dish into a crate on the dining table. "I really do wish we were going along."

"Absolutely not," Titus said from across the room.

"I could go," Miriam volunteered once again.

Daniel glowered at her. "Your hands are full enough. You're watching my girls, and Delilah's too sick of a morning to lift her head off her pillow."

"I need you to keep Alisa from overexerting," Titus added.

"And no one but you can feed Caleb," Gideon finished as he handed her their infant.

"You men planned that. I can tell!"

"Auntie Miri-Em, are they being Chance men again?" Polly asked.

"Yes, we are." Daniel set the girls down. "And you are to be Chance girls. That means you're to be nice to each other and obey your aunts."

"You 'ready told us to be good," Ginny Mae said.

"Daddy, you going to see Miss Lovejoy?"

"I'll be busy building. I'm not visiting with the women."

"My mouse got untied." Polly fished the scrap of material from her pocket. "Will you ask her to make it again?"

"I'll try to remember." He tucked it in his pocket and forgot all about it when they reached the MacPherson ranch and started building the cabins.

Plenty of men showed up to help, just as they had on the day Chance Ranch built cabins. Coming here and helping out was part of paying back a debt. It wasn't his debt—he hadn't wanted Miriam to stay on Chance Ranch and didn't help with the construction. Then again, the MacPhersons hadn't lived in Reliable at the time, so they hadn't helped, either. That didn't much matter, though. Folks here banded together. Lent a helping hand. Favors were bartered, and every last man here knew if he needed assistance, folks would turn out for him.

The MacPhersons hadn't anticipated building three more cabins this soon, so their supply of logs would be insufficient. Logan and Bryce had both gone over the past three days to help fell trees. They'd reported that other men had also shown up to do the same. By the time the work teams showed up on Thursday, they had enough logs to build two.

"Gonna need us more timber," Hezzy commented as everyone gathered to discuss the plan.

"We're nigh unto tripping over each other." Daniel scanned the crowd. Word had spread that there were several unmarried women at the MacPhersons'. Plenty of the men in the area figured that until the happy couples found their way to the altar, an opportunity still existed to get a woman to change her heart and mind. A handful of those men were already making pests of themselves.

"Todd Dorsey. Aaron Greene. Hookman." Daniel rapped their names out. "Marv Wall and Garcia—you men, too. Let's let these scrawny men build the cabins. We'll apply ourselves to downing more timber."

"You callin' me scrawny?" Obie's eyes narrowed.

Logan cackled. "I'd call you love struck."

Things were well under way by noontime. Obie let out a shrill whistle then hollered, "Grub's up!"

Gideon went through the line and filled his plate. Lovejoy smiled at him. "It shore was kindly of yore missus to let us borry her plates. Don't rightly know what we woulda done."

"You put out a fine spread. Men would have stood at the table and eaten with their hands." Gideon chuckled and snagged the last biscuit.

Lovejoy called, "Eunice, get t'other basket of buns. These men need plenty of vittles to keep a buildin' your place." Giving Daniel a steady look, she lowered her voice. "That was a right fine thing you done today. Mostly, these men're fine bucks, but a couple. . ." She shook her head. "They was a givin' me fits."

"Lonely men do foolish things." He grabbed a biscuit from the new basket and strode off.

By the end of the day, three new cabins stood on the MacPherson ranch. Men straggled away, but Dan stayed behind. "Reckon yore here to claim the dishes," Eunice or Lois said. He hadn't yet figured out a way to tell them apart.

He nodded.

"Lovejoy and Tempy are packin' 'em up in the old cabin."

Daniel went to the door of the "old" cabin and stood in the doorway like a slack-jawed wantwit. He'd already seen the extensive gardening the women had accomplished in one slim week. This cabin showed a level of industry he couldn't fathom. Leaves, flowers, roots, and small bags hung from the roof. A bowl on the table held an arrangement of grapes, oranges, and cinnamon sticks. A wreath of drying flowers dangled from the buck's antlers over the fireplace.

"Take a seat." Tempy waved toward a chair. "We'll be done with the dishes in a trice."

Daniel watched Lovejoy tuck a dish towel between a pair of plates and remembered Polly's request. He yanked the scrap of material from his pocket. "When you're finished, could you please make a mouse for Polly again?"

" 'Course I will. Want me to show you how?"

Daniel shook his head. He'd already tried, though he'd never confess it to a soul. Bitsy things like that never worked right for a man with big hands.

"Bryce said the lassies lost their cough and are right as rain." Lovejoy looked up at him and smiled when he nodded, then she went back to handling the plates with uncommon care. "Never seen me such pretty dishes. China, they are, delicate as a bird egg, but all a-matched up. You Chance men take mighty fine care o' yer women."

"I counted. Forty-five plates." Tempy handed the last one to her sister.

Daniel's gaze went from Lovejoy's hands to a shelf just over her shoulder that held a jumble of wooden, pewter, and glass dishware. He looked back at the blue willow plate Lovejoy dried so carefully. "Two dozen were my mother's. Alisa inherited the other half. They're a mite different, but the same company made them and the color's the same."

"Staffordshire," Lovejoy read from the bottom of the plate in a reverent voice. "Please give your women our thanks for sharing their finery." After packing it in with the others, she smiled up at him. "Now how 'bout I make you a mouse?"

The light brown square looked much bigger in her hands than it did in his. In a mind-boggling series of intricate folds, tucks, flips, and knots, it became Polly's mouse again. "You cain make this little feller move and jump if you hold him jist so and do this." She demonstrated cradling him in her hand and coordinating a stroke and carefully timed squeeze. Sure enough, the mouse wiggled and flipped.

He grinned at the sight.

"Dan, you ready to push off?" Paul was leaning against the doorjamb.

"Paul Chance!" Lovejoy called over to him. "How's Delilah's belly?"

Delilah's belly? Daniel nearly choked at her coarse question.

"She's sick as can be morning, noon, and night." Paul's mouth tightened with worry. "Have any suggestions?"

"That poor gal. She sippin' ginger tea like I tole her to?"

"Yes." Paul's shoulders slumped.

"She keepin' anything down a-tall?"

"Not much."

Lovejoy crossed the cabin and picked up a forked stick. She used it to hook the strings on a small muslin bag hanging from the ceiling. "I'll mix up some tea. Y'all have any melons?"

"Yes." Paul and Daniel exchanged puzzled looks.

"Real problem is her growin' parched. Boil a teaspoon of this till the brew turns the same color as this here leaf I'm putting in the jar. I want her to have a cup of tea laced with honey every other hour. Try her eatin' melon. It's mostly juice, but it might sit in her belly better than the tea. Tell her I'll be holdin' her up to Jesus, and you come git me if'n she don't start keeping more down."

Paul accepted the half-pint jar she'd put in his hands.

Daniel hefted the crate of dishes and made sure the little cloth mouse peeping out of the edge wouldn't fall out. Polly would be delighted to have that simple toy again. "Let's go."

"Y'all ride safe. Afore ye go, I wanna say I niver seen a man wield an ax like you did this day, Dan'l Chance. Them trees left standin' out there are prob'ly gonna start a-shuddering in fear when you ride past."

At first her praise sat nice, but as Daniel rode home, he changed his mind. That little widow had plenty to say, but it was always good. Such compliments and flattery from a woman added up to only one thing—she aimed to nab herself a husband. Daniel determined then and there to keep his distance.

Chapter 8

T here, now. Such a grand girl you are," Lovejoy crooned to the sorrel mare Obie lent her for the day as she saddled her. The girls were busy hitching a pair of sturdy workhorses to the buckboard so they could all go to town.

Yesterday the men worked from can-see to can't to make up for the house buildin' day. The gals worked alongside their men as was fitting—taking care of the barn critters, mucking stalls, gardening, milking, collecting eggs. They'd dug right in and done more baking and laundry, too.

"We 'spected you'd be fixin' the houses today," Obie told them at supper.

"We picked the feed sacks we liked best to make curtains," Lois said.

"Until you all speak your vows, these gals are gonna sleep in this cabin." Lovejoy set down the law. "You men cain decide if you want to all pile down together in one of them cabins or out in the barn. That way you'll all avoid temptation."

No one argued with her, and to her utter amazement, Mike said, "I paid White for potbelly stoves. He's only got one in stock, so he'll bring all three up soon as the others arrive."

As if that news hadn't been enough to stun them, Hezzy dug around in his pockets and dropped five double eagles on the table. "We ain't had time to make furniture and sech. Mike says yore gonna need stuff. This'll be our weddin' gift to you."

The three brides stared at the gleaming coins in shocked silence. One hundred dollars. Lovejoy doubted any of them had ever held more than two bits.

"Go on with you now," Obie said. "Lest you think we're rich, though, best you know that's 'bout the last of what we got."

Tempy shoved it back. "We got what we truly need. You keep that and send it to your pa through the comin' years."

Lois and Eunice held on to one another. Though their faces were pale as dandelion fluff, they both nodded. "Kin comes first."

Mike took Tempy's wrist and turned over her hand. One by one, he stacked the glittering twenty-dollar gold coins there. "When a man and woman marry up, they put each other first, above all. We got faith that the good Lord's going to provide. He's never failed us. Now you go spend smart, sweetheart."

Spend smart. The girls were up most of the night assessing what they'd brought and what the men already had on hand, then making a list. Lovejoy tried to stay out of their discussion. They were grown women, and they needed to be making their own decisions. Judging from the list Tempy carried in her pocket, they'd proven themselves worthy of that trust.

Lord, those gals are heading toward the altar. Their hearts and minds are set, and from all I see, the men are good 'uns. Don't let me be blinded by this wealth of supplies or smooth talkin'. If there's reason for any of these couples not to wed, I'm beggin' Thee, please drive them asunder right quick.

Daniel got a sinking feeling as he rode Cooper up to the MacPherson cabin. It didn't look like anyone was home. Asking for help went against his grain. He hated relying on anyone, but he had no choice.

By breakfast, he knew he couldn't ask Miriam to watch the girls. Their coughs had returned with a vengeance and turned into nasty colds. Miriam's baby was cranky and feverish, too. Paul said Delilah was so green around the gills, she could barely lift her head off her pillow, and Alisa wasn't weathering her pregnancy any better. The way she looked reminded Daniel of how bad his Hannah had gotten whilst carrying Ginny Mae. He finally admitted to himself that his plan to avoid the Widow Spencer wasn't going to work.

So he bit the bullet, came seeking help—and no one was home. *Maybe she and the brides-to-be were all chattering up a storm and didn't hear me.* Dish towels flapped in the breeze on the clothesline, but that was the only sound. He knocked, opened the door of the main cabin, and found it empty. *Not empty, vacant,* he corrected himself. Lovejoy's "yarbs" filled the place.

Faint singing made him shut the door and turn around. Sopranos were singing "Oh, how I love Jesus." With their accent, it sounded more like, "Oh, how Ah luuv Jay–sus." This time the hillbilly accent brought relief. The women were in the stable—well, make that coming out of the stable.

Daniel noticed none of the gals on the seat of the buckboard was Lovejoy. He looked at Tempy. "Where's your sister?"

"I'm right here, Dan'l Chance." Lovejoy rode straight to him then skillfully nudged her horse to sidestep so as not to have it splash in a puddle near his feet. Her smile faded. "What's a-wrong?"

"Is it Delilah?" Tempy asked.

"Yore little girls?" the other two asked in unison.

"Both, and Miriam's little Caleb's taken ague, and Alisa's just too puny. Can you come check on them?"

" 'Course I will. Lemme fetch my healin' satchel."

Not wanting to waste any time, he lifted her out of the saddle and set her to earth away from the mud. She scurried into the cabin and called over her shoulder, "Don't you worry yourself so hard, Dan'l. Ain't nobody bleedin' or dyin'."

As far as reassurances went, it was as odd as the woman who gave it, but it worked. Relief flooded him.

Accustomed to making sick calls, Lovejoy had everything down to an art. She always kept her satchel packed for emergencies. By simply tossing in her night-dress and other dress, she met her personal needs. Knowing the children had colds and the women were suffering maternal difficulty led her to grab specific packets, then she latched the valise. Normally she wore her knife, but she'd planned to leave it at home for the trip to town. Binding the sheath to the side of her apron, she whispered a quick prayer, then slipped the knife into place. Valise and gathering sack in hand, she exited the cabin.

Daniel Chance hadn't stood around whilst she was in the cabin. Hardworking, helpful man that he was, he'd busied himself checking to be sure the team was properly hitched. Though somewhat amused that he thought they might not know how to hitch a team, Lovejoy was also touched by his kindness. Women in his family probably didn't know how to saddle or hitch up horses—they were all fine ladies.

"You gals go on ahead." She tilted her head toward the road. "You know what to do, and we need to get a wiggle on."

Daniel lifted her onto the dainty sorrel mare and took the canvas valise. Once he mounted up, Lovejoy kept her mare going at a lively canter right beside him. "I'm a-tellin' you, this land is surely wrought by God. Don't it just take yore breath away?"

"Fine land."

He didn't seem overly talkative, but Lovejoy figured he was worried. "I don't mean to boast, but I'm able to ride without followin' a path. If'n you got yourself a shortcut, we cain take it."

"You got lost following the road the first day you were here," he reminded her wryly.

"Now there's the truth. Onc't I've traveled a place, I cain find it again, though."

"Straight off, or after you've wandered awhile?"

Lovejoy laughed. "Now there's a poser." They rode a bit farther, then she pulled back on the reins. "Whoa."

"What're you stopping for?" Daniel scowled at her as she dismounted.

"I'll jist be a minute."

"We don't have time to waste. Didn't you hear me? Women and children are sick!"

"We'll have need of these." She didn't pay no nevermind to his grumpy ways—men ofttimes got that way when a loved one was ailin'. If anything, it did her heart good to meet a man who showed such devotion to the children and women in his life. It was an admirable trait. Lovejoy took out her knife and har-vested rames of mustard and put them in her gathering sack. It took such little time to glean a fair supply, and mustard—even dried mustard—made effective poultices. Whatever she didn't use in the next day or so could be preserved.

Daniel growled under his breath, "You're liable to step on a snake out here."

"Nope. The horses are too calm." She tucked her knife back in the sheath.

Vexed as he was, Daniel minded his strength and gently boosted her back into her saddle. "No more stops."

"Fair enough. I got what I need now." She patted his hand. "You got yourself five brothers, but I got myself five sisters. I know what it is to love and fret o'er family. I promise to look after 'em for you."

Lovejoy didn't bother to ask where everyone was when they reached Chance Ranch. She could hear the girls' coughs from the barnyard. "Hoo-oooo-eeyy. They's a-barkin' all right."

"It's not whooping cough, is it?" Worry tightened his features as he dismounted.

"Rest your mind. That ain't nothin' like the whoopin' cough." Lovejoy accepted her valise from him after he helped her down. "I aim to make poultices for the lassies. They'll reek to high heaven, and the smell's likely to send poor Delilah into spasms. Best I prepare them o'er in your cabin. We cain have Miriam bring her babe in there, too."

Some things could be done by rote. Dicing onions and mustard, frying them in lard, and fixing them into poultices was stinky, but Lovejoy did it automatically. The girls stumbled along on their own, and Daniel brought along the cradle as Miriam toted Caleb into the girls' cabin. "Tuck 'em in and be shore they all have socks on their feet."

"I don't wanna eat that. It's yucky," Ginny Mae whined.

"You don't have to eat it," Lovejoy promised. "Now clamber into the bed with your sister. Dan'l, I want their heads up higher. How 'bout you go stuff a couple feed sacks with hay? Those'll be right fine extry pillows."

"I've got extra pillows."

"Don't aim to use 'em. The stink'll get a-holt of the feathers and won't turn loose. Oh, one more thing: I got a mind to put together a stock of essentials for this ranch. Keepin' the girls out of the stuff's important. What say I use that loft up there?"

"As long as you move the ladder afterward so they can't climb up."

Once Daniel stepped out, Lovejoy pointed her chin toward the chair. "Miriam, go have a seat. I venture your son ain't sucklin' none too good, what with his nose all stuffy."

"He's not, but I know he's hungry."

"Wipe his nose best you cain. I aim to have him catch a whiff of camphor. That'll holp."

A few minutes later, Miriam had a shawl over her shoulder. "It's working. He's doing better."

The plasters worked, too. By suppertime both girls still coughed but were able to eat soup and a biscuit. Caleb wasn't as cranky, either. Miriam decided to take him back to her place. Daniel fetched himself a cup of coffee and brought back a mug for Lovejoy. She smiled her thanks.

"So are they cured?"

"Nope. We got the symptoms reined in. This'll play out another two, three days. Coughs like to stay 'round for 'bout a week all told. Gotta keep 'em sippin' warm drinks, breathin' steam from the teakettle, and lying 'round. Don't want it to sink into pneumonia."

"You'll come back tomorrow?"

Lovejoy gave him an amused look. "I aim to stay here. If you'll keep an eye on the sprouts, I'll go see 'bout holpin' the mamas-to-be."

"But you can't stay here. This cabin and mine are connected."

"I'm a proper woman, and I 'spect yore a proper man. Decent folk ain't gonna imagine any horseplay, 'specially with sick young'uns at hand. Come bedtime, you'll kiss your daughters and go mind yore own business for the night, and I'll bolt yon door that goes to yore place."

✿

Booted out. She'd gone and done whatever she deemed necessary for Delilah and Alisa then had come back and booted him right out of the girls' cabin. Daniel sat on his bed and strained to hear if they needed him. All he heard were his daughters' coughs and the soothing murmurs of a mountain woman.

He didn't like this one bit.

Two minutes later he slammed his door and walked out through the yard to the door of the girls' cabin. He didn't want to go through the hallway. No skulking around for him, no sir. He was heading out there where every last man jack on the place could see and hear him so no one would misconstrue this as anything improper.

He raised his hand to knock, but before his knuckles made contact, the door opened.

Lovejoy let out a surprised squeak. "Is something a-wrong?"

"What's wrong is, those are my girls. I don't leave 'em with strangers. They need me."

"They need water." Lovejoy stuck the bucket she'd been holding into his hands and promptly shut the door again.

Chapter 9

Vexed that he hadn't gained entrance, yet equally irritated with himself for not having seen to such a basic need, Daniel stomped to the water pump. Water splashed over the brim and dampened his fingers. His temper cooled. If anything, this gave him an excuse to march straight back into the cabin.

The door opened. "Thankee, Dan'l." Lovejoy reached for the bucket.

He ignored her and brushed right past. Wordlessly, he topped off the pitcher on the washbasin and sloshed more water into the empty pot on the stove.

"That's kindly of you." Lovejoy shut the door but stood by it.

Daniel knew she wanted him to leave; he turned away, picked up a log, and opened the grate on the potbelly.

"I just added a log. The fire's fine."

"It'll grow cold soon." He prodded the log already in there to make space.

"When that time comes, I'll add to the fire. No use wastin' wood or makin' the cabin smoky."

Any other woman saying those words would be quibbling; Lovejoy said them so calmly and quietly, Daniel couldn't very well grouse.

"No use having a hardworkin' man chop more wood when the fire's already fine." She gestured toward his daughters. They'd slept through the whole exchange. "Peaceable as a pair of played-out kittens."

"They're coughing."

"Aye, they are. I'm not aimin' to stop all the coughin'. Best that they bring up what ails 'em 'stead of keeping down low in their lungs. You needn't fret, Dan'l. I'll keep a weather eye on your precious lasses."

"You're a stubborn little woman, aren't you?"

Lovejoy hitched one shoulder. "Reckon there's a heap of truth behind that. I wrastle the enemy called sickness. Gotta be just as hardheaded and dauntless as him. If'n you went to battle, you wouldn't want no one marchin' alongside you that would turn tail and run at the first skirmish. You come and got me to fight for your daughters. I ain't gonna flee jist 'cuz you suddenly ain't shore I cain stay awake on my watch."

"I'm not a man to ask others to fight my battles. They're my daughters."

"No one said contrary. Problem is, you're a-comin' to this battle unarmed. You ain't got the proper weapons for the enemy of illness. Like it or nay, your daughters need me. You fetched me; standing here all night argufying ain't doin' them a lick of good."

Her words carried a sting of truth. Daniel looked over at his precious babies. "They're sleeping fine now."

"That they are. I give 'em another hour or so; then they'll be needin' some elixir. 'Round 'bout the wee hours, they'll start barkin' regardless of what they already took. Onion and mustard poultices again then. The bitty one, she's got a raw edge to her cough. I reckon she'll need sommat to soothe her wee throat then. I'm fixin' to whip up some sage gargle for her. Come first light, they'll settle down and want to sleep; but afore I let 'em, I'll have to get a pint of apple cider mulled with yarbs into each of them."

"You sound mighty sure of yourself."

Lovejoy took her shawl off the peg closest to the door.

Daniel's heart lurched into his throat. *What kind of idiot am I? My girls need help—*

"I'm fixin' to check them dog roses Delilah planted to see if'n I cain spy another hip. They're a right fine thing to give these young'uns. Mild enough for Miriam's little man-child, too. I aim to go get what's needed. Best you take a few minutes here with your lassies and decide what you want to do. I cain't fight you and the sickness."

The door shut. She'd left, but with the implied promise that she'd return. Plainspoken as she'd been, her voice never took on a bite. She kept a soft tone so the girls wouldn't be disturbed. Daniel stood over his daughters and fingered the sweet little twirly curls that invariably sneaked from their braids and framed their cherubic faces.

They need their mama so badly right now.

The door whispered open and shut. Lovejoy's raggedy skirt swirled about her ankles as she set the latch. " 'Tis a wicked cold wind for a summer night."

"When it blasts from the ocean, that happens." He frowned as she went to the washstand and set down a single rose hip. "One? You only got one?"

Her head bobbed. "One's what God provided. 'Twould be a waste to get more, anyhow. Moon-gathered hips carry a moisture that causes them to mold. I took just what the young'uns require this night. Tomorra I'll search about. If I spy more, I'll gather them, 'cuz they cain be stored away."

Thin shoulders rising and falling with a deep breath, Lovejoy said, "Whilst I was outside, I did some soul searching. Those be your lassies, and you've done a right fine job with them, Dan'l Chance. That's saying a mouthful, seein' as you do it on your lonesome. Cain't be easy on you or them. Cain't say as I blame you for frettin' 'bout leaving them in a stranger's care."

She tugged her shawl about herself more closely and continued. "Back home, folks know me. I earned their trust. To you I'm nothing more than a hillbilly woman with a sackful of leaves and twigs and a boastful mouth. What say I meet you halfway?"

"Halfway?" He couldn't fathom how perceptive she was.

"I'll brew up the elixir and make ready everything for the plasters now. Onc't I'm done, we'll give the girls a dose, and I'll stay out in the stable. When I judge it time for the plasters, I'll come in and fry 'em up for you."

"You're not staying in that stable!"

A sad smile lifted the corners of her mouth. "Dan'l, lotsa places in Kentuck got grand houses full of book-learned folks a-wearin' fine clothes. The holler ain't like that. Your stable's better built and likely warmer than any shack back in Salt Lick Holler. Won't bother me none."

"You can't do that. You can't sleep out there."

She started concocting her elixir. Amusement tinged her voice. "Sleepin' wasn't in my plans for tonight."

The door jiggled. "Lovejoy?"

"Miriam," Lovejoy murmured the name just loud enough to acknowledge her presence, yet calmly so as not to disturb Daniel's daughters. She'd wheeled around and gotten the door unlatched before Daniel made it around the girls' bed.

"He's sleeping, but that rattle in his chest—" Miriam's voice broke.

Gideon followed his wife in and wore an equally anguished expression.

"Let's have us a look-see."

Dan stood behind Miriam and Gideon as Lovejoy pulled what looked to be an old-fashioned powder horn from her satchel. "Now you jist hold that sweet little man-child 'gainst you. I aim to loosen his swaddling clothes and have me a listen." Lovejoy pressed the wide, open end of the horn to Caleb's tiny back and rested her ear to the opening of the horn. She moved it about to listen a few other places then straightened up.

"Well?" Gideon rasped.

"Mullein ought to do him right fine. I got me some leaves. Makin' the tea's the easy part. Think you cain get him to drink it if'n we put it in a salt shaker?"

Miriam clutched her son tightly. "We'll do anything."

"Gideon Chance, I'll be askin' you to fetch a rockin' chair for your wife. A quilt, too, on account it's gonna be a long night. Cain you do that?"

While Gideon went on that errand, Lovejoy found what she wanted in that satchel of hers. "Best I not fix things in the same pot. Dan'l, do you have a pot or kettle o'er in that cabin o' yourn?"

It wasn't long before Lovejoy had several things going on the potbelly stove. Though he'd seen women at a stove much of his life, Daniel hadn't watched one do it to end up with the collection she arranged in tubes, vials, cups, and a pie tin. The mullein tea stayed in a cup, but Lovejoy carefully measured a few teaspoons into an emptied saltshaker. Binding a handkerchief over the opening, she said, "No race to get this down your wee man-child. Let him nuzzle it down through the cloth."

Later, though the kids didn't seem much better or worse, Lovejoy fried up the plasters. Daniel's eyes burned—partly from the fumes of the onions, partly from the fact that weariness left his eyes grainy. When that treatment was finished,

Lovejoy nudged his boot with her foot. "Them lasses are wantin' your warmth and comfort, Papa. Kick off them puddle stompers and shimmy betwixt 'em. If we keep their heads raised, their breathin' will stay eased."

Daniel didn't crawl beneath the blankets. With the fire going, the cabin felt like a giant oven. He lay atop the bed, and each of his daughters wiggled and squirmed until finally nestling into his side.

Lovejoy went to Miriam and held out her arms. Miriam kissed her son and handed him over. "What should we do next?"

"Drag the rocker to the far corner. I'll plop down a crate so's you cain put up yore feet. Time's come for you to grab a bit of shut-eye. We cain't have you takin' sick."

"I'm healthy as a horse."

Daniel absently rubbed his thumbs down his daughters' bumpy braids and listened to their raspy breaths while watching Lovejoy coax Miriam into wrapping up in a quilt for a rest. Daniel glanced away then looked back. By an odd twist in life, he and Gideon had ended up wedded to sisters. When Miriam arrived a little over a year ago, Dan mistook her for Hannah. Any similarity between them no longer registered. All he saw now was a frazzled, weary woman.

"Miriam." He cleared his throat. "Go on through the hallway to my bed. You'll sleep better there."

She rested her head against the pressboard back of the oak rocker. "Thank you, Daniel, but knowing Lovejoy's just a step away makes me feel Caleb will be safe. I wouldn't be able to close my eyes if she weren't here."

"You prob'ly didn't sleep none last night," Lovejoy said as she walked the floor with Caleb over her shoulder.

"No, I didn't." Miriam yawned.

Hannah never lost a night's sleep when Polly was sick. The thought stunned Daniel. His hands stilled. He'd been the one to hold their sick babe through the dark hours. But Hannah was frail. Ginny Mae let out a raspy sigh, and he tugged the blanket up closer. Unbidden, the thought slipped into his mind. *Polly was well past her first year before Ginny was conceived. In those months, when Polly sprouted a new tooth or had the croup, Hannah slept while I tended our girl.*

Lovejoy nuzzled Caleb's temple and hummed softly as she swirled her hand on his back.

She's doing more for another woman's baby than Hannah did for our own. Daniel shook his head. Never once had he said or thought an uncomplimentary thing about his dearly departed wife. It was just weariness and worry.

Lovejoy eased Caleb into the cradle and approached the bed. "We need to turn the gals. Gotta move 'em so's any water in the lungs cain't settle. Think we could turn them with their backs to you, or will they sleep better if they just swap sides?"

In the end he sat up and slipped Polly across to his left side while Lovejoy carried Ginny Mae around to his right. While Polly started to burrow into a new place, Lovejoy coaxed Ginny Mae to have a few sips of water, then popped her into place and efficiently tugged up the blankets. Daniel's arms curled protectively about his precious daughters, and Lovejoy nodded.

"Yore a good man, Dan'l Chance. Them girls don't know how lucky they are to have a daddy who holds 'em close in his arms and in his heart."

By the time morning broke, Daniel held the conviction that Lovejoy would tend his daughters with diligence and care. He'd dozed off and on, but each time he opened his eyes, Lovejoy was checking his girls, stoking the fire, cradling Caleb, or measuring out a dose of something.

Lovejoy pulled on her shawl, picked up her gunnysack, and strapped on her ridiculous-looking sheath.

"What do you think you're doing?" he asked in a hushed tone.

"Now that the sun's ready to rise, the wee ones will stay sounding fair to middlin'. Onc't we hit sunset, 'twill be like last night. I've a few things to gather and get done. I shouldn't be long a-tall."

<hr />

I'll come along. I don't want you getting lost. . . . Daniel's words echoed in Lovejoy's mind as she let herself into the main house where Gideon and Miriam lived. From the time she'd been here before, Lovejoy knew everyone ate as one big family in this kitchen. She set coffee to boiling, started a broth, and searched in vain for grits.

"Mrs. Spencer? How's my son?"

She turned. "He's holdin' his own, Gideon Chance—which is more than I cain say for myself. Where do y'all hide the grits?"

He chuckled. "No one can stand them. One of us can see to making oatmeal. Don't trouble yourself."

"Them gals ain't lifting a hand to do work for a few days till we get them straightened out. Your Miriam's sleepin' like the babe in her arms after a rough night. Fact is, she's comin' down with the sniffles, and I don't want her sharin' them with anyone. Alisa needs to rest, and it's been a coon's age since I seed me a gal half as green 'round the gills as Delilah."

"I didn't think the women ought to. The Chance men survived on their own cooking for a couple of years."

She located the oatmeal, started it, and put beans on to soak for a meal later on. "I'm fixin' to go gather me more yarbs. You shore you cain keep watch on the breakfast?"

"We'll manage the food—I just don't want you going out there alone. We've got snakes and poison oak."

"You Chances mollycoddle women. That strappin' brother of yourn already fussed over my plan to go gathering." She laughed and touched her sheath. "I got me my knife. I'll watch where I walk, and if'n a snake takes a mind to say howdy, he'll make a fine lunch."

Gideon gave her a stunned look.

"Oh, now don't you be a-tellin' me yore truly afeered of pizzen oak. Onliest things I touch or harvest are things I ken. Them nasty leaves o' three. . .well, I leave them be!"

The corner of his mouth kicked up. "Miriam learned that lesson the hard way. Just promise me you'll stay to the path and in sight of the homestead."

"Fair's fair." She nodded and left. Walking along the edge of the yard, she took note of a few places where she could show Miriam to gather a few essentials, but a spot of land by the vegetable garden had her aching to plant an herb garden.

'Mornin', Lord. I'm givin' Ye my thanks for them young'uns makin' it through the night. I could pert near feel the angels stirrin' the water on the stove, jist like they did in them healin' pools in that Bethesda place in the Bible. . . .

Hands busy collecting yarbs, she carried on her morning prayer time. Granny Hendricks back home taught her that praying whilst she gathered carried a special blessing—that a healer who listened and spoke to the Almighty would hear His voice, follow His leading, and pick the essentials for whatever ailments and accidents lay ahead.

She'd told Daniel it wouldn't take long, but the bounty of this landscape exceeded her wildest imaginings. It took no time whatsoever to fill her gunnysack. Since Daniel gave her permission to use that loft, she might as well lay by a good stock of yarbs. "Lord, I'm thinkin' on bethroot. Ain't seen me none hereabouts. What with two gals a-carryin' babes, I'd shore like to lay in a supply."

"I talk to myself, too."

Lovejoy let out a surprised yelp as she spun around. "Bryce Chance, I swan, you 'bout skeered the liver outta me!"

"Sorry." He scratched the back of his neck. "I aim to take that sorrel back to the MacPhersons' 'less you say otherwise."

"Now that's kind as cain be. I'm shore Obie has need of her."

Bryce took the gunnysack from her. "Dan said not to let you go far afield."

Lovejoy tried not to gape. "Dan'l sent you to hover over me like a guardian angel out here?"

"He said a stiff wind could blow you straight to Texas." He frowned as he looked at the bag in his hand. "This is too heavy for a dab of a woman."

"Your big brother worries too much." Though she said the words, something deep inside warmed at the thought that Daniel didn't just pay lip service to her safety—he'd needed to stay with his daughters, but he'd made sure his brother shadowed her.

"Can't blame Dan. Mama and Hannah are both buried yonder. We're all antsy 'bout womenfolk."

"Hannah was his wife?"

Bryce nodded curtly.

"I'm sorry. Did she pass on recently?"

"Nah. Little over two years past—right after Ginny Mae was born. Best you not talk of her. Dan's been half-crazy with grief."

They walked back to the barnyard in silence, and Bryce handed her the gathering sack at the pump, then headed toward the stable. Lovejoy paused at the pump, washed her hands free of the sap and dirt, and rinsed the blade of her knife. Stretching and looking about, she let out a sigh and whispered, "Dear Lord in heaven, look down on me. I'm a-needin' strength and wisdom. Plenty needs doin' 'round here, and my mind's whirlin' round foolish thoughts."

The foolish thoughts didn't go away. As the day progressed, Lovejoy reminded herself that she didn't ever want to marry again—not even if someone as stalwart as Daniel Chance asked. Besides, he wasn't asking, and folks back home relied on her. They needed a healer in Salt Lick Holler.

Chapter 10

Red flannel?" Daniel echoed Lovejoy's request as soon as he took a gulp of oatmeal. Someone hadn't tended the pot, and the cereal tasted scorched. It was the first time since Miriam had come that one of the brothers had made breakfast. Daniel hoped it was the last.

Logan made a face and dumped sugar in his bowl; Titus opted for drowning his in milk and salt. Paul plopped a blob of butter in his, but it was all in vain. No amount of doctoring would fix their breakfast.

Lovejoy took a bite and bobbed her head. "Yes, yes. Red flannel. Gideon, thankee for makin' the meal. It makes me warm clear through."

"Glad you like it." Gideon smiled, but Dan figured he had reason—he'd gotten a fair night's sleep.

Alisa suppressed a shudder and washed down the only bite she'd tried with some ginger tea. "I have some white flannel. You're welcome to it."

"That's powerful nice of you to offer, 'specially seein' as how you need that flannel to stitch baby gowns, but I'll turn it away." Lovejoy rose. A moment later she returned with a little bowl filled with berries and a cup of cream, which she set down in front of Alisa, effectively nudging away the oatmeal. She patted Alisa's arm. "Not often I'm picky, but this is one of them times. I'm wantin' red."

It's not like her to be so persnickety. Dan shook his head at how she sat down, took another bite, and swallowed without letting on just how foul the stuff tasted. If she could be satisfied with this, why couldn't she be satisfied with white flannel?

"Red makes the best poultices and plasters. Need lemons and lemon drops, too. Whichever of you bucks moseys into town, I'll be asking for them as well."

"Lemons?" Bryce echoed.

"Lemon drops?" Logan looked like he didn't know whether to be confused or thrilled at that order.

Calm as you please, Lovejoy took another spoonful of oatmeal, downed it, and confirmed, "Aye. I recollect seein' a whole bushel of lemons in Reba's mercantile. They smelled dreadful good."

"Get her whatever she wants," Paul muttered.

"It's for that bride o' yourn," Lovejoy said. "Lemonade or suckin' on them drops helps with the sickness."

Paul shot to his feet. "Why didn't you say so? We have horehound—"

"Lemon's the onliest candy that'll do."

Paul accepted that outrageous notion without batting an eye. "Fine. What else do you need?"

"That's it, unless they got a library."

"A library?" the Chance brothers asked in unison.

"I reckon I may as well learn me a bit 'bout the yarbs what grow in this place. Some stuff don't grow but in special places, and I have a hankering to take advantage of this opportunity. I'll collect a passel o' whatever's beneficial, leave some here, and take the rest back home when I go."

"You're not staying?" The words tumbled out of his mouth before Daniel could hold them back. That sleepless night was making him do stupid things.

"I aim to change your mind," Titus declared. "I want you around when Alisa needs a midwife."

"And when Delilah does, too!" Paul slapped his hat on his head and glowered at Lovejoy. "I'm going to get red flannel, lemons, and lemon drops. One more thing: I'm going to see if White's Mercantile has a spare pair of handcuffs, because I'll do whatever I have to, to keep you here!"

Lovejoy merely laughed. Plainly, she didn't understand just how serious Paul was. *The man is besotted by his bride. Just like I was. . . .*

As his brothers divvied up the chores for the day, Daniel ignored their plans. He'd work in the barnyard, the stable—anything close to home. Whenever his girls were under the weather, that was a given.

"Dan'l." Lovejoy's voice jarred him out of his thoughts. He looked up from his barely touched oatmeal. "The young'uns are gonna give us fits again tonight. 'Member where the mustard was when you brung me? I'd take it kindly if'n you got a mind to gather a passel more on account of, by tomorrow, we'll use up all I cut."

"I know where there's some mustard," Alisa said. "I'll get it."

"Nope. Ain't gonna see you walking farther than the yard. Yore ankles done swoll up over the night. Most you oughtta be doin' is stitchin' and readin'."

Alisa blushed to the roots of her hair. Dan couldn't be sure whether it was because she was trying to keep it a secret from Titus or if it was because Lovejoy spoke of such anatomy in mixed company.

Titus gave his wife a horrified look. "What's wrong? Why didn't you tell me—"

"I'm fine, I'm sure," Alisa murmured.

"Don't bother growin' gray o'er that, Titus," Lovejoy said. "Her hands ain't swoll a-tall. It's when a mama-to-be's hands and face get swoll up that you got cause to fret. I niver seen me men who clucked like hens over their women and kids like you Chance boys."

"They're very good men." Though Alisa included them all in her words, Dan noticed she kept her gaze trained on Titus.

Lovejoy chuckled. "Cute as a litter of speckled pups, if'n you ask me."

"I'll get the mustard on my way home," Paul said.

Alisa started to giggle. "Look for a few bones, too."

⤜⤐⤏⤐⤚

"You even chop vegetables purdy."

Alisa looked across the table at Lovejoy and laughed. "I do?"

"Looky there." Lovejoy gestured at the colorful heap. "You don't hack at 'em with your blade; you cut 'em all of like size. And you got it arranged in an arc about you like a rainbow with the stripes a-going up and out 'stead of side to side."

"I feel ridiculous sitting here while you're working."

Lovejoy took two pots and a kettle over to the table. "Beans in here," she said as she scooped half of the tomatoes into the larger pot then put the rest of the tomatoes and vegetables in the kettle. "You're doing plenty of important things, Alisa Chance. First off, you're carrying a new life. Ain't anything more important a woman cain do than that."

"Any woman can carry a child."

Lovejoy looked her in the eye and felt the waves of pain wash over her for an instant before she resigned them to the Almighty. "Not every woman, Alisa."

Dumping her last handful of beans into the pot, Alisa sucked in a sharp breath. "Oh, Lovejoy. I'm sorry. That was—"

"Now don't you start frettin'. I need you to be clear-thinkin' on account of I need to know what Delilah's been able to tolerate so's we cain perk up her appetite."

"Other than an occasional soda biscuit, she's not keeping much of anything down. I figured on making biscuits to go with the soup you're planning."

"That's a right fine idea. After you take a nap, I expect it'll be 'bout time for you to start in on that."

"Nap!" Alisa gave her an outraged look. "I'm not going to lie around while you work."

"Yup, you are." Lovejoy started stewing the tomatoes and said over her shoulder, "Never did see me any reason to beat 'round the bush, so here goes: The ox is in the ditch here. This is a big ranch with plenty that needs doin'. All three young'uns are ailin', and Miriam's hands are full with them today. You and Delilah best behave yourselves, else you're risking the lives you carry. 'Stead of frettin', why don't we praise Jesus that I'm strong and cain fill in?"

"Fill in? Lovejoy, you did laundry, too!"

"Day's fair and sun's strong. Good time to let the whites bleach on the line." She stirred sautéed onions into the tomatoes and added in broth and a sprinkling of mild spices. Last night's leftover rice finished the recipe. This would be for the children and women. The menfolk would be having a hearty Brunswick stew. "I ken 'tisn't Saturday night, but seems to me Delilah would feel a far sight better if we tubbed her. No use lettin' the hot water go to waste, so what say you have a soak? It'll loosen you up afore your nap."

"You're doing too much."

Lovejoy laughed. "One of these days when the shoe's on the other foot and my Tempy's in a fix with Lois and Eunice, you'll return the favor."

"You'll be there—"

"She said she would be leaving soon," Daniel said as he came in. He lifted his chin toward Lovejoy. "I put another pair of onions in the girls' cabin for tonight."

"Thankee, Dan'l."

He crossed the kitchen, lifted a spoon, and took a taste of the soup she'd started for the children. Humming appreciatively, he grabbed a mug, dunked it, and started drinking. He turned to Alisa. "You found Ma's recipe!"

"Who cares about a recipe! Daniel, she can't leave. We need her! I need her." Alisa started to cry.

Wincing, he gave his sister-in-law an awkward pat. "Now, Alisa. . ."

"Folks back home are expecting me," Lovejoy said in a level tone. She'd found sympathy usually made a maternity patient worse instead of calm. "Widow Hendricks is fillin' in as the healer, but it's temporary."

"But they'll have her. We don't have anyone." Alisa took hold of Daniel's sleeve. "Tell her, Dan. Tell her how we need her to stay."

Daniel looked like he'd gladly give up his best horse to anyone who'd bail him out of this situation.

"Things have a way of working out. I've tended well o'er a hundred births, so I speak from experience. Why, look right under your nose. Miriam and Caleb seem to be just fine."

"But Dan's wife died." The words curled in Alisa's throat.

Lovejoy tilted her head and frowned. "Dan'l, is that the gospel truth?"

Chapter 11

Dan's wife died. Alisa's outburst shocked him. No one mentioned Hannah's passing. Ever. He wouldn't put up with it. As if that wasn't bad enough, Lovejoy expected him to talk about it.

"If'n a woman passes on in the first ten days, it's the childbearing. That's why I'm askin'."

He managed to mumble something about two months.

Lovejoy plopped down, disentangled him from Alisa's terrified grasp, and pulled the weeping woman into her arms. "See? You've been worryin' for naught. May as well have yourself a fine caterwaul. Cleanses the heart. Dan'l, we'll see you at supper."

He got out of there fast. Never once had it occurred to him that by keeping silent about Hannah, he'd given Alisa cause for worry. *Worry? Panic. Alisa was scared half out of her mind. Come to think on it, Paul went to fetch Delilah for Miriam so she'd have some support.*

"Dan?" Miriam called to him from the girls' cabin. "I need to go get a few things. Would you mind staying with the kids?"

He paced to his cabin and frowned. "Sounds like you're catching what the kids have."

"No need to worry, Dan. I'll be fine. It's nothing much, and I have no doubt Lovejoy will concoct something to help me improve. I won't be but a minute; I need to fetch diapers for Caleb."

Dan thought about Alisa crying in Lovejoy's arms. "Diapers on the line ought to be dry by now."

Miriam smiled. "Lovejoy's mother should have named her Mercy. I declare, the woman has more compassion than anyone I've ever met."

Polly and Ginny Mae were growing restless at their dolly tea party and started dressing Shortstack in doll clothes. The kitten seemed remarkably tolerant of that indignity, so Daniel didn't put a stop to it. When Miriam returned with a stack of diapers, he left. Plenty of chores needed doing and kept his hands busy, but his mind stayed far busier.

He could say exactly—to the day—how long Hannah had been gone. Two years, one month, and three days. Some days it felt like it was just yesterday; other moments he felt as if he'd lived a lifetime since then. Day by day he made it through for his daughters' sake. Today, though, reality smacked him in the face. Everyone else was still doing things for his sake—not tasks or favors, but shielding

61

him as if he weren't man enough to deal with his sorrow.

And I haven't been.

The thought staggered him. Grief was normal. Even Jesus wept when He learned of Lazarus's death. The emptiness inside wouldn't change, but Dan determined not to cause others sorrow because of it.

Hearing Lovejoy say anything past ten days probably wasn't related to the birthing released him of a burden he'd been carrying for more than two years now. Reba White was gone when Hannah went into labor with Ginny Mae, and Dan had to deliver their child. When Hannah didn't spring back after the birthing, he'd worried he'd done something wrong. But Lovejoy said she'd tended over a hundred births. Surely she would know whereof she spoke.

I've been troubled by that for years. The relief is unspeakable. He cast a glance back toward the house. Scrawny little Lovejoy's plainspoken words had lifted a burden from his shoulders that he'd carried for far too long. With his guilt assuaged, the sorrow persisted. . .but it was almost bearable.

Alisa shouldn't have had to worry all these months. The least I can do is give her and Delilah peace of mind when it comes to them being in a motherly way. And I'm going to be certain Lovejoy stays to attend them when their time comes. She's got a merciful heart and a gentle touch. Add to that, she's capable. I'll do anything to safeguard my brothers' wives and make sure Titus and Paul never carry the burden I have.

In the distance, he watched Lovejoy and Delilah take the wash off the clothesline. Delilah seemed to have perked up a bit. Having Lovejoy here was a good idea. She'd managed to rescue them all from a bad situation. *I'll keep her here to be sure things go well.*

❦

Having her here is a disaster. Daniel glowered at Lovejoy two mornings later. He'd slept in his cabin last night and come to check the girls this morning. One look, and he'd been livid. Fortunately, the girls were well enough to go to the main house for breakfast, so he'd sent them ahead. Now he blocked Lovejoy's exit. "What were you thinking?"

She hitched her shoulder in a careless manner. "Things that need doin', need doin'. I've got me a strong back and willing hands."

"It doesn't give you the right to meddle." He gestured wildly at the girls' cabin. Since last evening, she'd rearranged the furniture, moved the dollhouse, and set a little box down by the washstand so the girls could splash around on their own. Lovejoy hadn't stopped there. She'd twisted and tied twigs to form a heart, then stuck little flowers in it and hung it up over the bed while tacking one of Delilah's paintings up on another wall.

"It didn't need doin'; it was unnecessary."

"Draft blowing 'neath the door used to keep some of the heat from radiating to their bed." She waved toward the little table and chair set the brothers had made for his girls. "Sun hits that table cheerful-like. It'll be easier on their eyes onc't they start readin' and cipherin'."

"There's time yet before then. You can forget feathering this nest, because you're not going to roost here."

Lovejoy laughed outright. "Roost?"

"We do fine, my daughters and I. We don't need another woman in our lives, so you can just march back to the MacPhersons'. They're interested in brides; I'm not."

"You're daft as a drunken duck if you figure I ever want to wed again. I got no need to."

He crooked a brow in disbelief.

"Think on it. I got me a marketable skill and make a fair living on my own. Fact is, you fetched me for holp, and holp is what I'm a-givin'. Since we've cleared the air, you cain just get out of my way, because I don't aim to scoot off until I'm satisfied everyone at Chance Ranch is on the mend."

Daniel stared at her.

She stared straight back. Amusement sparkled in her eyes.

"You're laughing at me."

Her head bobbed. "That's a fact. If'n you come up with more of those crazy notions, I'll be in trouble. The yarb I use back home for pullin' a bent mind straight don't grow here."

"You're a pushy woman. I don't like pushy women."

"To my way of reckonin', Dan'l, you don't like most anybody. I seen you with your kin, and I seen you at Sunday worship. Onliest man I ever knew who scowled more'n you was Otis Nye from back home. He done lost both legs in the War 'twixt the States, and he spends all his time carvin' wood into the ugliest owls ever seen. Has his cousin put them up on the barn to scare folks away, but I never saw the reason. Ain't a soul who wants to pay visits to such a cantankerous coot."

"Are you calling me cantankerous?"

She sucked in one cheek and chewed on it a second as she studied him then nodded. "Yup." She dusted off her hands as if she'd just handled a gritty task. "Now you gonna move so's I cain go holp with breakfast?"

He stepped aside and watched her go toward the house. She paused at Delilah's flower garden, plucked a few flowers and leaves that she promptly tucked into her apron pocket, and disappeared into the house.

There's nothing wrong with me, and I'm not cantankerous. As he reached to shut the cabin door, he caught sight of himself in the just-rearranged washstand mirror. He was scowling.

❧

"I've been five days gone, and I cain scarce believe this is the same place." Lovejoy turned and looked about the MacPherson spread.

"We've been busy." Tempy gave her a hug.

"Hezzy turned over more ground," Eunice said, "and we put in even more of a garden."

"And just wait till you see my cabin." Lois took on a dreamy look. "Aunt Silk would swoon if'n she got a gander at how fine it is."

Lovejoy laughed with delight. "It's a fine thing to hear all's goin' so well. So why don't you gals show me what you done in those cabins?"

"First off, we made sure to take care of the larder," Tempy said as she led her to the main cabin.

"Keep a man warm and fed, and he's happy," Eunice chimed in.

Lois giggled. "With them in the stable and us all in here, I don't think they're warm at all."

"And it's going to stay that way till you all speak your vows," Lovejoy said as she gave Lois a playful poke in the arm.

Tempy raced to the shelves in the cabin. "Look, Lovejoy. We got us nice dishes. We're going to set our men a fine table."

Lovejoy watched as the girls showed her what they'd gotten—flatware, mixing bowls, a generous supply of canning jars, and a sadiron. They'd laid in a wise selection of food, too. "My, you gals did yourselves proud."

"We prayed," Tempy said. "When you rode off with Daniel, we prayed for his kin, for our men, and to have wisdom so we'd be wise stewards and good wives."

"God surely answered your prayers."

"Can we show her the cabins now?" Lois could scarcely contain herself. "We ain't seen each others' yet. It just seemed like more fun to have a grand show."

"Let's look at yourn first." Lovejoy locked arms with her.

They went to Lois and Obie's. Lovejoy stood at the door in shock. "You got an above-the-ground bed!"

"Couldn't not," Eunice explained as she reverently ran her fingers over the carved oak headboard. "Miz White o'er at the mercantile, she made us a fine deal. Bed, dresser, and—she used a highfalutin name—'commode' came to fifteen dollars a set. Even included a ticking."

"Tempy told us to add clover to the hay to keep 'em smelling sweet."

Lovejoy cast a smile at her sister.

Tempy pointed at the blankets atop the bed. "Good, thick, wool covers."

"And the pillow slips you brung look fancy as cain be," Lovejoy praised.

They went to Eunice and Hezzy's cabin next. Lois got excited at the sight of the tintype of their parents. Lovejoy admired the pitcher hanging from a peg. "The daffodils on that are enough to cheer up any mornin'."

"The washbowl's just plain white." Eunice didn't look the least bit sad. "Unmatched sets was half the price. Bought me my verra own hairbrush and comb. Lois cain keep the old ones."

Finally, they ended up in the cabin that would belong to Tempy and Mike.

Seeing the first two should have prepared Lovejoy for the last, but it hadn't. She stepped into what would be Tempy's bridal bower, and tears flooded her eyes.

"Mama's crown-of-thorns quilt!"

Tempy snuggled into her side. "You like it?"

"Oh, Temperance, it warms my soul. Mama would be so pleased."

"Mike has books, too." Tempy gazed at the shelf on the far wall with glee. Between them, they boasted nine books.

"Tempy, you brought good stuff from home." Eunice turned around. "Asa Pleasant whittles them swan-neck towel pegs, and that tatted dresser scarf couldn't have taken any room a-tall in your satchel. They make this place look dreadful fine."

"Lovejoy, will you weave me a flower wreath? I'd like one over there." Tempy indicated a spot on the wall not far from a crate she'd covered with a green calico feed sack and used as a table to hold a kerosene lantern.

"Surely I will." Lovejoy didn't mention she'd just made one over at Daniel Chance's; she was just glad this one would be a welcome addition.

She went back to the main house to help fix supper and only half listened to the list of things the girls rattled off. They'd bought ammunition so the men could hunt, kerosene, wicks, molasses, paraffin. . . .

"So what do you think, Lovejoy?"

"Huh?" Lovejoy gave Lois a guilty look. "I confess, I got lost in my thoughts."

"I said, they built a smokehouse. Hezzy's takin' me huntin' tomorrow for black-tailed jackrabbits."

"Rabbit stew sounds mighty fine. I hope you come back with a whole slew of 'em."

"You're plum tuckered out, and we're talkin' your leg off." Tempy frowned. "You hungry?"

"Not in the least. I'm tired, though. Think I'll nap a bit." Accustomed to grabbing sleep when and where she could, Lovejoy curled up on a pallet in the corner and slipped off to sleep. The next thing she knew, a rooster crowed.

Tempy stirred and sat up. She turned and tucked the blanket back around Lovejoy's shoulders. "You sleep in. I'll see to breakfast."

Lovejoy thought to protest, then decided against it. She lay there and watched as her baby sister set to doing a woman's work. Her moves were sure and steady. Pride and pain warred in Lovejoy's heart.

Time's come. Time's come for me to let her fly. My baby sister's a full-growed woman, aglow with love. God, I'm askin' Thee to shine on her and the other gals. Let the happiness they have now last a lifetime. I'm thankin' Thee for answerin' my sup-plications for them—that they'd come and find men who'd be good husbands. Thou art faithful, Lord. Now holp me as I turn loose of them. Amen.

Eunice and Lois got up, primped a moment, then went to work. All three of them moved quietly in deference to the belief that Lovejoy was still asleep. While

Lois went to gather eggs, Tempy and Eunice planned two supper menus—one if Lois and Hezzy brought back rabbit, another if they didn't.

"I brung my button tin. Obie's shirt was a-missin' a button last night. You gonna mind if'n he don't have on his shirt at breakfast so's I cain fix it? His other shirt's filthy."

"He can wear his Sunday best at the table," Tempy said in a muted tone. "We need to make our men new shirts."

Lovejoy squeezed her eyes shut tight to keep tears from overflowing. Tempy needed a new dress—really needed one; yet here she was, putting Mike's needs ahead of her own. Lovejoy had just enough of her own money to pay for her trip back home. *Pa gave me money when we left.* . . .

Lovejoy didn't know precisely how much money he'd given her. He'd shoved it into her hand, and she'd been afraid of any of the passengers on the train seeing her hold those greenbacks. Pretending to check on something in her medicine satchel, she'd stuffed the money into a small inside pocket. Since then she'd been so busy keeping an eye on the gals and on the folks over at Chance Ranch, Lovejoy hadn't troubled herself with seeing what she had.

Maybe if I'd have had me a new weddin' dress and spoken vows before a parson 'stead of having the judge pound his gavel and shoutin', "You're hitched," Vern might had honored our marriage.

Lovejoy sat up.

"You go on an' get a little more shut-eye." Tempy wagged a spoon at her.

"Eunice, will you please get me my medicine satchel?"

Tempy's eyes widened. "Are you ailing? Did they have something catchy?"

"No, no. I'm fine." Lovejoy took her satchel from Eunice and gently worked the clasp until it opened. She pulled the paper money out of the pocket, yet kept the bills inside the bag. No use raising hopes prematurely. Could be they were nothing more than bank notes from somewhere back home—and those would be useless out here.

Peeping down into the dim satchel, Lovejoy smoothed a bill and felt her heart plummet. The Confederate note wasn't worth the paper it was printed on. *Good thing I didn't say anything to Tempy and get her hopes up for naught.*

Her fingers curled into a fist, crumpling the bill. Lovejoy started to withdraw her hand, but her heart skipped a beat when she spied a different bill. Legal Tender Note. This one was a Legal Tender Note. One whole dollar. . .and another. . . and a two-dollar note, too! Four dollars. She should hold one back to pay for food on the way home, but three dollars ought to buy enough material and ribbons to outfit all three brides.

Lois came in, set down the egg basket, and started to laugh. "We'd best make it a good breakfast. The menfolk are unhappy."

"Then why are you laughing?" Eunice gave her sister a baffled look.

" 'Cuz from the sounds of the bellowin' in the barn, they was all a-tryin' to wash up. Someone didn't latch a stall right, and a horse come over and drank up the water in the basin!"

They all started laughing, and Lois plopped into a chair. "I don't know if it was Obie or Hezzy—" She gulped in a breath and finished. "But he threatened to shave the horse's tail!"

"It had to be Mike. Obie and Hezzy have beards," Lovejoy pointed out.

Tempy whooped with laughter.

Hair combed and shirts tucked in, the men arrived for breakfast. Obie's upper lip bore stubble, and Mike's whole face looked like sandpaper.

Before everyone started eating, Lovejoy cleared her throat. "If'n y'all don't mind, I'd like to ask the blessin' this mornin'. Afore I do, I wanna say, I came here to be shore things'd work out—that these gals would be happy and you MacPhersons would treat 'em right. Well, I've come to a decision."

Lovejoy heard her sister suck in a quick breath.

Mike slipped his arm around Tempy's shoulders.

"For whatever it's worth, y'all have my blessing. But it's gotta be a real weddin' with all the trimmings. Onc't I got you all to the altar right, tight, and proper, I'll be headin' back home."

Chapter 12

"Hey there, Dan'l Chance. You're a hardworkin' man to be out so early of a mornin'."

Dan turned around and dipped his head in a curt greeting. "Mrs. Spencer."

"You come to gather mustard? Are the lassies ailin' again?"

"No." He felt utterly ridiculous standing there with an armful of bright yellow flowers. Because he didn't know diddly-squat about plants, he'd come to this spot because it was the only place he could be certain he'd harvest the right stuff. "Miriam wanted a supply to dry—just in case."

"She's a smart gal. I reckon you come to do the chore so's she cain keep an eye on all the Chance women." She didn't head straight for him. Instead, she veered to one side and clipped some leaves, zagged another way and plucked a few little flowers, then approached him.

He wasn't feeling overly talkative, but he managed another curt nod.

Lovejoy chatted as she wandered closer. " 'Tis a fine thing to hear your daughters are on the mend. I'm on my way to see how Delilah and Alisa are farin'."

"You're walking?"

"That's why God gave me feet."

"God made horses with four feet so they could go farther faster." As soon as he made that ridiculous comment, Dan fought the urge to make a strategic retreat. He'd already made an utter fool of himself.

She drew closer, and merriment sparkled in her eyes. "Tell you what, Dan'l Chance. If'n you don't tell that to the woolly worms, spiders, and centipedes, I won't. They all got plenty more feet than the both of us combined, but we got 'em beat in a race."

He let out a disbelieving laugh.

"Now don't you be a-laughin' at me, Dan'l." She continued to smile broadly and opened her gunnysack. "Woolly worms and me are right good friends. Their stripes always holp me decide what to gather on account they tell me how bad the winter's gonna be."

He accepted her implied invitation and dumped the mustard flowers into her sack. "You're friendly with worms?"

"You're friendly with horses," she countered with a feisty grin.

"I've seen you ride a horse." He tugged the bag from her and held it as she gathered more mustard. Her moves were spare and efficient. "You ought not be walking out here. It's not safe."

"I got my knife."

He resisted the urge to finger the hole in his hat that Delilah had put there with her knife. Of all the women he'd ever met, Daniel felt certain Lovejoy was probably the only other woman who could wield a knife with such speed and accuracy. Even so, that didn't count for much—not out here. "Snakes and bears wouldn't much care about your knife—not to mention the two-legged variety of wolves around here."

"You back to countin' legs again, cowboy?" She slanted him a quick look.

"Polly's learning her numbers."

"And her critters, too, from the way you're going about it."

"You're full of sass and vinegar, but this is a wild land. It takes more than a sharp tongue and a sharp knife to be safe." Taking her arm, he led her beside his horse. After shoving the nearly full bag back into her hands, he cinched his hands about her waist.

Lovejoy clamped her hands about his wrists. "Wait just a minute, there. What're you up to?"

"One of us has to exercise some common sense."

"If'n you're so all-fired sure snakes are about, then why don't we share your horse? I cain ride pillion. You ride a grand horse. He shouldn't have no trouble with the extry weight."

"Fine." Dan turned loose of her, wondering what extra weight she meant. Lovejoy was a mere wisp of a woman. He didn't have all day to stand in a field of flowers jawing with a woman—however feisty or clever she might be. Leather stretched and eased as he swung himself into the saddle.

Spry as could be, Lovejoy simultaneously lifted her foot onto his and slipped her hand about his wrist. One small heft, and she swung up behind him. Her full skirts swirled with the action, then settled. She continued to clutch her bag in one arm and wound the other about his waist.

"You got this horse trained." Admiration filled her voice. "He didn't move an inch."

"I prize him." It was no understatement. Of all the brothers, Bryce had a knack with the beasts—but this horse was Daniel's. They'd taken a shine to each other from the start. "Cooper's good with my girls. Ginny Mae has a habit of squealing, but he doesn't mind."

Lovejoy hadn't stretched the truth when she claimed she could ride pillion. Perched behind him, she not only kept balance but quickly sensed the horse's rhythm and moved naturally instead of going all stiff. It felt unsettling to have her arm about him, though. Other than his daughters' hugs, no one touched him.

"Why'd you name this here gelding Cooper?"

"After a Cooper's hawk."

"That 'cuz he moves so fast you pert near fly, or on account of his coat being the exact same shade of gray?"

"His coat."

"Don't the sun feel glorious?"

From the way her cheek brushed against his shirt, he could tell she'd turned her face upward. How many times a day did he do the same thing? Different as they were, it struck him that they were alike in such personal ways. They prized time alone in the morning and sun on their faces, and each had five siblings to love and worry about. She liked birds, too.

"Well, speakin' of hawks, looky there. That red-tailed hawk's ridin' a current. Powerful sight, ain't it? And hear that? You got yourself a woodpecker!"

Dan didn't have much to say. The trip home was short, but in that time, Lovejoy identified several birdcalls and imitated them. "That 'un's a sparrow. Cain't tell from the sound if'n it's a Lincoln's sparrow, a house, or a fox sparrow. Surely ain't a song sparrow."

He didn't know, either. Dan pulled his horse to a quick halt as a covey of quail skittered by. "California quail. The meat's tender but gamey."

"It'd take a mess of them to feed a strappin' man like you. Do you set a box trap or do you net 'em?"

"Too much trouble to pluck them. We don't bother."

She managed to imitate several more birdcalls and viewed the landscape with unfeigned appreciation. *Not many women are content with such simplicity. It's a fine quality. Then again, from some of the comments she makes about life back home, Salt Lick Holler doesn't offer much.*

If any other woman told him she didn't want to remarry, he'd bet his bottom dollar she was lying. Violet Greene had come to town the same time Alisa did, and though her brother told all the men in Reliable that she was observing a year of mourning, the only thing Dan thought she was observing were the men so she could weigh their worth. On the other hand, Lovejoy didn't seem to have a bit of guile in her. *She's a pleasure to have around.*

A few minutes later, just before they reached the barnyard, Lovejoy tugged on his shirt. "How 'bout you halt this horse out of sight? I aim to put my hand to work here. What say whilst I grab what b'longs to your lassies, you venture into your kid brothers' cabin and fetch me their dirty clothes? Ain't fittin' for me to prowl around there, and I aim to have the wash pot boilin' afore I give my greetings to the women. Thataway they cain't shilly-shally when I add in their laundry."

As plans went, it was a sound one. Selfless, too. Daniel remembered having to do the laundry before Miriam came to stay with them. It was a hot, tiresome, and thankless chore. "Okay. But I'll set the fire and fill the pot."

"Now there's the spirit!"

Lovejoy Spencer didn't believe in letting grass grow under her feet. By the time Dan had a fire set and the pot over the fresh flames, she'd exited the girls' cabin with her arms full. She hadn't just gathered clothes. She had towels and sheets, too. "How 'bout soap?" she whispered.

"Bryce keeps a supply in the tack room."

"Dandy. I'll fetch it."

He went into Bryce and Logan's cabin. By the time he'd plowed through the mess in his kid brothers' cabin and emerged, Lovejoy had finished shaving lye soap into the kettle. He gave the rope at her feet a glance. "It's an old myth that snakes won't cross a rope."

" 'Course that's a bunch of nonsense. I got me that length of rope thinkin' as fair a day as we got, I'll air out the blankets and quilts. I cain start at that far end of the clothesline, loop through the fork in yon tree, then—"

"I'll do it." As tasks went, it would take no time at all for him to rig the line; Lovejoy would have to climb the tree to wind a rope about the branches. She'd do it, too. Dan snatched the rope from the ground.

"I'd take it kindly if you'd string up the full length." She smiled as she dropped shirts into the wash water. "Get me near a kettle and a washboard, and I'm a wild woman."

"No one likes to do laundry."

"No one but me, then. It's a time to pray for the folks who wear the duds and thank God for His provision." She looked over at the cabins and nodded. "I reckon the kinfolk of yourn could use some prayers."

"They do plenty of praying."

Lovejoy gave him a long, shrewd look. "They do? You're not on speakin' terms with the Almighty?"

"No use talking to someone you don't trust."

"You surprise me, Dan'l. I figured you to be a man of his word and a believer."

He glowered at her. "I am."

"Now that don't make no sense a-tall. What're you doin', not talking to the Lord who holds your heart and soul?"

"He holds my wife." The raw words tore out of him.

Lovejoy stirred the wash with a wooden paddle that was as long as she was tall. "Not a one of us loses a loved one that we don't think God shoulda let us keep. Faith ain't a fair-weather thing. Fact is, faith is all we really, truly got."

"It wasn't all I had. I had a happy life with a woman I loved."

She bobbed her head in understanding. "Sad fact is, family, friends, possessions—they cain all be gone in an instant. That feller Job in the Bible found that out. If'n you meant it when you knelt at an altar and put your soul in God's hands, then you gotta leave it there. 'Specially when life brings hurts."

Daniel glowered at her. She thought having Hannah ripped from his life was simply a hurt?

"Grief's ugly. It bubbles up like this here lye soap. You cain swim in grief for a time and come out clean, or you cain stew until it eats at your seams and tears you to shreds." She lifted a shirt, inspected it, and dunked it back in. "Mayhap I was wrong. I come here today to wash and pray for the womenfolk. P'rhaps 'tis you I'm supposed to be holding up to Jesus."

"If all it took to make your grief go away were a couple of prayers, then you must not have loved your husband the way I loved my wife."

Lovejoy didn't say a word. She set down the paddle and walked off.

Daniel paced over and knotted the rope to the end of the clothesline stake. *Mousy hillbilly woman doesn't know what she's talking about. Simple things like plants and laundry are fine for her, but that's her limit. So what if she can ride both pillion and alone?* He paced several feet, passed the rope through the fork of a tree, and wound it twice so it'd stay taut. A voice deep inside taunted, *Hannah never learned to drive a wagon, let alone ride.* He banished that frustrating memory and reminded himself that Hannah was a lady. *So what if Lovejoy can copy the whistle of every bird in the township?* He headed toward another tree. *No lady whistles.*

Anyone can go pick mustard and make a poultice. The rope burned through his hands as he savagely yanked it around a branch. *Hannah never did—not even when Polly was Caleb's age and sick like this. Well, Miriam hasn't ever made her baby son a plaster. . .actually, she did fix a turpentine one.*

No matter what thought registered, a contradiction followed. None of those counterpoints portrayed Hannah as a paragon. All along he'd been remembering her as the perfect wife and mother. But in the last week, he'd had memories of a woman who had both strengths and flaws. Instead of being a paragon, she'd been. . .well, she'd been the woman he'd married and loved.

Lovejoy's soft, hillbilly twang haunted him. *You cain stew until it eats at your seams and tears you to shreds.* Wasn't that the very nature of grief? It was impossible to lose a love and still be whole.

Lovejoy's words echoed in his mind. *A man of his word and a believer. . .not talking to the Lord who holds your heart and soul?*

He finished stringing the extensive clothesline and called himself ten kinds of fool for bringing her here. He picked up his ax and headed for trees that needed to be cleared. That odd little woman could fuss over everyone else—she'd just better keep away from him.

Chapter 13

"There." Lovejoy smoothed the quilt in place on Miriam and Gideon's bed and straightened up. "Now where was I?"

"You were telling about Tempy's wedding dress," Delilah prompted as she tugged at the other side of the quilt. They'd gone from cabin to cabin, putting the fresh linens and aired blankets back on the beds. Miriam had helped with all the other beds, but Caleb decided he was hungry, so she sat in the rocker to nurse him while Delilah stepped up to help.

"Tempy and Eunice and Lois is all getting married," Polly said importantly. "I know 'bout weddings 'cuz Auntie Miri-Em had a wedding and so did Auntie 'Lilah. Auntie 'Lisa got married in San Fur-isco."

Lovejoy smiled. "Oh, that's right. Well, that dress—it's dreadfully beautiful. Brings tears to my eyes just thinkin' on it."

Alisa finished pulling a sun-baked case on a pillow. "She'll make a lovely bride."

"They all will. Smart, too. Did I tell you 'bout what they done for the fabric? I cain't recollect who I tole what to."

Alisa folded a towel and slipped it on the towel rod at the side of the washstand. "You made me take a nap. I haven't heard a word about the weddings."

"You needed that nap." Delilah frowned at Alisa. "Titus said just the other day that you're not sleeping well."

Lovejoy folded her arms akimbo. "Alisa, I aim to tell your man he needs to hog-tie you. Them ankles of yourn are too swoll up."

"You said it was all right for them to be puffy."

"That was when they was turnip sized. You're up to muskmelon, and I aim to put a stop to it. If'n that was all, I'd be holdin' my peace, but them hands o' yourn are plumpin' up."

Alisa looked down and fiddled with her wedding band. "Miriam said her ring got tight when she was carrying Caleb."

Miriam looked at Alisa's hands and gasped. "Not tight like that!"

Lovejoy pursed her lips and waited a few moments. "You wantin' me to spout off platitudes so's you'll stop worryin', or you want me to speak the truth?"

"You not a spout. You a girl." Ginny Mae gave her a perplexed look.

"I am?" Lovejoy made a show of spreading her skirts and looking down. "Well, fancy that. I am! Since we've settled that, why don't you take me to the kitchen so's we cain finish makin' supper?"

" 'Kay." Ginny Mae took her hand and led her through the doorway.

Lovejoy shot a look over her shoulder at Alisa and mouthed, "Later."

Not long thereafter, Lovejoy put some lemonade in front of Delilah and a cup of tea down for Alisa. "You gals drink up."

Delilah sipped from her glass. "The lemon's such a big help. As long as Paul keeps me in lemon drops, I'm not nearly as queasy."

As if on cue, Paul came in. "You talking about me, darlin'?" He gave her a kiss on the cheek.

"Unca Paul, Miss Lovejoy's going to spout on Auntie 'Lisa." Polly wound her arms around his thighs. "Did you come to watch?"

Paul's brows furrowed.

"I'll be speaking to Mrs. Chance alone," Lovejoy announced.

"They's all Mrs. Chances, Miss Lovejoy. Which one you wanna talk to alone?"

"Why does Lovejoy need to speak with someone alone? What's wrong?" Gideon clomped into the room with Titus on his heels. He sucked in a loud breath. "The last time she took one of you aside, it was to tell Delilah—" He turned to his wife. "Miriam, are we going to have another one already?"

"Miriam's in the family way again?" Logan let out a low whistle.

"No! No, I'm not." Miriam glowed with embarrassment.

"Then what is it?" Titus stepped over toward Alisa and gave her a stern look. "You're too pale."

"You all sit down and eat. We got a nice meal a-waitin' for—"

"Lovejoy Spencer," Titus growled, "don't you dare think you'll get us to ignore something by waving food under our noses. It won't work."

Miriam let out a mirthless laugh. "Unless it's cobbler or gingerbread."

"Or—"

"Alisa." Titus's voice halted her from adding to the list. "Now what's going on?"

"Good thing 'bout big families is they care; bad thing 'bout big families is they hover." Lovejoy bustled through them and thumped the coffeepot down on the table. "Nobody's entitled to know nothin' that somebody wants to keep secret about their body."

"Huh?" Bryce gave Logan a bewildered look. "Did that make sense to you?"

"Someone's keeping secrets about bodies," Logan answered.

"What's this about secrets and bodies?" Dan straggled in and swept Ginny Mae into his arms and held her protectively. "Was someone done in?"

"Bloodthirsty lot, these Chance men," Lovejoy muttered as she headed toward the stove. When she turned back with a bowl of zucchini in her hands, an arc of men surrounded her.

"We decided something today," Gideon started.

"You're staying here." Titus added, "After your sister's wedding."

"Our wives need you. The children need you." Paul took the bowl from her and handed it to Logan, who promptly passed it to Bryce. "You can't go."

"We voted." Bryce swiped a slice of the vegetable and popped it into his mouth before setting the bowl aside.

"And you thought I didn't make sense?" Lovejoy gawked at them. "You cain't go voting on makin' a body stay someplace."

"Sure we can." Titus shrugged. "We've done it three times already. You're the fourth."

"Y'all voted?" Lovejoy couldn't fathom this turn of events.

"All but Dan. He was off choppin' wood. Don't matter, anyway. All five of us agreed, and the ladies already made their wishes clear. Majority rules."

"Dan would vote for you to stay." Paul's voice carried grave, unwavering certainty. "He knows what it's like for a man to worry about his wife during her carrying months. He'd want you here for Alisa and Delilah's birthings."

"You said you have someone back home filling in as the healer," Miriam interrupted.

"The very woman who trained you," Delilah added. "So you have every confidence in her ability. She'll take care of them; you'll be here to take care of us."

"Ain't right for me to presume on Widow Hendricks."

Daniel hadn't joined his brothers when they surrounded her. That fact hadn't escaped Lovejoy's notice. He'd stayed back by the door holding Ginny Mae. The man still looked as bleak as he had when he stomped away this morning; nonetheless, he locked gazes with Lovejoy. "You're needed here. I'll send a telegram."

⁓⁓⁓

"Where did all these come from?" Daniel stared at the wagon Lovejoy drove into the yard. Hannah always bemoaned the dearth of flowers in California, but Lovejoy managed to fill the entire buckboard with blossoms.

"They're all about you." Lovejoy swept her hand toward the pastures. "Poppies everywhere, curly dock, fern, and daisies. Pretty as it is, mustard don't seem quite right for a weddin', so I didn't go for any of it. Found me a passel of pasture roses, seep monkeyflower, elderberry. Delilah offered anything we wanted to cut from her flower garden, too."

He checked to be sure Lovejoy set the brake, afraid she'd been so excited about the blossoms that she'd forgotten something basic—only she'd been diligent. "Where do you want the flowers?"

She laughed. "Alisa's cabin, if you please. She and Delilah are gonna holp arrange them. The both of them have an eye for beauty."

"What's this?" He thumped on a closed crate.

"Vittles. The gals are bringin' up more in t'other wagon. Did I remember to thankee for having the grooms come set up the benches? Couldn't abide having them shuffle 'round there today. Men shouldn't see their bride on the weddin' day afore they reach the altar."

Like a hen with too many chicks, Lovejoy squawked and scurried about all morning long. Daniel minded his daughters because Miriam and Lovejoy were busy icing the wedding cake. By noontime, neighbors filled the benches, and the parson stood up front.

Lovejoy sat off to the side up front, her dulcimer in her lap and a wreath of flowers on her head. Her light brown hair shone in the sun. In the weeks that she'd been here, she'd had enough to eat, and it showed in the soft curve of her cheeks, the sheen of her hair, and the feminine form filling her dress.

Her dress. She'd changed to her other dress—the one Daniel knew was her Sunday best. The woman owned two gowns, both worn beyond redemption. He'd already spied the brides. They all wore new gowns—Lois in yellow, Eunice in green, and Tempy in blue. Why didn't Lovejoy get a new dress for herself? She needed one.

Someone must have gotten hold of Parson Abe's black suit, because it was neatly pressed instead of rumpled. He stood up front and nodded at Lovejoy. Once she started strumming her dulcimer and singing, the MacPherson men lined up at the altar. All three wore love-struck smiles.

Weddings. The " 'til death us do part" promise of his wedding vows came far too soon, and seeing others find love and expect a long, happy future made his heart ache. How could God give love, only to take it away?

Daniel hadn't attended Gideon and Miriam's wedding, because it was just too painful to remember the day when he and Hannah took their own vows. When Titus and Alisa got married in San Francisco, relief flooded Daniel. He'd been spared having to decide how to handle another ceremony and managed to put in an appearance at the reception they'd held back here at the ranch two weeks later. That should have been enough, but it wasn't. In a rash moment, he'd promised Paul that he'd escort Delilah down the aisle. He kept his word, but that stretched him to the limit.

Flowers and rings, vows and kisses—he knew firsthand those sacred moments truly forged two hearts into one. He also knew the pain of having death tear that heart asunder.

"We're ready now!" Ginny Mae's excited squeal loosened the tension.

Dan stood toward the back and couldn't help smiling when Polly and Ginny Mae started down the aisle. Each held a basketful of flower petals. Polly strewed hers with notable grace; Ginny Mae picked up clumps and dumped them onto the ground every now and then.

He squinted, then his smile nearly cracked his sun-weathered face. Instead of tying ribbons on the handle of Ginny Mae's basket as she had with Polly's, Lovejoy had wound wire or thread around a little brownish-black something-or-other to make one of Ginny Mae's beloved "worms."

Woolly worm aside, the color plan suddenly made sense—Polly in pink, Ginny in lavender, and the brides all lined up. . .a rainbow of pastels.

He looked at Lovejoy. One stripe short of the rainbow. It was how she had described the land, but at the moment, it also explained the wedding party. Well, that rainbow was missing a color. Something. . .orangish. Maybe the color of a peach or apricot or, well, anyway, a dress out of that would have suited Lovejoy.

Only she didn't seem to mind the fact that her gown looked as exciting as mud. As the brides and grooms paired up, she softly plucked the strings of her dulcimer and started to sing a hymn.

"By vows of love together bound,
    The twain, on earth, are one;
One may their hearts, O Lord, be found,
    Till earthly cares are done."

Since Obie was the eldest, the parson had him and his bride speak their vows first. Once the ring was on Lois's hand, Lovejoy sang the next verse of the hymn.

"As from the home of earlier years
    They wander hand in hand,
To pass along, with smiles and tears,
    The path of Thy command."

Hezzy and Eunice came next. Hezzy wouldn't let go of her hand long enough to slip the ring in place, so the parson helpfully accomplished that task.

"With more than earthly parents' care,
    Do Thou their steps attend;
And with the joys or woes they share,
    Thy loving kindness blend."

Mike and Tempy came last. Ginny Mae tugged on the parson's pant leg. "Him not Micah. Him Mike." Likewise, "Her Tempy, not 'Rance." The congregation muffled chuckles. Daniel didn't bother. He laughed aloud.

Instead of being weepy, Lovejoy beamed at her baby sister's wedding, and as soon as Daniel started laughing, Lovejoy looked into his eyes and laughed, too. She quickly regained her composure and sang the next verse as the parson served Holy Communion to the couples.

"O let the memory of this hour
    In future years come nigh
To bind, with sweet, attractive power,
    And cheer them till they die."

The hymn had been downright nice up till that last line. Then Daniel decided Lovejoy exercised lousy judgment in her choice of music.

"You MacPherson men may greet your brides."

"It's about time!" Obie shouted as he yanked Lois into his arms.

Everyone cheered as the newly wedded couples kissed.

"Wait a minute. My turn!" Polly motioned to Davy Greene.

Daniel took a second to realize his daughter thought she was going to either kiss or marry that snot-nosed, spoiled brat of a kid. He hiked up the aisle just as Davy reached Polly's side. Bending down so he rested his hands on his knees, he said very distinctly to the chunky kid, "Go back and sit with your mama."

Polly's face lit up. "You wanna marry me, Daddy?"

"I wanna marry Daddy." Ginny Mae glowered at Polly.

"I married your mama. She was the only bride I'll ever have." He scooped them up in his arms.

"Parson," Lovejoy called out, "how 'bout if you declare Dan'l Chance and those lassies father and daughters?"

Parson Abe cleared his throat, and his voice deepened to sound important. "I now pronounce you father and daughters. You girls each kiss your papa."

His daughters both placed a peck on his cheeks. Dan gave them each a squeeze and a kiss. He was glad he'd come to the wedding, after all.

Chapter 14

He slept through the night," Miriam whispered as she tiptoed into the room.

Lovejoy chortled softly as she finished changing Caleb's diaper. "You talkin' 'bout your son or your man?"

"Both!" Miriam yawned. "I did, too. What did you do?"

"Not a thing. That's the trick. At his age, he don't need to suckle at night. He just got used to wakin' up and wantin' company. He fussed a moment, then decided since nobody was a-gonna pay him no mind, he'd lief as well go back to sleep." Lovejoy handed the baby to his mother. "He's hungry as cain be."

Miriam took her son to her bedroom, and soon the homey creak of a rocking chair filled the cabin. Lovejoy washed up, got dressed, then plaited her hair.

Somewhere along the line, someone had mentioned they'd recently doubled the size of this cabin—mostly because with the brothers marrying and neighbors dropping by, Paul had built a much-needed second dining table. Adding on allowed a small parlor and let Gideon and Miriam have a room that would be for their children. Lovejoy had moved into that nursery and shared it with Caleb.

She scanned the room and wrinkled her nose at her reflection over the washbowl. Though never one to put on airs or long for fancy things, she was the sorriest lookin' woman in the county. All the Chance women wore their hair pinned up, and once Tempy and the gals went to town, they'd followed suit. *My hair looks like a silty river a-runnin' down my spine bone.*

Since I don't care to catch myself a husband, my appearance don't much matter, but it surely would be wondrous to move and talk so ladylike. These here women are like queens. Lovejoy laughed at herself. None of that mattered. When she went home, those kinds of trappings and pretenses would be out of place. *Who am I kiddin'? I'm just an ol' hillbilly woman, and a plain one at that.* She tied on her boots and went to see about starting breakfast.

As she cooked, she asked Delilah, "Why do ya'll go a-buyin' what grows free?"

"Like what?" Delilah started setting the tables.

"Yarbs and such. Thyme, sage, rosemary—why, you could have nice, fresh stuff 'stead of this bitty box you got at the mercantile."

Delilah laughed. "The MacPhersons gave me a bag of seeds for my birthday. Paul and I planted most of the flowers, but I didn't know what to do with the herbs."

"Yore lookin' pert today. What say we fix up a yarb garden?"

"Oh, I'd love that. I enjoy gardening so much!"

By afternoon Delilah, Lovejoy, Polly, and Ginny Mae were dirt-streaked and delighted. They shared a pitcher of lemonade and watched Shortstack stalk Daniel as he put up a chicken-wire fence around the carefully laid-out plot. "How's about we go for a nice walk? I been readin' that book Paul got me from town. I'm thinkin' we cain gather up some of the edibles and usables."

Daniel straightened up. "Usables?"

"That book Paul got me in town says there's plenty hereabouts that's handy if a body knows what to do with it. Yesterday I seen a bunch of broom. Broom's wild, and I reckon we cain gather up sufficient for me to make up some brooms—maybe even little ones for small hands." She cast a smile at his daughters.

"Poison oak's bad this year," he warned. "No going off the path."

"I'll take good care of yore loved ones, Dan'l."

"But who's going to take care of you?"

Lovejoy slid her hands down her skirt. "You needn't fret o'er that. The dear Lord does a fine job."

❦

Daniel watched them go. Delilah and Polly held hands, and each swung a basket in the other hand. Lovejoy carried Ginny Mae on her left hip and carried both a bucket and her ever-present gunnysack. Suspecting Lovejoy would find things she wanted to transplant, he shifted the fence line she'd paced off. Five more feet wouldn't make a hill of beans' worth difference to him, but she'd be pleased.

And he wanted to do things for her.

Lovejoy had faith God would take care of her soul, but that woman needed someone to fill in the little things here on earth. Self-reliant as she might be, that mountain girl needed to learn that others could help her so she didn't have to scrape by. She put her heart and hands to helping others, and the result was she didn't pay much attention to her own needs.

She'd come here and quietly filled in wherever they needed her. Before they'd moved here, Ma had an herb garden. It would be a nice sight, and he recalled how flavorful her cooking had been. She would have loved knowing the place boasted an herb—or as Lovejoy called it, a yarb—garden. Lovejoy was full of ideas and nifty tricks.

Her latest idea to make little brooms for his daughters was charming. As soon as he finished the fence, he'd go find saplings or thin branches that he could whittle into broomsticks. Maybe he'd whittle a special hook for her medicine satchel. She was always careful to put it up high, out of the girls' reach. The brass latch on that satchel had been hanging by a small wire she'd threaded through where the prongs had been, but he'd repaired it good as new last night with four small brads and a reinforcing plate. He wondered when she'd discover that. It wouldn't be a secret when she did. Lovejoy noticed little things and always appreciated them.

"Hey, Dan!"

Daniel turned toward the stable. He didn't see anyone, but it had been Bryce's voice.

"The blue's in a bad way." For Bryce to call out a problem meant something was drastically wrong. He normally doctored the animals by himself.

Dan left the bright summer sun and entered the cool shade of the barn. They'd sunk a tidy sum into buying the blue roan last week. For being just weaned, it already stood twelve hands and boasted a sweet disposition. They had big plans for him. "What's wrong?"

"Colic." Bryce grunted.

Daniel immediately grabbed the halter and started pulling. "I'll walk him." Bryce eased away. "Have at it. He's been fighting me."

Clenching the halter tighter, Daniel hauled the beast up the center aisle of the barn to the doorway and back. They paced that same route several times. He kept his gait steady and slow, careful not to exhaust Blue.

"I already gave him hot water and mineral oil," Bryce said.

It took the two of them to keep Blue upright. The colt tried desperately to lie down so he could roll, but that would be the death of him. His coat grew slick and dark with sweat.

"He's sufferin' something awful," Bryce said as he tried to wipe down the horse.

Daniel heard the edge in Bryce's voice. Calm as Bryce stayed in the worst of cases when the animals sickened, that boded ill. "Walking isn't working." Unable to think of anything else to do, Daniel asked, "Think we ought to give him another dose of mineral oil?"

"I gave him plenty. It didn't work. Only thing left is an old horseman's remedy."

"We're going to lose him if we don't do something quick. Let's do it."

Miriam came into the stable. "Did you need some lunch or help?"

"Coffee. Strong as you've got it," Bryce ordered. "I want two quarts. Ginger tea, too. Same two quarts."

Miriam got a puzzled look on her face, but she didn't stay to ask why he'd made such an odd request. Something in his tone sent her flying.

"Keep him upright," Bryce said. "I need whiskey."

"Bryce, drinking—"

"For the horse." Bryce shot him an irritated look and headed toward the tack room. When he came back with two sizable bottles, he added, "Seein' Logan fall off his horse and brain Miriam the night she arrived should have made me swear off the stuff. I was too hardheaded to figure it out, but being drunk as a skunk when Titus brought Alisa here finally made me see the light. I haven't had a drop since. I keep a store of it for medicinal purposes."

Miriam reappeared bearing the coffeepot. Alisa accompanied her with a pitcher. "Lovejoy made ginger tea for us this morning."

"Empty them on in here." Bryce had taken the caps off both bottles and was dumping their contents into a steel bucket.

Fearing the horse might kick one of the women, Daniel rasped, "You women best get out of here."

"We'll be praying," Alisa said as she and Miriam scurried away.

Pouring the remedy into a suffering colt took brute strength and perseverance. As soon as they succeeded, Daniel and Bryce started the horse in motion again.

"How long before we know if that worked?" Daniel looked over the colt's withers at Bryce for the answer.

"Twenty minutes or so." Bryce's brow furrowed. "It's amazing that we already had that ginger tea. Coffee, we always have, but the tea. . .well, that was nothing short of heavenly providence."

"Lovejoy made it."

Bryce rubbed the blue as they shuffled along. His voice was slow and thoughtful. "Never seen a woman like her."

"She's one of a kind."

"You startin' to have feelin's for her, Dan?"

Dan snapped, "I've already had a good woman."

"Yup, you did." A second later Bryce added, "Good, not perfect. Hannah loved you, and she bore you two children."

Chest tight, Daniel waited for the other shoe to drop.

"I won't recite her shortcomings, Dan. I'm just going to say she had some. We all do. Grieving makes us remember folks fondly."

"There's nothing wrong with that."

Bryce heaved a sigh. "Tell me, which horse is better? This here blue or Cooper?"

"What kind of nonsense is that? This one is young and untried. He's worth a bundle. Cooper is trained and useful. He's proven himself over and over. They're entirely different. I can't compare them."

"Hannah was like this blue—beautiful, sleek, and young. She meant the world to you. Lovejoy's like Cooper—ordinary, hardworking, and loyal, but you're blind to that. She can't measure up because you've let your memories turn a regular woman into a saint."

"Who says I'm blind?" As soon as the words were out of his mouth, Dan stopped in his tracks. He stared at his brother. "I can list plenty of Lovejoy's virtues. It doesn't mean I'm ready to get hitched to her, though."

"I didn't ask if you were ready to get hitched. I asked if you're startin' to have feelings."

At that moment the blue managed to get down to business. Bryce nodded wearily. "He'll make it. I'll keep him walking awhile yet. You can go on."

Dan headed toward the wide-open door. He stopped in the big sunlit square and looked out. His daughters both wore wreaths of daisies in their hair and about their necks, and they each had hold of Lovejoy's skirts. Drawing in a deep breath, Dan turned back toward Bryce. "Yeah. I've got feelings for her."

Chapter 15

R eliable is one fine little place," Tempy said as she latched a lid on a jar of
berries.

"Purdy as a fawn's coat." Lovejoy scooted over and made room for
Delilah at the table. Two days ago the Chance women had gone to the MacPherson
spread to help put up vegetables. Today the MacPherson women were returning the
favor after they'd all gone berry picking.

"And the folks hereabouts are neighborly as cain be." Lois came out of the
bedroom carrying Caleb, with Ginny Mae and Polly following behind her. The
children's cheeks were flushed from their nap.

Reba White had come, too. Priscilla refused to join them, but no one pointed
that out. Lovejoy had learned Priscilla had refused Titus's marriage proposal, so
she figured it was for the best that Alisa wouldn't have to spend an awkward day
with a disagreeable woman.

The Chance families couldn't begin to imagine how blessed they were to
have tables laden with plenty and not know what it was to be hungry, to sit at
that table where love, not strife, ruled. Lovejoy smiled at Tempy. The true blessing was that her own sister had married up, and the Lord seemed to be smiling
down on her in the same way.

A knock sounded on the open door as someone said, "Is Miz Spencer
here?"

"Yes, she is, Todd." Miriam motioned her neighbor to come inside.

"I heard tell she's good at doctoring. Chris Roland got a gash on his head
that needs stitching."

Wiping her hands on her apron, Lovejoy headed toward the bedroom. "Let
me get my satchel."

⸎

"What do you mean, you let her ride off with him?" Daniel glowered at his brothers
as they got ready to sit down to supper. "This can't continue. Two days can't pass
without someone wanting her attention."

Gideon elbowed Titus. "It's mostly Dan's fault. Chopping all that wood, he
gets some pretty wicked splinters."

Daniel ignored that jibe. "If folks want Lovejoy's help, they can come here
instead of expecting her to wander all over Reliable Township. It's not safe."

"She's scrappy." Bryce plopped down and swiped a biscuit. "I reckon she can
handle herself."

Logan snorted. "He reckons anyone who can lance a boil on a horse can do anything."

Paul cast a quick glance at Delilah and whispered hotly, "Watch what you say. Delilah's barely keeping her meals down. I won't have you spoil her appetite."

"Well, I'm taking a stand," Daniel announced. "She doesn't pay house calls unless it's an emergency, and if that's what's up, one of us men will escort her."

He kept busy with his daughters at the table, then took them to their cabin. It didn't surprise him in the least when Lovejoy knocked on the door. "I come to smear some salve on the girls' arms. They got scratched up a mite pickin' berries today."

Daniel stood back and watched Lovejoy minister to his daughters. Once he'd thought her to be a mousy-looking woman. He couldn't have been more wrong. Compassion shone from her hazel eyes, and her mouth perpetually tilted into a warm smile. The string she used to tame her hair into a simple plait snagged on a button of Polly's nightdress and slipped off. Instead of fussing with her own hair, Lovejoy fretted over a scratch on Polly's arm then kissed it better. Dan caught himself wishing the braid would unravel entirely.

"There, now. Sweet dreams, lassies." Lovejoy turned and pulled one of her dynamite vials out of her satchel. "You'll probably need this."

"What is it?"

"Dr. J. H. McLeans Volcanic Oil Liniment. I poured half into this for you and gave the bottle to Bryce. After fighting that colicky colt yesterday, it stands to reason yore shoulders might be squawkin' a mite."

"I take care of myself. I don't need you to coddle me."

Polly sat up in the bed. "Miss Lovejoy cuddles good, Daddy. Why don't you want her to cuddle you?"

❧

He said coddle, not cuddle. It means to fuss and pamper, Pollywog. I don't expect no one's gonna cuddle your pa, on account of him bein' prickly as a berry bramble.

Lovejoy woke early the next morning and groaned over the memory of what she'd said to Polly last night. If she hadn't given her word that she'd stay and help Delilah and Alisa with their birthings, she'd gladly pack her bags and run off.

Facing Daniel after she'd said that was going to test her composure. *Why is he different from every other man? I cain hold my own with any other buck in the world, but Dan—well, he just manages to take me by surprise.*

She dressed and searched in vain for another scrap of string to tie her plait. Miriam slipped into the room. "I thought I heard Caleb."

"He'd jist started stirrin' a bit." Lovejoy lifted him from his cradle. "He's a fine boy."

Miriam took him and rubbed noses with her son. "That's because you take after your daddy, don't you?"

The one thing Lovejoy missed about Salt Lick Holler was that she never had any solitude. Why, back home, when she was feelin' a mite blue, she could go out all on her lonesome and natter with God about her achy heart. Most days she felt happy with her lot in life, but every now and again she struggled with being a lonesome, barren woman surrounded by blossoming families. Watching the folks at the MacPherson and Chance ranches hip-deep in love. . .well, now that was a right wondrous thing. But it also hurt. Times like this, her arms ached to hold a young'un of her own, and there were times she wished she wouldn't be going back home to an empty house.

But what about how I acted last night? I could end up just as bitter as Daniel if I let this briar patch of self-pity hold me fast.

"It looks to be a fine morn. I'm gonna go gathering."

"Why don't you wait till after breakfast? Delilah or I could go with you."

Lovejoy shook her head. "No need." She slipped her knife in her sheath and hastened away before Miriam asked any questions.

"Lovejoy didn't go pay a house call on anyone, did she? It's not like her to leave others to do the cooking."

"Are you kidding?" Gideon gave Daniel a cocky grin. "We know better than to let her off the property without your approval."

"She went to gather more 'yarbs,' " Miriam said. "Don't worry. She has her knife, and one of the dogs was trotting alongside her."

Miriam looked at Delilah and Alisa. "Do either of you have any fabric? Lovejoy's dresses are in tatters."

"I'm doing nothing but sitting around." Alisa perked up. "I can sew for her."

"I'm goin' to town." Bryce propped his elbows on the table. "I suppose I could get material."

Dan nearly choked on his coffee.

Logan hooted as the women exchanged horrified looks.

"Mrs. White would help me," Bryce muttered.

"Fine. Have her help you." Dan nodded curtly. "Get something pretty—orange and flowery." He stood abruptly, suddenly feeling ridiculous. As if to provide an excuse, he tacked on, "She won't take payment for healing my girls. At least this way I can cover my debt."

Paul elbowed Delilah. "We owe her, too. Are you going to be picky about the color?"

"I'll go along and see what she has."

The table conversation ebbed and flowed. Daniel ignored it and secretly hoped Lovejoy hadn't gotten lost. The woman didn't seem to possess much of a sense of direction. By midmorning he couldn't stand it anymore. Lovejoy hadn't returned—he'd been keeping a lookout for her and determined it was time he tracked her down. What if a snake bit her or she fell and got hurt?

Daniel followed her tracks. It wasn't hard at all. Lovejoy wore sturdy, albeit badly worn, boots. The Chance women all had dainty lady's shoes that left narrow heel imprints; Lovejoy's small footprint was the only one with a broad heel. It wasn't long before he discovered where she'd gone.

Her gunnysack bulged with whatever she'd harvested, and a pail of berries sat beside it, but for the first time ever, he saw Lovejoy sitting still. The woman was always in motion—working, helping, rocking a baby. Even for church, she'd either play her dulcimer or keep one of his girls content on her lap. The oldest mutt they had lay with his head in her lap, but she wasn't stroking him. Something was wrong.

Chapter 16

L ovejoy?"

Her posture straightened, but she didn't turn around.

Dan hastened closer and noticed the distinctive motion a woman used to secretly wipe away tears. "Did you get hurt?"

She shook her head and wouldn't meet his gaze.

Dan couldn't very well ignore her red eyes and tearstained face. He didn't know what to say, though. *Talk is overrated.* He'd forgotten his father's tenet until now, but it fit. Sometimes talk just didn't suit the situation and wouldn't improve it any.

Dan sat beside Lovejoy under the tree, reached over, and silently pulled her into the lee of his body. It was a bittersweet time, her resting against him, neither of them saying a word. Somehow they were sharing the deep hurts of life. After a while, Lovejoy took a deep breath, but he didn't let go. "Some days are rougher than others, aren't they?"

She nodded.

"I got mouthy last night when you were trying to be kind. I said harsh words, and it made things harder for you. It's not you. It's me."

❦

Well, isn't that just the way God works? She'd just about given up hope of being around Daniel—not in a romantic way but just as a friend—and here he'd sought her out, waded in the creek of sorrow along with her, and given consolation. Pa and her husband always blamed her, told her everything was her fault. Here Dan sat a-sayin' 'twas his doing.

"I get upset, and I chop wood." He cupped her head to his chest. "You can't go tromping off when you're uneasy. It just isn't safe. I'll put a bench by the tree at the curve in the creek. You can go sit there when you need a spell."

She eased away from him. " 'Tisn't necessary. I won't be stayin' all that long, Dan'l."

"I'll do it because I want to." He brushed her cheek with his thumb. "Now let's take you home."

When she stood, her hair unraveled more. Only a soiled dove went about with her hair all wild. Lovejoy grabbed it, quickly twisted it, and jammed a twig through to keep the heavy tresses at her nape.

Daniel pulled it out. "Don't go putting an ugly stick in such pretty hair."

Lovejoy couldn't think of a reply to make to such an outrageous comment.

Daniel had just proven himself to be a man who could own up to his flaws and share someone's sorrows without prying. For him to pay her a compliment was like. . .well, sort of like sprinkling sugar atop a pie even though it wasn't needed. She smiled at that thought because Daniel's flattery was especially sweet. No one else had ever spoken a word of praise about her appearance. She'd cherish those words for the rest of her days.

Once they got back to the barnyard, Dan followed her into the house. "Miriam, how are we set for ribbons?"

"The girls have plenty. Why?"

"Lovejoy needs some for her plait." He turned to leave then said over his shoulder, "And don't go trying to put it up all fancy."

As the day progressed, Lovejoy heard him sawing and hammering. Late in the afternoon he popped Ginny Mae onto his shoulders. "Polly, take Lovejoy's hand and come see what Daddy did."

They walked to the bend in the creek, and Lovejoy let out a cry of surprise. Dan grinned at her. When he said he'd put a bench there, she simply assumed he'd drag one of the benches they kept in the barn and used for church meetings. Only the church benches didn't have a back to them.

"You built those!" He'd not built one small bench or chair by the tree; he'd made three benches.

"Yep. You're going to stay until the babies are born, so it's only right that there are seats for when your sister and friends come to visit."

"Oh, Dan. Thankee."

Nothin' better than fresh air and sunshine to perk up a body." Lovejoy sat back on her heels and lifted her face to the sky. "Ever think on how God made light first?"

"Can't say that I have." Delilah dusted off her hands. "Until this year, I didn't even believe in Him. It's a wonder they took me in. I couldn't cook, garden, or pray."

"Seems to me you've learnt plenty." Lovejoy reached over and patted Delilah's tummy. "And you're gonna be a good mama and teach your young'un all those things."

"You'll have to teach me that trick you used so Miriam's baby sleeps through the night."

"Time did that, I didn't. A babe's born wee little, so his belly cain't hold much. Give him three, mebbe four moons, and he fills up right fine and cain make it through. Caleb's next fit'll come when he's a-fixin' to cut teeth. I'll check in that book your man give me. See if'n there's sommat growin' hereabouts to holp with that."

"We have plenty of time," Miriam said.

"Not by my reckonin'. I aim to spend the next week or so gathering."

Lovejoy plucked a sprig of mint, dusted it off on her sleeve, popped it between her teeth, and bit. The taste burst in her mouth. "Moon's on the rise, so the flow tide in the stems will make the flowers and leaves best to pluck."

"Daniel's likely to throw another fit if you go out at night." Delilah giggled. "He about pounded a hole in our door when he couldn't find you."

"I have to agree with him," Miriam defended. "It didn't seem wise to go out on a moonless night."

"Dark is when the roots are strongest." Lovejoy shrugged. "It's jist a fact—like putting in the root vegetables for cold seasons and above-the-ground crops during summer. There's still plenty of room in the loft for me to dry things. I'm trying to put by plenty for Tempy and for you folks as well as gather up stores for folks back home."

"Won't the lady who's filling in for you do that for the people in Salt Lick?" Alisa sat in the shade. The curls around Ginny Mae's face danced in the breeze Alisa's fan stirred up.

"Widow Hendricks is nigh unto fifty. She's got rickety bones and her back's twistin' like a gnarled tree."

"If you show us what you need, we can help gather," Delilah offered.

"Might be I'd take Miriam up on that offer, but you and Alisa cain't go a-traipsin'. Reckon I could talk you folks into lettin' me have one of them empty crates to fill up and take back with me?"

"We'll fill it up and send it back by train," Alisa decided. "That way the Widow Hendricks can have whatever she needs on hand, and you won't worry about leaving." She swished the fan again and sighed. "How can I possibly be so tired? All I've done is sit around all day."

"That's a sign you need to be abed." Lovejoy got to her feet. "Like it or nay, that's just the fact." She walked over and eased Ginny Mae's head onto the blanket they'd spread on the ground near the garden and reached down to help Alisa up. "I'll go get Alisa situated. Miriam, think you could start lunch? 'Lilah cain keep an eye on these here lassies. I worry lest a snake slithers up on 'em whilst they sleep."

"She's never seen you toss your knife, Delilah," Alisa teased.

"I'll see to lunch." Miriam headed toward the main house. "Alisa, you lolly-gag and dawdle."

"I can't bear just lying around while you all work."

Miriam laughed. "You did the hard work and made me rest when I carried Caleb. Now the shoe's on the other foot."

"What foot?" Alisa muttered.

Delilah glanced down at Alisa's hem. Her face went taut for a moment, then she shot Lovejoy a quick look. "Alisa, you're not making this easy. We want Lovejoy to fuss over you instead of finding more to do. The woman never rests."

"Best you start a-prayin' for forgiveness after telling that falsehood, Delilah."

Lovejoy waggled her finger. "I niver slept like I do here. Why, I'm like a queen in that fancy above-the-ground bed!"

"If a bed makes a woman a queen, then why am I barefoot?" Alisa looked down then made a wry face. "I can't see my feet."

A few minutes later Lovejoy set a basin down on the floor and guided Alisa's feet into it. "Soakin' in that water'll cool you off and holp the swollin' go down."

"That's what Titus said last night. He's taken to washing my feet at bedtime." Alisa got teary-eyed. "He said Jesus served those He loved by doing the same thing."

"You got yourself a fine man. Loves you. That's a blessing beyond words."

As Lovejoy lifted Alisa's feet onto a towel in her lap, Alisa whispered thickly, "I'm worried."

Lovejoy looked up at her. "I niver saw the right in fibbin' to reassure folks. I'm not pleased with how yore farin', and that's a fact. I aim to put you abed and keep you there."

"Will my baby be okay?"

"God willin'."

"Titus left last night."

Daniel's blood ran cold at Gideon's so-called greeting when he and the girls arrived at breakfast.

Miriam poured coffee in the mugs on the table. "Alisa's no worse, but Titus couldn't bear to wait till this morning to go."

Dan was so sure of his next statement, he didn't even look around to confirm the fact. "Lovejoy's with Alisa."

"I wanna go be with them. We played tea party on Auntie 'Lisa's bed yesterday, Daddy."

Dan hunkered down and held Polly's hands. "Aunt Alisa is sick, and Lovejoy needs to pay attention to her. No more visiting until the baby is born."

Delilah put a dish of scrambled eggs on the table. "How about if you girls paint a picture with me today? We can have Uncle Titus hang your picture up in their cabin so Auntie 'Lisa knows you miss her."

"That's a great idea." Dan pasted on a smile. "You love to make pictures with Aunt Delilah."

"Auntie Miri-Em and Auntie 'Lisa don't make pitchers; they sew." Ginny Mae worked with her hand a moment and held up two chubby fingers. "Miss Lovejoy gots two new dresses tomorrow."

Delilah smiled. "We gave them to her yesterday. Just wait till you see her in them. She's downright pretty."

"Pretty is as pretty does." Polly singsonged the adage.

"Then Lovejoy's beautiful," Miriam said.

Daniel didn't comment, but he had to agree. The woman had a heart of gold. He just hoped her skill would be sufficient for the task that lay ahead.

With Titus gone, the brothers reassigned chores to cover for him. Knowing he needed to keep his hands busy to stay sane, Dan volunteered to do the hardest, dirtiest tasks. Miriam had packed lunches for the men as usual. He had to give her credit—whatever she packed was always tasty and filling. But today he didn't have much appetite. He knew how Titus must be feeling—that sick dread in the pit of his stomach, knowing his wife and child's lives hung in the balance.

After dragging a stubborn calf out of a mud bog at the edge of the creek and wrestling another from a thicket of scrub oak, Dan's patience had been tested to the limit. Logan was no better. He'd gotten thrown from his horse when it got skittish because a rabbit bolted from its warren. By the time they rode in for supper, Dan figured his clothes could stand up in the corner once he shucked them, and he'd best sluice off and change for supper. But first he needed to know how Alisa and Titus were.

Dan caught sight of Titus standing outside his cabin.

"He looks worse than the two of us put together," Logan murmured.

Dan halted Cooper and dismounted. Without saying a word, he stepped in front of Titus and yanked him into a tight embrace.

"Doc's in there with her," Titus said as he squeezed back.

"How long have you been home?" Logan asked.

"About two minutes."

Dan finally eased his hold. He stepped back but kept his hands on Titus's shoulders. Looking him up and down, he growled, "Let's get you cleaned up. No use in your wife seeing you looking as bad as the road you've been on."

Titus didn't want to leave the doorstep, but Dan and Logan dragged him off. None of the usual brotherly teasing filled the air. Five minutes later, with Titus washed up and wearing clothes he borrowed from one of his brothers, Dan walked him back to see what the doctor had to say.

They'd barely made it back to the porch when the door opened. The doctor came out, and the look on his face made Dan's heart drop to his knees.

"We'd best speak in private," the doctor told Titus.

Titus shook his head.

"I'm sorry. There's no hope for me to save both of them. You have to decide who you want to save. I can perform a cesarean tonight and save your wife, but the child's too small and won't survive. Women with this syndrome can worsen in a matter of hours. If she grows worse, she won't pull through. You can wait and. . .ahem. . .rescue the baby on the slim chance that your wife can last a few more weeks."

Chapter 17

Lovejoy stepped outside and took in the situation in a single glance. The doctor's bleak silence, Titus's shocked pallor, and Dan's face lined with determination and grime as he braced his brother's arm.

"Titus, Alisa sent me out here. She knows the baby won't survive if the doctor operates tonight. She won't allow that."

"Doc," Titus said, "there's got to be another choice."

When the doc gave his head a single, decisive shake, Dan rasped, "He loves his wife. They can have other kids."

"Not necessarily."

Lovejoy wrapped her arms around herself and noticed how Daniel bristled at the doctor's curt response. Clearly, he shared her horror at the man's complete lack of compassion. She tried to fish for vital information. "Doc, I know each day makes a powerful difference. How much longer would Alisa have to carry the babe afore it'll have a fighting chance?"

He shrugged. "May as well be two years as two weeks. You don't just need time; you need a miracle."

"We believe in the God of miracles." Dan spoke the words with a certainty that took Lovejoy by complete surprise. "Titus, this is your call. I'll support you in whatever you decide, but if I had things to do over again, I would have done a lot more praying."

Titus heaved a sigh. "How soon do you need an answer, Doc?"

"Morning's as long as we can wait."

"Dan'l, the doc's gotta be hungry as a three-legged wolf. Think we could take him on over for supper? I'll come along for the prayer and bring back a plate for Titus. That way he and his missus cain have a few minutes alone."

They went to the main house where Miriam and Delilah had a meal waiting. Gideon said a heartfelt prayer.

The doctor piled food onto his plate and groused, "I don't see any use in this woman using any of her herbal remedies. They haven't cured the malady."

Lovejoy didn't argue with the sour-faced stranger. To her surprise, Daniel did.

"Alisa's hanging on. That says plenty to me about how well Lovejoy's treatment works."

"I can't pull a miracle out of my medical bag. I don't know why you bothered to come get me if you believe she can." The doctor shoveled another bite into his mouth. "Then again, nothing's going to make her condition any worse than it already is."

"Paul, there's hawthorn by the mercantile. Cain I send you to town to fetch me some?" The uncertain look on his face forced a smile from Lovejoy. "I'll show you a picture in that book you bought me. I cain tell you 'zactly where it is, so you don't have to fret on whether you picked the right thing."

"Doc, you look like you could use some rest," Logan said. Bryce nodded. "You can bunk down in our place."

Lovejoy couldn't decide whether the Chance brothers truly believed she'd pull Alisa through this crisis or if they were just so angry at the doctor's heartless attitude that they were banding together to keep him at bay.

She brewed black haw bark that she had traded for back home to make a tea and handed the cup to Delilah. "You go pour this down her. I'm out to fetch dandelion leaves and valerian."

"Miriam, will you watch my girls?" Daniel stood up. "I'll carry the lantern for Lovejoy."

◦◦◦❧◦◦◦

"Oh, Lord, please holp us."

Daniel stood by Lovejoy and wondered what happened to the calm she had displayed until now. She'd knelt to dig up some dandelion and suddenly burst out with those words. She didn't stop there, either. An intercessory prayer poured out of her.

Daniel knelt, cupped her close, and sheltered her from the cold of night. He set down the lantern and reached to hold her hand. When her prayer ended, he haltingly added his own plea. "God, it's been so long since I came to You. I'm asking a lot of You—to forgive me for being so headstrong and stubborn. And please heal Alisa. Lord, spare my brother the grief I've known. Protect their baby. Give Lovejoy the wisdom and stuff she needs to do Your work. In Jesus' name, amen."

Lovejoy looked at him with tears glistening in her big eyes. "Guess since we asked the Almighty to do His part, we best get busy and do our share."

The next morning the doctor reassessed Alisa. "I don't know what you gave her, but the herbs have helped Mrs. Chance to some degree. Her swelling's gone down, but she's still in poor condition. I can't stay here while you dither. Either I operate or I leave."

Titus wavered about what to do. He spent a few moments in privacy with Alisa then came out. "Doc, Alisa won't let you operate. I can't betray her wishes any more than I can give up on either my wife or my child. Sacrificing one for the sake of the other—I can't do that."

Doc left, muttering about how he didn't know why they bothered him in the first place.

Daniel wound his arm around Titus's shoulders. "You've made the only decision you could. We have faith in the Lord, and Lovejoy's been blessed with a healing touch. We'll take it one day at a time."

⟵∽◦∼⟶

Dabbing the pencil tip on her tongue, Lovejoy frowned at the paper. She struck out yet another line with the moistened pencil lead. Many of the herbs she needed didn't grow here, or if they did, it was the wrong time to harvest them. White's Mercantile didn't carry a supply of compressed dried herbal cakes, so she was sending a telegram back home.

At three dollars for ten words, she struggled to compose the briefest message possible. No matter how she tried, what she needed couldn't be phrased in ten words. *I never noticed how many herbs have two-word names.* Red raspberry, black sampson, and lady slipper alone took up a total of six precious words. Was Virginia bugle-weed two words or three? She tapped the pencil on the page and sighed. Up to nine words at that point. Then came bethroot, false unicorn, peach bark, and yellow dock. *Delilah has fennel growing in her garden. Blessed thistle, too. But I'll need marshmallow. Cain't use rye ergot on Alisa, but I might need it for Delilah. . . .*

"Lovejoy?"

She jumped and turned around. "Dan'l! Does Alisa need me?"

"No, Titus is with her. I've never seen you scowl. What's wrong?"

"Miriam tole me to write up a telegram so's I cain have Widow Hendricks send essentials. I'm parin' it down best as I cain. White oak bark's available here. So's butcher's broom, dandelion, and rose hips."

"Hold on." He took the paper from her and joined her on the bench. Their arms brushed.

Lovejoy didn't want to scoot away. Since the day he'd found her crying and lent her his warmth and strength, she'd sensed a profound shift in him. He wasn't so caught up in his sorrows that he was oblivious to anyone else. Papa never was one to pay any mind to a female's feelings, and Vern—well, Vern never cared one bit how she was. Plenty of times she'd seen other men support their womenfolk; she wasn't Daniel's, but he'd cupped her head to his sturdy chest, and suddenly the burdens she'd been carrying didn't feel half so heavy.

And here he was again.

He studied the paper, took the pencil, and circled all the things she'd struck out. "Stop fussing and order everything you need. Ask for plenty. With Delilah also in the family way, you ought to have a generous supply."

"This is already nineteen words!"

He shrugged. "Make it forty—even sixty. I don't care about the cost; I want my brothers' wives well. Money in the bank's no good without loved ones to share it with." With that, he handed back the paper and smiled at her—smiled!

He walked off, and Lovejoy was glad he did. She didn't think she could hide her amazement. *Why, Dan smilin' is nigh unto bein' a genuine miracle!*

In the end her telegram ended up being thirty words—a nine-dollar, thirty-word telegram. No one in Salt Lick would believe such extravagance. "Lord, if Thou art of a mind to bestow miracles, Dan's perkin' outta his sorrow is right fine. Might be Ye did that jist to keep from listenin' to me yammer on 'bout him, but I been burdened for him. Whilst Thou art at that miracle business, if'n Thou wouldst protect Alisa and her babe, that'd be wondrous fine."

God listened. They took things one day at a time. Things remained touch and go, but Alisa didn't worsen. Casting a quick look back at Alisa as she napped, Lovejoy prayed the herbs would arrive the next day. *Widow Hendricks'll either figure Alisa's in grave condition or that I've gone 'round the bend, but either way, I hope it makes her shake a leg and send the stuff.*

Delilah quietly tacked Polly and Ginny Mae's latest drawings up on the wall for Alisa to appreciate. "How much longer before the medicines come?"

"Best I cain guess, the packet ought to arrive next day or so," Lovejoy said in a low tone. "Train from back home to San Francisco took five days. Stage to here took another day."

"Paul sent the telegram the day you wrote it, so I guess it just depends on how long it takes your Widow Hendricks to gather up what's needed."

Lovejoy nodded. She still couldn't believe the telegram she'd sent. She drew closer to take a gander at the girls' colorful pictures. "You got them having a right fine time with those fancy Farber colored pencils. Drawin' alongside you is a dreadful treat for them."

"They miss you." Delilah gave her shoulder a nudge. "I'll stay here. You can go on outside for a while. You can play with them or go have a little time to yourself."

Stepping outside Alisa's cabin, Lovejoy heard children's laughter. Miriam was hanging clothes on the line, and the girls were chasing chickens about the yard. The instant they spied Lovejoy, they cried her name and ran to her.

Nothing ever felt half as precious as the way Daniel's daughters flung themselves into her arms as she knelt down.

❧

"Howdy, Daniel Chance."

"Mrs. MacPherson." He nodded at Tempy. In hopes that the things Lovejoy ordered might have arrived, he'd mounted Cooper and was heading toward town.

Her eyes lit at him calling her by her married name. Atop the sorrel mare he'd seen Lovejoy use, Tempy tilted her chin up the road toward Chance Ranch. "I aim to go pay a call on my sister."

"She went off on a walk with my girls."

Tempy smiled. "You sure are nice to share your lassies with her. Fills in some of the ache in her heart."

"Because she misses her husband?"

Tempy let out a mirthless laugh. "Vern Spencer wasn't worth the cost of the copper pipe he paid Pa for her."

"Your father sold her?"

Tempy folded her arms across the pommel as pain flickered across her features. "Yes, he did."

Daniel frowned as Lovejoy's words echoed in his mind. *Them girls don't know how lucky they are to have a daddy who holds 'em close in his arms and in his heart.* He couldn't fathom what Tempy had just admitted. "What was your father thinking?"

Tempy paled and got a stricken look on her face. "Forget I said anything."

Daniel regretted his outburst. "I didn't mean to alarm you. Whatever happened wasn't your fault."

Her jaw lifted. "It's over and done with, and it's none of your business."

If he hadn't seen the tears sparkling in her eyes, he would have mistaken her resolve for stubbornness. Daniel couldn't let it go. "I'm making it my business."

"Nothing but hurt will come from you digging into my sister's past, Daniel Chance. Best you leave things alone. She's built herself a life again, and I won't let anyone hurt her."

He sat there and weighed his words carefully. "Your sister matters to me. I wouldn't hurt her—ever. It tears me apart to think your father treated her that way."

"What do you mean, Lovejoy matters to you?"

"I care for her." He paused. "A lot." The admission didn't come easily, but he knew from the guarded look on her face that he had to be more forthcoming. "I care enough that I've discussed it privately with one of my brothers."

Tempy's eyes widened. "Really?"

Daniel smiled wryly. "I'm not sure who's more surprised—you at the news or me for confessing it."

"Are you declaring your love and intentions, Daniel Chance?"

"It's not like when I fell in love with my Hannah, so I can't say it's true love." He let out a long, slow breath. "Time will tell, but I can tell you this much: I hold a deep tenderness and respect for her."

"Better you're honest about that and taking time to be sure than that she gets her heart broke." She studied him at length. "Lovejoy hasn't told you a thing about her husband, has she?"

"No."

"I'm going to trust you, Daniel. I'm not sure why."

"It's because you want your sister to have the same happiness you've found." He relaxed his grip on his reins.

She nodded. "That would be a grand miracle."

"So tell me." He fought to keep an angry edge from his voice as he bade, "Start with why your father sold her."

Chapter 18

Pa needed the copper and sugar. Lovejoy was sixteen, so he reckoned he could get a bride price and not have to feed her anymore."

Aghast, Dan stared at Lovejoy's sister.

"Pa ran—runs—a bootleg still. It broke down, and he needed the copper tubing to make it work again. That and four pounds of sugar. He traded his firstborn daughter for them."

Daniel dreaded asking, but he had to. "Did her husband treat her any better?"

"Worse. After she lost the babe—"

His mind reeled. Daniel held up a hand and blurted out, "Lovejoy had a child? She's never said—"

"No." Tempy stayed silent for a moment then sighed. "Almost seven moons into the carrying, Lovejoy came down sick, and Vern was off somewhere. He'd take off for weeks at a time. She was all by herself when she lost the babe." Tears choked her voice. "It was an awful time."

Daniel wiped his hand down his face as if it would clear the horror from his mind. Lovejoy loved babies. She'd been alone and lost her very own.

"When Widow Hendricks said Lovejoy couldn't have more children, Vern tried to sell her back to Pa."

"He didn't deserve Lovejoy or any of her children."

"I agree. Might be wicked of me to say, but I thought about dancing on that man's grave for what he did."

His grave. Lovejoy was a widow, and that fact took on a whole new significance. Daniel felt a small spurt of satisfaction and relief. "He died. When?"

"Four years back."

Daniel's brow furrowed. "She got married at sixteen."

Tempy didn't make him ask. "My sister's twenty-four. She put up with Vern Spencer for four long years."

Four years of a horrible marriage. The thought staggered him. Scrambling to reassure himself things had gotten better, Dan nodded. "So after he died, Lovejoy apprenticed herself to a midwife?"

Tempy clamped her lips together.

His heart wrenched. Lovejoy had endured so much, yet Daniel sensed there was more bad news.

"Lovejoy didn't wait that long. Once she buried her own babe, she went to Widow Hendricks and learned her healing ways in order to be there for other women so they wouldn't be alone in their times of need." After a pause, she added on quietly, "Even when those women were having babes Vern Spencer fathered."

What was a man to say in response to such a revelation? Dan wanted to bellow in anger that Lovejoy had endured so much.

Uneasily shifting in the saddle, Tempy wiped away tears. "I shouldn't have said anything. It was wrong of me."

"No, Tempy. I needed to know."

"Lovejoy never talks of it. Please don't say anything to her."

"Everything you've said was in confidence. You have my word."

"Don't even tell her you saw me." Tempy gulped in a noisy breath. "I'll just go visit another day." He no more than nodded, and she turned the mare and raced back toward the MacPherson spread.

Lovejoy. Daniel kneed Cooper toward town. What an incredible woman. Life battered her, but she'd come through with a sunny attitude and an open heart. Admiration for her filled him.

The first time they met, she'd been singing. Since then she'd had a kind word for everyone.

And she wasn't one just to talk. The woman jumped in with both feet and helped in countless ways, always with a cheerful heart. Just last week Bryce remarked that if she was any busier, she'd have to be twins.

The thought of Lovejoy patiently tending Alisa took on a whole new significance. She alone knew the loss Alisa might face, yet she kept her own experience a secret so Alisa wouldn't have more cause to worry. Lovejoy bore the burden of that worry in complete silence. Her courage humbled Dan.

Suddenly, the words he'd said to Lovejoy as she did laundry weeks ago shot through his mind. *If all it took to make your grief go away was a couple of prayers, then you must not have loved your husband the way I loved my wife.*

He groaned aloud at the memory of those words. What kind of man would be uncaring and unfaithful to his bride? Instead of being cherished, she'd been treated like chattel. Her marriage was a nightmare, not a dream.

How could I have known? Lovejoy always finds the good in people and appreciates everything around her. She never acts as if she ever walked through the valley of the shadow of death. Every hope a woman held dear was taken from her—the babe she carried, the ability to ever bear another one, the love of a mate, the simple dignity of being treated with respect. . . .

Beneath her practical, capable exterior, Dan knew Lovejoy had the tenderest of hearts. How could she deliver other women of her own husband's children? How did she stand seeing them day in and day out? Marriage brought her nothing but humiliation and heartbreak, yet she'd overcome it.

The truth hit him. *I've been so caught up in my sorrow, I kept looking at my loss. I never stopped to thank God for the blessings I had.*

"Lord, You gave Hannah and me three happy years of loving one another. The girls, Father—You gave me two daughters to cherish. I've been lost in grief, but it never occurred to me that the very depth of that sorrow showed how deeply You'd blessed me. Lovejoy talks about rainbows, and all I saw was the rain. Help me to look up."

Cooper whinnied and cantered by a clump of yellow flowers. Mustard, one of the many plants Lovejoy used to heal others. She was like those flowers—sunny and turning her face toward heaven all the day long. What was that verse? The one about mustard seed. . .faith just the size of a mustard seed was enough to move a mountain.

Dan determined then and there to exercise his faith. His mountain of grief had already been shifting and crumbling. Lovejoy told him days ago that she'd hold him up to Jesus. *Well, I'm going to do that same thing. I'm going to hold her up to You, God. I'll have faith that You can heal the hurts in her heart.*

≈≈≈

The children and Miriam were perking along right fine. Now that Delilah was over her morning sickness, she'd bounced right back, too. If only Alisa were doing as well. Lovejoy was doing her best to keep Alisa and that wee babe fine.

Daniel went to town yesterday and came back without the things from Salt Lick. No one said a word about it. They all felt the tension, but yammering over it wouldn't change a thing. Today Daniel hitched up the buckboard and took Miriam, baby Caleb, and the girls to town with him. It would be a nice outing, even if the shipment hadn't come yet.

Please, Lord, let it come. Alisa's squeakin' by one day at a time. Each day is a gift, but we're all so worried. Keep her and that babe in the palm of Thy hand and rock 'em tenderlike.

"Lovejoy?"

"I'm right here, Alisa." Dipping the rag in the pan of water and wringing it out, Lovejoy made sure she wore a serene expression. "The heat sappin' you, honey?"

"You're just as hot as I am." Alisa pushed back a russet wisp of hair. "I'm worried about Titus."

Instead of filling the cabin with chatter, Lovejoy quietly sponged off the pregnant woman. Experience had taught her folks would talk when they were good and ready.

"One of the things I love about him is how he always sings or whistles. . .or hums." Alisa's smile didn't reach her eyes. "He's stopped."

"A gal in this condition's supposed to lie in a hushed, dark room. Your man's probably trying to be quiet on account that he loves you and wants to do his part."

"I'm afraid that if the baby and I don't pull through, he'll end up brooding like Daniel."

"Then let's pray on that. I'm a scrapper, and you gotta fair bit of fight in you. Betwixt us and the heavenly Healer, I'm a-plannin' to dandle your babe on my knee by the time you and me get Delilah through her birthing."

"You always say the right thing."

Lovejoy chuckled softly. "Wish I felt thataway. Listenin' to you Chance gals talk, I always think on how wondrous fine you sound. I'm a plainspoken hillbilly woman, and I niver heard genuine ladies' conversation till I got here. My words are like grains of sand on pasteboard, and every word trippin' off yore tongues is like diamonds and silk."

"In Matthew, Christ said, 'Out of the abundance of the heart, the mouth speaketh.' You have an abundant heart, Lovejoy."

"See there? That's what I mean. Now here. Time for you to have another cup of this tea." After her patient emptied the cup, Lovejoy grinned. "Now afore we pray, I gotta tell you something wondrous fine since you mentioned Dan'l's brooding nature. You've been laid up and not seen it, but he's a-climbin' out of that dark sorrow. The man's got a smile, after all."

It wasn't long before Lovejoy saw Daniel's smile again. The buckboard pulled into the barnyard, and moments later she heard heavy footsteps. Though they left the door open for fresh air, she'd hung a midnight blue blanket inches from it to block out the light. In cases like this, light wasn't good for the mama. Sunlight flooded the cabin, then the blanket fell back in place, leaving Daniel standing there. His smile lit the whole place.

"This came for you." He set down a box and pulled the bowie knife from his belt. A flick of his thick wrist, and the twine fell away.

"Thankee, God!" She scurried over and knelt by the box. Lifting the lid, she added, "And thankee, Dan'l. 'Twas good of you to go fetch this."

"How is she?"

Lovejoy cast a look back to assure herself Alisa was sleeping again. The sedative in the tea seemed to be working well, but she'd used the very last of what she'd originally brought in her satchel. "With prayer and all these yarbs, we got a fightin' chance now. This here's lady slipper to keep her sleepy and calm. The honeysuckle'll draw off the swollin'. My, my. Widow Hendricks sent hawthorn for Alisa's headache, even though I didn't even ask for it."

Relief flooded her as she tucked the packets and vials into her apron pockets. "If'n you send Delilah or Miriam here, I'll go to the kitchen and start brewin' up what all we need."

Three days later, even with all the medicinals she'd requested on hand, Lovejoy worried. She knew she needed a bit of time to collect her thoughts and calm her nerves. If Alisa lost the baby, it would be a terrible tragedy—one that Lovejoy related to all too keenly.

I need to take time to shed my own woes, or I'll only add to Alisa's anxiety. The Good Book says a cheerful heart doeth good like medicine. Believing that proverb,

Lovejoy left Titus at his wife's side, fetched her dulcimer, and went to sit on the bench at the bend in the creek.

Having tucked the girls into their bed, Daniel stepped outside. Soft music carried on the breeze. Lovejoy was playing her dulcimer, and it was a mighty pretty tune. It didn't take but a second to surmise she'd gone out to that bench he'd made for her by the creek.

Congratulating himself for having thought to make more than just one bench, Daniel started walking. He figured he'd go sit a spell and listen. If Lovejoy wanted privacy or an opportunity to think over a difficult matter, she'd not be making music.

Taking the nearest bench and dragging it closer, Dan motioned to her to keep playing and singing. Her brows rose in surprise, but she continued as he plopped down. The last lines of "He's Gone Away" faded into the night air.

"You out for a stroll after makin' sure yore lassies are snug as bugs?"

He nodded. "It's nice to see you catching fresh air. Much as you like being outside, it must be making you chafe to be confining yourself to Alisa's side."

"She's the one who's plowing the rocky field." Absently, Lovejoy plucked a few strings. Soon the notes to "Lorena" hovered in the air.

Hannah had loved that song. She'd hummed it now and then as she straightened up their cottage. The memory made him smile—he'd forgotten how he'd teased Hannah about the fact that she followed the biblical injunction to make a joyful noise all too well. Then, too, she hummed because she couldn't ever keep the words straight if she kept on key as she sang them. The memory brought him pleasure instead of pain. *Almighty Lord, thank You.*

The last measure trembled in the air. "What are you going to play next?"

Lovejoy's right shoulder hitched. "Don't have anything particular callin' to me. You have a tune or a hymn on your mind?"

"Hmm." He thought a moment. "What about 'Rock of Ages'?"

She nodded and found her fingering, then started singing. Dan noticed her voice quavered slightly on the second verse. "Let's sing that verse again."

"You'll be a-singin' with me?" Her eyes widened.

He started singing, and she joined in.

"Not the labor of my hands
    Can fulfill Thy law's demands;
Could my zeal no respite know,
    Could my tears forever flow,
All for sin could not atone;
    Thou must save, and Thou alone."

Lovejoy's hands stilled. "I ken the hymn's about salvation, but 'tis fitting for

Alisa's situation. No matter what I do, Dan'l, 'twill be Jesus who decides whether to save or take her."

"I know." He leaned forward. Resting his forearms on his knees, he managed to be at eye level to her. In the dim evening light, he could see the glistening tears. "But we're thankful for all you're doing, and we're relying on the Rock of Ages."

Chapter 19

A thin wail shivered in the air. Daniel held Titus back. "Half an hour. You agreed to Lovejoy's rule."

"I'm not waiting. That's my wife and babe!"

"And you owe them both to God's grace and Lovejoy's skill. There are medical details she needs to tend to in there."

Titus groaned. "I'll credit God for Alisa and the baby making it. I'm thankful for all Lovejoy's done, too. But that ax. . ."

Daniel folded his arms across his chest. "What's wrong with my ax? I like to think it helped."

"It's hillbilly nonsense. Putting your ax under the bed didn't cut Alisa's pain."

Though he secretly agreed, Dan goaded his brother to delay him from bursting into the cabin. "Of course it did. I just sharpened it."

Paul started chuckling. "It's one thing to be crazy about a woman; it's another thing to be plumb crazy."

"Fine." Dan smirked. "When Delilah's in labor, I'll take my ax and go chop wood."

Paul snorted. "You'll be lucky if she doesn't swipe it and keep it under our bed from now until our baby comes." He poked Titus. "Notice Dan didn't deny that he's crazy about Lovejoy."

Titus kept craning his neck so he could keep the door to the cabin in view. He grumbled, "She's dead set on going back to Salt Lick. If she doesn't let me in there in the next five minutes, I'll personally stick her on the next stage out!"

"You can't mean it." Paul glowered at Titus. "Delilah's going to need a midwife."

Daniel rocked back on his heels and shot his brothers a smug smile. "I aim to coax her to stay forever, but Delilah's a good excuse in the interim."

Titus jolted. "Forever? Dan, are you saying—"

Dan jerked Titus around. "The door's open!" *Whew. I hushed him up just in time.*

"Titus, yore family's a-waitin' to greet you." Lovejoy beamed as she stood there. Miriam slipped on out, and Titus raced in. Lovejoy stepped out and closed the door to allow them a moment of privacy.

"Well?" Dan prompted.

"Mother's a tad weakly and the child's smallish, but I estimate they'll both be right as rain within a week."

"What is it?" Delilah rushed over, holding both Daniel's girls by their hands.

"It's a baby," Polly said with certainty.

Dan chuckled and looked to Lovejoy for the answer. "Boy or girl?"

"Cain't say. 'Tisn't my news."

"It's a girl, Daddy." Ginny Mae shimmied up his pant leg like a bear cub climbing a tree.

"How do you know that?" He wound his arm around her and planted a noisy peck on her sun-kissed cheek.

"Auntie 'Lisa sewed gowns, not pants," Polly explained.

He tweaked her nose. "Baby Caleb wears gowns, and he's a boy. All babies wear gowns."

The door opened once again. Titus stepped out into the morning sun and beckoned them in. "Come meet Tobias!"

Lovejoy waited as everyone else hastened to see the baby. Dan wrapped his free arm about her shoulders and walked her to the door. "Tobias, huh?"

"It means 'God is good,'" Titus explained.

"And He is," Dan agreed.

Everyone admired the baby and said sweet things to Alisa. Dan didn't like how she looked at all, and he was more than glad Lovejoy planned to stay and attend her. After a handful of minutes and plenty of praise, Lovejoy shooed them all out and told Miriam, "I'd count it a favor if you'd fetch me them jars I made last night of the Virginia bugle-weed and the black sampson teas. Alisa needs to drink them now."

Dan lagged behind. As she nudged him out the door, he whispered, "Yell if you need help."

She nodded.

His gaze held hers. "You're something else, Lovejoy Spencer. Without you, Alisa and Tobias wouldn't be here."

"That's God's blessing, not my doin'. He listened to yore prayers."

"I'm talking to Him plenty these days." Daniel barely kept from adding on, *And often it's about you.*

⌘

A week later Lovejoy sat on the beautiful red and gold Turkish rug in Alisa's parlor. She and the girls played with dolls while Alisa and Miriam both nursed their sons in the bedroom. Delilah sat on the settee, sipping Lovejoy's special raspberry-lemon tea after hanging dozens of diapers on the clothesline.

"One, two, free, seben," Ginny Mae counted.

"One, two, three, four," Polly corrected in an exasperated tone.

"I's playing on the floor, so I don't have to say it."

Lovejoy tickled their cheeks with the tails of their braids. "The both of you are getting grumpy. Naptime."

"Do we get a tea party when we wake up?" Polly's eyes lit with hope.

"Are you offerin' to pick the pine needles and wash 'em up?"

The girls' braids danced as they nodded emphatically. On the way back to their cabin, both girls filled their little hands by stripping a fistful of pine needles from a low bough. Lovejoy had them rinse the needles in a pie tin she kept by the pump. "Now that'll do us just dandy. Pollywog, see if'n you cain spy a rose hip. We could add that in."

Delighted that they'd helped, the girls galloped into their cabin, took off their gingham aprons, and scrambled onto the bed. In a matter of moments, they fell fast asleep.

Brewing the tea took hardly any time, but Lovejoy tried to get everyone to have either berries, something lemon or orange, or this tea each day. Pine needles and rose hips contained that same component as citrus and kept scurvy at bay. The pungent taste didn't much appeal, so she took to adding a wee bit of black-strap molasses. Not only did it sweeten the drink, it also built up blood.

"Yoo-hoo!"

Lovejoy raced out of the cabin. "Tempy!"

"We come callin'," Eunice said as the sisters hugged. "Wanted to see the new babe."

"He's a grand little man-child." Lovejoy gave the three visitors a stern look. "Alisa's still catawamptiously chewed up. Best you all sing yore praises short and sweet. We cain visit more out by the bend in the crick."

Mindful of Lovejoy's edict, Tempy, Lois, and Eunice oohed and aahed over little Tobias, then came back out. Miriam accompanied them and promised to keep an eye on Polly and Ginny Mae.

As the MacPherson women settled on the benches by the creek, Tempy sighed. "We hoped we'd be taking you home with us today. I miss you."

"It does my heart good to see you, too. I been busy here, but thangs ought to settle down in another few days. I'll come back to the MacPherson spread, least-ways till Delilah's child arrives. Even then, y'all are fairin' well. I aim to traipse back over here every couple of days and lend a hand."

"We understand," Lois said. "Day'll come, one of the Chance women'll come bail us out."

Tempy grabbed Lovejoy's hand and squeezed it. "Even if they never end up setting foot on our spread, we'd still want you to help them."

"Aunt Silk is fit to be tied," Eunice blurted out. "We got us a letter Asa Pleasant writ for her. She said you promised you'd stay with us."

Lovejoy added on, "Until I got you settled. I'd never promise more than that. Salt Lick won't have a healer if'n I stay here."

"Widow Hendricks is doing fine," Tempy argued.

"Widow Hendricks is spry of mind, but her back and joints won't let her go on much longer." Lovejoy shook her head. "This don't bear no chatter. Facts is facts. Now let's us not waste our breath or time on that when you cain tell me 'bout what y'all been doin'."

They had a lovely visit, and when it was time to leave, Eunice and Lois decided to scamper ahead and peep in on the baby once more. Tempy lagged behind.

"It does my heart good to see you lookin' this happy." Lovejoy needlessly smoothed her sister's collar. "Aglow—that's what you are. Aglow with love. God be praised."

"And you!" Making a sweeping gesture, Tempy continued, "Scrumptious as a peach in that new dress and a ribbon to match." She waited a beat then added, "Seems Daniel's name tripped off your tongue quite a bit today. Are you falling in love?"

"Temperance MacPherson! What kind of nonsense is that?"

"He's the kind of man you can ride the river with."

"I'm not getting into the marryin' boat! I'm fixin' to go home, and I'll thankee to remember that."

After her sister left, Lovejoy sat back down on the bench and stared at the sunlight sparkling on the creek. Daniel Chance was a fine man. As Widow Hendricks would say, "a man you cain tie to." *Well, he is that steadfast and dependable. Goodhearted. God-fearing. But just because he's a man a woman could tie to doesn't mean I'm tying the knot with him. Like he said at the wedding—he's had him a bride already. He don't have a heart for marryin' up again.* She sighed heavily. *Don't reckon I need to think on it, anyway. I promised to go back home.*

But the thought of leaving him left her close to tears.

Chapter 20

C ould you hold still a moment? I'm getting seasick watching you bob up
and down."

Lovejoy let out a throaty laugh and pinned another diaper to the
clothesline. "Got two babies here, each using a dozen of these a day. Better you
get seasick than drown!"

Dan nudged the laundry basket aside with the toe of his boot. "I heard you're
thinking of going back to the MacPhersons', but I'd like to discuss an alternative."

"Go ahead and talk." She scooted around him, bent, scooped up a diaper,
and reached for the clothesline again. "Might be, you ought to close yore eyes if'n
I make you dizzy. Weather's a-shiftin', and I want these dry afore them clouds
take a mind to sprout leaks."

"I've been thinking—"

"Think to tell Polly not to get her sister wet over at the pump."

Dan glanced over his shoulder. "Polly, cut it out and get away from there.
Ginny Mae, step back. The last thing we need is for you to have muddy shoes."

"What's the first thing we need, Daddy?" Polly shouted back.

He gladly took that question as a segue. Hooking his thumbs through belt
hoops, he looked at Lovejoy as he called back, "We need Lovejoy to stay and
mind you girls while I deliver cattle to Fort Point. I want you girls to behave so
I can ask her."

Lovejoy finally stopped working.

Polly and Ginny Mae dashed over. "Ask her, Daddy! Ask!"

He cleared his throat. "Mrs. Spencer, I'd—"

"You said you was askin' Miss Lovejoy, Daddy." Ginny burst into tears and
grabbed hold of Lovejoy's skirts. "I want Lovejoy."

She stooped down and gathered the girls into her arms. "It would take a
hardhearted woman to turn down a plea like that."

Daniel dared to reach over and slide a single fingertip down her cheek. "And
you've got the softest heart of anyone I've ever met. You'll stay?"

"I'm honored you trust me with your treasures."

Daniel walked off feeling quite smug. His plan couldn't be working better.
Day by day, week by week, he was going to court her with all the reasons she
should become his wife. Lovejoy understood this message loud and clear: He
trusted her with his beloved daughters. What better thing could a man tell a
woman than that?

Covers rustled. The soft, wet sound of Ginny Mae sucking her thumb in her sleep. Polly mumbled a few garbled words, and Lovejoy smiled. Even in her sleep, Polly couldn't stay silent. With Daniel gone, Lovejoy could have slept in his cabin and left the connecting hall doors open so she'd hear the girls if they cried out, but she didn't. Accustomed to a pallet on the floor, she slept each night close by them just to relish these sweet sounds.

During the day she missed seeing Daniel. And his brothers, too, Lovejoy belatedly added. Except for Titus, who stayed behind and couldn't stop smiling and humming. Having a strong, protective provider around was a novelty—not, she hastily reminded herself, that Daniel was her man. He was just, well. . .

No use hoping or dreaming his attention and help were caused by anything more than the fact that the other Chance men were involved with their wives and babes. It was natural that Dan and she became friendly on account of her minding his lassies.

At nighttime Lovejoy filled her heart with the simple things mothers took for granted—how each of the girls said "amen" with such certainty at the end of bedtime prayers, the extra tight hug around the neck one last time before lying down, the way tiny toes curled under on a cold floor the next morning.

"Lord, Thou blest me with those gifts early on when I had little sisters. 'Specially my Tempy. I reckon I didn't appreciate them then, and I'm sorry. I 'spected I'd have a passel of young'uns and would relish it all then. This time I know it's just a few nights, but I'm gonna fill up my heart with this."

She drifted off to sleep and woke the next morning to warm little knots of knees and elbows on either side of her. Opening her eyes, she whispered, "What is in my bed?"

"A Pollywog." Polly giggled.

"Pollywogs are wet little critters. I'm hoping yore not wet."

"I not wet, Miss Lovejoy." Ginny Mae wiggled around and trapped Lovejoy's braid beneath herself. "I a big girl!"

"Yes, you are. Dumplin', you're a-layin' on my hair. Since you got plenty of yore own, what say you let me have mine back?"

Asking Ginny Mae to move was akin to asking the ocean to have a tide. The child was in motion all the day long. No longer trapped, Lovejoy turned onto her back and gathered the girls in her arms. "How did I get me a pair of lassies?"

"We snuck," Ginny Mae boasted.

"Daddy told us we could." Polly sounded quite proud. "He said you might be scared, sleeping somewhere new. We're 'posed to make you not be a-scared."

"And you done a fine job." She lay there and fingered the scalloped texture of their braids. *Dan'l did the selfsame thing those nights when they got so sick.*

"Do we getta go on the gathering walk this morning?" Polly's upturned face lit with hope.

" 'Course you cain. It's like I get to carry sunbeams with me when you come along."

Funny how something could become a habit in just a few days, Lovejoy thought as she tied Ginny's little blue gingham apron. Being a make-believe mama felt so right. Never one to be overly fanciful, Lovejoy reminded herself this was just a fill-in week, a pretend time. Once Daniel made it back, she was going to go back to live at Tempy's.

But I'm going to love every minute of this while I cain.

"Polly-my-wog, fetch me the brush. Yore hair looks like a haystack gone sidewise."

"Daddy says my hair is pretty as a princess's. Soft and light as a moonbeam."

"Just like Mama's," Ginny Mae tacked on.

"Then yore mama must've been comely as a china doll." Lovejoy took the brush and got busy. She'd gone through this routine each morning now. The first time, surprise speared through her that Daniel spoke of his wife to his daughters. He was always so closed-mouthed about that. By the third day, she understood it was a father-daughter ritual. For just a moment today, Lovejoy felt a pang of jealousy. Hannah had wed and loved Daniel and cherished these sweet babes. *Oh, what I wouldn't give to have been blessed like that.*

Practicality took over. *If'n Hannah hadn't been blessed like that, I wouldn't be a-havin' my turn with these girls now.*

Once dressed, Lovejoy put on her sheath and slipped in the knife as the girls claimed their pails. Somewhere along the line, they'd each been given smallish lunch buckets. Before the walk was over, Ginny's would be dragging on the ground. That didn't matter. She looked adorable, clutching it in her chubby hand. Lovejoy slipped the edge of her gunnysack under her belt and stepped out into the morning, thrilled by the feel of a little hand in each of hers.

"Good mornin', Lord!"

Dirty and bone weary, the Chance men headed for home. Normally the married ones pushed to reach home right away; the single ones took an extra day or two of freedom. This time Daniel led the pack to get home.

"You'd think someone was holding a lit match to Cooper's tail the way Dan's racin' ahead," Paul teased.

It wasn't the first time Daniel had taken the brunt of some ribbing on this trip. He didn't mind, either. Fact was, he'd forgotten how good it felt just to hear a baby's first cry, to tease his brothers, to enjoy simple pleasures. In the past few months, life had turned around. He didn't have to haul himself out of bed in the morning. Lovejoy was right: Starting off by greeting each day and asking the Lord's guidance made all the difference.

Each of the men had a bedroll tied to his saddle, but the two horses that carried supplies on the way to Fort Point now bore packs with things the men had bought in San Francisco. Imagining Lovejoy's delight at what he'd gotten for her, Dan rode on.

When they reached the ranch, Gideon and Paul both vaulted out of their saddles and swept their wives into whirling hugs. Dan dismounted and immediately had a daughter wrapped around each leg. Lovejoy remained in the vegetable garden and simply waved at him. In the past this reception had felt empty—he'd keenly suffered Hannah's loss. This time he didn't mind. With the certainty of a man who'd found his mate, Dan knew the next homecoming he'd have Lovejoy in his arms.

After the men had taken long, hot baths and eaten a savory meal, the Chances remained around the table. Gideon started by handing a paper-wrapped parcel to Alisa. "Titus placed this order. Hope it's all right."

Alisa murmured her thanks, opened the package, and let out a cry of delight as a sand-colored, merino wool shawl spilled into her lap. "Oh, it's so soft! Thank you!"

Miriam and Delilah both accepted dresses from their husbands with voluble delight.

Polly and Ginny Mae tore the paper off their package: a new children's game called Snakes and Ladders. Eager to play it right away, they danced about while Titus read the instructions and Delilah arranged the pieces on the board.

While they were occupied, Daniel put a package in Lovejoy's arms. She gave him a stunned look. He grinned. "Go on ahead. Open it."

"It's for me?"

"Of course it is."

She looked bewildered. "Ain't niver gotten a present afore."

"Then it's well past time." He motioned for her to get started. The fact that she'd not experienced such simple delights bothered him. Daniel promised himself then and there that he'd make up for all the birthdays and Christmases she'd done without.

Lovejoy painstakingly unknotted the twine, wound it about her fingers, and tucked it in her pocket. "Cain use that later." Likewise, she unfolded the paper carefully. "This here paper's enough for letters and envelopes for months to come."

"Hurry, Lovejoy. We wanna play our game!"

Lovejoy gasped as the burgundy leather satchel came into view.

"When I fixed the latch on your other satchel, I noticed the tapestry was getting frayed." Daniel said the words in a low tone.

She ran her fingers over the beautifully tooled leather. Tears glistened in her eyes, turning them molten, and a beguiling pink suffused her cheeks. Looking up at him, she said, "Thankee, Dan'l. 'Tis enough to steal my breath."

"I knew you'd be able to use it."

She nodded. "When I go back home, it'll remind me of you."

When I go back home. When I go back home. The words echoed in her mind as Lovejoy tried to fall asleep in the above-the-ground bed back in the room she shared with baby Caleb. She flipped over and stared at the rafters. Admitting to herself that lying here was useless, she dressed and went for a walk. She ended up out on her favorite bench by the bend in the creek.

"Lord, I'm in terrible trouble here. Terrible. I'm needed back home. Widow Hendricks cain't last long, and it's just plain wrong to leave the folks in Salt Lick without a healer. When I started learnin' my yarbs, I pledged to Thee that I'd minister in Thy name and touch in Thy loving care. Well, far as I cain see, that sends me right back home.

"Only it don't seem like home no more, God. That's the problem. Well, that's part of the problem. See, my heart's here in Reliable. Tempy's gonna end up in the family way and will need my holp. Mama put her in my care long ago, and now it's not feelin' right to leave her. And the other folk here, they need my holp, too.

"And bein' dead-level honest, Father, somewhere along the line, I done lost my heart. Dan'l is a fine man—and I love him. I know he's not interested in me for more than a friend; that's a sore spot, but I reckon I cain settle for that. It's plenty more than I ever had. His daughters are a joy, and he's needin' holp with 'em.

"It's nigh unto tearin' my heart in twain. I need to go, but I'm a-longin' to stay. Thou knowest best, but I'm beggin' you to ease my heart and mind so I cain do what's right. Amen."

"We've taken a vote," Daniel announced at the breakfast table the next morning. He gulped down a bite of Delilah's incomparable flapjacks and stared at Lovejoy. "You're to stay here."

"It wasn't just the Chance men who voted, either." Miriam held Caleb in one arm while drizzling syrup on Ginny Mae's flapjack.

Logan groused, "Women voting. What's the world coming to?"

"It makes sense for you to stay," Daniel continued, ignoring his brother. "You've filled that loft with all sorts of stuff. Folks come here for you when they need assistance."

"And we love having you here." Alisa cradled Tobias close to her bosom. "You've made all of the difference."

"Now hold yore horses. God makes the difference—not me. I'm nothing more than a plain, old hillbilly woman with a knack for usin' yarbs."

Daniel studied her from the top of her shiny, fawn-colored hair down the length of her peachy dress. "Only a blind fool would call you plain or old."

"So it's settled," Bryce cut in. "You'll stay here."

"I'll think on it."

An hour later, Bryce shouldered Daniel. "She'll think on it. I'm trying to decide whether that's a good or a bad thing."

"We have time. She promised to stay until Delilah has her baby. No use rushing her. I'm going to sneak into her heart one step at a time."

◦∽৹৶৹৴৹

"We come to fetch ourn." Obie MacPherson's comment rumbled through the barnyard. Eunice sat beside him on the buckboard and nodded.

"Lovejoy is settled in nicely here," Miriam protested.

"She belongs with her kin."

"Now, Obie," Delilah reasoned, "we all understand she's Tempy's sister. You have to admit, the women of both families have been doing plenty of visiting back and forth."

Lovejoy felt Ginny Mae and Polly clutching her skirts.

Obie turned his gaze on her. "I pledged to Mike that I'd fetch you back. Your place is with kin. Tempy's setting up a place in the first cabin. You cain put all your healin' stuff there. Folk'll learn to come call for you there if'n they's a-needin' holp."

I prayed, Lord. I asked Thee to let me know Thy will. Thou art taking me away from Daniel. Thou art taking me away from these girls. Give me grace to do this.

She squared her shoulders. "I'll pack up."

Chapter 21

G one?" Daniel roared the word in disbelief. He stomped into his daughters' cabin and looked upward at the loft where Lovejoy kept her healing supplies.

Empty. Not a berry, scrap of bark, leaf, or vial remained. His heart felt just as empty.

"You was supposed to make her stay," Bryce said from the doorway.

"I'm sure she'll come visit," Miriam soothed.

Dan didn't bother to hide his glower. "What do those sneaky varmints think they're doing, dragging her away from us like she's some kind of pup and they get the pick of the litter? She's a woman—my woman."

"Yes, but—" Miriam began.

"I'm getting her back."

"We'll watch the girls for you," Delilah volunteered.

"Nope. I'm taking them with me. She can't resist them."

Miriam planted herself directly in front of him. "You're doing nothing of the kind."

Dan lowered his voice. "Miriam, I loved your sister, and I was a good husband to her. Hannah's passed on. It's no insult that I've fallen in love again."

A bittersweet smile lit her face. "I've been praying you'd find happiness, Dan. I don't begrudge you that at all. It's just that though Lovejoy loves Polly and Ginny Mae, you don't want her to think you're after a nanny. Either you go on your own, or you shouldn't go at all."

He gave her a quick hug. "I'll bring her back."

❧

The stool teetered beneath her feet as Lovejoy reached to hang a bunch of leaves.

"Obie pounded them up there for you, hisself," Lois said as she handed up another bunch.

"It was shore clever of him to bend them so's they make hooks. It's right handy."

"Tempy tole him to put in lots." Eunice stayed over by the stove and took out a loaf of bread. "Obie started funnin' her, on account it's gonna look like a dyin', upside-down garden in here."

"But it all smells so good." Tempy inhaled deeply.

"That's my cookin', not the plants and such."

Lovejoy forced a smile. The easy companionship and contentment at the MacPherson spread was an answer to so many of her prayers. God had graciously blessed the gals and settled them into loving marriages. In truth, that's what Lovejoy had asked of the Lord when she set out on this trip.

I got no business, askin' or wantin' anything more.

". . . pintail ducks and pheasants. They had themselves a great time."

"Hmm?" Lovejoy realized she wasn't keeping up with the conversation.

"Chances took down as many as our men. Smokehouses are gonna be full unto bustin'."

"That's the last of it," Eunice called up. "Got every last thing put away now."

"A letter came for you, Lovejoy." Tempy helped her big sister hop down from the stool and gave her the folded paper.

Running her fingertip over the edge of the page, Lovejoy smiled. The spidery script brought back pleasant memories of Widow Hendricks writing labels to paste on jars and vials. Wheat flour, a pinch of salt, and water mixed together made the paste for those labels, just as it sealed the carefully folded edges of the letter. No one back home used fancy stationery and envelopes like the Chance women did.

"Widow Hendricks sent all sorts of yarbs on Alisa Chance's behalf," Lovejoy said as she carefully coaxed open the paper. "And the Chances holped me gather and send back a whole crate in return."

"That's fitting," Lois said. "What with her spinebone being so twisty, she prob'ly won't be able to keep up on stock."

"I know." Lovejoy sighed. "I'm frettin' over how thangs are back in Salt Lick."

"You promised you'd stay for Delilah's birthing." Tempy gave her a startled look. "You won't go back on your word."

" 'Course not. I aim to get busy and gather up sufficient for Reliable and Salt Lick, though."

Eunice started laughing. "Get busy? You cain't sit still any sooner than I cain catch a weasel asleep."

Lovejoy sat on the stool, one foot on a rung and the other on the floor, since the silly thing rocked a mite. She read silently—partly because Widow Hendricks might tell her something private about one of their patients and partly because the outspoken old crone didn't mince words when she spoke of others. Some things didn't need to be passed on.

Dear Lovejoy,

That box came in right handy. Them mule's ear roots work grand on Otis's rheumatiz. Mine, too. Send more if'n you cain spare them. Had the Pleasant young'uns gargle with yore kind of slip elm and healed soar throt right quik. Other than that, folk are chipper as cain be. Mayhap we cain trade boxes of yarbs now an agin.

Which is why I writ this. Lots of prayer wint into this, so listen with yore heart. Tempy writ and said there's a widower there with two lassies. You been helping his kin, and she tells me the both of you got on real good. He sent telegrams. First one tole me the whole story in just a few words. "Lovejoy needed. Difficult maternity cases. Request you continue serving Holler."

Then and thar, my heart tole me the truth. Yore needed there, and I'm needed here. May be, 'tis just yore talent they need. Silk Trevor has conniptions whenever she thinks on you leaving her gals. Yore sisters are keeping watch on your pa, but Tempy's there, and she'll need you to deliver her babes as the years roll on.

Parson preached on Titus last month bout old women helping the younger gals. He brung Hattie Thales to me that week.

Hattie Thales. Lovejoy bit her lip. At thirteen, she'd been married off to a man twice her age. She'd lost a babe halfway through the carrying three times in a row. A deadwood fell in a stiff wind and half crushed her man a year back. She'd tended him till he passed on just before Lovejoy left to come here.

Nobody wants Hattie. She cain cook and clean, but a man wants sons. I took her in. We been in yore house, and she's got a clever mind. Learnt yarbs on our first walk and recited them back the next day. I got me a few good years yet to train her up, and this'll give her a happy life.

'Tis yore nest, but I'm fixing to push you out. Less you say otherwise, me and Hattie'll keep serving Salt Lick, and you cain serve God where He sint you.

You been like a dotter to me, and I will alwuz holt you in my heart.

Fondly,
Willomena Hendricks

Lovejoy stared at the letter. Tears blurred her eyes. *Heavenly Father, I've been a-prayin'. Even afore I knew how much I wanted to stay here, Thou wert makin' it possible. It near takes my breath away. About Dan'l, Lord—*

"What's a-wrong?" Eunice gave her a stricken look.

"Bad news from home?" Tempy bustled over and wrapped her arms around Lovejoy.

"No. No, it's not." Lovejoy tried to blink back the moisture and carefully fold the letter on the same creases to keep it in good condition. She didn't dare look up, else Tempy would read her face just as clearly as she'd just read these words.

"Ever'body's okay?" Lois asked. "Aunt Silk?"

"Widow Hendricks said folks are fine." *And for the first time in my life, maybe things will turn out fine for me, too.*

"That's all?"

Lovejoy wanted to go off on her own. Think. Pray. Hope and dream.

Eunice tugged on her sleeve. "More's gotta be happening than that."

"Well, yes." Her voice quavered as the realization of God's provision washed over her anew. "She's taken to training up Hattie Thales."

"Hattie!" Tempy jolted upright. "Who would have imagined that?"

"Her man was sick a good long while. I swan she's good at handlin' sick folks." Eunice nodded.

"But nobody's half as good as you, Lovejoy." Lois wiped her hands on her apron. "You got the healin' touch. Don't be sad. Folk's are always gonna seek you first."

Tempy let out a squeal. "This means you can stay! You won't be going home!"

Lord, Thou hast shewed me Salt Lick ain't home anymore. Thou hast been a-changin' my heart and mind all this time.

"You belong here," Tempy chattered on. "Obie, Hezzy, and Mike have been champing at the bit to bring you back from Chance Ranch. This here cabin's to be yours."

"See?" Eunice beamed. "Yore sister's right. You belong here."

"No, she doesn't," a deep voice said from the doorway.

"Now ain't that a fine howdy-do." Eunice gave him a sour look. "Our Lovejoy's been a-workin' her fingers to the bone for yore kin and—"

"Eunice, hobble your mouth," Tempy said, nudging her away.

"I'd like to speak with you." Daniel directed his words at Lovejoy then cast a meaningful glance at the others. "Privately."

Lovejoy slipped off the stool.

Tempy stepped in front of her big sister. "She'll be out directly."

"If she wants to," Lois tacked on, then rudely shut the door in Daniel's face.

Daniel stood there and grinned. He'd grown up with five rowdy brothers and knew that stubborn, protect-our-own look. Well, he'd let them have one last time to do it, because after this, Lovejoy was going to be his.

Minutes passed.

Daniel scowled. He could hear soft murmurs from the other side of the door, and he started considering the possibilities of either banging on the door or eavesdropping at the window. *What's taking so long?*

The door opened, and a woman stood there. For a moment he barely recognized Lovejoy. It was her, all right, in her peachy-colored dress. But her eyes and red nose tattled she'd been crying. And her hair—the MacPherson women all standing behind her had messed with her hair. Instead of her customary plait that danced along her spine or slipped over her shoulder and hung to her waist, they'd taken out the braid and twisted sections and pinned them into a cameo-sort-of look.

A virulent rush of red flooded Lovejoy's face, and she slammed the door shut again.

Dan shoved it open and plowed past Eunice and Lois, who clucked like a pair of upset hens, to get to Lovejoy. She stood in the center of the cabin, back turned toward him as she tore out the hairpins. He stepped behind her, stilled her hands, and murmured, "Let me."

One by one, he slid the pins from her hair and let them ping on the plank floor. Tempy patted his back, then she and the others scooted out the door. Lovejoy shuddered as he pulled out the last pin.

Forking his hands through her hair, he purred, "That's more like it." He crushed the thick waves in his palms then combed his fingers through the length. "There. Better."

She sidestepped and yanked her hair over her shoulder. Quickly dividing it into three portions, she muttered, "Couldn't convince them. No use trying to prettify—"

He pressed his fingers over her mouth. "You're right."

She tried to blink away moisture in her eyes.

"There's no use trying to prettify a woman who's already perfect."

Beneath his fingers, her lips parted in shock. He brushed his thumb across her lower lip. "I planned to take the months until Delilah had her baby to court you. I thought I had plenty of time to take things slow and easy."

"Court me?" Hope flickered in her eyes.

"But I'm not about to be separated from you—not even by a single fence. I'm taking you home with me. Today."

Suddenly, all the color in her face drained away.

Daniel chuckled and wrapped an arm about her waist. He'd shocked her speechless.

Lovejoy shook her head. Tears started to seep down her face, yet she leaned into him.

Daniel wouldn't figure out what was going through her mind, but something told him these weren't tears of happiness. He was sure of his feelings for her. *Did I speak too soon? Rush her when she needed that slow courting? Maybe that time was more important than I knew after her father and husband treated her so badly.* "Sweetheart, if you just want a little time—"

Despair filled her voice. "It cain't be."

"Anything's possible when you love someone." Whatever the problem, he'd solve it. Daniel refused to let anything come between them.

Pain flickered across her face.

"Salt Lick Holler doesn't need you like I do. To the depths of my soul, I swear that's the truth."

" 'Tisn't that at all. Widow Hendricks is trainin' up a new gal to holp."

He glided his hand along her neck and slipped his fingers into her hair until he cupped her head and tilted her face up to his. "Then stay here. Be my wi—"

"No!"

Daniel stared at her in stunned silence.

She tried to pull loose of his hold, but he held her fast. "What's wrong?"

"Yore offerin' me every dream I could ever have, but I cain't give you what you deserve." Her face crumbled and anguish filled her voice. "Men want sons."

"Sons? What does that have to do with me loving you?"

"I'm barren, Dan'l." The confession left her sobbing. "Widow Hendricks. . . Hattie. . .men and sons."

Broken words poured out of her broken heart. Daniel couldn't stand it. He dipped down and pressed his lips to her mouth to silence them. For a moment, she clung to him, then she tried to push away.

"Shhh." He held her tight.

"I won't ask you to sacrifice—"

"I want a wife, not a brood mare." He tilted her face up to his. "I want you, Lovejoy. I love you."

"But sons," she moaned.

"With five brothers, Chance Ranch is bound to have plenty of boys running around. We already have Caleb and Tobias. Even if they're the only ones, we can hire help. I've got you, and I've got my daughters. I'm more than blessed."

"You really feel that, Dan'l?"

His lips hovered a breath away from hers. "I lost my heart to you."

Wonder and hope lit her features. "It really don't matter to you?"

"The only thing that matters is, God brought us together."

A soul-deep sigh shuddered through her, and she cuddled close. "Truly, Dan, I love you."

"Be my wife."

"Yes." She barely whispered her breathless assent, and he pressed his lips to hers.

❧

The very next Sunday, Daniel pulled Lovejoy into his arms and kissed her again.

"Daddy, you're 'posed to do that after Parson Abe tells you to. It's at the end, not now," Polly scolded.

"I can't believe it's drizzling." Delilah handed Lovejoy her bouquet. Eunice and Lois both picked up Daniel's daughters to carry them into the barn where they always held church during bad weather. As matron of honor, Tempy stooped to gather up Lovejoy's skirts so they wouldn't become muddy on the trek to her wedding.

"I've got her." Daniel swept her into his arms.

"Oh, looky there, Dan'l! We got us a rainbow on our wedding day!"

He stopped in the middle of the yard, looked at the expanse of color, then grinned at his bride. "And it's not one stripe short."

Epilogue

Six years later

S o Jesus fed five thousand with just that one little boy's lunch." Lovejoy folded her hands. "Uncle Paul's gonna pray; then you young'uns scamper off to bed."

After Paul said the prayer, the cabin burst into a flurry of nighttime hugs and kisses. The Chance clan now boasted a full dozen children, and Miriam, Alisa, and Delilah all blossomed with the promise of another babe apiece in the coming months.

Lovejoy nuzzled a kiss on Miriam's youngest toddler's cheek then laughed as Bryce and Logan loaded up kids to piggyback them off to their cabins.

Delilah stood next to Lovejoy and said, "I read a verse this morning that fits you."

"Oh, what is it?"

Delilah smiled. "Psalm 113:9—'He maketh the barren woman to keep house, and to be a joyful mother of children. Praise ye the LORD.' Your hands have caught all of these kids, and you add so much to their lives. I'm praising God for you."

"Now wasn't that jist the best verse I ever heard? Thankee, Delilah." Lovejoy gave her a hug.

After they tucked Polly and Ginny Mae into bed, Daniel gathered his wife into his arms. "I was watching you again this evening, and something struck me anew."

She hugged him back. "What was that?"

"Your name—how fitting it is. You brought love and joy back into my life."

She stood on tiptoe. "Praise ye the Lord."

CATHY MARIE HAKE

Cathy is a Southern California native who loves her work as a nurse and Lamaze teacher. She and her husband have a daughter, a son, and two dogs, so life is never dull or quiet. Cathy considers herself a sentimental packrat and collects antiques and Hummel figurines. In spare moments, she reads, bargain hunts, and makes a huge mess with her new hobby of scrapbooking.

Chance Adventure

by Kelly Eileen Hake

To my mother, who has supported me through every word I've written since I learned the alphabet and encouraged me to pursue a career in writing. Without her guidance, patience, wisdom, and passed-on love of literature, this book wouldn't exist. Thank you, Mommy. I love you.

Chapter 1

Logan Chance rubbed his sore legs and groaned before pulling off his boots. Hard days in the saddle had never fazed him before his older brothers all suddenly decided to make him an uncle. Not four years ago, the six Chance men had had their hands full with just Polly and Ginny Mae—or so they'd thought. Now, thanks to Miriam, Alisa, and Delilah, they sported no fewer than nine little bundles of joy. It would be ten any day now—not counting the McPhersons' growing brood, which ended up on Chance Ranch more often than not. Seventeen children, and each one demanding a "horsie" ride from Uncle Logan as soon as they could talk.

No wonder Logan was restless—he didn't even have a wife, and he was already tied down! He rubbed his neck as the door opened and Bryce came in, bringing with him a gust of rain-soaked wind and muddy boots smelling of the stables. They were the last two bastions of bachelorhood, he and Bryce. If they didn't watch out, they'd be trapped just like their other four brothers. With all the womenfolk around, you never knew what new female would pop up with a smile on her face and a bare ring finger. After all, that's just what had happened to Gideon, Titus, Paul, and even surly old Daniel.

Not that he didn't love each and every fuzzy head and gummy smile, but Logan ached for some excitement before he gave in to the inevitable. After all, his brothers had waited until they were years older than he was now, and all of those years had been spent in a man's world of riding, ranching, hunting, and building. Logan just wanted some of the same, but there was no way he'd find it at Chance Ranch. It was 1874, and the world was growing so fast there was no end to the adventures out there.

"What's got you lookin' so serious?" Bryce's voice interrupted Logan's thoughts.

"Awww. . .nothin'." It was one thing to think about his dissatisfaction but entirely another to give voice to it.

Bryce pinned him with a level stare. "When're you goin' to admit that it's getting to you?"

"What do you mean?"

"You're chomping at the bit here, so why don't you go and do something about it?"

Logan shook his head in disbelief. Bryce, so often oblivious and awkward socially, still surprised him with his uncanny ability to see straight into his head. "Like what?"

"I don't know, but it seems to me that if you don't set out soon, you never will. You'll be needed for the calving season, but the end of spring would be a good time to go stretch your legs and satisfy your curiosity."

Logan mulled that over for a minute. "And what about the Chance vote?" If the others didn't want him to go, the situation could get ugly.

"Seems to me this isn't a voting issue. You may be the youngest, Logan, but you're not a boy any longer. Men make their own decisions, and since this one won't hurt the ranch, everyone will respect that." Bryce spoke with an authority Logan was unaccustomed to hearing from him.

"You think it'll be that easy, huh?" He flopped down onto his unmade bunk and shoved his boots underneath.

"Nothing worthwhile ever comes easy, Logan. If I were you, I'd start praying."

❦

"Get up."

Logan awoke with a start when a wadded-up sock hit him smack-dab on the nose. Giving a huge yawn, he lobbed it back at his brother, who caught it easily and stuck it on his foot.

"What? Breakfast bell hasn't even rung yet." He pulled up his blankets farther around his neck and scowled at Bryce.

"I know." Bryce looked annoyingly alert already. "Unless you dreamed up a plan last night while you were sleeping, you've got to nail down some particulars before breakfast."

Logan scratched the stubble on his chin. "What for? I haven't even made up my mind to go yet. No rush."

Bryce snorted. "You've got to tell everyone as soon as you can, get them used to the idea. Best try it in the morning when Gideon, Daniel, and Titus are a little groggy."

Seeing the logic in Bryce's advice, Logan sat up and started running through options. "Where should I say I'm goin'?"

"San Francisco? Big growing city like that'll give you plenty of opportunities."

"Nah." Bryce obviously wasn't thinking big enough. "I don't want to be a city slicker—what's the fun in that? Besides, it's too close to really count as an adventure."

"So you want someplace that's not too civilized and not too close?" Bryce summarized.

"Yep."

"Any other requirements?"

"I should know something about the place before going in."

"That's a mighty tall order, but I think I know just the place." Bryce looked mighty pleased with himself, but he didn't say another word.

"Well?" Logan prodded.

"Sounds to me like you're going to Salt Lick Holler." With that, Bryce walked out the door, leaving Logan to scramble into his clothes and tromp after him to the breakfast table.

As the women looked after the children and the men started making plans for the day's labor, Logan tried to recall all he knew of Salt Lick Holler.

The MacPherson brothers, known more commonly as Obie, Hezzy, and Mike, owned a spread neighboring Chance Ranch but hailed from Hawk's Fall. When they tried en masse to court Delilah—long before she wed Paul—she cleverly encouraged them to write back home for brides. They couldn't think of any girls from Hawk's Fall, but Mike remembered girls from the neighboring Salt Lick Holler. So Lovejoy had hauled Eunice, Lois, and her sister Tempy from Salt Lick to Reliable to wed them off. Somehow she wound up filling the hole in Daniel's heart.

They were all upstanding people with an easy freedom Logan envied. They'd settled well here but kept ties back to the holler—Lovejoy, in particular, wrote to their healer. It was far enough away to be a journey, foreign enough to be an exploration, but familiar so the Chance clan wouldn't protest. Salt Lick Holler was perfect.

Salt Lick Holler was far from perfect, but it was home, and Hattie Thales loved it. She took a deep breath of crisp mountain air tinged with the scent of freshly fallen rain. Spring had come again, bringing along with it the promise of new life.

Spring meant she'd be needing to shore up her stock of medicines. She'd have use for black haw bark, motherwort, cramp bark, and fennel seed before long. Hattie didn't know what meant more work for her—the babes born after a cold winter, or the scrapes and sprains collected by men and young'uns jumping around like crickets to be outside again. Come to think of it, she'd best keep an eye out for any goldenseal, heal-all, and larkspur.

Widow Hendrick had taught her all the yarbs and medicines she knew, so Hattie would be ready. Her favorite part of healing was walking through the lush country in search of yarbs, roots, and berries to put in bags, vials, teas, and poultices for later use. This winter she'd even received lessons in reading and writing, which she'd taken to like a duck to water. She'd come far in the past two years.

Who would have figured Hattie Thales would ever be so book-learned? Not her pa, who'd wed her off to Horace Thales as soon as she'd become a woman. Horace had been a good man, but he'd boasted more than twice her years and less than half her joy in life. For six years she'd fetched, cooked, mended, cleaned, and carried for him with nary a word of thanks for any of her trouble. Then a widow-maker deadwood branch had fallen on her husband and crushed the life from them both.

He hung on nigh a year, and she nursed his body but couldn't touch his bitter heart. As his health declined, so did the life Hattie had built for herself. She carried out all her household duties, stayed faithful to Horace, and tried to make him comfortable, but nothing she did could make up for the way she'd failed him. He knew he was fixing to leave this world, but he had no one to pass his name to before he died. Horace never said a word, but that bitter knowledge tainted the very air around them.

It had been over a year since he'd passed on, and Hattie could have married again—but no decent man would have her. She didn't hold it against them. Who could blame them for wanting sons? A body couldn't deny nature's way: The woman brought forth children, and the man provided for them all. Once a woman lost a babe the way Hattie had, she'd never be able to carry another. Her miscarriages didn't only mean she'd failed as a woman; they meant that any husband of hers wouldn't have the chance to be a man in the eyes of his kith and kin.

So she'd left her home to a new couple just starting out with every hope in the world and moved in with Widow Hendrick. Miz Willow, as Hattie had come to call the elderly healer, had outlived everyone she'd known so far and was glad for the company. Besides, since Lovejoy Linden had fetched her sister and the Trevor gals out to Reliable and landed herself a Chance husband, somebody needed to tend to the health of the holler. If Miz Willow had her way, she'd be around forever and a day, but the older woman needed more help as her capable hands grew stiff from rheumatism and her back twisted with age.

Hattie spotted some burdock and stooped to dig up some of the root. It helped with joint pain, and she'd used up most of her supply this winter. The cold always brought aches to the older folks. She'd need some devil's claw root for Miz Willow's rheumatism, too.

The sun hid behind a heavy cloud, casting the meadow into shadow. It seemed as though they were in for another shower. Hattie hurried to gather as much of the precious root as she could without killing the plant. She tucked it into her gathering bag and turned back toward home.

As she made it to the door, the heavens opened. She stomped her feet on the threshold to loosen the mud, then stepped inside and shut the door before taking off the worn boots. She hung up her cape and carried her gathering pouch over to where Miz Willow sat in her old rocker.

"I was askeered you wasn't gonna make it in time," she chided. "M' bones say it'll be a gully warsher for shore."

"And I know those bones o' yourn never tell tales." Hattie bent down and gave the old woman a kiss on her leathery cheek. "I'll fix you some devil's claw tea to ease the ache." She busied herself with the old kettle and added more wood to the fire.

"Thankee, child." Only Miz Willow could call a twenty-one-year-old widow-come-healer a child and give no offense. "I'm a-fixin' to write a letter for Lovejoy. Roads oughta be openin' agin soon. Anythin' we'll be a-needin' from them parts?"

Hattie thought for a moment, picturing the jars and vials of the storeroom in her mind's eye. "Not much. I harvested devil's claw and burdock today and have my eye on a patch of motherwort and some fennel. Could use more of the mule's ear root for Otis's rheumatiz. Wouldn't turn down some witch hazel, iff'n she cain spare it. I have plenty of rusty rye to trade."

She waited while the widow painstakingly scrawled out the list, pen clasped tightly between her pale fingers. There was a time when Hattie would have envied Lovejoy her good fortune in finding a husband despite her barren womb, but Lovejoy's marriage had given Hattie a place and purpose back in the holler. Hattie could only thank the good Lord for the gifts He'd seen fit to give her. She had a home and a respectable living. She'd never want for food or warmth, and she'd touch the life of every child in the holler even though she'd never have one of her own. What more could a body want?

Chapter 2

Adventure. It loomed on the horizon, as glowing and enticing as the setting sun. It beckoned to him, and Logan nudged Britches to trot so he could present his plan to the family.

The gelding had earned his name by being pure white up to his rump and hindquarters, where the white gave way to a rich chestnut brown. Logan's father had given Bryce the runt to nurse back to health if he could. Bryce's calm voice and gentle care had seen the pony through, though he would never be a large horse. Since Logan was the youngest brother and had the shortest legs, it made sense for him to ride Britches at the time. Now, years later, it was an undeniable fact that Logan had gotten too big for his Britches.

But the horse was loyal and shared his rider's love of open spaces, cool streams, and fast runs. Logan could have his pick of any horse on the ranch, but he couldn't bring himself to leave behind a companion that had served him so well—same as he'd stayed on the ranch for the past two years even though it had become increasingly obvious he was a round peg surrounded by square holes.

At least he wouldn't have to worry that Britches would be put out to pasture when he left. Mike MacPherson, the smallest of the MacPherson brothers, had an affinity for the horse and had been dropping hints lately. They'd be a good fit together. It never hurt to keep one's relatives happy, and Mike was his brother's wife's sister's husband, after all.

Yep. Logan's family tree had grown as tangled as Polly's hair when he'd tried to braid it yesterday. It had taken Delilah and Lovejoy the better part of the afternoon to straighten out that mess. The fact that he'd been reduced to messing with a little girl's hair proved he needed a change of pace.

He hadn't brought up the issue at breakfast—he'd needed some time in the saddle to think it over. He was already known as the loose cannon in the family, so he had to be as logical and serious as possible when he brought up the plan. If it sounded like he was just going off half-cocked, the family would veto his plan. After all, he was the youngest brother, and they might not take to his suggesting he leave them in California to travel across the country.

Now he knew how he'd broach the subject.

Logan slid out of the saddle and led Britches into the barn. As he removed the horse's tack, rubbed him down, brushed him, and gave him water and hay, Logan reviewed his plan of attack once more. It was crucial to wait until everyone had eaten their fill. Knowing everyone would feel warm and full after a long day's work, he figured the end of supper would be the best time to bring it up.

First, he had to wait until an opportunity presented itself. It might take a couple of days, but this was important enough for him to be patient. He'd ease into it on the sly by asking Lovejoy how things were back at the holler and what it was like this time of year. She was bound to talk about how beautiful it was and say something about one of the folks back there to make them all laugh. With everyone smiling and off guard, he'd casually mention how he'd like to see it for himself. Bryce would back him up. Then everyone would realize he meant it. The whole thing should go off without a hitch.

Hattie woke up early in the morning to the *pitter-pat-plink* of rain striking the wood and tin roof. She stretched carefully so as not to wake Miz Willow asleep in the bed beside her, then snuggled deeper beneath the warm covers.

Once more she reveled in the way their home boasted no leaks. Growing up, she'd helped Mama put pots and jars beneath the tiny streams of water pouring in from the roof. She remembered wondering if they'd reach far enough to find one another and become one long fall of water. When she'd wed Horace, she'd slept in a true, above-the-ground bed for the very first time. The Thales's cabin was a far cry from Papa's shack, but tiny drips still found their way through the walls and under the door, muddying the floor.

But the healers' hut was something else altogether. Vern Spencer had been a prideful man. A woodsmith by trade, he determined to have the best home in the whole holler. To that end, the place even had the luxury of two rooms. The offshoot served as the healers' storeroom now, and the other held the fireplace, table, and bed for everyday living. It was one of the soundest buildings standing in the holler. The only thing that weathered the storms of life any better was old Miz Willow herself.

The rain petered out, and Hattie eased out of the bed. She pulled on her overdress and stockings before stoking the fire and putting on a kettle for morning tea. She was just starting to fry the eggs when a knock sounded at the door.

"Mornin', Nessie," Hattie said, ushering the visitor inside. "What cain I do for you?"

"Pa's feelin' poorly agin and sint me ta fetch some o' yore medicine." Nessie kept her head down, refusing to look Hattie in the eye.

Rooster was feeling the effects of his brew again. Drink held that man in its grip tight as could be. Peddlin' moonshine to other fools was only the beginning of the things for which he'd have to answer to the good Lord on Judgment Day. The way she'd dealt with her father made Lovejoy Linden—now Lovejoy Chance—an even more amazing woman.

"Nessie, look at me."

The girl barely peeked up before returning her gaze to the floorboards, but it was enough to prove Hattie's fears.

"He was samplin' his own wares again, was he?" Hattie knelt down and pushed Nessie's hood back off her face to get a better look at the purple bruise coloring the girl's left cheek.

Nessie nodded wordlessly. Rooster Linden had gotten worse in the past year, but it seemed there wasn't a thing anybody could do about it. He'd always been unpredictable after drink, but lately he'd tended more to angry and violent. Hattie got up and went to the storeroom and came back with a poultice of marshmallow and burdock root.

"This should holp with the swellin' and soothe the skin a bit." Hattie paused but had to ask. "Did he hit you anywhere else?" At the shake of Nessie's head, she said, "I'm powerful sorry he took out his wrath on you. You ken 'tisn't yore fault?"

"Yes, thankee." Nessie cleared her throat. "Cain I have Pa's medicine now?"

Hattie rocked back on her heels and prayed. *Lord, I want to do Yore will, but I don't know what that is. Mr. Linden's hurtin' himself and others. As a healer, I'm s'posed to holp wherever I cain—but iff'n I make it so his drinkin's easier, who does that really holp? Not Nessie or even Rooster. But iff'n I don't, he'll be riled as a bear and drink more. Then Nessie'll suffer his anger agin. How do I protect her?*

"Here you go, Nessie." Miz Willow took the decision from Hattie's hands by handing a packet to Nessie. "That'll clean him out right quick, though he won't thank me for it till after."

"Thankee, Widow Hendrick." Nessie shrugged her hood back on.

"Wait a minute. Have some of this." The older woman passed the girl a mug of tea. "It'll keep yore bones warm on the walk back. And when yore pa feels better, you make shore you ask him to come down and visit with Widow Hendrick." A steely glint lit her usually twinkling eyes. "We have sommat to discuss, him and me."

Logan breathed deeply as he stepped into the main cabin. *Smells like pot roast, mashed potatoes, and could that possibly be. . .*

"Muck!" Alisa's voice interrupted his thoughts. He was surprised to see her tapping her tiny foot and glaring up at him. "Go wipe off your boots, Logan. I just cleaned the floor!"

He obligingly loped back out the door, stomped his feet, and came back in. Little things like that didn't seem like much, but he heard those kinds of remarks every day. "Wipe your feet." "Don't put your boots on the chair." "Hold the baby for a minute." "Not like that!" "Why aren't you washed up yet?" "How'd you get these so dirty?" "Where'd you put the. . .oh, never mind." "*Another* hole to mend?" The endless refrain was enough to set a man's teeth permanently on edge.

He spotted the apple pies he'd been smelling earlier and reconsidered. Having women around wasn't all bad. It definitely had its compensations! His mouth watering, Logan filched a biscuit from one of the baskets, only to have his knuckles rapped with a wooden spoon.

"Ow!" He dropped it like a red-hot poker.

"You know better than that, Logan Chance." Miriam shook the wooden spoon at him.

There was a time when he would've flashed her a smile, waited until she turned around, then crammed it into his mouth while she wasn't looking. Now it wasn't worth it. The mischief had been all but scrubbed and chided out of him. Things had come to a sorry state indeed.

He took a seat and bowed his head for the prayer, then shoveled forkfuls of meat and potatoes into his mouth while everybody chattered away. Chomping on a buttery biscuit so light it could've flown, Logan promised himself he'd ignore the domesticity of it all and enjoy his family before he set out. When plates of apple pie came around, Logan judged the time was right.

"So have you had any letters from Widow Hendrick lately?" He addressed the question to Lovejoy before trying the pie. The taste of cinnamon and apples lingered as sweet as victory while Lovejoy started speaking about the holler.

"As a matter of fact, had one jist this week. Seems the spell of whooping cough is over—they lost two young'uns and one older fella." She shook her head sadly.

This wasn't going the way he'd hoped. He tried to steer the conversation into more pleasant territory. "Could've been much worse. How's everybody else doin'?" He held his breath until she smiled.

"Well, there're at least three babes on the way for this spring, so Hattie's busy harvesting and offered to send me some rusty rye." She paused for a moment before continuing. "Isn't it just like the good Lord to send three new lives after taking the same number? Keeps it all in balance."

"Balance?" Logan jumped on his opportunity. "Seems to me they're a bit short over there since Reliable snatched Obie, Hezzie, Mike, Eunice, Lois, Tempy, and yourself."

"Now if that doesn't just prove it, I don't know what will, Logan. See, God sent out three men, but the loss of eligible bachelors would've been hard to bear, so He paved the way for their brides, too." She beamed across the table as all the women nodded in agreement, Paul nudging Delilah with his elbow.

"I just meant that Salt Lick Holler's sent a bunch of wonderful people out to Reliable"—Logan leaned back to appear nonchalant—"but Reliable hasn't returned the favor."

"There's some truth to that." Daniel put an arm around his wife's shoulders. "We're keeping 'em, too."

Murmurs of agreement sounded around the table, punctuated by one of the babies banging a spoon against the table. If Logan didn't do something immediately, the conversation would be over and he'd've lost his chance.

"I bet it's nice this time of year." He shrugged and gobbled the last bite of his pie.

"Shore is." Lovejoy's eyes went a little dreamy. "You cain smell things a-growin' from the earth in spring. It's fresh and green. Birds sang at ya; butterflies flit around through the air. The sun's so bright, you walk under the trees to keep cool until a breeze picks up. Baby critters pop their tiny heads up around every corner, and the sounds of life rustle alongside the ring of wood bein' chopped." She gave a wistful sigh. "At night the stars glow like it's their last time, and glow-worms dart 'round the trees an' ruffle yore hair iff'n ya git too close. It'll be that way till the middle of summer."

"Oh, Lovejoy, that sounds beautiful." Alisa reached over to pat her on the arm.

"I'd like to see all that," Logan burst in before Lovejoy could start assuring them all how wonderful Chance Ranch was and how she'd rather be here anyway.

"Everybody should." Lovejoy smiled at him. "But it's a better place ta visit than ta call home."

"I've already got a home. Seems like I'm missing a place to visit." Logan sent up a little prayer. "Would that be possible?"

"You mean it, don't you?" Delilah looked at him in surprise.

" 'Course he doesn't. He's got everything he could want right here." Gideon brushed the idea away like a pesky gnat, and Logan felt his freedom slipping away.

Chapter 3

I don't know about that." Every head turned toward Bryce.

"What are you talking 'bout, Bryce?" Daniel drew Lovejoy closer.

"I'm just saying we all remember moving out here to start Chance Ranch, making a home and a place for ourselves with Ma. Logan was barely eight, though. It makes sense he'd like to stretch his legs and take in a few sights before he settles down." Bryce cast a meaningful look around the table at all the children.

"There is something about being in a new place that makes a person learn to follow God's will and grow into oneself." Delilah spoke thoughtfully, obviously thinking of the time she'd spent in San Francisco to sell her art. While away from Chance Ranch, she'd found God.

"You've got a point. Stickin' where things is familiar ain't always what's best." Lovejoy grinned at Daniel, who relaxed a bit.

"I don't see why it wouldn't be an option after calving," Titus offered.

"Me, neither," Paul agreed. "I think it might be a nice change of pace for everyone—we'll get to hear all about what you get into instead of having to witness it and pull you out of it!" Everyone laughed.

"I don't suppose you two could get into too much trouble," Daniel assented.

"Two?" Logan had missed something, he was sure.

"Yeah." Gideon jerked a thumb toward Bryce. "Like he said, you guys have grown up here. You both need the experience of making your own way in the world for a while."

"Whoa. How'd I get dragged into this?" Bryce held out his hands, palms up, as though trying to shove away a skunk without getting sprayed.

"Oh, come on," Titus chortled. "You two are like Frick 'n' Frack. Always have been."

Logan kept his trap shut and thought about it. Of all his brothers, Bryce understood him the best and bothered him the least. He'd be fairly quiet, and besides, he usually went along with whatever Logan decided anyway. Plus, it was a six-day trip, and he could use some company on the way. Sounded good to him.

"We'd feel more comfortable with two of you going," Alisa encouraged Bryce.

"I'll send off the letter tomorrow making arrangements," Lovejoy determined. "There's not a moment to lose!"

"Time for an official vote." Gideon called them to order. "All in favor of

Bryce and Logan visiting Salt Lick Holler for the summer after the calving season, put up your hands."

Logan watched everyone vote for his adventure and gave Bryce an apologetic smile as he followed suit. It was settled. They'd both go.

∽≫≪∽

"Wait, Hattie!" Hattie turned to see Nate Rucker rushing up to her.

"Was thar sommat else I should know 'bout the babe, Mr. Rucker?" Hattie's smile fled. Abigail Rucker was due any week now, and Hattie had taken to checking up on the woman almost every day. She seemed fine when Hattie left her just moments ago.

"Nah. Abigail and I are beholden to you for yore care. Yore a fine healer." He put his hands on his knees to catch his breath. "It's jist that thar's a letter for you and Widow Hendrick. I plumb fergot about it on account of the babe."

He handed her a slightly smudged envelope. Hattie recognized the fancy paper and loopy print as being from Lovejoy.

"Thankee for yore quick memory, Mr. Rucker."

"Welcome. I've gotta go, but I'll be seein' ya afore long." He gave a jaunty wave and turned back, leaving Hattie to her thoughts.

It was Nate and his wife's first babe, scarcely a year into their marriage. They'd moved into Hattie's old home when she went to live with Miz Willow. Now the place would have the child she'd never been able to bear. It would be a real home. Such bittersweet thoughts, but at least she'd have a hand in bringing the babe into the world. That was something to make her give thanks.

"How's Abigail Rucker doin' this fine spring day?" Miz Willow asked as soon as Hattie stepped inside.

"Restless as a raccoon in a river, but farin' well." Hattie smiled and brought out the envelope. "I've got sommat for you!"

A grin broke across the widow's face, deepening the lines given to her by years of honest living and laughter. "How nice. How 'bout you read it to me. It'd be good practice."

Hattie slid a finger beneath the corner of the delicate paper and lifted open the glued flap of the envelope. She pulled out the sheet of paper, unfolded it, and carefully shaped the words with her mouth as she read it aloud:

Dear Miz Willomena and Hattie,

Praise be that th' whooping cough has ended. I keep you in my prayers ev'ry day. Thankee for the valerian root you sent. Little Polly says it helped with 'er head poundin's. Yore so good to us.

Night past, we was talkin' 'bout how much Salt Lick Holler has sent down to Reliable, and we come ta the truth that we ain't returned the favor. Important as it is to keep strong ties with yore kin, we wish to rectify our negligence. (Lookie thar—Delilah learned me that word.

Means we ain't been watchin' out like we should.)

Hattie stumbled over the bigger words and sounded out the new one. "Well, live and learn. That thar's a fancy phrase."

The widow was obviously pleased with both her students—Lovejoy for making good use of her lessons, and Hattie for learning them.

"You want I should keep on?" Hattie wondered if Miz Willow would like to read the letter herself, seeing as how it was a real link between her and her friend. Letters were special, something to touch and still almost hear a voice, too.

"Please do."

> *Tempy an' Lois are expectin' again, so's none of us cain come down. 'Sides, we don't know what good could come a leavin' all the young'uns with Obie, Hezzie, and Mike. So's the best we cain send you is our love.*
>
> *But Logan and Bryce Chance (Dan's least brothers) are fine young lads with God in thar hearts and adventure in thar eyes.*

Hattie paused as she saw the next line, then kept on.

> *Iff'n yore agreeable, they'd like to visit come end of spring thru summer. Bryce charms anything with fur or feathers, and Logan does better with folks with two legs. I was thinkin' they could sleep in yore barn, and in return for their keep, they'd be happy to holp any way they could—huntin', fishin', buildin', choppin', an' such.*
>
> *Pray on it. You both have to be fine with it. I know Hattie's still a bonnie young lassie, so's it may be awkwart ta have them around her. They're right respectful bucks, but none of ourn want to impose. All our love regardless of yore decision.*
>
>

Forever yores,
Lovejoy Chance

"Well, I'll be." Miz Willow just rocked in her chair, looking thoughtful.

Hattie didn't venture much of an opinion but pointed out, "That's jist a few weeks from now, I'd imagine."

"True, true. We'd hafta git ready mighty quick." The widow caught her gaze. "Iff'n you say it's fine by you."

Rather than just agree as the widow obviously wanted, Hattie thought about it for a minute. She'd gone through so much change in the last two years and finally settled here. She had everything she could want and praised God for it. Did she really want two young men stepping into their lives and setting the whole holler aflutter?

It wasn't her first choice, but then again, it wasn't her decision. It was Miz

Willow's. Besides, there was plenty to keep her busy and out of their way.

"No skin off my nose, Miz Willow. I cain think on a few gals who'd be mighty pleased to hear 'bout two new fellas comin' for a visit."

Widow Hendrick nodded. "And I know Silk Trevor will want ta know the type of folks who've taken her nieces into their family. Come to think on it, so do I." She rocked a bit more and reached for a pencil and paper. "So do I."

⁂

The barbed wire bit through the tough leather the moment Logan looked away. He tugged the glove off with his teeth and sucked on his finger till the bleeding stopped, then kept right on mending the fence.

Served him right for daydreaming on the job. He'd been wondering what the mountains were like, whether the train would feel as quick as a fast gallop, if all the folks in Salt Lick Holler would sound like Lovejoy—gentle and kind of musical. What did the men do to pass the time? How did everyone make a living?

He'd know the answers soon enough, but for now he needed to keep his thoughts on the work at hand. Otherwise he'd end up like Paul—everyone knew back in his courting days that he'd fallen off his horse and broken his arm because he was busy thinking about Delilah. *Well, at least I'm not being distracted over a woman.*

He heard Bryce coming before he saw the horse and winced. They'd started in the middle, and both were supposed to reinforce two miles' worth of the safeguard. Logan blamed his slow pace on his oft-pricked fingers.

Bryce swung out of the saddle and came over to help him finish up. They worked side by side until the job was done. Not a word passed between them. After they finished, they sat and guzzled some lukewarm water from their canteens.

"How long you gonna be mad at me for something I had no control over?" Logan decided it was time to clear the air. Bryce had been even quieter than usual the past month—ever since the Chance clan had decided they'd both go to Salt Lick Holler if the Widow Hendrick and Hattie Thales let them.

Bryce blinked, then drew his bandanna across his forehead. "I'm not mad at you, Logan."

"Then why've you been so all-fired quiet lately?"

"I've never been much of a talker. You know that."

"But you always talked to me." Logan grumbled this, not wanting to sound too whiny.

"What's done is done, little brother." Bryce slugged him on the shoulder. "It's not what either of us thought it'd be, but I won't be the hitch in your plans."

"Thanks." Logan's voice went gruff as he thought about how his brother was willing to take this trip for him, even though Bryce would always be happy to stay at home—well, in the barn, anyway. "I'm glad that's settled." He got up and dusted off his seat.

"Who says it's settled?" Bryce grinned as they went back for their horses. "Maybe they won't want us."

"Now why would you say something that crazy?" Logan grinned and waggled his eyebrows. "Who wouldn't want us?"

Chapter 4

Dear Lovejoy and Chance Family,

Sorry bout my writin—I'm new at it but Miz Willow says I don't git nough times to practice, so here goes.

We're glad the valerian roots holped Miss Polly's head and have sent more along with some rusty rye. Already used some of this batch last year on one of Silk Trevor's daughters—Katherine. She's delivered of a healthy son an she says to make shore I tole you to tell Obadiah MacPherson she's named her chile after him. She says Hezzie and Mike 're next since she's done run outta names from her man's kin.

Everyone's all aflutter here bouts since we tole em how Logan and Bryce'll be comin. We figgur iff'n y'all write back rite quick we'll know they're comin bout a week afore they git here in the end of May. Sowry we cain't offer nuthin better'n a barn for 'em, but I'll clean out the loft and make it as nice as I cain. Miz Willow reckons a barn were good nuff for Jesus Hisself so it'll do jist fine.

We cain't hardly wait to meet you boys! Everyone's excited. The mensfolk plan on takin you hunting and the women want to have a doin's to celebrate yore arrival, but Widow Hendrick tole em they'd hafta wait till yore a bit more settled.

God be with you all.

> *Truly Yores,*
> *Hattie Thales and Willomena Hendrick*

Logan gave a whoop as Lovejoy finished reading the news, then reached for the letter. He reread it quickly and gave a silent prayer of thanksgiving.

Lord, it wasn't easy coming to this decision, much less convincing the others to support it. You've warned that the road we are to follow is narrow and hard, not simple. But now my journey begins, and I ask for Your continued guidance so that I follow Your will. I pray I'll be of use to the folks in Salt Lick Holler so this journey is fruitful. Amen.

"Perfect. This is going to be so much fun." He slapped Bryce on the back. "They even want to throw us a shindig."

"Now you *know* they haven't met us." Bryce's grin belied the words.

"They will soon enough."

⌒≈⌒

Hattie eyed the lopsided old ladder with misgiving. The rest of the barn had been kept up well, but the loft hadn't been used in a coon's age. She'd been working at the building steadily since they'd received Lovejoy's letter. She'd swept, scrubbed, and laid fresh hay, and was running out of other things to tackle.

Today she'd moved the few critters left—the milk cow and old mule—over to the farthest stalls so they wouldn't be scared by the men moving around above. Now there was nothing to do but to ready the loft itself. Hattie had never been fond of climbing, and the way the boards for the ladder's rungs were nailed down all cockeyed didn't much help the matter.

She took in a deep breath and chided herself. *How're ya ever gonna make it to the heights of heaven iff'n yore afeared of a plain ole loft, Hattie Thales?*

With that, she twitched her skirts, steadied the ladder, and started up. Eleven rungs later, she planted her feet on the wooden floor and looked around. It was clear not a soul had been up here in years. Dirt caked the walls and the sloping roof. Moldy hay littered the floor in knee-high clumps decorated with bits of old twine.

Cleaning the barn first had been a mistake. Once she pushed this mess over the ledge, she'd have to redo most of what she thought she'd already finished. After grabbing a dusty pitchfork leaning against the far wall, she started hefting the hay. Finally about done, she heard the pitchfork thunk on something solid. Hattie cleared the rest of the gunk from around the object—a still-sturdy bench with a fair-sized trunk stuck beneath it.

Hattie glanced down before dropping the pitchfork off the loft and had to close her eyes for a moment before turning back to the matter at hand. She wrestled the trunk away from the wall and apart from the bench. It was heavier than she'd thought it would be, and she hesitated before opening it. Should she ask Miz Willow before she stuck her nose in?

She could, but that would mean an extra trip up and down the ladder. Besides, Miz Willow had already told her just to throw away anything she found up there unless it could be put to good use. Reassured, she pried open the cracked leather straps and lifted the lid. Two old blankets took up most of the room, and she pulled them out. They were clean, and once she aired them out, they'd be good to make up pallets. Beneath them she found a ball of twine and a small folding knife. She pulled out a bag and a carved wooden box, deciding not to open these without Miz Willow.

She laid the blankets on the bench, put the knife and twine in her pocket, looped the string of the bag over her wrist, and clasped the box under one arm before slowly stepping down the ladder. With her feet firmly on solid ground, she put everything down. She tossed a straw broom up into the loft, wound some of the twine around her waist to tuck in a few cleaning rags, and made her way back up the ladder.

She got to sweeping and scrubbing everything in sight, then grabbed the blankets and descended from the loft for the last time that day.

The sun was setting by the time she'd cleaned up the mess left on the barn floor and aired out the blankets. She dusted most of the dirt off her hem before going to the house. As she walked through the door, the warmth of simmering stew made her stomach growl.

"Smells good in here, Miz Willow." Hattie placed the burlap bag and wooden box she'd found on the table. This was part of the reason she loved living with the old woman—they cared for each other and shared the cooking and cleaning. Not to mention that having a healer's knowledge of yarbs made ordinary dishes full of flavor.

"Thankee kindly. Since you missed yore dinner workin' in that ole barn, I figured you could use sommat to stick to yore ribs. Got biscuits waitin' in the kettle oven, too." The widow began ladling dinner into two wooden bowls while Hattie dusted ash off the Dutch oven, lifted the lid, and took out the biscuits.

"Shore right 'bout that." She nudged Miz Willow's chair closer to the table before taking her own seat. "Would you like to pray?" Hattie bowed her head at Miz Willow's nod.

"Good Lord up above, we come to thank You for the bounty on this table and in our hearts. Thankee for my Hattie who done brought this ole woman so much joy. She and Lovejoy is like the daughters I niver had. We ask for safe travelin' for our visitors from Californy an' hope all goes accordin' to Yore will. Amen."

A comfortable silence filled the room as they ate their fill of the hearty stew and honey-drizzled biscuits. Hattie leaned back and patted her full stomach.

"That was a meal fit for a queen, Miz Willow."

"I allays was partial to possum myself, but this were a mighty tasty squirrel in our pot tonight." The widow picked her teeth with a sharpened twig, then used it to gesture to the far end of the table. "What've you got there?"

"I don't know. They was in the trunk I found in the loft. I didn't feel right openin' 'em without yore blessing." Hattie brought over the bag and box and set them before the older woman.

"Right thoughtful of you, Hattie." She stared at the objects for a long moment before adding, "But they ain't none of mine. This was Lovejoy's house with her first husband. She invited me into her home after that husband of hers passed on." The widow's mouth puckered as it always did when she thought of Lovejoy's first husband.

Hattie didn't know much about Vern Spencer. He'd left the holler an awful lot, always coming back with things to trade—usually sugar for Lovejoy's father's still. He trapped a lot, most often coming in from the woods with a few poor critters strung up, but he must not have sold their pelts for much, because he and Lovejoy hadn't lived high on the hog. No one ever talked about it, but folks knew he'd done his wife wrong and fathered a string of babes with other women.

"Should we jist send this stuff on down to Reliable without openin' 'em?" Hattie pushed aside her curiosity.

"Seems a risky thing to do—iff'n you don't know what yore a-sendin', you'll niver know iff'n it arrived." Miz Willow leaned forward. "We could write Lovejoy an' ask her what she wants done."

"But iff'n she don' know what's in 'em, neither?" Hattie prompted, running her fingers over the carved wood.

"Reckon that might be a bother. Let's us open 'em an' then decide whether whatever it is be worth the trouble." Miz Willow reached over and undid the drawstring on the small sack. A handful of braided leather ties spilled out onto the table.

"Those'll come in right useful here'bouts." Hattie gestured toward the storeroom.

"Right you are, Hattie. Ain't nothin' important to write Lovejoy about." Her lively blue eyes fixed on the box. "That's a purty piece for shore. Cain't imagine she'd leave it behind."

"She didn't know she wasn't comin' back when she left," Hattie offered, tracing the swirling design with one forefinger. It looked to be the work of a master craftsman.

"True, but iff'n it were close to her heart, I figgur she woulda asked for it to be sent. Go on ahead an' open it, dearie." She craned her neck as Hattie flipped the latch to lift the lid.

"Mercy," Hattie breathed as a pile of golden coins came into view. She pushed the treasure trove toward the widow.

"Well, I'll be," Miz Willow declared. "Cain't think Lovejoy even knew 'bout it. She wasn't one to set on sommat as could holp others so much. You'd best fetch me pencil and paper, Hattie. This is worth more'n any letter I cain write."

⁓⸝⁓

Logan inched toward the door, hoping that no one would notice. His hand closed around the handle, the sliver of sunlight he exposed welcoming him outside.

"Logan!" He winced at Lovejoy's voice. "Where'd you put that sack of slippery elm I handed you?"

Wistfully he shut the door. Obviously he wasn't going anywhere, certainly not today. He cast a glance around the unusually cluttered main cabin and reassessed. If the women couldn't get everything together, he and Bryce wouldn't be leaving for Salt Lick Holler tomorrow, either.

"The brown bag about so big." Lovejoy motioned with her hands before rushing past him. "Here it is!" She snatched one of a pile of bags and waved it triumphantly.

Logan quelled the urge to groan aloud. He and Bryce were packed and ready to go with one saddlebag apiece to hold two pairs of britches and three fresh shirts. They'd be wearing everything else they'd need, and the horses would go on a stock car. It should have been light traveling, but Lovejoy and his other softhearted sisters-in-law had other plans.

He, Bryce, Gideon, and Mike had ridden down to White's Mercantile with all the MacPherson and Chance women yesterday—and walked out with near half of it. Material, bandages, sacks, needles, knives, a teakettle, candy, leather, buckles, French-milled soap, cotton batting, wool blankets, a magnifying glass, razors and strops, fishing hooks, bandannas, brushes, hairpins, two shawls, chalk, ribbons, stockings, and pocketknives. Every bit of it was supposed to go with him and Bryce to the holler, along with the quilts and hooded cloaks the girls had all been stitching furiously since the decision had been made.

So tallied up with the wool the MacPhersons bundled up and the dried flowers and such Lovejoy measured out, two packhorses were added on to carry the gifts. The Chance men unanimously decided that the two horses wouldn't be returning, either. One would stay with Hattie and Widow Hendrick, and the other would be given to whomever Logan and Bryce deemed needed it most. The only exception was Lovejoy's father. She said, "Though I love my pa greatly, I won't be holpin' him carry his moonshine to other poor folks, and you cain bet that's jist what he'd do with the animal."

Logan pulled out his train ticket and stared, willing the date to change. No such luck. He was stuck here for another day while everybody rushed around packing. It was almost enough to make him and Bryce regret how they'd balked at the women's initial plan to just send along a list of what went to whom. Now they scurried around trundling items into packages with Delilah's fancy script designating some lucky citizen of Salt Lick Holler.

He could scarcely believe it when he thought of how he and Bryce would be hauling around more than twice as much baggage as Eunice, Lois, Tempy, and Lovejoy combined brought when they first came to Reliable. Two packhorses. He shook his head.

"Put this in that great big burlap sack for Silk Trevor's family." Miriam thrust a bundle into his arms and pointed across a veritable obstacle course.

Logan bit back a groan and trudged across the room. Tomorrow couldn't come quickly enough.

Chapter 5

Logan woke up with a smile on his face. Today his journey would begin. He jumped out of bed, shaved his whiskers, and flung on his clothes in record time before realizing Bryce hadn't joined him.

"Come on. Get up!" He thwacked his brother on the shoulder with his hat. "You're the morning person, remember?"

"Nope. No recollection of that." Bryce pulled the covers over his head. "Breakfast bell ain't even rung."

"Now let me think back to what you told me when I said the very same thing the morning you decided Salt Lick Holler was the place to go. Oh, that's right. I know!" Logan yanked off the blankets and hunkered down to grin at Bryce.

"If I'd only known then how that whole thing would turn out. . ." Bryce's grumble died off as he yawned.

"That's just it," Logan retorted. "Neither of us knows how this whole thing will turn out!"

Three hours, two loaded-up packhorses, one train, and thirty-one hugs later, they were on their way. Bryce snoozed in the aisle seat while Logan kept his nose against the glass window, determined to remember every bit of Reliable so not even a twinge of homesickness would come between him and all the adventure that lay ahead.

Sure, he'd miss Gideon, Titus, Paul, Daniel, Miriam, Alisa, Delilah, Lovejoy, Obie, Hezzy, Mike, Eunice, Lois, Tempy, all the kids, and even Britches, but it would only be for a few months. Who knew what he'd see and do and who he'd meet in between? God had something for him, Logan was sure of it. And no man could regret following the road the Lord laid before him.

He took his Bible out of the pocket inside his coat, and it fell open to the story of Jacob. He read, feeling the presence of the Lord in the words, until a couple of verses stopped him cold: "So the Lord alone did lead him, and there was no strange god with him. He made him ride on the high places of the earth. . . ."

He brushed the fragile paper with his fingertips and mouthed the words. This had been Mama's Bible. His brothers had decided to use Pa's as the household scripture and gave Ma's smaller version to Logan. They thought it was only fair, since Logan hadn't had as much time with her. Ma's faith had been a big part of her, and Logan could feel her love right along with God's whenever he opened this Bible.

He had everything he needed, and now he was heading toward whatever the Lord planned to show him.

వ౨౮౨౨౨

Hattie picked up the flour, salt, and water that served to make paste for the medicine labels. She combined the flour and salt but hesitated to add the water. She'd done this three times already today, and three times the paste had dried before she could put it to use. It wasn't because folks needed help. No, 'twas that they were curious and hoped to be the first to meet the men from California.

Sure enough, a knock sounded on the door. Miz Willow was off at the Peasley place helping clear up a case of poison oak. Usually that would leave Hattie alone with her thoughts and the sound of the rain. But not today. She bit back a sigh as she swung the door open.

Bethilda Cleary sailed out of the rain and into the cabin with her daughters, Lily and Lark. All three were cleaner than Hattie had ever seen them, and the girls were wearing shoes. From the looks of their tiny steps and periodic winces, the shoes were far too small.

"Good day, Mrs. Cleary." Hattie gestured for them to sit down. She'd prefer they stated their business and went along, but she couldn't let those poor girls stand in their pinched shoes for even a second. Besides, no potion Hattie could concoct would soothe the afflictions of Bethilda Cleary—two unwed daughters.

"Thankee kindly, Hattie." The woman peered into the corners of the room as though what she sought would magically appear.

"What cain I do for you and yourn?"

"Well, on account of our fine health," Bethilda's voice rose on the last two words before continuing, "we ain't had cause to visit you. So's we reckoned we should come an' see you on this. . .glorious spring day." She faltered at the end as Lark squeezed a handful of water from the sodden hood of her cloak onto Hattie's clean floor.

"I see." She didn't hide her smile. She might as well appreciate the humor in this visit, after all. "Pity yore visit hadn't waited a couple days. By then you coulda been introduced to our visitors." Hattie saw Bethilda's shoulders slump and blithely added, "We're expectin' their arrival any day now, ye ken."

"Yep. Mawma sayed as how those two rich city bachelors would be here, we'd git first dibs on account of the rain iff'n we—ow!" Lily broke off as Mama Cleary kicked her under the table.

"Well, that shore is a shame." Bethilda smiled wanly and stood up. "It'd be nice to have some new blood in these hills."

Hattie pushed back the thought of a mother mountain lion hunting for her cubs. The poor Chance brothers probably had no idea that every family with so much as one single daughter viewed them as fresh meat for the pouncing.

"You'll be shore to come on by once they get here." Hattie wasn't extending an invitation, just stating a fact.

"That's right neighborly of you. It's good to hear you won't be keeping the gentlemen all to yorself, Hattie Thales." Bethilda looked at her daughters. "Gotta give the young girls as could make 'em good wives the opportunity to meet them boys."

Hattie excused herself to the storeroom for a moment. The woman had all but accused her of having designs on the visitors and having no right to do so since she couldn't be a proper wife. As if Hattie didn't know that though she was a good woman, she wasn't a whole one. When a man took a wife, he wanted sons. Her hands fisted for a moment as she prayed for forbearance.

Good Lord up above, You know I've made my peace with the life You've seen fit to give me. I don't angle for another husband, Jesus. I'll never bear a child, but I protect the lives of all who're born into this holler. That and Yore love are more'n enough to fill my heart. Holp me to remember all the blessings You've bestowed upon me rather than my failures. The Chance brothers bring with them excitement and possibility. Please don't let me begrudge my neighbors those things. Holp me to forgive Bethilda her hurtful words and not let old sorrows taint the present. Thank You for Yore constant goodness. Amen.

At peace once again, she took a deep breath and reached for the medicine she'd come for. She took out the large jar of salve and scooped some into a smaller tin. Made with ground ivy and marshmallow root, the cream would help soothe the blisters Hattie was certain the Cleary sisters would soon be nursing. She took a deep breath, pasted a smile on her face, and went back to the table.

"It shore was nice of y'all to come and visit me. I cain't holp but notice those fine shoes yore gals is wearin', Mrs. Cleary." Hattie waited for the older woman to nod. "But when it's wet, sometimes the leather cain rub somethin' awful. Here's a salve just in case yore gals need it."

Mrs. Cleary spoke through tight lips and gritted teeth. "That's right kind of you, but my gals are used to such things. I don't think—"

"Thankee, Miss Hattie!" Lily snagged the tin and put it in her pocket before her mother could refuse.

The glower in Bethilda's eyes warned Hattie that the woman would make her daughter sorry she'd spoken up. She thought hard for a moment before consoling her. "Well now, I ken yore right, Mrs. Cleary, but I'd shore hate to see Lily and Lark miss out on meetin' the fellas at the doin's iff'n their delicate skin should take an exception to the weather."

"Good thinkin', Hattie." Bethilda's brow unfurrowed, and she nodded sagely. "Shore am glad to have such a long-sighted healer. Sounds like the rain's lettin' up a mite, so we'll be takin' our leave."

After a flurry of good-byes and a hug from Lark, who whispered her thanks for the salve, the Cleary women set out. Hattie sank down in Miz Willow's rocking chair and buried her face in her hands. The Clearys had been her fourth visitors that day alone. What would happen once the Chance brothers actually arrived?

"We'll be pullin' in soon." Bryce, who'd somehow managed to sleep through most of the five-day trip in his thinly padded seat, tipped up his hat brim.

"Praise the Lord," Logan said fervently.

"Goin' a bit stir-crazy, are you?" Bryce grinned.

"Maybe a little," Logan admitted, "but today we saddle up and ride on to Salt Lick. I can hardly wait to get there."

"Me, too. It'll be nice to sleep lyin' down again."

"What?" Logan stared at his brother in disbelief. "You slept through the whole trip!"

"Not lyin' down." Bryce shrugged. "Besides, I think you did more dreaming than I could lay claim to."

The whistle cut off Logan's response as the train slowed on the tracks. The better part of the next hour was spent unloading everything from the train. Then came the onerous task of fitting everything onto the backs of the two pack animals. Finally, they were ready to set off.

Logan left Bryce with the horses and sauntered up to the only other fellow around.

"Excuse me, could you point us to the road to Salt Lick Holler?"

The old-timer chewed steadily on his straw before nodding and pointing. "Over yonder's the path. Ain't no road, but it'll git you and yore animules thar. 'Bout half a day's ride. We don't git many foreigners up these parts." He stared at Logan, obviously waiting for an explanation.

"Visiting some kinfolk." Logan smiled as he remembered Lovejoy's word for extended family. The man just shrugged and walked off, but it was clear the answer had been understood. Logan rejoined Bryce, and they swung up into their saddles.

Over to the west of the train tracks lay a dirt path, now overgrown from a long winter and wet spring. They set out more slowly than Logan would've liked, avoiding ruts and puddles as they followed the winding way through the mountains. Evergreens of all shapes and sizes spread thickly across the ground, punctuated by wild grass and blossoming shrubs. Squirrels and rabbits darted to safety as they rode by, chipmunks chattering at them all the while.

Occasionally they'd have to stop to clear deadwood out of the path, fallen branches Logan remembered Lovejoy warning them about. She'd said they were called "widow makers," and one of them had caused the death of Hattie Thales's husband. With that in mind, Logan kept an eye out for dried-out trees. He didn't see many, but he did see birds flying, singing, courting, and building among the needles of practically every bough.

Overall, Logan and Bryce passed the pleasant ride in silence. It was best to take in their surroundings and enjoy the crisp fresh air for now. Besides, after five days on the train, they didn't have anything new to say to each other. That was fine. There'd be plenty to keep them busy in Salt Lick Holler.

Be polite and considerate, Logan dutifully reminded himself. *Remember that your actions reflect on Lovejoy and the Chances in general. You aren't here solely to have a good time roaming around the hills. It's not like recess at school—you're going on this trip to find what God has in store for your life. You'd better be certain you're not too busy having fun that you miss the message.*

All the same, Logan couldn't help but smile. It was going to be an eventful trip.

The sun had long since set by the time they reached the valley. They squinted to find the fork in the road Lovejoy had told them would lead to the healers' place. They inched along in deepening darkness, the only light coming from the waxing moon and more stars than Logan had ever seen before. The soft hoots of owls underscored the chirps of lovelorn crickets.

They guided their horses to the right and went a few hundred yards before spying a comparatively large structure to their left, exactly as it had been described. There. The cabin. Regardless of the weariness of cross-country travel, Logan felt a surge of excitement.

Chapter 6

Hattie rolled out of bed and slipped on her overdress almost before she was awake. She grabbed her satchel and padded across the floor in her bare feet to answer the door. If someone was calling in the dark of night, it must be urgent. She opened the door to a blast of frigid night air and a man on her doorstep.

"What can I do for you?" Hattie placed her satchel between them and tried to make out who it was in the dim flicker reaching from the fireplace.

"I'm looking for the healer's home." The stranger took off his hat. "By that satchel you're holding, I'd guess I found it. You must be Miss Thales. I'm Logan Chance. I believe you're expecting me and my brother?"

"Nice to meet you, Mr. Chance." She dipped her head.

"So you two young bucks made it all right." Miz Willow hobbled up next to Hattie and squinted through the door. "Where's yore brother?"

"You must be Widow Hendrick." Logan smiled and gave a little bow. "Bryce is watching the horses. We weren't positive we were at the right place."

"You shore are. We'll have you come in and warm up after we see to yore animals. Hattie, why don't you show 'em to the barn while I brew some tea?"

Hattie fetched two lanterns and stepped outside as the first brother motioned for the second to follow. She could scarcely believe her eyes when she saw not two but four horses. Two of them were loaded down with more than she'd ever owned in her whole life. They had just enough room in the barn for the animals. Good thing she'd put fresh hay in all the stalls.

She opened the barn door and went ahead to light a few hanging lanterns so they could get the horses situated. She gestured to the wall of empty stalls.

"They can stay here. While you unload 'em, I'll fetch some water." She grabbed a bucket and went out to the well, making four trips to see to every horse's thirst.

She'd never seen the barn so full. Their mule and milk cow looked at the newcomers curiously. The chickens ignored the entire proceedings as the opposite half of the barn suddenly became occupied, and the final empty stall filled with all the gear the Chance brothers had hauled up the mountains.

"This here's the ladder to yore loft, where I've made up some pallets for you. You should be plenty warm, but if yore needin' more blankets, jist let me know straightaway." She put her hand on the ladder but didn't climb up it to show them their beds. She figured they could manage fine on their own. "Miz Willow's made you some tea inside to warm you up, iff'n you'll follow me." She blew out the hanging lanterns and left the barn.

When they reached the cabin, one of the men hurried to open the door for her. It was the first one, Logan. She'd studied their faces in the lantern light as they took care of their horses. Both had dark hair and comely features, but Logan boasted a stronger jaw and wasn't quite as tall as Bryce.

"Thankee." She acknowledged the gentlemanly gesture and walked over to where Miz Willow was rocking in her chair. The kettle steamed over the fire, while a loaf of bread warmed in the niche.

"You've both met Hattie by now, and I'm Willomena Hendrick. Most folks in these parts call me Widow Hendrick, but when folks lodge with me I prefer Miz Willow. Hattie started callin' me that, and I like it right fine. Ain't that right, Hattie?"

"True 'nough." Hattie placed a jar of blackberry preserves on the table and nodded. "I don't like bein' called Widow Thales, so I reckoned Miz Willomena probably didn't shine to it after all these years, either."

"And Willomena's a mouthful and a half, so's she shortened it to Willow." The old lady rocked contentedly.

"Because it's fittin' for a healer to be named after a soothin' yarb." Hattie finished telling the story and placed the warm sliced bread on the table along with freshly brewed tea. Then she motioned for the men to sit at the table.

"We'll be happy to call you Miz Willow. It suits you. This is Bryce, since you didn't get to meet him before we took care of the horses."

"Nice to meet you, Miz Willow. Miz Thales." Bryce took a swig of tea and raised his eyebrows. "Say, I'm more of a coffee man, but this is pretty good!"

"No arguments here. We're much obliged for your hospitality." Logan slathered his bread with jam and took a large bite.

"Yore welcome, Mr. Chance." Miz Willow beamed and rocked more quickly, the runners giving tiny squeaks on the wooden floor. "Both of you Mr. Chances."

"You can call us Logan and Bryce. Everyone in Reliable does, since there are six Chance brothers." Logan grinned. "No one'd know who you meant back home if you called any of us 'Mr. Chance.' Plenty more for the next generation, too, so we just stick to first names."

Hattie blew on her tea to avoid saying anything. These good-looking men came from a large family that was getting larger all the time. How different they would find it here, with just her and Miz Willow and no little ones to play with or cuddle.

Not that it would matter. The older youths of the holler would keep them plenty busy. Abner MacPherson and Rooster Linden would want to meet their kin. Silk Trevor's boys, Ted and Fred, would take them hunting and trapping. Asa Pleasant was teaching his Albert the best spots for fishing, and his two girls, Sky and Lizzie, were of the right age to be courted. Not to mention the Cleary gals. Hattie had a sneaking suspicion that Logan, with his bright blue eyes and easy grin, would be much in demand. Both of the handsome brothers would be before they went back home to their nieces and nephews to start having babes of their own. If any of the folks of Salt Lick Holler had their way, the mothers of those babes would be their very own daughters.

∽≈∾

When Miz Willow tried to hide a yawn, Logan knew they'd stayed and chatted long enough. He swiped one last piece of bread.

"Much as we'd like to stay right here at this comfortable table with you lovely ladies. . ." Logan glanced at Hattie when he said the words. Sweet wisps escaped the long braid down her back. They caught the red glow of the fire and framed her young face. She moved quickly and gracefully; those deep blue eyes seemed to catch every detail. He realized he'd paused too long and covered it with a yawn of his own. "It's been a long time since we hit the hay." He stood up and waited for Bryce to follow suit.

"Thanks for your warm welcome and delicious treats." Bryce rose to his feet.

"Here's a fresh lantern for you. There's another in the loft. I left water in the bucket should you wish to fill the pitcher I left on the bench up there." Hattie handed the light to him.

"Thanks. We'll do just fine. Good night."

He and Bryce made their way back to the barn and climbed the ladder to the loft. Surprised at its size, Logan held the lantern high to look around. Two pallets made of fresh hay beneath clean blankets looked homey and inviting. Several blankets piled on the end would ward away the nighttime chill. A sturdy bench held the lantern and pitcher Hattie spoke of, as well as a basin, two hand towels, and a tin cup. A large empty trunk sat in a corner where the sloping roof kissed the loft floor, and a few nails were stuck in the wall to serve as hooks. Everything was clean as a whistle.

Someone—no, not someone—Hattie had taken a lot of time to clean up this place and make it comfortable. It fit with the way she watered the horses and took care of the tea and such. Hattie Thales had a kind heart to match her pretty face.

"Nice digs." Bryce lit the other lantern and hung up his hat. He grabbed the pitcher and started down the ladder to get the water Hattie had left for them. Logan caught the bundles Bryce slung up to him. They'd want fresh clothes in the morning.

Bryce came back up to the loft and plunked down the pitcher while Logan put their clean clothes in the trunk, along with his Bible.

Then they each sank onto a makeshift bed, pulled off their boots, and gratefully stretched out under the comforting warmth of a heap of blankets. Logan shut his eyes and immediately started to doze.

"What's going. . . You've got to be. . . Are you whistling?" Logan raised up on his elbows to peer at Bryce, who was giving a jaunty rendition of "She'll Be Comin' 'Round the Mountain."

Bryce finished the tune before answering. "Not anymore."

"Good," Logan grumbled. "Now let's get some shut-eye."

"You go on ahead. I'm not a bit sleepy."

"I'll do that. Just don't whistle anymore." Logan settled back into the warm bed and breathed deeply, waiting to drift off again.

Thrum-dum-dum-bum-thrum. The sound made Logan crack an eye open. It was too close for one of the animals to be fidgeting. "What are you doing now?"

"Hmmm. . . Oh, I guess I was tapping my fingers on the floor. Sorry." Bryce didn't sound at all repentant.

"Something on your mind?" Logan gave up trying to pretend Bryce wasn't there.

"A lot. Pretty country, ain't it?" Bryce, the most silent of all his brothers, sounded downright chatty.

"Yes, and I want to get a good night's sleep so I can explore it tomorrow." Logan yanked his blankets higher and tried to get some sleep. The sooner he fell asleep, the sooner morning would come—and with it, new faces to meet and places to explore.

"Miz Willow's a spry old gal. Did you see the twinkle in her eyes?"

"Yep." Logan thought of the wispy snatches of white hair covering the widow's head, like she was so full of energy her hair couldn't lie flat. But now wasn't the time to think about it. "Go to sleep, Bryce."

"Can't. Don't know why."

"Because you only woke up to stuff your face for the past five days." Logan glared in his brother's general direction. "If you can't sleep now, it's your own fault. As for me, I'm gonna ask you to be quiet so I can rest. There'll be a lot to do and see tomorrow."

"True. Maybe Hattie'll show us around. What did you think of her?"

Logan realized Bryce's yammering had managed to make him too alert to sleep. He sat up and ran his hand through his hair.

"Why? You're usually the one who's more interested in animals than people." Logan was actually interested in Bryce's opinion.

"Yep. But she's kinda hard to read. She's got a servant's heart—I mean, look at how she fixed up this place for two strangers. She was awful nice about helping us in the middle of the night. I don't think they have a pump. She had to draw all that water for the horses out of a well. Reminds me of Rebekah in the Bible, but she's pretty quiet, too. I guess I'm used to hearing Miriam, Alisa, Delilah, Lovejoy, Temperance, Eunice, and Lois all gabbing to each other and directing the kids. Hattie's pretty enough. Why isn't she married?"

Logan thought it over for a while.

"She was, but he died, remember? And if she's on the quiet side, maybe it's because we met her in the middle of the night and we don't know her yet." Logan wondered what she'd be like in daylight. Would her hair still hang in a tidy braid past her waist? Would her voice still sound soft, husky, and musical?

Bryce rolled over. "She's as pretty as Eunice and Lois, and as kind as Lovejoy. I'll bet she's about as good a healer, too."

Logan thought that over. Was she smart like Tempy? He remembered the carefully slanted script and strange spelling of her letter and how she'd mentioned just learning to read and write.

"Well, I—" Logan broke off when he realized Bryce was snoring. He shook his head and lay back down. "Figures."

Chapter 7

Hattie came awake when the cock crowed, and she got out of bed straightaway.

Would the Chance brothers—*Logan and Bryce,* she reminded herself—sleep late after their journey? She'd best make enough breakfast just in case.

After slipping on her dress and rebraiding her hair, she made bread dough and left it to rise under a blue and white gingham towel. She dashed out to the smokehouse and fetched a side of bacon. Logan and Bryce looked like they could pack away a lot.

She sizzled the bacon and left it in the small oven to keep warm, then shaped the loaf and put it in the niche of the hearth wall to bake. By that time, the early dim had given way to morning's brightness, and Miz Willow had woken up.

"Why don't you go on ahead and fetch some eggs and milk whilst I put on some coffee? My old mind seems to recall one of those brothers mentioning it yester-eve."

Hattie picked up the small basket she used to gather eggs and took her time getting to the barn. She'd be as quiet as she could just in case the Chances were still asleep. Cautiously she opened the door and stepped over to the chicken coop, trying to shush the clucking birds as she searched for their brown eggs.

"Mornin'." Logan's head popped over the edge of the loft, startling her.

"Mornin'. I didn't know if y'all was awake yet." She focused her attention on shutting the coop before picking up the three-legged stool and milking pail.

" 'Course we are. We'll be down in just a minute, and I'll take care of that for you," Logan offered.

"No need." Milking cows was woman's work, but offering to help didn't make him any less of a man. She finished and stood up, leaving the pail of fresh milk on the barn floor. "Y'all cain come into the house soon as yore ready. I've got breakfast started."

"Sounds good!" She recognized Bryce's voice before she left the barn.

She gave the eggs to Miz Willow, who immediately started scrambling them once she heard that the men were on the way. Hattie strolled out to the well, pulled up the bucket, and lifted a pail of chilled milk from where they kept it hanging down by the cool water. She drew a bucket of water for the house.

By the time she poured the milk into a pitcher and put it on the table with the bacon, Logan and Bryce were knocking on the door. Real gentlemen, they were, to knock rather than just saunter in. Even though they knew they were welcome, the gesture showed good manners. Logan set down the pail of fresh milk.

"Come have a seat," Miz Willow invited, putting the eggs and coffee next to the plates and mugs.

Hattie sliced the cinnamon bread and put out some butter before joining them at the table. She sat next to Miz Willow, across from Logan.

"Would one of you gentlemen like to bless the meal?" Miz Willow invited.

"Certainly." Logan surprised Hattie by reaching across the table to take hold of her hand so they all formed a circle.

She noticed his clean hands and face, shaved jaw, and combed hair. He honored their table by coming to it as though ready for a banquet. His brother looked just as neat. These men had more manners and common sense than most folk—and they probably suffered illness a lot less.

"Dear heavenly Father, we come before You this morning and thank You for all You've given us. We praise You for the safe journey and warm welcome we've experienced, and thank You for the hands that prepared this food. We pray for those who aren't with us now and ask You to keep them close. Amen."

Hattie smiled to thank him for his beautiful prayer. He'd blessed them as well as the food and remembered his family, too. If all the Chance brothers had been brought up as well as these—and Hattie figured they must have been—then Lovejoy was well taken care of as she deserved to be.

"Mmmm, this hits the spot." Bryce jabbed a fork into his eggs as though to punctuate the comment.

"Delicious." Logan agreed. "Thank you for getting up early to make all of this for us. Nice of you to go to the trouble." He directed this last comment to Miz Willow.

"Much obliged." Bryce reached for another slice of cinnamon bread, and Logan passed him the butter.

"Hattie do have a way 'round a fire," Miz Willow praised. "Her cinnamon bread's a favorite of ourn."

"I can see why." Logan took an appreciative bite and washed it down with some milk.

This man kept on surprising her. Most lads she knew wouldn't bother to think of how she and the widow didn't need to make so much food for just the two of them. Pa and Horace hadn't seen any need to thank her for cooking or anything else. That was her place. Not that she minded doing it, but it was nice to be appreciated for her efforts.

⌧

Logan helped himself to some more bacon and passed the platter to Bryce, who did likewise. The smoky flavor of the meat was rich and filling, but he had plenty of room left over for the melt-in-your mouth flavor of Hattie's warm, buttery cinnamon bread. He was glad to see he and Bryce weren't going to strain their food supply. All the same, he'd find ways to repay them for their hospitality.

According to Lovejoy, the widow and her apprentice made a steady living. Their home featured wooden floors, two windows covered with clarified hide, a real bed, and a separate storeroom. Everywhere he looked, he saw the tiny touches of love that made this place a home.

A rag rug covered the center of the floor. Fresh flowers filled a jar on the bedside table, where a Bible held the place of prominence next to a tallow candle. Cheery curtains lined the tops of the windows, keeping out drafts and letting in some light. The bed was neatly made, and a sampler hung above it proclaiming, A MERRY HEART DOETH GOOD LIKE A MEDICINE. He only noticed it because the same type of thing had snuck its way onto Chance Ranch with each new bride.

He wasn't able to think of anything to help Hattie and Miz Willow that Lovejoy hadn't already included in her packages. They had an outhouse and a smokehouse. The milk this morning was nice and cool, so they might have a spring-house, he figured. Then again, they might keep it dangling in a well bucket.

"I don't think they have a pump. She had to draw all that water for the horses out of a well." Bryce's observation from the night before tickled Logan's brain. Maybe he could get and install a pump. Living with Lovejoy had taught him just how much fresh water a healer could need, and the childhood memory of hauling buckets on Chance Ranch reminded him how much easier a water pump made the daily chore. The idea had merit.

"Now that yore bellies are full, I've a mind to ask you how that Lovejoy of ourn is farin' back in Californy." Miz Willow's lively voice interrupted his thoughts.

"Just fine, ma'am." To Bryce, those three words summed it all up.

"We're awful glad to have her," Logan jumped in. "She's worked wonders with Daniel."

"No foolin'," Bryce offered. "He'd been downright surly for about three years through. Sore as a buckshot bear."

Logan shoved the coffee in front of his brother to make him stop talking. What was Bryce thinking? Didn't the alarmed look on Hattie's face clue him in? They needed to hear how well Lovejoy and the MacPherson brides were getting along.

"There's some truth in that." Logan smiled to soften the admission. "But Lovejoy came into our lives and pushed away his grief. She's a mother to Polly and Ginny Mae, and the only woman I know who could've worked her way into Daniel's heart. She's a blessing to Chance Ranch."

"Heh," the old woman said, slapping her gnarled hand upon her knee, "that's Lovejoy for shore. Has a way of cuttin' through the muck and taking care of the wounded." She gave a decisive nod. "Sounds like she's found the place God intended for her to be."

Hattie shot the old widow a questioning glance, and Miz Willow asked her next question with such cautious nonchalance that Logan could tell something was in the works.

"Don't suppose she sent a letter or word with you boys 'bout a small matter we writ to her. . ." Her voice trailed off, but her eyes flickered with surprising intensity.

"Not that I know of, but she and the others packed so much stuff for us to bring, it could be in some bundle or another." Bryce shrugged and leaned back. "We've gotta unpack it all and figure out what goes to who anyway, so we'd be glad to keep a lookout."

Miz Willow looked at them expectantly. Logan knew whatever she was expecting must be awfully important, because she stood up and rested her weight on the table.

"Well, Hattie and I've got to clear the dishes. Why don't you boys git to it. When yore done, Hattie an' I'll help you track down the folks it's intended for."

Logan reckoned that was about as close as she could politely come to a blunt, "What're you waitin' fer?" He stood up and nudged Bryce on the shoulder.

"Sounds like a good idea to me. Good way to start meeting people. C'mon, Bryce." He led the way back to the barn, where they both stared at a veritable mountain of bundles and sacks.

Each package was bound with string and adorned with a note detailing what family it was intended for. Occasionally a list of what was for whom also hung from the string. Lovejoy's neatly cramped script, Miriam's elegant letters, Alisa's grand flourishes, and Delilah's calligraphy brought back a sense of home. It seemed as though they'd packed something for every family in these parts.

Logan realized Bryce was staring at the pile with the same hopeless expression he probably wore. He could just imagine Hattie and Miz Willow coming back after they'd done all the dishes to find both of them just standing there, scratching their heads. Miz Willow just might poke them with her cane. Though twisted with age, she still held a presence that was both fun and formidable.

"Let's start laying them out so they're not just in a big heap." Logan couldn't really think of anything else to do without knowing where each family lived.

They worked for a while, finding that while some families had one package, others had more. Logan combined these smaller individual bundles into neat piles.

I can't believe how long this is taking! We should be out of this barn by now, riding the countryside or fishing with other men of the holler. Instead, my adventure today is going to be sorting packages like a fussy old maid.

He and Bryce had just about finished laying all the things out when the women walked in.

"Howdy, Miz Willow, Miz Hattie." Logan tipped his hat. "We put yours aside over by the door."

"Thankee much, both of you. We'll git to 'em later. For now I figgur we'd best git all this organized." Miz Willow gestured expansively.

"We sure could use your help." Logan smiled. "We've already divvied it up by surname, if that's any use."

"Shore will be." Hattie nodded and stepped forward, glancing at Miz Willow. What she saw slid the small smile right off her face and made Logan realize just how tightly the older woman was clutching her cane.

"Oh, Miz Willow, I jist had a worry. What iff'n someone comes for the healer and cain't find a one of us? I'll bet Otis Nye's near run out of the devil's claw tea we give him for his rheumatiz. Why don't you go inside and brew up a batch so he cain have some straightaway iff'n he comes to call?" She gently turned the older woman to the door.

"I s'ppose you've the right of it." Miz Willow started back to the house. "Jist you let me know when yore ready. I might have some salves or poultices to send out with you." She left.

"Nice of you to find a way she could rest." Logan tried to encourage her.

"It's my fault she needs to." Hattie blinked a few times. "I forgot to make the tea to soothe her joints this mornin'. It holps with her pain and makes it so she don't swoll up so bad."

"Seems to me she's doin' just fine," Logan said, consoling her. "She can make the tea for herself now and not feel as though she's not pulling her weight. You saved her the pain of her joints and the humiliation of having to admit she needed to sit."

"I reckon." Hattie shook her head as though to clear it, making the deep red of her braid bounce along the pale yellow of her cotton dress.

Logan couldn't help but like her better for her tender heart and the way she watched over the saucy old woman. Of all the people he'd meet in the holler, he had a funny feeling he'd be glad to have met these two remarkable women first.

Chapter 8

W ait a minute." Hattie lifted up a small parcel. "Did you two miss this?" She recognized Lovejoy's writing and smiled. "It's got yore names on't."

Bryce held out his hands, so she tossed it to him. He made short work of unwrapping two shiny harmonicas. He picked one up and handed a slip of foolscap to Logan.

"It says here you'll know who's best to teach us how to play these." Logan waved the paper. "Any ideas?"

"Yep. Li'l Nate Rucker'll learn you how. I'll introduce you later." Hattie couldn't help but grin. Li'l Nate was the burly blacksmith of the holler. It did a body good to see such a bear of a man make a sweet tune on his harmonica. "It's a good way to get to know some folk, 'specially since they're plannin' to have a sang real soon."

"A sang?" Logan repeated doubtfully.

"We have us a sang when we want to celebrate sommat. This case, yore arrival's all the reason these folks need. It'd be swell iff'n you could play a song or two by then."

Hwaaaang. Bryce gave an experimental toot. "I hope it's a ways off, in that case."

They all shared a chuckle before finishing the work at hand. It seemed as though Lovejoy, Tempy, Eunice, Lois, and the MacPherson boys had been determined to send something back for every last kinsman in the holler. She'd thought it looked like a heap of goods when the brothers first rode up, but spread out, the bundles filled the barn floor and then some. Hattie could only imagine what the packages held, but if she knew Lovejoy and those gals, everything would be useful and appreciated. The gifts would also go a fair way to making even those most distrusting of outsiders warm up to the new men.

"Seems to me we ought to see about gettin' some dinner before we load up yore horse," Hattie said. They'd decided to just start making the rounds today. Hattie thought it best for the men not to strut around with two horses packed full of goods. It might make these men seem uppity, even though she knew they weren't.

"Agreed." Bryce scrambled up the ladder.

"We'll be along soon as we're washed up." Logan shot her a grin before following.

Hattie picked up the bundles bearing her and Miz Willow's names and went into the house to wash up. Maybe she'd make some sandwiches or something that wouldn't need to cook long. Bryce hadn't left any doubt as to whether or not he was hungry.

The door was open and the window covers rolled up when Hattie came inside. She could smell the faint sulfuric tinge in the air signaling boiled eggs. Miz Willow had fixed egg salad sandwiches and sliced apples for dinner.

"You've been busy." Hattie nodded toward the table as she laid the bundles on the bed. She was glad to see Miz Willow moving around with ease. "Need me to fetch some cool water?"

"That'd be nice, dearie. I'm just going to make a few more of these here sandwiches. Those boys shore cain pack it away." Hattie heard the fondness in Miz Willow's voice and knew she enjoyed having the Chance men around. Hattie was starting to feel the same way.

She took a wooden bucket made smooth by much use and filled it with the cool mountain water. As she walked back to the cabin, Logan and Bryce joined up with her.

"I'll get that." Logan smoothly snagged the bucket without sloshing over any of the water. His thumb brushed the back of her hand, warming her.

Logan clasped the handle of the bucket, feeling how warm it was from Hattie's hand. The rope was rough, a definite contrast to her soft hand.

They ate a pleasant lunch of tart apples with egg salad sandwiches on thick slices of bread. The crisply fresh water Hattie had drawn from the well washed it all down.

"We were going to bring in your packages when we came in for lunch, but Hattie beat us to it." Logan spotted them on the bed. "Maybe you ought to open 'em before we set off. There might be a note from Lovejoy that tells us something we need to know."

He couldn't dismiss the meaningful looks between Hattie and Miz Willow this morning.

"That might be a good idea," Hattie said slowly, raising her eyebrows in a silent question to the widow.

"Reckon so." With Miz Willow's nod, Hattie crossed the room and brought the parcels back to the table.

Logan made sure to move all the dishes out of the way before she got back. He and Bryce scooted as far down as they could so as not to intrude.

Miz Willow painstakingly untied the string and unfolded the neat brown paper to reveal her treasure. Although Logan could see a box and a shawl, she first picked up the note Lovejoy had written to her. She slid a wrinkled finger beneath the edge of the envelope to open it. Her mouth moved silently as she read to herself; then she put it down.

"No mention of it, Hattie. I reckon our last letter didn't make it afore these two"—she jerked a thumb at them—"took off."

Logan registered Hattie's disappointment and could hardly restrain his own curiosity.

"What were you lookin' for?" Bryce held no compunction.

Logan didn't know whether to kick him or slap him on the back for the blunt question, so he just waited for the response.

"I reckon it's up to Lovejoy to let you know. We don't have all the facts yet, but I figgur we cain tell you when yore sister-in-law gets word back to us." The widow's vague answer only raised more questions, but it would have to do. An awkward silence hung in the air.

"Fair enough. Why don't you go on and see what they sent you?" Logan ended the uncomfortable pause.

They all watched as the widow opened the pasteboard box and took out a gleaming new copper kettle.

"Ain't that a sight?" She held it up and looked at it from every angle. "I cain see ever wrinkle on my face, but it's beautiful just the same, 'cuz it's the same color as yore hair, Hattie!"

Logan privately thought Hattie's hair a much richer shade but held his peace. It wasn't the type of thing to mention.

"It'll shore come in useful for you, Miss Willow." Hattie gently took the proffered kettle and placed it in a position of prominence on one of the shelves.

Miz Willow drew out a soft-looking woolen shawl in bright purple. Hattie held it up. "Now ain't that the prettiest thing you ever clapped eyes on?" she asked before tucking it around the old woman's shoulders.

"I've been needin' a fair-weather wrap." Miz Willow stroked the fabric lovingly. "Ole one's plumb wore through."

"Don't you look a sight in yore violet shawl." Hattie stepped back to admire the color while the widow pulled out a thick hooded cloak in a deeper shade.

"Trust Lovejoy to remember my favorite color," she said with a chuckle. "Give me airs to wear the color of royalty." She handed the cloak to Hattie, who hung it on a peg near the door.

The last things in the bundle were small labeled bags Logan guessed were the healing herbs, since Hattie picked them up and carried them back to the storeroom.

Next was Hattie's turn, and she deftly untied the string to find a rose cloak identical to Miz Willow's purple one. She immediately stood up to try it on.

"Oh, it's so warm and soft!" she gasped. "I do believe they made these special for us, Miz Willow!"

Now Logan never would have thought to give any living soul anything pink, but the deep rose cloak brought a glowing blush to Hattie's cheeks. It was a good choice.

She kept it on as she unwrapped a small package of needles and a set of sharp knives. She tested the weight of each knife in her hand.

"These are wonderful. They'll shore come in handy, and this one fits my palm jist right!" Logan watched as she removed an older knife that had seen many sharpenings from the sheath around her small waist and replaced it with the new one of the same size. "Good for gathering," she explained when she noticed him looking.

"It's a good thing to have around, period." Logan suddenly realized how often Hattie must walk around alone. The healer would treat folks from all around, including men. Pretty as she was. . .well, he wasn't sorry to see her carry a knife.

❧

"Go on, off with you young'uns. I'll do the dishes and rustle up some rabbit stew and corn pone for supper. Hattie'll know when to come back." With that, Miz Willow shooed them back to the barn like they were a flock of ornery chickens.

Hattie found herself out in the barn, holding the head of one of the pack-horses as Bryce and Logan lifted on all the parcels. "Shore is a fine animal—not so tall as yore ridin' horses, but sturdy strong. Glossy brown coat, too." She patted the mare's nose and gave her a carrot from the basket on the wall. Whickering, the horse tickled Hattie's palm with her soft nose, looking for more of the treat.

Blossom brayed from the stall directly opposite, and Hattie went to offer the old mule a carrot. Blossom ignored her favorite vegetable and snorted, throwing her head up.

"What's wrong, girl?" Hattie opened the gate and stroked the mule's side, but Blossom edged away. She gave a high-pitched sort of whinny and raised her left foreleg.

"Shh. . ." Hattie patted her reassuringly and bent down to see if something was caught in her hoof. It had been awhile since she'd been shod, and Hattie thought she might need reshoeing.

"She okay?" Bryce quietly stepped beside her.

"I don't see anything wrong." Hattie peered at Blossom's hoof. "I thought she might need shoeing since it was a long winter, but it seems fine."

"But she's favoring that foreleg." Something about the way Bryce said this made Hattie look at him.

"She never has before. Maybe she has a cramp." She turned back to the mule. "Guess I won't be riding you today, huh, old girl?"

"Might be worse than a cramp. She's a bit long in the tooth." Bryce walked beside Hattie and squatted for a closer look. He ran his hands expertly over the mule. "What's her name?"

"Blossom." Hattie figured she'd best get out of his way.

"Blossom here might be coming up lame." Bryce stood up and pushed back his sleeves. "I'll pack her with mud today and tomorrow put some liniment on it.

Why don't you and Logan go on ahead? You can ride Blaze." He jerked a thumb at his own gray gelding, whose forehead held a white blaze.

"I don't know. . . ." Hattie wavered. Blossom was a good old friend, but her neighbors would have her hide if she didn't bring around at least one brother today. She chewed the inside of her lip in consternation.

"Bryce is about as close as you can get to a vet." Logan gently guided her toward the horse. "He has a way with animals. Besides, Blaze here's more interested in clover than running, so you don't have to worry about him being hard to handle."

"All right. To tell the truth, if I didn't show you around, I'd get in a mess of trouble with folks hereabouts." She turned to Bryce. "Before we go, is there anything I cain get to help you?"

"Nah. I know where the well is, and you've got some clean rags in the corner that'll serve. You two go on ahead without me and tell me all about it at supper."

I hope folks don't git the wrong notion with it jist bein' Logan and me ridin' *alone.*

Chapter 9

Logan led the packhorse; Hattie led the way. He watched her sway ahead of him, completely at ease in the saddle. The winding mountain lane gave way to a makeshift bridge over a full stream where they let the horses drink a little before continuing on their way.

"I'm leading you out to meet the Trevors. Eunice an' Lois've probably mentioned Silk to you. Jist their aunt, but reared 'em like a mother hen. The Pleasants live in the same area, so you'll meet them, too. It's fittin' that you meet up with yore kinfolk afore anyone else."

"I can hardly wait to meet them," Logan assured her. *I can hardly wait to meet everybody. I want to get to know every person in the holler—what they do, why they do it, how I can learn it. After six days of travel and a morning of unpacking, I'm finally going to have some excitement!*

"The Trevors got two twins, Ted and Fred, who're close to yore age. They're 'bout nineteen this season. You oughtta get along right well. Katherine married up with the oldest Pleasant boy, and they live here'bouts, too. Charlie'll be happy to show you the good trappin' spots." She reined in her mount.

"I ain't quite shore how to say this, but I feel you deserve a wise word or two. You know that folks up here is excited to meet you and yore brother. It's not 'cuz they'd ever in a million years thunk you brung 'em sommat, mind. But they do hold the notion they might have sommat valuable you'll take a shine to, iff'n you know what I mean." She stared at him with an undeniable intensity.

"No, not really." He hated to admit it, but he didn't have the faintest idea what she was talking about.

"Do you reckon that Eunice, Lois, and Tempy were the only unmarried women in these parts, Logan Chance?" She sighed. "Fact of the matter is, you might have a care around families with young ladies. Do you know what I mean?"

Whoa. Why didn't I see this before now? My perfect adventure has one huge hitch.

Hattie shifted in the saddle and started talking again. "You see, there ain't too many fresh faces around here, and yore two good-lookin' young bucks with a decent living and no wives attached." She looked away. "Maybe I shouldn' have mentioned it, but the cat's outta the bag now."

"Oh, no—thanks for the warning! It hadn't even crossed my mind. Now I'll know to watch my words." He waited for her to look at him again. "Hattie, I'm grateful. I'll be sure to pass this on to Bryce. See, back home it's the other way around—'bout six men to every woman. We've never exactly been in demand before." *No way she knows how truly grateful I am. The last thing on earth I hope to find in Salt Lick Holler is a bride. I need a break from children, not my own factory for 'em!*

❦

If that wasn' the most awkward conversation I've had in my whole entire life, I don't know what was. Hattie reached to pat Blaze's neck as they kept riding. *All the same, I'm glad I did. Poor guy hadn't any notion what lay ahead. He and his brother woulda been absolutely ambushed iff'n I'd hobbled my mouth.*

"Down thar's the Pleasant place." She pointed from atop the hill. "We'll go on to Silk's first and then stop by on our way back."

As they came into view of the modest cabin, Hattie thought to warn him of the dogs. "Ed Trevor breeds hound dogs. The minute you dismount, each and ev'ry blessed one of 'em'll sniff you up an' down, but they're well trained. Ed's the best breeder in the hills." As she finished, Hattie realized that the dogs weren't the only ones who'd be sniffing him over before the day was done. But he'd been warned, so she wasn't going to stew about it.

Silk Trevor came out onto the porch when they arrived, wiping her hands on a dishcloth. She waited as they tied up the horses and unloaded two packages.

"Afternoon, Hattie." Silk wrapped her in a hug and waited to be introduced to the stranger.

"Silk Trevor, this is Logan Chance." Hattie smiled as Logan held his hat to his chest.

"Nice to meet you, ma'am. Eunice and Lois tell me to give you their love." He stopped to grin mischievously. "Obie and Hezzy send their thanks. They're a happy bunch."

Silk took a deep breath as though to stop from crying. Then she changed her mind. "Aw, stuff it." She enveloped Logan in a hug.

Hattie bit back a laugh at his surprised look as Silk disengaged and held him at arm's length.

"I'm that glad to see you." She studied him head to toe. "Yore words do an aunt's tender heart some good. Why don't you two come and sit on the porch a spell? Ed and the boys'll be back afore long."

They all settled into the chairs before Silk realized they were short one brother. "Weren't there supposed to be two of you Chance men?" she asked as she started to rock.

"Yes, ma'am," Logan agreed, only to be cut off.

"Oh, you cain call me Silk."

"That's nice of you, Silk. I go by Logan, just so you know." His friendly invitation earned a nod from Silk.

"Bryce came with me, but he's down at Miz Willow's place right now."

"That's right," Hattie explained. "He thinks Blossom might be coming up lame."

"That's a sorry shame, Hattie. Blossom's been 'round long as I cain remember.

Maybe there's sommat cain be done."

"If there is, Bryce'll know it. He has a way with animals," Logan said, repeating what he'd told Hattie earlier.

"Just like our Hattie has a way with holpin' people." Silk's compliment made Hattie's cheeks go hot, so she ducked her head for a minute.

"I believe you're right," Logan said. Hattie could feel Logan looking at her, so she reached down and picked up the package labeled "Silk."

She passed it to Logan, since it had been placed in his trust. Besides, she had no business giving the gifts of others.

"Right." Logan bent to pick up the one marked "Trevor Men" and held them both toward Silk. "These are from Eunice, Lois, and their husbands, I believe."

"Thankee for bringin' 'em." Silk put a hand over her eyes and looked out into the distance. "I think I see Ed and the boys, so how 'bout we wait a minute?"

In no time at all, Silk was introducing Logan to her husband and sons. "This is Ed, and these are our boys, Ted and Fred. Meet Logan Chance from Californy."

They all shook hands before taking a seat, the twins hanging a brace of rabbits from the roof.

"Nice place you got here," Logan praised. "Good land."

"Thankee." Ed beamed at him. "Hear tell you Chances don't do too bad yoreself." He cast a look around. "Say. . ."

"Bryce is at Miz Willow's, tending to her mule. I'll bring him up this way later in the week," Logan promised.

"Yore welcome anytime, anytime." Ed put his pipe between his teeth. "Me an' m' boys was just emptyin' our traps." He glanced proudly toward the rabbits.

"We'd be happy to show you an' yore brother around," Ted offered eagerly.

"I'd like that." Logan nodded. "Hattie tells me you know the best hunting and trapping spots in the hills."

"Shore do." Fred puffed out his chest. "Why don't you both come 'round early tomorra an' we'll go lookin' for deer?"

Hattie gave a slight shake of the head, hoping Logan would pick up on the signal. There were plenty more folks she needed to take Logan and Bryce to see afore they went off gallivantin'.

"Nice offer, but since we just got here, I think we still have a lot of people to meet." Logan leaned forward. "Can we take you up on it a bit later? We'll be here through summer."

"Like I said"—Ed blew a ring of smoke in the air—"anytime."

❧

Logan rubbed the grit from his eyes and flexed his feet. After meeting the Trevors and Pleasants, they'd set off for home at dusk. Once they'd shared a hearty dinner, he and Bryce had groomed all the horses and given them a good rubdown. Now he and his brother sat in the loft, winding down but not ready to sleep.

"How's Blossom going to fare?" At dinner Logan had heard Bryce assure the women that their mule was feeling better and would be even more improved the next day. But that only meant the animal wouldn't be in pain—not that she'd be able to work.

"Better. We'll see how it goes after the liniment, but she wasn't suffering from cramps." Bryce shook his head. "The old girl's coming up lame in that foreleg, if I'm not mistaken."

"You rarely are." Logan paused before giving voice to his next thought. "We intended to leave behind the packhorses. I can't think of anyone I'd rather give one to than Miz Willow and Hattie."

"Yep." Bryce settled the matter with one word. "Speaking of which, tell me more about the folks you met today."

"Good people, every one. They aren't well-to-do by any stretch of the imagination, but they're willing to share what they have." Logan leaned back and rested his head against his hands.

"I believe it. Sounds like you're describing Hattie and Miz Willow." Bryce lay back. "Fits in with Lovejoy's ways, too."

"Silk Trevor's a warm soul. She's the one who reared Eunice and Lois. Looks like them, only softer around the eyes with age."

"Sounds 'bout right, since she's their aunt." Bryce nodded.

"Her husband, Ed, is a straightforward man. Raises hound dogs. Takes care of his family best he can. Smokes a pipe." Logan remembered the perfect rings of smoke. "Their two sons are twins, Ted and Fred. Both are blond and freckled, and I can't tell 'em apart. Offered to take us hunting and trapping once we've met everybody in the holler. They're probably a year or two younger than I am."

"Good. I'd like to explore the land a bit, stretch my legs." Bryce rolled over onto his side. "It'd be good to bring back some game to replenish Miz Willow's smokehouse."

"Just what I was thinking," Logan agreed. "Their daughter, Katherine, married the oldest Pleasant boy. He might come along when we go hunting, might not. His wife's expectin' again. It's her third. Hattie went inside with her to check up on everything. She's doing just fine."

"If she's anything like Eunice and Lois, she'll barrel through it like a champ." Bryce grinned. "Reckon Lois might've delivered by now. When we left, she looked liable to pop at any minute."

"Could be. Lovejoy will write when it happens." Logan worked a crick in his neck. "Last stop today was the Pleasant place."

"Sounds nice," Bryce mused. "The Pleasant place. Could be a fancy hotel."

"Not by a long shot. It's a cabin smaller than Miz Willow's and not as well built. Asa and his wife, Mary, still have three children home. His son wants to take us fishing." Logan looked forward to the shade and clear mountain stream. Fresh fish was one of his favorites.

"I'm up for it. Will the other two kids come along?"

"Sky and Lizzie are young ladies, Bryce." Now came the time to tell Bryce about Hattie's warning. "Actually, there's something Hattie mentioned I need to pass on."

"Yeah?" Bryce sat up.

"Before we visited that family, she gave me notice that there's more than one family around here with unmarried young ladies."

"Well, that's to be expected," Bryce said with a snort.

"I guess. I just never thought about it," Logan admitted. "Truth is, Hattie said they don't get a lot of visitors up this way."

"Coulda told you that by the almost-empty train." Bryce lay back down. "That's what makes it an adventure."

"Still, she was saying they don't meet new men very often, especially well-established bachelors."

"Stands to reason."

Logan could tell the exact moment Bryce got it, because he shot up like his pallet was covered in fire ants.

"You mean they'll be makin' eyes at *us*?" Alarm and disbelief painted Bryce's question.

"Yep." Logan made use of Bryce's favorite answer.

"Did Hattie tell us what to do about it?" Bryce did his best to pace around the loft, without much luck.

"Just watch what we say so we don't put any ideas into their heads."

"Sounds to me like they had ideas before we even got here!" Bryce walked into the bench, banging his shin and sloshing water onto the floor. He sank back down onto his pallet and used one of the hand towels to mop up the spill.

"Take it easy. Hattie just thought we deserved advance notice. Don't spend time alone with any of 'em, is all." Logan blew out the lantern and pulled up the covers.

Bryce groaned. "Sounds to me like this is gonna be more of an adventure than we reckoned."

"I'll watch your back," Logan bargained. "You watch mine."

Chapter 10

After serving up and polishing off a breakfast of flapjacks and sausage, Hattie began clearing the dishes.

"Bryce and I'll go muck out the barn and load up Legs." Logan handed her his plate.

"Sounds fine." Hattie added the plate to the pile as the men took their leave.

"Did he just call one of those packhorses Legs?" Miz Willow started wiping off the table.

"Yep." Hattie smiled. "His legs look too long for his body, and when he's loaded up, they say that's pert near all you cain see of him."

"Probably should've made him a racehorse," Miz Willow suggested.

"Too broad in the shoulders and flanks to summon enough speed. Bryce said it's kinder to give him work he cain accomplish and be valued for." Hattie went outside to wash the dirty dishes.

Lord, in a funny way I'm sorta like Legs—at first glance, it seems like I was meant to be a wife and mother, but the fact is I weren't made for it. Instead, You've given me a purpose and work I cain accomplish. I know I come up short, but in Yore arms I cain reach out to holp others. I thank You for that, Jesus. Let me not lose sight of the blessings You've given me.

She finished the dishes with a light heart, humming under her breath. Then she went inside to put them away.

"Is there anything I should be on the lookout for as we ride today, Miz Willow?" Sometimes the widow knew odd spots where valuable yarbs grew. Hattie hadn't managed to memorize them all just yet, but she was working on it.

"Not today, Hattie. I figgur you'll have yore hands full enough. Now I've packed some salted meat, biscuits, and apples in that thar saddlebag for dinner, though I've a notion you might be invited somewhere. Not good to rely on such things, though, so thar's plenty for all three of you." Miz Willow kissed her on the cheek. "I'll be seein' you afore supper, I reckon."

"Depends. We're going to visit Rooster, and I'll have a look-in on Abigail Rucker, since her husband's on a trip to Hawk's Fall this week." Hattie paused. "But we pass the Cleary place, so if they git a-holt of us, it'll take forever."

"I suppose. Jist do yore best to be gone in a trice." Miz Willow grimaced. "Iff'n that don't warsh, jist don' let Bethilda corner 'em."

"I cain't make any promises."

Logan finished mucking out the last stall, then walked over to find Bryce hunched over, rubbing Dr. J. H. McLean's Volcanic Liniment on Blossom's ailing leg.

"How's she comin' along this morning?"

"Hard to say." Bryce frowned in concentration. "She doesn't shy away when I touch her, but she still stays off it."

"Any chance of improvement?" Logan pressed.

"A little. She'll probably be able to use the leg a bit, but she'll favor it a good long while. If it's a bone split, she won't ever carry weight again." Bryce stood up and rubbed his hands on a rag. "Fact is, she's old, Logan. Too old to work."

"You've done what you can. We'll see to it that Hattie and Miz Willow are provided for." Logan lifted a saddle off the stand. "C'mon and help me saddle the horses—Hattie's taken a liking to Legs, so we'll load up the other one."

"She can ride Blaze again."

Something about Bryce's too-casual air made Logan turn around. "You'll have need of Blaze today," Logan stated matter-of-factly.

"I was thinking. . ." Bryce edged back toward Blossom's stall, and Logan knew what was coming.

"Oh, no you don't." He pinned his brother with his best glare. "No way you're hiding out in this barn and leaving me to meet everybody on my own."

"If there's a need, it'll be accepted." Bryce looked at something beyond Logan's shoulder rather than meet his brother's gaze.

"There's not. Yesterday you were needed. Today Blossom won't need liniment again until this evening. You're coming." He punctuated the order by hefting Bryce's saddle at him. "No brother of mine's gonna turn tail over meeting a few gals. Get going."

"Fine." Bryce straightened his shoulders. "I'll go. But I ain't talking to a one of 'em."

"Deal." From what Logan had seen, he wouldn't have to. Folks 'round Salt Lick Holler were anything but shy. They saddled all the animals and were finishing loading the packhorse when Hattie showed up.

"Are y'all ready?"

"You bet. We've loaded up everything for Abner, Rooster, Goody, and Nessie." Logan gestured to the packhorse.

"Blossom's leg is covered with some liniment, so we saddled up Legs for you." Bryce led the horse around. Hattie rested her medicine satchel on the pommel and swung up.

"Thankee." She stroked Legs's mane and crooned at him for a minute. "We get along just fine."

Logan rode alongside her while Bryce led the packhorse and brought up the rear. They went the opposite direction from the path they'd taken yesterday. The road wound uphill. The higher they climbed, the more trees crowded along the path, so full of birds it seemed as though the plants themselves sang to them.

"We'll be passin' the Cleary place. I reckon it's jist early enough not to bother them." Hattie's tone took on an unfamiliar flat note. "We'll probably be seein' 'em on the way back."

Logan turned around to make sure Bryce had heard the message; Bryce nodded. They saw a ramshackle old cabin, the wood bleached white by sun and rain, sitting in a clearing peeking through the trees. He figured that must be the Cleary place and noticed how Hattie picked up the pace as they passed it.

They reached the stream he remembered crossing the afternoon before and figured it must wind through the hills. Since there was no bridge, Hattie led them to a shallow embankment, and they crossed through the water. Legs carried Hattie across, and Logan and Bryce made it through with damp boots as they coaxed the packhorse across.

"It's jist past this turn," Hattie told them as they let the horses have a drink. "Don't quite know how to say this. . ."

"It's all right." Bryce grimaced. "Logan already told me how it is."

Logan watched Hattie's cheeks turn bright pink. It must be something different.

"What is it, Hattie?" Something about Lovejoy's dad tickled the back of his mind.

"I don't know if Lovejoy told you." She hesitated, and her voice dropped. "Mr. Linden owns a still."

"Yeah." Bryce nodded. "I remember Lovejoy sayin' her pa made moonshine."

"Well, Rooster says he takes pride in his work, so he keeps a close eye on the. . ." She searched for words. "The quality of his product."

"Samples his own wares, eh?" Logan said.

Hattie nodded sadly. "Folks call him Rooster. Used to be he'd jist git jolly, but of late, he's taken a different turn." She jutted her chin toward the curve in the road. "I'm not shore what mood he'll be in."

Logan could feel his own frown. What Hattie was trying so hard to state delicately was that the man had become a mean drunk, and she'd been around him enough to know it wasn't an occasional occurrence.

"Is 'Rooster' his real name, or do folks just call him that because he gets roostered?" Bryce's voice made him pay attention again.

"You know, we've all called him Rooster for so long I cain't remember iff'n he has a proper name." Hattie shrugged. "Since Nessie's fella up and ran off, she's done her best to take care of her pa. Goody pitches in now and then, too."

Nessie and Goody were, if Logan remembered right, short for Gentleness and Goodness. Ma Linden had named her girls for the fruit of the Spirit in an effort to raise them well in spite of her husband's dubious occupation. Lovejoy was firstborn, Peace had died young, and Kindness was stillborn. Temperance was Micah MacPherson's Tempy, and these were the other two of the sisters. Lovejoy must not have known about Nessie's husband running off, or she would have mentioned it. She wasn't the type of woman who'd leave one of her sisters alone to fend for herself with an angry drunk for a father.

"I see." Logan met Hattie's gaze to let her know he fully understood the problem.

"Sorry to hear that." Bryce shook his head. "Glad to know in advance, though."

Hattie just nodded and got back in the saddle. Logan felt the blood pumping in his veins, and his eyes narrowed. Whatever was to come, he'd be ready for it.

I wonder what we'll find once we round the corner.

"Hattie, I'll take the lead now."

Hattie pretended not to hear Logan. Instead, she nudged Legs to go a bit faster so the brothers were a few paces behind.

"Hello!" she called loudly so Rooster wouldn't think they'd snuck up on him. "Nessie, Rooster! It's Hattie Thales, and I brung you some visitors!" Best to warn him so he didn't think he had a pair of trespassers on his land. When Rooster was soused, it wasn't completely out of the question that he'd answer company with a shotgun—especially if they were strangers.

Logan pulled up beside her and shot her a dark glower before he scanned the area. "Don't try that again."

She smiled at him innocently. If he didn't like her precautions, well, he'd have to live with them.

Nessie came out of the house to greet them. Bryce busied himself tying the reins to a tree while she spoke.

"Howdy, Hattie. Mister. Mister." She cast a nervous glance toward the barn. "What cain I do for you folks?"

"Mornin', Nessie." Hattie patted the girl's arm to reassure her. "These are Logan and Bryce Chance, Lovejoy's kin. We come to visit you and yore pa, iff'n he's feelin' up to it."

"I reckon it's a good day for a visit." Nessie gave a slow nod. "Why don't you wait in the shade whilest I fetch 'im from the barn."

"Shore thing."

They waited as Nessie hurried to the barn. When she opened the door, a string of curses fouled the air before she swung it shut again.

"If she says it's a good day for a visit, then he ain't riled. He'll put on his manners for yore company." Hattie caught Logan and Bryce sharing a meaningful glance, and she gave a tight smile.

At least they'd taken her words to heart. Facing a man in the grip of drink was a bitter thing. No less taxing than telling his daughter in Californy that her old man had taken a bad turn. She and Miz Willow hadn't managed to work up the nerve yet, for fear Lovejoy would fret over things she couldn't change. Now maybe Logan and Bryce could help do something about the situation. Maybe not.

Rooster burst out of the barn, slapping his hat on his head and stumbling a little to meet them. Nessie carefully shut the barn door behind her and followed at a little distance, wringing her hands.

"Howdy." Rooster vigorously pumped Logan's hand. "Niiish ta meetcha." He turned to Bryce and did the same. "You, too."

He stood back to get a good gander at them, puffing out his gray-streaked red beard and putting his hands on his suspenders.

"Which one of you whippersnappers married m' girl?"

Chapter 11

The man reeked of whiskey and all but fell over when he leaned back to look at them. Logan and Bryce exchanged another look, neither one too eager to answer their brother's father-in-law.

"Pa," Nessie spoke in a low whisper. "Neither of them—"

"What?" Rooster reared back and reeled forward. "Which one of you low-down polecats be livin' with my Lovejoy in sin? Come on, take it like a man." He brandished unsteady fists and danced around—the better to roar at each of them.

Logan had seen about enough. On a handful of occasions, he'd taken a nip of the hard stuff and knew how it could change a man. Since he'd gotten right with the Lord, he'd laid off the stuff. This man needed to have his head dunked in a trough a few times, followed by a pot of strong coffee and a long talk with a brother in Christ.

For now, there'd be no reasoning with him. Logan started to roll up his sleeves and saw Bryce do the same. The water trough stood about twenty paces to their left. He only hoped the thing was full of enough water to cool Rooster's hot head.

"Now then, Rooster." Hattie stepped in front of Logan. "Jist calm down a minute."

"Calm down! These heathens done ruint my firstborn!"

Logan put his hands on Hattie's upper arms and made to sweep her behind himself. She didn't budge, so he tried to step around her. Then she moved—back in front of him. He gritted his teeth as she kept talking.

"No, Lovejoy married *Daniel* Chance. These are Logan and Bryce, come to tell you what a good wife yore daughter is to their brother."

It took two repetitions before understanding banked the fire in the old man's eyes. He swiped off his hat and scratched his head. "I've made a right ole mess of things, ain't I?"

"You've raised fine daughters, Mr. Linden." Logan finally succeeded in gently pushing Hattie behind him. "But your actions aren't doing them proud."

"Oo-ee." Rooster sucked in a shallow breath. "That do cut to the quick." He hung his head. "You don' need to tell anybody 'bout my lack of manners. I'd hate to shame Lovejoy. Schhee's been good to me." He slung his arm around Nessie, who had to take a step forward so as not to buckle. "We miss her 'round here."

"I'm sure you do, Mr. Linden," Bryce acknowledged, "but that's no reason to ply yourself with liquor."

"Here now." Rooster drew himself up. "Don't be castin' as–asp–aspursi, uh, sschoe black on m' good name."

"He jist tole it like he sees it, Rooster." Hattie came forward again, and Logan didn't try to stop her. The old man's humiliation had sobered him up a bit. " 'Tis barely even noon." Her voice lowered to such a soft whisper that Logan had to strain to catch it. "Miz Willow's been wantin' to speak with you about it for a long while now."

"Did yer brung me shum of my headache tonic?" Rooster shrank into himself, looking thin and frail. "I've need for more."

"No, Rooster." Hattie patted his shoulder. "You need to come down to the cabin so we cain talk 'bout what's best to cure them headaches."

"I been doin' tolerable." Rooster jerked a thumb at his daughter. "Nessie here'll go on down for some more tea."

"No, Pa." Nessie's small voice hung in the wind.

"We're happy to see Nessie anytime. Like Logan said, you've raised fine gals, Rooster," Hattie soothed. "But Miz Willow and I cain't be givin' you yore medicine when you don't come in. As healers, we need to make shore we're a-givin' you the right treatment. Why don't you come on down, and we'll talk about it?"

Logan realized what she was trying to do. She and Miz Willow planned to confront the man about being jug-bit, but Rooster avoided them. Now Hattie wouldn't treat his ale head until they'd discussed the real problem. Logan only hoped that when the man came to the healer, he'd be in such bad shape he'd agree to almost anything. He'd seen men who had to hit rock bottom before drying out and staying sober. He was only glad the Lord had spared him from being one of them.

One thing's for certain: I'll be there when Rooster Linden comes to call. The man's a threat. Poor Nessie looks worn down. Under no circumstances will I allow Rooster to be alone with Hattie or Miz Willow.

⌘

By the time Rooster had settled down and agreed to stop by and have a long-overdue chat with Miz Willow, the sun shone high in the sky. Hattie took Nessie aside for a little chat after Bryce handed her a parcel. They went and sat at the base of an old elm while the men talked and Rooster opened his package.

"I've not seen you in a while, Nessie." Hattie kept her voice light. "How are you getting along?"

"Fair to middlin', I suppose." Nessie toyed with the end of her string. "You know how it goes."

"Nessie." Hattie waited until she looked up. Hard to believe Nessie was two years younger—life had her looking careworn as an old quilt. "I do know. That's why I ask."

"Oh." A tear slid along the side of Nessie's nose. "Pa's never clear these days.

Usually he's jist melancholy and sits alone jawin' at himself, and some days he's right cheery and gits out his jug to play awhile. Then he's pert near tolerable. But when he's riled. . ." The floodgates opened. "I know he don't mean the things he says, but a girl cain only hear it so many times afore it seems true. I jist stay outta his way as best I cain and make shore there's sommat for him to eat iff'n he wants it. Thar's nothin' else I cain do to holp him. I jist hafta watch him drink hisself into an early grave."

"Here you go, honey." Hattie put her arm around the gal's shoulders and handed her a clean hanky. A healer was never without a few clean cloths. She waited for Nessie to cry herself out a bit.

"I mean, he only hit me that once, and it were an accident 'cuz I was a-pullin' him away from the fire and his arms was flailin'. So don' worry yerself 'bout that a-tall. He really ain't a violent man." Having said her piece, Nessie stopped talking.

"Why don't we put it afore the Lord, Nessie?" It was the best advice Hattie had. "I'll pray with you for yore pa, iff'n you want."

"Thankee, Hattie." Nessie twisted the handkerchief a few times before letting it drop in her lap.

Hattie took Nessie's hands in hers and gave a reassuring squeeze. She could only hope that she and Miz Willow were successful in talking turkey with old Rooster when he finally came to call. If he didn't want to change, there was precious little they could do about it except pray.

"Dear heavenly Father, we come to You now in search of Yore guidance. We know You call Yore children to walk 'with longsuffering, forbearing one another in love,' and we ask for Yore holp in putting that into practice. Nessie's pa is in a bad way, Lord. He dug hisself a hole so deep that his daughter cain't hardly look after him and see the light herself. We know of Yore words on those who abuse likker: 'Woe unto them that rise up early in the morning, that they may follow strong drink; that continue until night, till wine inflame them!' Well, Father, I reckon Rooster's feeling that woe, and we pray it brings him back to Yore love. Let Yore glory inflame his heart and displace the cheap lures of moonshine. Amen."

Nessie gave her a watery smile and leaned back to dry her eyes. The both sat in silence for a minute, and Hattie was grateful for the time they had alone. The men never need know how much Nessie needed support.

"Thankee. I don't know what I'd do without you, Hattie Thales. I think the Lord gave this holler a great blessing when He called you to be a healer. There's wounds as cain't be seen by most, but you've the gift of carin'. You remind me how the Lord is always with us." Nessie reached out to stop Hattie from smoothing her braid. "Now don't be fiddlin'. I know yore modest, but it does no justice to you nor gives glory to the Lord to dismiss earned praise. It's honest appreciation, Hattie." Nessie's eyes grew moist again, and her voice dropped to a whisper. "It's all I have to give you."

"Don't you start up again." Hattie shook a finger at her before enveloping her in a hug. "Else you'll git me goin', too." She pulled back and smiled. "Besides, we have this here parcel from yore sister to open." She tapped the package. "Why don't you have a look?"

Nessie carefully untied the string and pushed back the blue calico fabric as though it were made of gold. She had to unwind it a few times before she was finished.

"It's so beautiful. There's enough here to make me a new dress." Nessie stroked a length of the material before picking up the note inside. "Lovejoy knows I cain't read, so I s'pose she reckoned on me gittin' some holp. How've yore letters bin comin' along, Hattie?"

"Just fine. I'd be tickled to read it to you." Hattie accepted the envelope and read Nessie the entire letter; Lovejoy wrote that she missed her and hoped she was well, that she was doing fine and so were Daniel, Polly, Ginny Mae, and all the others. She said she hoped the things she sent would come in useful and finished off by giving her love and prayers.

"It does my heart good to hear from her." Nessie smiled and returned her attention to the package lying open on her lap. She pulled out a pack of needles, a pair of ribbons the same shade of blue as the calico, and a fawn-colored hooded cloak just like Hattie's rose one, Miz Willow's purple one, and Silk's buttercup yellow one. When she unfolded the cloak, she found French-milled soap, two pairs of stockings, and a new hairbrush, exactly like the other three had. They'd just not held them up in front of the menfolk.

"Mercy. Lovejoy weren't foolin' when she said she's livin' fine." Nessie couldn't stop smiling as she refolded the package. "There's not a thing here I cain't use— and so many luxuries, I'll feel like a queen." She stood up. " 'Tween yore prayer and Lovejoy's package, I feel so loved and blessed, I cain hardly stand it."

"S'pose we ought to join the menfolk. I've still got to check on Abigail Rucker this afternoon." Hattie stopped to give Nessie one last hug. "Remember how yore feeling now and know yore never without holp. The Lord takes care of His own."

Chapter 12

Hattie heard the cock crow and snuggled under the covers for a mite longer. Logan and Bryce had gone off to Hawk's Fall to visit Abner MacPherson, whose three boys had married Tempy, Eunice, and Lois. They'd set out yesterday morning and wouldn't be back until tomorrow night—just in time for church on Sunday.

She and Miz Willow were happy with some boiled oats and brown sugar, so she could afford to snuggle in for a little bit this morning. When the flames in the hearth began to gutter, she got up to lay on some more wood. No matter what the season, evening through morning in the mountains could put a chill in a body. She slipped into her clothes and set water to boil for the oatmeal before she went to milk the cow and bring in fresh cream to add to their breakfast.

"Mornin'." Miz Willow was up and stirring the oats when she got back in, her pretty new shawl wrapped around her shoulders.

"Mornin'." Hattie nodded toward the pot. "Have I got time for a quick barn muckin' afore it's ready?" In addition to their milk cow and Blossom, who was on the mend, they still housed the two packhorses Bryce and Logan had left behind since they'd only had one or two packets for Abner.

"I reckon you'll be done by the time it's cool."

Hattie went back to the barn and got straight to work. After breakfast she and the widow planned to do the wash while the brothers weren't around. Miz Willow had told the men to leave out anything they needed cleaned before they left, and Hattie found a neat bundle of shirts and britches in the barn.

She finished lickety-split and went back to the bowl of creamed oats and brown sugar Miz Willow had already served up for her. It was perfect with cool milk. The widow favored hers with tart cranberries; she said it woke her up. Hattie remembered her mama saying each bowl of oatmeal was special to the person who ate it.

I wonder why Lovejoy warned us that Logan hates oatmeal. It's one of my favorites. There's so much you cain do with it—add honey, raisins, preserves, cinnamon, maple syrup, berries. . . . Oh well. I'll jist enjoy it today and tomorra, seein' as how we won't make it for what's left of spring—or most of the summer.

After breakfast she started heating water and hauling it to the washtub outside while Miz Willow cleaned the dishes. Soon enough, the scent of strong lye tinged the mountain air as Hattie put the washboard to work. Then she let the clothes soak in the washer before rinsing them in clean water. It took all morning to finish the clothes.

"I figgur we'd best stop for some dinner." Hattie hung the last few items on the clothesline with the clothespins Asa Pleasant had fashioned for them. It would do Miz Willow good to sit a spell before they tackled the towels, sheets, and rags. Everything in the healers' house had to be kept clean as a whistle.

"Sounds good to me."

They retrieved some salted fish from the smokehouse and used the last of the bread they'd baked the day before, washing it all down with lots of water.

"Warshin's a thirsty work." Miz Willow poured her another cupful of water. "Always seems like the smell of the lye gets caught in yore throat."

"But it feels powerful nice to sleep on fresh sheets and put on a crisp, clean dress." Hattie wiped off the table and set more water on to boil.

She was bringing out a kettleful of piping hot water when she saw the Clearys opening Miz Willow's garden gate. "Seems we have us some visitors," she muttered to Miz Willow, who straightened up as best she could.

"Good afternoon, Bethilda."

"Afternoon, Miz Willow. Hattie." She sailed toward them across the yard, Lily and Lark in tow.

Hattie could see the tight lines around Bethilda's mouth. Suddenly, working over a vat of hot lye water seemed like a fine way to spend the afternoon. She took a deep breath and pasted on a smile. "What seems to be the trouble?" Hattie knew the problem wouldn't be medicinal.

"Silly girl." Bethilda gave a forced laugh. "This be a social call."

"Well, in that case I s'pose we'd best set in the shade awhile. I cain make us some tea." Miz Willow ushered them to the porch, but Bethilda followed her inside.

"We went to visit Abigail Rucker t'other day." Bethilda sat down at the table, and her daughters followed suit. "Bless her heart, poor thing's bigger'n a bear. She mentioned as how Hattie'd been to see her jist the day afore, and how nice it'd been for Hattie's visitors to wait outside like gentlemen while they talked 'bout the babe to come."

Hattie closed her eyes for a moment. Bethilda Cleary knew she'd been up her way and hadn't stopped by to introduce the Chance brothers. Hattie reached for the chamomile—anything soothing couldn't hurt. Upset, Bethilda Cleary resembled a riled polecat—the stink she raised would cover everyone around.

"And I asked myself, how was it we hadn't seen you or yore new friends?" Bethilda's tone sounded sticky as honey but held none of the natural goodness.

"To tell the truth, Bethilda, we counted on stoppin' by but owed it to Rooster and Nessie to see them first, seein' as how he's their brother's father-in-law." Hattie saw Miz Willow nodding in support. "Took a mite longer'n we reckoned, and it were dark when I'd finished lookin' in on Abigail." She wouldn't mention how she'd taken Logan and Bryce through the meadow instead. "We wouldn't want to impose on you—and with no warning whatsoever!"

"I'm shore I done made it clear as a mountain stream that we was anxious to meet the bachelors." Bethilda's eyes narrowed. "Lily and Lark are bound to get along with 'em like peas and carrots. That bein' the case, I've got to ask why yore keepin' 'em away."

"Fiddlesticks, Bethilda Cleary," Miz Willow broke in. "You know better. Hattie cain't control the sun, and happens right now, the boys went to Hawk's Fall."

"Aw," Lily groaned, "you didn't scare them off, did yer, Hattie?"

"We was itchin' to meet 'em." Lark sounded downright mournful.

"They went to visit Abner MacPherson and take him word from his sons back in Californy." Hattie poured the tea into five cups. "That's all."

"I heard they brung more'n words." Bethilda peered around. "Caught wind that Lovejoy and the MacPhersons done sent gifts to everybody in the holler."

"They brought things for kin and such," Hattie clarified. Clearer than a cloudless night, the Clearys were hopin' for something from Californy in addition to husbands.

"Oh?" Bethilda glanced slyly at the two cloaks hanging by the door before nodding at the copper teakettle. "Didn't realize you was kin."

"Lovejoy an' Hattie is kindred spirits. All healers are. 'Sides, Hattie's the one what's takin' care of her brothers."

"I see." Bethilda stood up. "Well, you'll be shore and let us know when they're back from Hawk's Fall. We wouldn't want Hattie to take all that *carin'* on herself."

Hattie bit her lip as the Clearys left, tamping down a surge of anger at Bethilda's implications. She emptied the teakettle and went outside to rinse the cups clean. Miz Willow followed her.

"Don't you let Bethilda Cleary direct her pointed words and pierce yore heart, Hattie. It reflects on her, not on you." Miz Willow waited until she nodded in response. "Now let's finish up this warshing. Bethilda's visit set us back."

"Shore did."

∽⟡∾

Logan and Bryce arrived at Hawk's Fall after dark and made their way to the MacPherson farm. Abner ushered them to the barn, where they saw to the horses, then bedded down in the loft.

Logan could scarcely believe this was the selfsame loft shared by Obadiah, Hezekiah, and Micah McPherson before they came out to California. He and Bryce barely fit in the space when they lay down. How three grown men had slept here was beyond him. Especially since Obie and Hezzy were absolutely mammoth. Logan now knew they'd gotten their height and girth from their father. It seemed as though Micah had inherited his mama's stature and his pa's smarts.

They got to know Abner better the next day when he showed them around. "You already seen the barn. Ain't as grand as the Peasleys' up yonder—they breed mules—but it serves." Abner puffed out his chest with pride. "M' boys set up in Californy and then sent me money for a new one."

"Sturdy animal." Bryce praised a nearby mule. "I'll bet he's good at pulling a plow."

"Right you are." Abner took them out to a shed behind the barn. "This here's the fancy plow m' boys wanted me to have." He took off his hat. "The Lord blessed us with fine sons. We raised 'em right in the sight of God, and now they share their blessings. Look 'round. We'll have us a bumper crop this year."

"Good to hear," Logan affirmed. "Obie, Hezzy, and Mike are well-liked back in Reliable. They got fine brides in Eunice, Lois, and Tempy, too. Done quite well out there."

"Knew they would." Abner gave a decisive nod. "Micah writes 'bout how holpful you Chance boys have bin." He slapped them each on the shoulder and pulled them close for a moment. "Yore like family to them. I cain't tell you how beholden I am to you an' yourn."

As quick as the emotion came on, it was over. Abner clapped his hat back on and took them inside for some dinner.

Logan and Bryce grinned. They'd made the right choice in coming.

Chapter 13

Y'all come back now, ya hear?" Abner MacPherson waved them off after an early breakfast the next morning.

"Yes, sir," Logan and Bryce answered dutifully as they rode out of the yard and turned onto the road. They'd decided to make an early start so they could stop by the Hawk's Fall General Store. Hattie had asked them to check to see if they had any messages. Logan hoped they did—he wanted to know about the mysterious "matter" they'd written to Lovejoy about.

"Abner's a good man," Bryce mused.

"True." Logan couldn't argue with that. "I'm glad we came, but it's nice to be getting back."

"Funny how quick Miz Willow's place feels kinda like home." Bryce gave him a slanted look. "I reckon Hattie has a lot to do with it."

"They both do." Logan wasn't sure what Bryce was getting at, but something warned him not to probe. Hattie was an upstanding woman, considerate hostess, devoted healer, kind spirit, and good friend. She couldn't help being pretty, so he wouldn't let that dampen his appreciation of her fine qualities one bit. He shot Bryce a smile. "Speaking of Miz Willow and Hattie, I have an idea."

❦

"Cut it out!" Bryce cracked one eye open to glower at him.

"Sure." Logan watched his brother close his eye again and try to burrow under the covers. He flicked more water. "Soon as you get up!"

"You can't blame a guy for wanting to prolong the best night's sleep he's had in three days." Bryce flung back his blankets. "After all, I had to sleep with your feet in my face in that loft!"

"And your feet were in mine. It was the only way we could both lie down without one of us running the risk of rollin' off." Logan started to shave. "We've got church this morning, so we'll meet the rest of the people from the holler. You'd best get going."

"All right, all right." Bryce rummaged through the trunk to pull out their Sunday best.

"What're you doin'?" Logan stopped him. "We've got to muck out the barn before we get dressed for church. Come on."

While they worked, Hattie came out to gather eggs. Logan stopped for a minute to look at her. Something was different. . . .

"What'd you do to your hair?" He blurted the question before he had a chance to stop himself. It was none of his business how she wore her hair. But it was all scraped back and pinned up so tight. Where was her long dancing braid the color of a sunrise?

"Hmmm?" Hattie shut the chicken coop and raised a hand to smooth back her hair. "Is it coming down?"

"No," Logan muttered. "It just looks different, is all."

"Of course it does!" She smiled at him and Bryce. "I cain't go to the Lord's house with my hair hangin' down my back in a braid. That's only passable for a young gal." She went to get the pail of milk since Logan had made a habit of doing that chore for her.

"You are young." Bryce joined the conversation.

"Kind of you to say so, but I'm no spring chicken." Hattie picked up the pail. "I'm a widow."

How did I manage to forget that she's had a husband? Maybe because she's like no widow I've ever met. I reckon scrapin' back your crowning glory isn't so awful when you're of Miz Willow's age, but Hattie? Now that's a crime.

"You both come on inside when yore finished here. Breakfast'll be on the table." With that, she left.

Telling himself it was a good thing she was gone so he couldn't stick his foot in his mouth again, Logan focused on the work at hand. He finished mucking out the stalls, then climbed the ladder to change. By the time he and Bryce left the barn, his stomach was growling.

As he filled up on country-fried potatoes and poached eggs, Logan reconsidered Hattie's Sunday getup. Her green dress wasn't faded like the yellow and blue he'd seen her wear for everyday, and it swirled a little at the bottom edge when she turned around. He still didn't like her hair pinned up, but the style did show off her slender neck and little ears. He was just wondering whether or not she could still carry her knife when she caught him looking.

"Ahem." He cleared his throat and turned to Miz Willow. "Couldn't help but notice how nice you ladies look this morning." He smiled at both of them.

"Thankee, Logan." Miz Willow beamed and smoothed the white wisps escaping her bun. "Nice of you to notice. I reckon everyone'll be gussied up today. Hattie and me need to hold our own."

Hattie shook her head but patted the old woman's hand. "You'd shore give any fella a run for his money iff'n he came sniffin' around, Miz Willow. But I wouldn't know what to do without you, so don't be gettin' any crazy notions."

"Heh, heh." The widow slapped her knee. "That I would, dearie. That I would." She smiled fondly at Hattie. "But I won't be batting my eyelashes at any whippersnapper who smiles my way."

Logan couldn't help but think Miz Willow wasn't the widow he'd like to hear that promise from.

CHANCE ADVENTURE

❧

It was a fairly short walk to the schoolhouse where they held church every Sunday. Hattie walked beside Miz Willow, holding her arm to keep her steady on the uneven road. Logan and Bryce walked on each side of them.

They were looking mighty handsome this morning. Hattie wasn't quite sure whether she'd forgotten how good-looking the brothers were while they were at Hawk's Fall or if it was their Sunday clothes.

When they got to the schoolhouse, women would be swarming all around them. Logan and Bryce's visit would be the high point of the year—whether or not they ended up hitched.

She knew they wouldn't. She loved the holler and wouldn't dream of leaving it, but Logan and Bryce were used to finer manners. She was well aware of how unpolished they all sounded, but these were her people. She knew Logan and Bryce were glad to visit, but the holler would never be home to them the way Chance Ranch was. Sad to say, but she suspected there was a world of difference separating California and Kentucky.

A crowd of people milled around the front of the building, and Hattie could tell when everybody caught sight of the Chance brothers. They stopped talking for a minute, then started whispering furiously.

Silk Trevor came up to them immediately, her husband and sons close on her heels. After a warm welcome—hugs for Hattie and Miz Willow from Silk and a lot of shoulder slapping and hand shaking among the men. Mary Pleasant came up to join them. Her husband, Asa, would be filling in for the circuit-riding parson today.

Hattie saw Nessie walking from the distance and motioned for her to come over. Rooster was nowhere in sight, as he hadn't been for the past two Sundays. Hattie hoped he would show up today after his first meeting with Logan and Bryce.

Lizzie and Sky Pleasant stood over with the Cleary sisters and a few other young ladies. At least they knew to wait for an introduction. After the service, everyone would stay around to chat and laugh before heading home to supper. Then she could introduce the Chances to Otis Nye and Li'l Nate Rucker—not to mention the Clearys.

They all moved into the schoolhouse, where benches formed rows down the narrow room. Hattie steered Nessie to her and Miz Willow's customary bench. Since Nessie's sister Goody had married up and joined the Peasley pew, Lovejoy had gone to California, and Rooster had stopped attending regularly, there wasn't a Linden bench any longer.

With the Chance men, it was a much tighter fit than usual, but they managed. Asa stood at the front and opened with prayer before asking them to rise.

His deep baritone led them in "Forth in Thy Name." The hymn, one of Hattie's favorites, swelled in the small schoolhouse:

"The task Thy wisdom hath assigned,
O let me cheerfully fulfill;
In all my works Thy presence find,
And prove Thy good and perfect will."

She loved the way a hymn could speak for so many. Every person had a task, but each was different. The words encouraged her, calling her to be a healer. When Hattie helped ease suffering or bring new life into the holler, she knew she was serving to carry out God's will.

Asa led them in "My Hope Is Built." The men and women sang in turns and joined in the chorus:

"On Christ the solid Rock I stand,
All other ground is sinking sand. . . ."

Hattie could hear Logan's rumble from where he sat on Miz Willow's left. The way his deep voice melded with her higher notes reminded Hattie that harmony came in many different forms.

The Chance brothers sounded different from the folks of the holler, but in the Lord, they all were joined in the family of God.

Chapter 14

Logan could pick out Hattie's soft soprano alongside Miz Willow's wavery alto. As they all worshipped, he was struck by the power of God's love to join people together in the bonds of faith. These folks weren't only part of Logan's adventure—they were part of God's plan for his life. He just didn't know how. The uncertainty made him shift a little on the bench as Asa began the sermon on the Sixteenth Psalm. He was glad Asa had chosen to speak on one of King David's psalms—the verses of praise in the Word of God never failed to give him focus. Asa talked for a bit on the joy and hope of having the Lord's guidance before reading directly from the scriptures.

"Verse eleven is David praising God directly: 'Thou wilt shew me the path of life: in thy presence is fulness of joy; at thy right hand there are pleasures for evermore.' " Asa paused for a moment to let those words sink in before expounding on them. "We cain only fulfill our purpose iff'n we follow the path God lays for us. Only then can we feel the full joy of His presence in our lives and be firm in our hope for the future."

And there it was. Logan sat up a bit straighter. He'd follow the path as far as he could see and trust the Lord for whatever lay beyond the next curve. Not knowing what came next was a part of the adventure, but knowing God controlled it was part of life.

Asa closed in prayer, and the service ended. Everyone stood up and shuffled toward the door. People milled around, catching up with the families they didn't see during the course of the week. Tiny girls with string bows in their pigtails took turns on the swings and seesaw while young boys chased each other, stopping only to pick up their hats when they fell off.

Hattie braced Miz Willow's arm and walked over to Abigail Rucker, gesturing for them to follow her. A hulking man stood protectively next to the heavily expectant woman. Logan wondered if he was her brother, since he remembered Hattie saying Abigail's husband was little.

"Logan and Bryce Chance, you've already met Abigail Rucker." Hattie nodded toward the giant. "This is her husband, Li'l Nate."

Little? There was nothing tiny about the man whose beefy hand all but squeezed the life out of Logan's in a hearty shake.

"Nice to meet you both." Li'l Nate beamed. "Abby told me you'd come to town. Wish I'd been around when you stopped by, but I was working at the smithy."

"You're the blacksmith." That made sense.

"Why do they call you Li'l Nate?" Bryce's curiosity got the better of him.

"Big Nate were my pa and the blacksmith afore me." Li'l Nate grinned. "It's from when I were growin' up, and it jist stuck."

"Li'l Nate's the best harmonica player in these hills." Hattie turned to him. "Logan and Bryce got two shiny new harmonicas but don't know how to work 'em."

"I'd be tickled to teach you boys," Not-So-Li'l Nate offered.

"Thanks!" Logan and Bryce answered in unison.

"Why don't you and Abigail come on back to our place for Sunday supper?" Miz Willow invited. "It'd break up yore walk a bit, an' you could give 'em a few pointers. Otis Nye'll be joinin' us."

"Thankee kindly." Abigail rested her hands on her back. "I'd be glad to eat someone else's cookin'!"

While that was settled, Logan saw a thick-waisted woman with salt-and-pepper hair make a beeline toward them. She all but shoved Hattie to one side to break into the circle.

"Mornin', Miz Willow." The woman gazed at him and Bryce out of the corner of her eye. "I see yore visitors came back from Hawk's Fall," she simpered.

"Yore right at that, Bethilda." Miz Willow's eyes twinkled. "Bethilda Cleary, meet Logan and Bryce Chance from Californy."

"Nice to meet you." Logan and Bryce took off their hats. Logan watched in disbelief as the woman sank into an awkward curtsy.

"Pleased to make yore acquaintance, sirs." Bethilda gave an unctuous grin. "It's shore a pleasure to have fine gentlemen visit our humble holler. Shame we didn't meet sooner." She shot a quick glare at Hattie.

Logan could see Bryce shift next to Li'l Nate, whose eyebrows reached near his hairline. One thing was clear: Bethilda Cleary was not the most pleasant of the holler inhabitants. But what could she want from them?

"I had hoped you handsome brothers would take an invite to Sunday supper so my family could get to know you."

Logan followed her gaze to a pair of young girls. One couldn't have been more than fourteen.

Bryce wouldn't look at Bethilda, and Logan saw Hattie shaking her head slightly but urgently. Now he saw which way the wind blew, and it was time to get out of the draft.

"Thank you for thinking of us, but we've already made arrangements." Logan kept the refusal as polite as possible.

"Oh, well, Miz Willow and Hattie won't mind, I'm shore." Bethilda trilled a fake laugh and shot another glare toward Hattie. "They've had you all to theyselves, haven't they?"

"No, ma'am. We've been meeting up with kin and have gotten to know the Trevors, Pleasants, and MacPhersons," Logan ground out. It was obvious the woman wanted to accuse Hattie of setting her cap for one of them. Ridiculous. Hattie was the one who had warned them about the likes of Bethilda Cleary.

"Spent half our time in Hawk's Fall," Logan went on. "And even if our plans only concerned Miz Willow and Hattie—"

"Which they don't," Bryce tacked on.

"We'd be hard-pressed to give up their company," Logan finished.

"I see." A steely glint lit Bethilda's gaze.

"I'm to learn 'em on the harmonica, Miz Cleary." Li'l Nate steered her attention to himself. "So as they'll be ready for the doin's."

"Wonderful!" Bethilda was all smiles once again. "But we must see you before Friday a week. Why don't you boys stop on by fer—"

"I'm shore they'll be seein' you, Bethilda." Hattie interrupted what was sure to have been another invitation and steered Abigail Rucker to the path. "We'd best git on our way now."

Logan smiled his thanks. There wouldn't be any way for them to refuse a second time, and the last thing he and Bryce wanted was to be stuck with Bethilda Cleary and her daughters.

❧

Hattie smiled as she mashed the taters, remembering the look on Bethilda's face when Logan and Bryce had refused her invitation. The woman had become so biggity she needed to be taken down a peg or two. Hattie knew Bethilda would make her sorry she'd interrupted, but she couldn't stand there and let the woman trap Logan and Bryce when Logan had stood up for her and Miz Willow like that—not that they couldn't take care of themselves, of course.

Abigail sat in the rocking chair, stroking her burgeoning belly and watching Otis Nye carve another perfect checker. The old man seemed gruff and crotchety most of the time, but underneath he just wanted to be useful. If only he'd stop carving those ugly owls of his and giving folks the stink eye when they couldn't think of anything nice to say about them.

Miz Willow put the biscuits in the ash oven and checked on the pot roast. She handed Hattie salt and butter to add to the potatoes. Hattie had already skimmed the cream from the top of the milk and poured it in. Soon enough, she was setting honey, butter, and jam on the table.

"Come on in now," Miz Willow hollered out the window at the men. "Dinner's ready."

Li'l Nate trailed Logan and Bryce to the washbasin. They'd been digging a hole for a pole they'd chosen for horseshoes. Bryce had remembered some old ones in the barn, and they'd decided to get up a game before the meal.

"Pass the taters," Otis grumbled at Li'l Nate, who was in the middle of taking another huge helping. It was a good thing Hattie had mashed about two dozen. She'd planned on making tater cakes with the leftovers but could see that wouldn't be happening.

"Shore are good vittles, ain't they?" Li'l Nate passed them on.

Otis sopped up some taters and gravy with a biscuit before grunting, "Passable."

Coming from Otis Nye, that was high praise.

"I say it's mighty fine eatin'." Bryce shoved some roast into his mouth and chewed emphatically.

"Right you are." Abigail took a sip of her milk and patted her tummy. "Babe's kickin' to make room for more." She grabbed Otis's hand and laid it on her stomach. He tried to pull away, but surprise flashed in his rheumy eyes as he felt the babe kick, and the lines around his mouth softened.

"Gonna be a strong 'un, Nate." Otis spoke the first compliment Hattie had ever heard from him. "You gonna make a fine mama, Abigail." Then he pokered up again. "Those biscuits ain't gonna et themselves, boy." He poked Logan in the ribs. "Give 'em over."

Hattie saw Logan bite back a grin as he followed the grumpy old-timer's command. Otis Nye's crotchety outside hid a soft spot wider than he'd like to admit. He was the exact opposite of Bethilda Cleary, whose fake smiles hid dark thoughts. Hattie would rather see Otis Nye any day of the week.

Dinner ended, but nobody was ready to leave the table.

"Yore food done broke m' breadbasket." Otis Nye glowered at them while he snatched the last biscuit and slathered it with honey.

"Yep. Between yore vittles and his child"—Abigail patted Nate's shoulder—"I'm thinkin' I'm too big to git up agin."

"Yore eatin' for two, Abby." Nate beamed at his tiny wife. "But I ken what you mean. I'm too stuffed to play a harmonica. Gonna have to let the food settle a mite."

"I'm with you on that," Logan agreed, and Bryce nodded.

Hattie got up to brew some coffee and then sat back down. She loved Sundays, the day the Lord Himself had set aside to enjoy hearty meals and good company.

Chapter 15

Logan and Bryce waved good-bye to Hattie and Miz Willow after breakfast a few days later. The Trevor boys were going to take them hunting, and they would meet halfway at the schoolhouse.

We've been here a week already, and this is the first time we're going out into the countryside together, just the men. We'll tromp around the hills all day, track animals, and maybe bring home supper. This is more like it!

"Nice day for huntin'," Ted said in greeting when they arrived. Or was it Fred? Logan couldn't really tell. Both of the twins wore brown buckskin trousers and cambric shirts faded gray from many washings.

"Sure is, Fred," Bryce agreed. Logan shot him a quick look. Was he bluffing, or did he really know which brother was which?

"We figgured we'd go up a ways, then double back on the meadow an' see if we cain't stay upwind of some deer." The other one—Logan decided it had to be Ted since they hadn't corrected Bryce—rocked back on his heels. Logan looked him over and tried to find a way to distinguish between the two. Impossible.

Bryce and Logan followed them up the trail for a while before cutting off into the forest. Logan gave up trying to tell them apart. It seemed as though he'd be doing a fair bit of mumbling—at least their names both ended with *ed*.

The two of them kept up a running dialogue as they passed various landmarks, keeping Logan smiling at the stories they told.

"That's where Uncle Asa got chased by Otis Nye's old ram. Ended up sprawled on the ground a few times afore he clambered up that thar tree." They pointed out a Fraser fir to their right. "Shore were a sight—that goat were as cantankerous as his owner."

A little farther in, they showed off a small cave in the mountainside. "Here's where we tracked the red fox as was killin' off our layin' hens."

After a while, they left off talking. Logan realized they must be getting close to the place where the twins had last seen the deer. Sure enough, they could catch glimpses of the meadow just a little ways off. The twins led them to a huge fallen log where they hunkered down to wait.

It was long past noon before anything moved. A few rabbits hopped around the clover, but they held off. One shot and no other animal would come near the meadow again. Then they saw it. A young buck, judging by his antlers, crossed the meadow kitty-corner to them. It put its nose out to test the air, but they were downwind.

Ever so slowly, they all aimed, careful not to move quickly and scare it off.

191

They shared silent nods and fired within seconds of each other. The buck fell immediately, and they hurried over. If they hadn't shot it in the head or heart, they needed to put it out of its pain as quickly as they could.

It was a clean kill, though, so they set to work. They picked out a fallen branch big enough to do the job and lashed the deer to it. They took turns, two at a time, holding either end of the branch to carry it back down the mountain. It was just the beginning of summer, so the buck hadn't had a chance to fatten up like it would have managed by fall. All the same, it was big enough to fill their need.

After they dressed it, the Trevor boys would take half home and leave half for Miz Willow, Hattie, Logan, and Bryce. It was a good start toward restocking the healers' larder, Logan realized. He and his brother had sadly depleted the smokehouse.

The women would stretch and cure the hide to make deerskin pouches for their herbs or scrape it thin to cover windows. The sinews would be dried and used as twine. Nothing would go to waste.

∿

Stooping to harvest useful plants, Hattie sang a verse of "Fairest Lord Jesus":

> *"Fair are the meadows, fairer still the woodlands,*
> *Robed in the blooming garb of spring;*
> *Jesus is fairer, Jesus is purer,*
> *Who makes the woeful heart to sing."*

The world around her was teeming with life and the things to sustain it. Today Hattie was looking for particular yarbs. The warm months always brought on rashes and poison ivy, so she'd need jewelweed and marshmallow for sure. She'd already added to her supply of yarbs to help with childbearing, and they were well set for coughs and fevers. It was a healer's duty to be prepared for everything possible.

After breakfast when Logan and Bryce had left to meet up with the Trevor twins, Miz Willow had given her a list of things to look for. From the plants listed and what Hattie knew of their uses, she had an idea why she was gathering them.

Dandelion root cleaned out the body and purified. Elderberry leaf was good for headaches. Milk thistle was a help for poisoning, whether snake, spider, plant, or drink. Lady slipper root took care of pain and sleep. Peppermint soothed the stomach, and scouring rush cleaned the bladder. Evening primrose could help with moodiness and ease the need for liquor in some.

The last one tipped the scale. Miz Willow was preparing for Rooster Linden. He hadn't come by yet as he'd promised, but they reckoned it was only a matter of time. Sooner or later, he'd make himself so sick, his body and his soul would overrule his habit—and when that happened, they'd be ready with all the help they could offer.

Gathering all of the necessary plants took Hattie through most of the holler, but she didn't mind. These were her very favorite kinds of days. Fluffy clouds moseyed along in the bright blue sky like they had all the time in the world to pass the mountains guarding the horizon. Everything around her was green and thriving. Birds sang to the bees in the blossoms. Flitterbirds sipped from the flowers just long enough to be seen, and butterflies danced along a breeze to tickle the tall grasses.

The sun warmed Hattie's hair and neck when she wasn't under the cool trees. When she took out her sack lunch of cheese and bread, she chose to sit near the stream. The water burbled along, clear and inviting. Hattie took off her shoes and dangled her toes in the cold water, flinging drops into the air to catch the light before they rippled back into the brook.

God was everywhere around her, just shining His love through beautiful things. This was her home, her holler. She could only wonder if Logan and Bryce Chance saw how special and precious it truly was.

⟡

"I'm glad yore back, Hattie-mine." Miz Willow pulled the door shut and waved a letter at her. "Lovejoy done writ us back, and I've been waitin' on you." The old woman practically danced around the cabin.

"All right. Let's hear—wait a minute." Hattie peered out the window. "Where're the menfolk?"

"They shot a buck up the mountain with the Trevor boys and brought it back here to butcher it. They took the horses and carried half of it all back to the Trevor place. They left awhile ago, so they'll be comin' home soon. I've already got venison stew ready and simmerin' in the pot, and corn bread keepin' warm in the fire." She pushed the letter into Hattie's hands. "Go on an' read it. I cain't keep still after that much waitin'!"

Hattie opened the envelope and began to read aloud:

Dear Hattie and Miz Willomena,

I shore was shocked when I got yore last letter. I don't know 'bout any trunk in the barn nor any carved wooden box. It's a mark of what fine folk live in the ole holler that you done tole me instead of puttin' what you found to use.

By now you've spent enough time with Logan and Bryce to see what manner of family I've taken on and to know you cain trust 'em as much as I do. So I'm gonna ask you <u>on</u> yore honor to give it all to them. The Lord will show them what to do with it. It's a jump of faith, but I know you both been stretchin' yore legs all yore life!

Yore in my heart,
Lovejoy

"That's shore a relief." Hattie refolded the letter and handed it back to Miz Willow.

"It's a good decision, I reckon." Miz Willow nodded. "So when we gonna tell 'em?"

"After supper, I'd say." Hattie went over to the fire.

Someone knocked on the door.

"Did someone say 'supper'?" Logan's voice sounded so hopeful, Hattie had to smile.

"Yep. Come on in." Miz Willow put the letter in her pocket, and Logan and Bryce tromped in.

"Good. I'm so hungry, I could eat Bryce's cooking." Logan grinned at the outraged look on Bryce's face.

"Hey! You've got no call to—" Bryce thought for a moment before giving a sheepish grin. "Nah, there's some truth in it."

"Set down, then." Miz Willow shook her head at their antics. They were just like the Peasley young'uns, scrapping around for a laugh.

Once the prayer was said, the food eaten, and the dishes cleared away, Logan went to bring out the checkerboard Otis Nye had made for them.

"Beautiful piece." Bryce ran his hands around the smooth pine board checkered with walnut stain and varnished over to gleam in the light.

"These, too." Logan held up one of the stained checkers and fingered the carved crown on the top. "Good craftsmanship. You've gotta give him credit—Otis Nye knows his way around a whittlin' knife."

"Shore does. It'd do him good to hear you say it." Miz Willow rocked. "But now's not the time for checkers. Why don't you both sit down for a minute, and we'll have us a little chat."

Logan shot Hattie a quizzical glance, but she refused to give him an inkling of what was to come. The widow would have it out in her own good time.

"Now when we heard you boys was a-comin' to Salt Lick Holler, Hattie here went and cleared up the barn an' loft for yore sleepin' space. Do you follow?"

"And a nice job she did, too," Logan praised.

"Real comfortable." Bryce nodded.

"What you might not know is that this ain't my property. Lovejoy didn't move in with me—I came to her home when it looked like she'd be marryin' up with yore brother. So when Hattie found a trunk in the loft—you know what trunk I mean?"

"Yes."

As Logan and Bryce agreed, Hattie could see interest light their eyes. They'd figured the general way things were headed.

"She came across a few things. I'll let her take it from here." Miz Willow leaned back and clasped her hands together as Logan and Bryce turned to stare at Hattie.

"I found a leather sack and a wooden box," Hattie elaborated. "We opened 'em both, and the sack held some leather scraps. But the box was somethin' we had to write Lovejoy 'bout."

"It's what we hoped Lovejoy would've written about in her letter to us that you boys brung on yore trip," the widow broke in. "But it hadn't been enough time."

"Today we finally got word from her about it." Hattie handed Logan the letter and watched as he and Bryce read it silently.

"So we're supposed to see to whatever's in the box," Logan prompted.

"Right you are. So we're honorin' her wishes." Hattie put the box on the table and opened the lid.

Chapter 16

Logan stared at the open box in front of him without speaking.

"Go on and shut that thing, Logan," Bryce ordered. "You've been lookin' at it since we got up here." He tapped on the loft wall. "It hasn't changed any, so stop lookin' at it, and let's talk about what we're gonna do with it."

Logan shut the lid on the money. Seventy-four dollars. It was a small fortune, and Lovejoy had just given it to them. But one thing bothered him. "Why didn't she tell Hattie and Miz Willow to keep it?"

"I dunno." Bryce shrugged. "But knowin' Lovejoy, she prayed on it before she made the decision. Like she wrote, the Lord will show us what to do with it."

"I don't think Lovejoy reckons we'll just keep it." The glimmerings of an idea sparked in Logan's imagination. "I think I might have a few things in mind."

"Good." Bryce put the box back in the trunk Hattie had found it in. "The way I see it, this is your adventure, Logan. I'm only along for the ride. I'm happy to help and curious about what you want to do, but that's the most I'm going to say on this subject."

"Lovejoy left it to both of us."

"And I'll help you with your plan, but I've got the feeling you're supposed to make the actual decision." Bryce pulled off his boots. "That's all there is to it."

"Fine." Logan shook his head in disbelief.

God must have a purpose for this money. And I'm supposed to find it.

"Bryce?" Logan wanted to run a few things by his brother. "I think we should use this money to help folks around here."

"Sounds like a good idea." Bryce paused. "Feels right. But how?"

"I don't think we should give it away to one person. I don't even believe we should divide the money evenly." Logan talked through his thoughts. "We should take a good long look at the people around here and what they really need."

"Makes sense." Bryce seemed excited by the idea. "But I don't think it's the type of thing where we just buy everyone some canned beans. We need to do something to help that will keep on helping after we're gone. Like the water pump you had us order for Hattie on our way home from Hawk's Fall."

"Yeah. Yeah, that's good." Logan chewed the inside of his lip and concentrated. "That's improving on something they already have, though."

"So what do the people of Salt Lick Holler have that can be used to make their lives better?"

Friday afternoon arrived far too quickly to Hattie's way of thinking. Where was the summer going? It seemed as though spring had barely begun, but here they were in June. She changed into her Sunday best to get ready for the doings. She figured it ought to be a lot of fun.

She helped Miz Willow put her hair up into a pretty snow-white twist and gave her another cup of burdock root tea. She'd be sitting on those hard benches for a while, and Hattie didn't want her rheumatism acting up. For good measure, she'd bring some more to the sang. Otis Nye might have use of some later on, and it wouldn't be noticed with everybody bringing something to share.

When the menfolk knocked on the door, Hattie handed Miz Willow her shawl and cloak. "It'll be evenin' afore we come back." She handed Bryce and Logan a pan of apple cobbler each before picking up her own cloak and satchel. With everybody excited by the doings, there would like as not be a few bumps and bruises. She'd be ready.

"Mmmm." Bryce sniffed the cobbler. "I say we stay right here and eat these ourselves."

"And you the guests of honor." Miz Willow waggled her finger. "Now don't you be tryin' to sneak a taste, neither."

"We would never!" Somehow Logan managed to sound affronted even as he chewed a piece of the crumb topping he'd broken off.

"Rascal." Miz Willow shook her head.

Hattie thought Miz Willow had the right of it. Logan Chance might be handsome, mannerly, and charming, but there was still a bit of the scamp about him. A woman had to be careful about that. She thought of Nessie's husband, a good-natured scapegrace who'd ducked out on her a year after the wedding. It just went to show—a boy made a mess; a man made a marriage.

Not that her opinion mattered much. As they drew near the schoolhouse, Hattie could see that every young gal from here to Hawk's Fall was already in attendance. It would be an interesting afternoon.

Hattie steered Miz Willow over to a bench along the side of the schoolhouse so she'd be able to lean back. She tucked her satchel under the bench and took the cobblers from Logan and Bryce.

"You two go on and chat around before the sangin' starts," Hattie said, leaving them to go put the cobblers on one of the tables set up for vittles. The tables were heaped full of bread, biscuits, corn pone, deviled eggs, mashed potatoes, green beans, carrots, stews, a couple of baked chickens, and one suckling pig. Jars of jams and honey sat alongside crocks of butter and pitchers of fresh milk. Pies, muffins, and cakes sat off to one side where Hattie put the cobblers, too. It looked as though everyone had gone all-out for the occasion.

The younger boys were putting together a bonfire in the middle of the wide circle of benches. They'd light it after the eating was done and before the singing began. By then it would be getting nippy, and the sun wouldn't stay out too long. She cast a look around to see if anyone was missing.

Miz Willow was chatting with Silk Trevor. Abigail and Katherine were comparing notes, trying to decide which babe would come first. Hattie would reckon on Kat for that—her first two had been quick births. The twins were playing the spoons—on each other's heads to make the children laugh. She didn't see Logan and Bryce right away—they were surrounded by a whole passel of folk.

What did she expect? After all, the Chance brothers were the main attraction here today. Just because she wouldn't set her cap for them didn't mean others didn't plan to. She could only hope Logan and Bryce didn't return their regard.

◦◦◦◦◦◦◦◦

"These are m' daughters," Bethilda Cleary said, clutching Logan's arm like a dog with a bone. Bryce had wisely slid out of range, but loyalty kept him close.

Lily and Lark made awkward imitations of the curtsy their mother had made the previous Sunday. He and Bryce tipped their hats, but the girls looked disappointed. Had they honestly expected bows?

"Nice to meet you, Mr. Chance. Mr. Chance." The younger one, Lark, giggled.

"We heard tell this is yore very first sang," Lily chimed in. "We'll be happy to git you anything you need."

"We brung the possum stew o'er yonder." Lark sidled closer. "I'd be happy to fetch you some."

"Maybe later." Logan pasted a smile on his face and looked around for a reason—any reason—to leave.

"My gals cook up a fine mess o' vittles." Bethilda smiled so widely Logan could count her teeth.

Lily was trying to talk to Bryce, who took a step back for every step she came closer. Any farther and he'd be cornered against the schoolhouse. Logan would've stepped in, but he was surrounded by Bethilda and Lark. He looked around out of pure desperation and caught the eye of one of the twins. Fred or Ted—Logan didn't care which—sauntered on over and managed to step between Lily and Bethilda to snag his arm. Logan saw the other Trevor walking over to Bryce.

"Ted and I need to talk to you Chance boys for a minute. I'm shore the Clearys will excuse you." Fred pulled Logan away before the women had a chance to protest.

When they were safely on the other side of the circle, Fred clapped him on the back. Ted burst out laughing. "Didn't anybody see fit to warn you 'bout that Bethilda Cleary?"

"Yeah. Pa'll sic his dogs on you iff'n you upset him, but Bethilda'll set her daughters after you!"

"I'm gonna ignore that since you helped us out of a tight spot." Logan grinned.

"Yeah." Bryce still looked a bit harried.

"No problem. 'Sides, Uncle Asa's 'bout to say grace so we cain tuck in."

By now Logan had lost track of which twin was speaking.

"Iff'n you know which thing the Clearys brung, keep away from it," one advised.

"Stew," Bryce said, casting a dubious glance at the kettle.

Asa called everyone to attention to say grace, and then people began to crowd around the food. Logan noticed that the women and children hung back, waiting for the men to finish. When he got to the table, he saw that most of the corn bread was gone, so he put two pieces on his plate alongside chicken, mashed potatoes, and green beans. He planned to have a healthy helping of Hattie's apple cobbler later on.

He and Bryce went over to where Miz Willow and Hattie were sitting and gestured for the Trevor family and the Ruckers to come join them. There were no seats available on either side of them when Bethilda led her daughters over. No one responded when she glowered around at the people taking up the three benches, much less offered to make room. Logan let out a deep breath when they huffed away.

As they were eating, Logan tipped a piece of corn bread onto Miz Willow's plate, then passed one to Hattie. He knew it was her favorite, and he'd been right to think it would be gone before she got there. She flashed him a surprised look, then a grateful smile.

"Thankee."

"Anytime." He smiled and leaned back. *This might just turn out to be a fun evening.*

After their early supper, the men gathered around to toss horseshoes and play checkers in the waning light while the women cleared up the tables—not that they had to take care of anything except dirty dishes. Not a speck of food was left in sight.

"Yeah!" Logan whooped as his horseshoe ringed the pole.

"Come on, everybody back to yore seats," Asa called out, ringing a bell to make everybody listen. "We're 'bout ready to light the bonfire."

Everyone quickly went back to the seats they'd taken for supper, but Logan didn't see Hattie. Lily and Lark looked at him and Bryce, and the men immediately sprawled out a little, taking up the whole bench. One of the boys lit the bonfire, and in the light it cast, Logan could see Hattie. She crouched in front of a little girl, spreading something on her hand and drying her tears. While the musicians tuned their instruments, she gave the child a hug and sent her scampering back to her mother. *She has such a big heart, my Hattie.*

My Hattie? When did she become mine?

Chapter 17

Logan pushed the disquieting thought aside as Hattie walked toward them and nudged Bryce to scoot over so she could sit between him and Miz Willow. She smiled and wiggled in, adjusting the cloak behind the older widow's back to make her more comfortable.

"What was wrong with the kid?" Logan nodded toward the little girl, now snuggled on her mama's lap.

"She took a tumble and scratched her hand." Hattie tucked her medicine satchel back beneath the bench. "I cleaned it and put some marshmallow salve on to take away some of the sting."

They stopped talking as the musicians began to play. Most were like no musicians Logan had ever seen. They sat scattered around the bonfire, so noise came from all sides. Fred and Ted rattled the washboard and boinged a mouth harp with youthful vigor. Rooster, who'd shown up just in time for the food, blew into a good-sized jug to add hollow hoots to the tune of Asa's fiddle. Otis Nye clacked on a pair of spoons with surprising energy and skill, while Silk plucked the strings of a simple dulcimer. Next to Logan, Li'l Nate wailed on his harmonica, making sweet music on the instrument so tiny in his big hands.

All together, they made the music lively and loud. Logan didn't know too many of the songs, but he pitched in when he could. Most of time he clapped along with the music, stomping his feet when his hands stung from the evening air and too much clapping.

"Any requests?" Rooster took a nip from the flask in his pocket and swayed a little on his tree stump.

"Equinoxial and Phoebe!" a woman called out. Logan didn't recognize her voice or the name of the song, so he sat back to listen:

> *"Equinoxial swore by the green leaves on the tree*
> *He could do more work in a day*
> *Than Phoebe could do in three.*
>
> *"So little Phoebe said to him, 'This you must allow.*
> *You can do the work in the house and*
> *I'll go follow the plow. . . ."*

Logan couldn't help laughing as the song progressed. The man got kicked in the head by the brindle cow, slipped in the pigs' mud, set the food on fire, and lost the hen before his wife came home. The last verse summed it all up:

> *"Now Equinoxial says, looking up to heaven,*
> *Phoebe could do more work in a day*
> *Than he could do in seven!"*

A great burst of laughter erupted from the circle, the women nodding vigorously as the men shook their heads and rolled their eyes. For his part, Logan saw the truth behind the words—not that women could do more than men, although some could, but that men didn't always value how hard women worked to hold everything together.

Hattie, for example, cooked, cleaned, laundered, sewed, and tended to the livestock like any housewife. In addition, she gathered, dried, crushed, and combined all the plants and things she used to heal the people around here. Hattie did with care and skill what he hoped to do with money—use the things the people in the holler already had to better their lives. If he did half as much good as Hattie managed, he'd have used the money well.

The musicians took a break, and people got up to stretch their legs. Logan went to get a drink of water and saw Hattie off to his right, cuddling a bundled baby. The smile on her face glowed brighter than the bonfire itself.

"Such a shame," Bethilda Cleary sidled up to his left.

Serves you right for not keeping on guard, Logan chided himself ruefully.

"What's a shame?" he asked as he wondered how he could get away before her daughters joined them.

"Hattie, of course." Bethilda widened her eyes. "Oh, I thought you knew." She made a *tsk-tsk* noise. "The way she's been hogging you, and now you cain't take yore eyes off her. . . ." The woman's voice trailed off as she shook her head.

"Hattie Thales is a good woman." Logan bristled. "She's been kind enough to introduce me and Bryce to everyone around."

"So yore not castin' glances at her?" Bethilda's eyes narrowed in challenge.

"I was just noticing how no matter where I go, women will always gather around a baby." Logan shrugged.

"True," Bethilda said, smirking. "Especially ones who cain't have their own."

Logan stalked away from the malicious woman and sank back down onto the bench, crossing his arms and scowling as Lily and Lark looked to come near.

So that's why Hattie hasn't married again. She can't have children. What's wrong with the men in these parts? Don't they have eyes to see that Hattie's a prize in and of herself?

Otis growled at them to name a song, and a few hesitant suggestions cropped up.

" 'The Old Maid's Song,' " Bethilda ordered, gazing directly at Hattie.

Logan leaned close to Hattie to try to make out the words of the song. Was it his imagination, or did he see a flash of sadness in those beautiful blue eyes?

The song moved through several verses about the type of man a maid wouldn't marry. Only unmarried women sang these, with the rest of the town repeating the refrain. He watched Hattie without her noticing as she sang the last verse with a wistful smile.

> *"But I will marry a man that's kind,*
> *Who's honest and wise*
> *And will always be mine. . . ."*

Then the refrain answered back:

> *"Then you'll not marry at all, at all,*
> *Then you'll not marry at all."*

Logan frowned at the words, which seemed to imply that no such man existed, or that if he did, he wouldn't want to marry the maid.

Says who?

❦

As they walked home, Hattie stayed quiet. Too much was turning over in her mind—like the way the Cleary sisters made eyes at Logan and Bryce all evening. But she'd been expecting that. What she hadn't expected was for Logan to be so attentive. It was thoughtful of him to bring Miz Willow and her some corn bread—it was her favorite. And how had he come to know her so well, anyway?

She remembered the way the firelight lit his golden tan, playing on his strong fingers as he clapped his hands to the music he didn't know. She wouldn't even have that memory but for the fact he'd saved her seat. She saw the way he'd elbowed Bryce to move over and make room.

He'd played the harmonica with more energy than accuracy that night and had a heap of fun trying out the washboard and spoons. The boy inside the thoughtful man came out and surprised her at times. Then he would look at her with a strange intensity, like when they sang "The Old Maid's Song." Why did it matter to her that he hadn't joined in the chorus?

You know very well why it matters, Hattie Thales. If he'd looked at you in the glow of the fire with his handsome blue eyes and ready smile and sang along, "Then you'll not marry at all, at all, then you'll not marry at all," whatever is left of the girl you once were would've just shriveled up and died.

❦

The next two weeks rushed by more quickly as Hattie kept busy treating cuts, rashes, poison oak and ivy, turned ankles, and the run of typical summer maladies. Every time she was called away to some home or another, she was aware of an air of expectation before they realized Logan and Bryce weren't with her.

It wasn't only the single girls who liked having them around, either. The Trevor twins, who at the advanced age of nineteen still provided an impressive number of the scrapes she treated, were always coming by looking for the Chance brothers to go fishing, hunting, trapping, or swimming. Edward Trevor swore Bryce could help him tame the orneriest hound dog alive, and Li'l Nate always stood ready to whip out his harmonica and teach them a few bars. At every house she visited, the children tugged on her skirts, begging for Uncle Logan and Uncle Bryce to give them horsie rides or play hide and seek. Even ole Otis Nye growled at her to bring the boys by for a game of checkers when she dropped off the tea for his rheumatism.

It was enough to make a gal feel about as wanted as a tagalong younger sister who followed after the boys. Hattie wondered whether the Chance brothers knew how much they'd come to mean to Salt Lick Holler. She'd gladly tell them, but they were hardly ever home, and when they were, they kept her laughing too hard to remember. When they left, they'd take a piece of the holler with them and leave behind a gap in the lives of everyone they knew.

❦

"We want to leave something behind that'll really change things around here." Logan paced in the loft—sort of. He managed about four steps one way before having to turn back around because of the slope of the roof.

"I thought we'd already gotten that far." Bryce stretched out on his pallet. "Hey, would ya quit walkin' over me?"

"Sure." Logan sat on the bench. "I'm edgy because we haven't gotten any further in deciding what to do with the money."

"Yep." Bryce nodded. "We've been kept pretty busy these past weeks."

"Don't I know it," Logan agreed. He'd hardly seen Hattie all week, with her out treating people and him and Bryce invited to so many houses.

"I like to think we're still doing some good," Bryce mused. "Those hound dogs of Ed's are shaping up to be a great bunch. He ought to fetch a fine price for them."

"True. I've never seen a dog obey so well as those pups." Logan raised his brows. "Ed vows it's all 'cuz of you, you know."

"I heard him say something like that." Bryce shrugged. "He's still the one who trains them. All I did was show him that rewarding the good behavior was a better track to take than punishing the bad. Dogs are like people—compliments over criticism."

"Only you could say something like that and make it sound right." Logan shook his head. "Well, you and maybe Otis Nye."

"Grumpy old geezer." Bryce smiled. "I think his carved owls are looking a lot better lately, since he doesn't make 'em tilted in the head anymore."

"And you've gotten a lot better at checkers." Logan winked at his brother.

"Someday you might even beat me at it."

"Don't be so proud about how wily you are. It's not always a good thing to be so sly," Bryce warned. "But I don't mind losing. It's almost more fun to look at the game than to play it."

"Only because Otis is a craftsman with those checkers of his. Did you get a gander at the latest ones with the circles carved on the bottom?" Logan gave an appreciative whistle. "I don't know how he does it with that rheumatism of his."

"Hattie's tea helps a lot," Bryce thought aloud, "but I think it's mostly his legs that bother him. His knees crack and pop something awful."

"True. His hands are as quick as his tongue—just not as sharp!"

"Yeah." Bryce snorted. "Speaking of sharp, did you notice how often he has to put his whittling knife to the whetstone?"

"Now that you mention it"—Logan scratched his jaw—"I reckon that's because he puts it to such use."

"And has for some time." Bryce was quiet for a minute. "Do you think he whittles so much because he's alone a good portion of the time?"

"Could be." Logan frowned. "I wonder if he knows that Asa Pleasant has taken up whittling, too. They could sit together."

"That'd be a good idea. Asa's swan-necked towel pegs are sturdy and a little fancy," Bryce said, "but I'm most impressed by those nativities he hides in his shed."

"The detail on those figures is incredible," Logan added. "I was thinking of asking him to make a set to bring home for the mantel."

"That's a pretty tall order." Bryce shook his head.

"True." Logan remembered how detailed the sets had been. "And baby Jesus can actually come out of the manger and fit in Mary's arms! It must take him a long time to make all that—especially since he does it so perfectly."

"You can see the fur on the animals and expressions on the faces of the people," Bryce pointed out. "You should offer to pay him."

"Of course!" Logan couldn't believe Bryce thought he hadn't meant to pay Asa. "But I'm not sure how much would be appropriate. I don't want to suggest too little—it's his art—but if I offer too much money, he'll think I'm showing off or want to give him charity. Either way it'll sting his pride."

"That's the last thing you want. I guess you'll have to think about it." Bryce blew out the lantern, but Logan lay awake for a long while.

Lord, there's so much to think about. What do I offer Asa? How can I use the money to help the holler? They're such good people, but the last thing I want to do is offend them. They should be appreciated for the things they do and the way they live their lives upright in Your sight. So how do I encourage them and help at the same time?

Chapter 18

"Hattie! Hattie!"

Hattie reined Legs in at the sound of someone calling her name. She was just returning from a visit to the Peasleys, where Grandma had felt a hitch in her chest and had been struggling for air. Hattie had made hot tea of black cohosh root and coltsfoot leaf to open the lungs and help stop the coughing. After she rubbed on some of Miz Willow's eucalyptus and peppermint salve and had Grandma breathe in the vapors, the old lady was doing just fine.

"I'm so glad I caught you!" Mary Pleasant rushed up. "I done heard some terrible news. Daisy Thales's place burned down last night. Looks like Jamie knocked over a candle or sommat."

Hattie froze. Daisy was her sister-in-law—another Thales widow who lived in Hawk's Fall. Her son, Jamie, suffered from palsy. They already had so little, and now their house had burned down?

Why, Lord? Daisy tries so hard to be a good mama, staying up and tatting lace to make ends meet for her and her boy. I've wished they were closer, but this ain't the way I'd hoped for it to happen. Please be with them, Lord, in this difficult time.

"Was it just the house?" A cold fear seized Hattie's heart.

"Mostly. Daisy got Jamie out all right, but she went back to get her workbasket and Jamie's favorite blanket. She got out, but one of her arms is burnt. I don't know how bad. Nobody else was hurt, but a lot of folk pitched in to put out the fire and keep it from spreading."

"Thankee for tellin' me, Mary." Hattie couldn't quite manage a smile. "I've gotta go right now, you understand." She didn't even wait for Mary's assent as she urged Legs into a run.

The morning was half over already, and she needed to get home before she could set out to Hawk's Fall. It was usually almost a day's ride, but if she rode hard, she'd make it just before nightfall. When she got to the barn, Bryce was sitting outside, practicing his harmonica.

"Bryce!" Hattie slid off the horse. "There's been an emergency in Hawk's Fall, and I need to gather up some things and get there as fast as I cain."

"I'll cool him down for you." Bryce took Legs into the barn. "He'll be ready when you are."

"Thankee." Hattie's throat felt thick. "And thankee for lettin' me take him to Hawk's Fall."

"No problem," Bryce assured her.

With that settled, Hattie sped to the house. She rushed right by Logan and Miz Willow, who were playing checkers, into the storeroom. She'd need marsh-mallow salve to soothe the burnt skin and lady slipper tea for the pain and to help Daisy sleep. Hattie just knew she'd been up all night fretting.

The folks who'd helped put out the fire would've breathed in a lot of smoke. She'd need more of the eucalyptus and peppermint salve, along with the black cohosh and coltsfoot leaf tea. She'd bring along some stevia to sweeten the taste. Smoke had probably stung the eyes, too, so she'd need some eyebright to make a wash.

"What's wrong, Hattie?" Miz Willow leaned into the store-room doorway.

"Fire at Daisy's place. She and Jamie got out, but she's got a burned arm and there'll be plenty of folks who need to git the smoke outta their lungs." Hattie took a deep breath. "There's nothing left, Miz Willow."

"I see." Miz Willow folded her into a hug. "Bring 'em back with you. I'll be glad to have Jamie close by. We've got plenty of room."

"Thankee, Miz Willow." Hattie's eyes filled with tears. Miz Willow had known Hattie couldn't ask her to take more people into her home, but it needed to happen. Miz Willow's big heart made room.

"I'll go with you." Logan put a hand on her arm as she went to the door. "You shouldn't be riding alone all that way."

"I've done it before." Hattie shrugged away his hand and the warmth it sent up her arm. "There's no place to sleep for the night, and another body will be an imposition. Besides, iff'n we traveled alone, tongues would wag."

"I don't care about that." Logan's eyes darkened.

"We do," Miz Willow stated. "Hattie's reputation as a woman of the Lord is needed for people to welcome her into their homes and tell of their ailments. You and Bryce'll be leaving Salt Lick Holler, but Hattie has to live with whatever people think."

"But she needs protection," Logan insisted.

"You'll jist have to settle for protectin' her reputation." Miz Willow handed Hattie her cloak. "Godspeed, child."

"I'll be back when I cain—prob'ly a couple of days." She kissed Miz Willow on the cheek and turned to Logan. "Take good care of everybody while I'm gone." She impulsively reached out to squeeze his hand. "I'm counting on you, Logan."

Logan could hardly believe it. Just that morning Hattie had been with them around the breakfast table, and in the twinkling of an eye, she was off. And she counted on him to hold down the fort while she wasn't around.

She'll only be gone for a couple of days. That's a drop in the bucket, Logan. Why are you so put out?

⁂

"I don' know what happened." Daisy sniffed back tears. "Jamie crawled over to wake me up."

"He's a hero," Hattie praised, ruffling the little boy's hair. "Now you drink up this tea, and then I'll have you put some salve on yore chest. It'll help with the coughin'. You've grown so big since I saw you last, Jamie!"

It was true. Hattie stifled a pang of guilt. Even if she'd visited more often, there wasn't much she could do aside from giving Daisy the right yarbs to make sure Jamie slept well. She surely couldn't have prevented the fire. It seemed as though a spark had jumped from the fire and lit up the hearth rug.

"He saved our lives." Daisy managed a genuine smile. "Yore my blessing, sweetheart." She went to hug him but stopped short since he was drinking the tea.

"How's yore arm feelin'?" Hattie glanced at the bandages covering Daisy's left wrist and forearm.

"Better since that salve of yores, Hattie. It helped with the stingin' after you cleaned it with that rinse you made."

"Good." Hattie would check and rebandage it in a few hours. It wasn't a pretty sight, but it hadn't gone deeper than the skin. So long as they warded off infection, Daisy would heal just fine.

"You need to put some of that salve on, too," Hattie admonished when Daisy tried to stifle a cough. "Otherwise I'll have to give you sommat stronger to clear yore lungs. I may still have to, as a matter of fact."

"Yes, ma'am." Daisy opened the jar and saw to Jamie before using it on herself. "Ooh, that is better."

"You took too much of a risk going back in." Hattie had to speak her mind. "You could've come out much worse for it."

"I know, but Jamie needs his blanket. He don't ask for much, Hattie." Daisy's eyes glistened. "And if I didn't get my tatting shuttle and thread, we'd have no way to feed ourselves."

"I ken what you mean, Daisy." Hattie patted her good arm. "But yore more valuable than either of those things—to Jamie and to me."

"Thankee, Hattie. Yore a good sister-in-law and a better friend."

"Do you know where to go from here?" Hattie gestured around the small barn where she, Daisy, and Jamie had spent the night. Daisy's mule was the only other occupant.

"I don't know." Daisy's head drooped. "We still have a roof o'er our heads, and I've got some lace I've already made that'll see us through until I cain make more. Folks have been kind enough to drop off food and blankets they cain't really spare. I reckon I'll jist have to lean on the Lord. We'll get by."

"Shore you will," Hattie reassured. "But Miz Willow and I reckon you and Jamie should come stay with us. We've got plenty of room, and we've been wishin' for a long while now you two was closer." Hattie could see Daisy struggle with the idea for a moment.

"My pride says no, but the truth of the matter is, yore invitation is a relief."

Daisy looked at her son. "I'll be glad to have Jamie in a warm home."

"Good. I'm glad that's settled." Hattie stood up. "Fact is, Miz Willow's rheumatiz is actin' up. I'd hoped it'd improve after the cold season, but she ain't doin' so well as I'd like. I'm away from home most days. I'll be glad to know yore there to keep an eye on her."

"I'd be happy to." Daisy smiled, and Hattie could see that the thought of being useful made coming to Salt Lick Holler easier on her.

"We'll head back tomorra iff'n you and Jamie aren't coughing still. For now, I'll go 'round and tend to the others." Hattie left Daisy to explain the move to Jamie. There were plenty of others with smoke in their eyes and lungs to see to.

Lord, how cain I convince Daisy to sell her land and stay with us permanently? She's already a humble woman, and I don't want to break what little pride she has left. Please prepare her heart and let the next few weeks go well. How cain I best holp Yore people, Lord?

Chapter 19

The answer came to Logan. After he and Bryce had talked about the money, and the conversation wandered around to the people of the holler, the way to spend the money became clear to him.

He hadn't said anything about it to anyone but Bryce, but he had high hopes. The way to help these people had been staring him in the face this whole time.

He'd written a letter to Jack Tarhill, an old friend from primer school who'd moved out to Louisville and opened an elegant shop there. He'd asked whether Jack would be interested in hand-carved nativities and checker sets or if he knew anybody who would. He also queried whether Jack had any connection with someone who used the fur pelts and skins collected around the holler by trappers. Today the reply had arrived, with good news.

Dear Logan,

Good to hear from you, buddy. Martha's doing well, and we have a brand-new baby girl. That's right. I've become a proud papa.

Finishing Touch is doing well—you wouldn't believe how many people will pay good money for trinkets and doodads that have absolutely no use. That's not to say that the things your friends make have no use—I pride myself on my checker playing. Besides, I've a healthy respect for anything that can turn a profit. Why don't you come on to Louisville and stay with me and the wife? Bring samples of the products, and we'll put them on display for two days. If they sell, I'd be happy to place an order. At any rate, it'd be good to see you.

Come over anytime—no need to write back. I hate to waste time. Hope to see you soon!

Sincerely,
Jack Tarhill

P.S. I spoke with my friend Barton Rumsford about the pelts. He's willing to pay for mink, otter, beaver, red fox, and some poor creature called the spotted skunk. I'll set up a meeting with him for you—bring a few along with you so he can check the quality.

"Whoo—ee!" Logan let out a whoop that had Bryce scrambling up the ladder. "What?"

"Jack Tarhill wrote back. He wants to give the checkerboards and nativity sets a trial run in his store. And he has a pal who's interested in the pelts—right now the Trevors aren't getting anywhere near their value."

"Terrific." Bryce clapped him on the back. "Well, you'd better go and ask Otis, Asa, Ted, and Fred if they're game."

"Let's go!"

*

"All right, I think that's everything." Daisy planted her hands on her hips and winced as she jarred her sore arm.

"Before we load it onto Fetch, we need to reconsider the traveling arrangements," Hattie suggested. "Since yore arm is botherin' you, you shouldn't hold Jamie and the reins. How 'bout he rides on Legs with me while you and Fetch carry yore things?"

"Good idea," Daisy agreed gratefully. "Let's load her up, then."

Together the two women situated the meager bundles that made up all Daisy and Jamie owned. The workbasket with Daisy's tatting, Jamie's blanket, and some dried meat and apples filled two saddlebags. Hattie's medicine satchel and extra supplies took up nearly the same amount of space.

They'd risen with the sun, and by the time they were ready to set out, the morning air was still chilly. Hattie saw Daisy shiver and was glad she'd thought to bring along her old cloak.

"Here, Daisy." She rummaged through a saddlebag to pull it out. It was worn and mended, but it would keep Daisy warm on the ride. Jamie would sit on Hattie's lap, and she'd wrap her cloak around him.

"Yore so good to me, Hattie." Daisy fingered the material.

"I'm jist passin' on the Lord's blessings. Lovejoy sent me this here fine new cloak, so I've no need of the other. It's old, but it'll still serve."

"I'm glad to have it." Daisy thanked her and shrugged it on. "Yore shore it's all right for me an' Jamie to come while you have visitors already?"

"Absolutely. In fact, it'll do Jamie good to meet Logan and Bryce. They're fine men. Besides, they'll be leavin' afore summer's ended." Hattie tamped down a wave of sadness. At least Logan and Bryce would still be there when she and Daisy brought Jamie home this evening.

*

He wouldn't be there when Hattie got home. The thought of not telling her he was going away for a while, of not seeing her before he left, sent a pang through Logan's heart. Later, when he told her why he'd had to leave, she'd understand.

If he waited for her to come home so he could say good-bye, it'd be another week before he could catch the train to Louisville. Too much was riding on this trip for him to wait to see Hattie before he left. Bryce would stay behind to keep watch over Miz Willow until Hattie got back. Besides, he'd understood Logan's need to go alone.

"Like I said before, this is your adventure." Bryce shrugged. "I'm here to help where I can, but it's your path to follow."

Otis Nye had given Logan three of the beautiful checker sets and mentioned he'd been working on chess ones, too. They weren't ready yet, though. Asa had been more than happy to send along two completed nativities. Ted and Fred danced a little jig at the thought of getting more money for the pelts they trapped and rushed to the barn to get one of every animal listed in Jack's letter.

They'd each given him their blessing and trusted him to work out the best deal he could. Logan only hoped he'd not give them reason to regret it.

"Go on, then," the old woman ordered. "I cain see yore itchin' to leave. It's sommat more important than the wandrerin' spirit that brought you here, I ken. I ain't about to keep you from followin' yore heart—'specially since you promise it'll bring you back to us!"

He hadn't felt right telling Miz Willow or anyone not already involved about the whole thing—if it failed, Otis, Asa, Fred, and Ted would already be plenty disappointed without having the whole holler know about it.

This trip was important to too many people for him to botch it up. This was a man's work, and he needed to shoulder the load. Back at Chance Ranch, he'd always been the youngest brother. The smallest, the jokester. Not the brother whom anyone would entrust with complicated business dealings or negotiations. Pretty much anything that demanded tact was delegated to someone else.

But the people of the holler saw him as a man. Asa, Otis, and the twins trusted him with their most valuable possessions and sent him to barter their skills and bring back a deal that would change their lives. Hattie entrusted to him the welfare of the holler. He wouldn't let them down. He couldn't.

He put his Bible on his lap and turned to 1 Corinthians 13. The circuit rider back home gave him the reference before he left, and now Logan wanted to read it again.

"When I was a child, I spake as a child, I understood as a child, I thought as a child: but when I became a man, I put away childish things."

There it was. God's words stood right in front of Logan. It was time to put away childish things and take on the responsibilities of a man. It was the only way he'd fulfill God's purpose for his life.

Lord, Hattie's become a dear friend to me, and I reckon she's become more important even than that. If that's Your will and part of the reason You brought me to Salt Lick Holler, then I ask You to work in her heart. Don't let her be hurt that I had to leave. You're leading me to Louisville same as You led me here, and I can only ask that You give me the focus to fulfill Your plan instead of dreaming up my own. When I return, I pray that I'll bring good news for the families of the holler, and, if it's Your will, a wedding ring.

❧

Hattie judged it would be a long day in the saddle. Daisy's old mule was slower than usual, loaded down with more than it was accustomed to carrying. Hattie kept Legs at a sedate walk, going nowhere near as quickly as she'd galloped to Hawk's Fall.

The animals were tiring by the time the sun shone high in the sky, and Hattie figured they deserved a break. They all did. Jamie had been quiet and still almost the whole way so far, snoozing through most of the morning. She knew of a small waterfall not too far ahead.

"Hey, Daisy," Hattie called back. "Thar's water a little ways up. How 'bout we stop for some dinner?"

"Sounds good to me," Daisy agreed. "Ole Fetch here could use a drink. So could I, come to think of it."

Not long after, they sat in the shade of an old oak, munching on cheese and jerky. Jamie scooted himself to the bank of the water. Hattie started to get up.

"No." Daisy's whisper stopped her. "Let me take care of it."

"Not with yore arm as it is," Hattie refused. "I'm jist gonna sit close to him to make shore he don' fall in. He should have a little fun—he's been so good through this whole thing."

"All right." Daisy leaned back against the tree and watched as Hattie walked over to Jamie and sat down beside him.

" 'At-uh." Jamie spoke the word and gestured.

"That's right. Water." Hattie dipped a tin cup in the water and handed it to him.

" 'Ank-oo." Jamie took a sip of the water.

"Yore welcome, Jamie." Hattie slipped him a piece of cheese. "Finish yore dinner."

"Yez, Hat-ty." He ate the cheese and took a few more sips of the water. "Here." He handed her the cup so she could drink.

"Thankee, Jamie." She smiled and took a big sip before refilling the cup. "How 'bout we take this to yore mama?"

"Ma," Jamie agreed. He put his hands on the ground and started scooting toward her. Jamie would never walk on account of his palsy, but he managed to move around just the same.

Hattie stayed beside him, keeping pace with him until they reached Daisy. She handed him the cup.

"Here, Ma." He carefully gave the water to Daisy.

"Jist what I needed," Daisy said appreciatively before taking a drink.

They packed up what was left of the food and saddled up again. Hours later, they came to the fork in the road that led to Miz Willow's house.

"We're almost home," Hattie whispered to Daisy so as not to rouse Jamie. "Logan and Bryce sleep in the barn, so we'll probably wake them when we take care of the animals. I'll put Jamie in bed first."

"All right."

Hattie carried the four-year-old into the house and tucked him in bed next to Miz Willow. She and Daisy would use the pallets Miz Willow had set up on the floor. She came back out to find Bryce leading Legs to the barn.

"Woke you up that easy, did we?" Hattie couldn't hide her surprise.

"Hadn't fallen asleep yet." Bryce led Daisy and Fetch into the barn first.

"Where's Logan?" Hattie didn't see him and wondered if he was still asleep.

"He had to go," Bryce confessed. "He said to tell you he's sorry he couldn't wait for you to get back from Hawk's Fall, but the train to Louisville left last night. He'll be back in about a week, give or take a few days."

"He's gone?" Hattie asked in disbelief. She'd been at Hawk's Fall for three days, and he'd left, just like that? "Why?"

"Well. . ." Bryce shuffled uncomfortably. "It's not my place to say. He asked me to tell you he's sorry, and he'll be back as soon as he can."

Hattie nodded as though she understood, but her thoughts roiled around in her mind as she helped unload the animals.

Why wouldn't he tell me why he was going? Did he wait until I wasn't here on purpose? I entrusted him with the holler—the people I care about. How could he have gone?

Chapter 20

I'll be with you in just a minute, sir—" Jack Tarhill looked up from the counter at his fancy shop, and a grin broke across his face. "Logan Chance! You got here in an awful hurry."

"Sure did." Logan smiled back. "Good to see you, Jack." He slapped his palms on the counter. "Nice place you got here." He gave a low whistle as he looked around at embroidered towels, ribbons, mirrors, pianofortes, music boxes, and the like.

"Frilly, more like." Jack shook his head. "But it keeps me in business. Speaking of which, I'm supposed to meet Barton Rumsford for dinner in about ten minutes. I was just about to leave. Why don't you come along?"

"If there's food, you can count me in." Logan's stomach rumbled, showing the truth in his words.

"I see." Jack laughed. "Well, let's go get that hollow leg of yours filled up."

An hour later, Logan groaned. "I can't put away another bite."

"Good," Barton Rumsfeld proclaimed. "Now we can get down to business."

"Fine by me." Logan liked Bart—he was a short man with a big laugh and the belly to match it.

"Let's go to my store, and Logan'll set out the things he brought in the back room," Jack suggested. "I need to be getting back."

About twenty minutes later, Logan unwrapped the bundle of furs and displayed them on a large flat table Jack said he used for products coming in and out of the store. Bart didn't say a word until he looked over each fur carefully, front and back.

"Good stuff," he decided aloud. "Skinned well, no bald spots. Clean, too."

"These are the types of pelts Jack mentioned in his letter," Logan explained, "but the Trevor twins also have the occasional white-tailed deer or bear hide. Lots of rabbits, too."

"I have all the rabbit fur I need. It's pretty common these days." Bard stroked his full beard. "The deer and bear might come in useful. If they have it, they can telegram ahead before they send it so I'll know if I've a place for it."

"So you're interested in setting up a deal?" Logan didn't press too hard but moved the meeting along.

"Yep. Otter and beaver skins are always in demand, and right now mink's all the rage for ladies' coats." Bart thought aloud. "I've got a friend who's using the spotted skunk skins. 'Course, that's on the basis that the quality is still high."

He started listing what he could pay per pelt depending on the size and type of animal. Logan nodded solemnly and accepted the terms. Bart offered more than twice what the Trevor twins were already getting. Logan would celebrate the good news later—for now, he didn't want Bart to lower his price.

"Sounds reasonable. I'll run it past the Trevors. They do pretty well, but I will tell you they stop trapping for a particular animal when the numbers get low."

"Smart boys." Bart nodded wisely. "Does no good to get them all at once, or there won't be any next time around. Can't tell you how many times that's happened. Awful thing." He stood up and held out his hand. "Let's shake on it."

Logan was more than happy to oblige. When Bart left, he took the furs with him and left money behind. Logan would go back to the holler with at least one family taken care of. Now for the others. He walked out onto the shop floor and waited while Jack helped a customer buy a gilded frame.

"Now that I've got a minute," Jack said as the woman left, "why don't we take a look at what you brought for me?"

This time Logan simply set out the boxes and let Jack unwrap the carvings inside, let him feel the smooth texture of the wood, notice the fine detail for himself as he uncovered each piece. The products would speak for themselves.

"Well, now." Jack gave a low whistle as he looked at the entire nativity spread out before him. "That'll make a fine display. Fine craftsmanship."

"The best," Logan agreed.

"Hold up a minute while I put it out." Logan helped Jack carry the pieces out to a prominent display area and watched his friend expertly set them up.

Logan sucked in a sharp breath when he saw the figure Jack wrote on the price tag. It was a lot of money. But Jack's store did quite well in Louisville. He'd know better about fine art than Logan did.

They went back to the table and opened up the checker sets. Jack ran his hand along the board, testing its weight and the smoothness of its surface before picking up the checkers and turning them over in his hands. "Good size. Perfect shape. The staining on the wood is even and precise." Jack squinted at the bottom of a checker. "He's even carved circles on the bottom of each piece! And that's nothing compared to the clean lines of the crown on the top."

They both heard a bell, and Jack walked out to help the customer. Logan finished unpacking all of the round checkers and set them up as though ready for a game. Jack came back in, smiling from ear to ear.

"Guess what just sold?"

※

He'd been gone for five days. Hattie could scarcely believe how much she missed Logan Chance.

Good thing he took off now so's I'll be prepared for when he leaves for good. I knew from the git-go he weren't goin' to stay. So I'll stop pining like some young maid after her beau. Logan's not my beau, and it's wrong of me to have let my feelings go so deep.

Besides, he up and left without a word. He didn't even explain to Miz Willow where he was goin'. It's that scamp in him that's made him hie off. Best I realize that now, so I don't make a fool of myself when he comes back.

Hattie had told herself the same thing every day since she'd brought Daisy and Jamie back to Salt Lick Holler and found out Logan had gallivanted off. She had no business missing him—it wasn't as though he was missing her. She beat the rug with more force than she meant to, sending a cloud of dust into her face.

See? If that ain't proof yore notions about Logan Chance are clouding yore vision, nothin' will be.

She heard a heavy pounding on the door and walked around to the front of the house to find out who was causing the ruckus. She tried to ignore the flutter of hope that Logan had come back, but her heart clenched when she saw Nate Rucker instead.

"It's time, Hattie!" Nate grabbed hold of her shoulder with one powerful hand and scooted her through the door Daisy had opened. His eyes were wide and frantic. "Abigail's havin' the babe!"

❧

"It's all right, Abby," Miz Willow crooned. "Breathe in and out, long and slow. That's it. The cramps'll let up in jist a minute."

"Hoo." Abigail let out a shaky breath, her eyes screwed tightly shut. "Ooh." She fell back against the chair as the pangs subsided. "That one were powerful fierce."

"You've got a bit afore the next one will come on." Hattie laid clean towels on the bed before pulling up the sheets and laying more towels for good measure. She went to the kettle to pour some motherwort tea.

Abigail sipped some of it before handing the mug back. "I'd like to walk a bit."

"Whatever makes you more comfortable," Miz Willow agreed.

"I've given up on comfortable," Abigail gritted out before doubling over with another onset of cramps.

"Yore doin' jist fine." Hattie held Abigail's arm to support her. "Think on yore precious babe. Yore gonna make a fine mother, Abby."

"I hope so." Abigail straightened up and paced around the cabin, letting gravity do its work.

"I know so," Miz Willow declared. Awhile later, Abigail's cramps were coming on much faster. She'd been in labor for nearly nine hours.

"I reckon it's time we git you to the bed, Abby." Hattie helped Abigail out of the rocking chair and winced at how tightly Abby clenched her hand as a spasm rocked her body. "Won't be long now."

"It's already been long enough," Abby moaned as she was put in bed. "Did Nate bring the ax?"

"Yes, Abby. It's under yore bed already to holp cut the pain." Hattie didn't know exactly how having an ax under the bed would help, but the thought seemed to comfort women in labor.

"Now, Abby," Miz Willow instructed after she examined the woman, "when the next one comes, I want you to push. Do you hear me?"

"Yes." Abby gritted her teeth and bore down immediately. The pain lasted longer, but the babe hadn't come yet.

"Now keep on pushing as hard as you cain every time you git the urge." Hattie mopped Abby's brow as she spoke.

About an hour later, Abigail's strength was flagging. "I don't think I cain push anymore," she wailed, tears trailing down her cheeks and splashing onto her nightgown.

"Shore you cain, honey!" Li'l Nate roared his encouragement through the shut door. From the sound of it, he'd been pacing back and forth the whole time, letting out groans when Abby yelled with the pain.

"You don't know what yore talkin' 'bout, Nathaniel Rucker." Abigail sat up and bellowed back. "Jist hobble yore mouth!"

"Yes, dear." Nate obeyed meekly. Hattie heard the sound of his boots as he started pacing again.

"One more time, Abby," Hattie encouraged. "Push as hard as you cain and don't stop until we say."

"AAARRRGGGH!" Abigail hollered as she pushed through the pain. The babe's cry hovered in the air.

A few minutes later, Abigail leaned back against the pillows, panting from exertion, her eyes closed. She smiled when Hattie laid the baby in her arms.

"I'm comin' in!" Nate pounded on the door.

"No, yore not, Nate. You know the rule. New father waits half an hour before comin' in." Miz Willow's dictum gave the midwives enough time to clean up the mother and the baby and gave the woman some time to rest up before her man saw her. Only then would he find out whether he'd been given a son or daughter. That was the mother's news to tell.

Abigail will fill my old home with love and laughter and children, Hattie thought. *It's only right to celebrate that. I won't think about how I never had the joy of telling my husband I'd given him a baby lad or lass. 'Twasn't to be so and never will be.*

Chapter 21

Logan stood at the counter of the biggest mercantile he'd ever seen. He'd been walking around the place for almost an hour now. The checker sets and nativities had sold in the two days, and Jack had ordered more. Logan would be coming back with good news for Otis, Asa, and the twins. But first he needed to pick up a few things to help get them going.

"What've you got here?" The proprietor wheezed and rubbed his hands together, like he was counting his money in his mind before Logan even gave it to him.

"Two whittling knives, one extra-large leather apron, four traps, a bolt of blue cotton, two cans of varnish, and a sack of peppermint sticks." Logan looked at the items and checked the list he and Bryce had thought up.

Asa and Otis would get a knife and can of varnish each. Li'l Nate needed a bigger leather apron, and the traps would go to the Trevor twins. He'd added the peppermint sticks for Hattie—she liked to use them to stir her tea. He figured that Hattie's friend whose house had burned down could put the fabric to good use. That made him think of all the things Lovejoy and the women had bought back in Reliable.

"Can I get a comb, a brush, a pack of needles, and a few spools of your finest thread in white, black, and blue?" Logan knew he probably hadn't thought of everything, but it was the best he could do at the moment.

"Sure. Anything else?"

"Yeah." Logan took a deep breath. "Do you carry wedding rings?"

Two hours later he sat in yet another train car, heading back to Salt Lick Holler. He kept sticking his hand in his shirtfront pocket to finger the small gold band inside, making sure it was still there. In a matter of days, he'd be back in Salt Lick Holler, where he could get down on one knee and ask Hattie to become his bride.

❧

"I'm home!" Logan all but shouted it through the front door.

No, you're not, Logan Chance. This isn't yore real home, and I have to remember it even if you don't.

"Well, git on in here so we cain see iff'n you still look the same!" Miz Willow called back.

Hattie had forgotten how tall he was until he had to stoop a little to get through the doorway. Had he been so handsome and dynamic the last time she

218

saw him? Surely not. Hattie grabbed the fennel seed tea she'd put together for Abigail Rucker. It would help her milk to come after yesterday's birthing.

"Hello, Hattie." The nerve of that man to smile at her like that after he'd up and left without a word of explanation! No scapegrace smile was going to make up for his leaving her and abandoning the people she'd entrusted to him.

"Welcome back, Logan." She gave him a perfunctory smile. "Miz Willow will introduce you to Daisy and Jamie while I run over to the Ruckers'. Abigail delivered her son yesterday." She slipped through the door without waiting for anyone to stop her.

She all but stomped in her frustration as she made her way to Abigail's home. It wasn't as though she'd expected him to frown when he got back, but to smile as though all was right in the world was too much.

That's not what's really upsetting me, she admitted to herself. *Even after what he did, after he let me down for a pleasure trip to Louisville, I still responded to his smile. It warmed me clear down to my toes before I pulled myself together. Logan Chance is downright dangerous. How could I have forgotten how charming he is? I'll have to guard myself against him until he leaves for good.*

Hattie ignored the sharp pang in her chest at the thought. *I'm jist winded. I've been walking so fast. That's all. Nothing more.* She could already see the Rucker place! Hattie took a calming breath before knocking on the door and giving Nate the tea. She stayed to chat with Abby and make sure everything was going well.

"He's sleepin' awful deep. Not very hungry," the new mother said worriedly.

"That's normal. It usually takes a day or so, Abby," Hattie reassured her. "I brung you some fennel seed tea to holp you make plenty of milk."

"Thankee, Hattie." Abigail turned to Nate. "Nate, let Hattie hold Bitty Nate." She smiled happily. "His papa will hardly put him down for a minute."

"That's right." Nate cuddled his son close for a second before carefully handing him to Hattie.

She nestled the tiny babe close to her heart. He smelled like just-dried laundry and newness. His tiny hands and even tinier fingernails were perfect and pink and clean. Dark swirls of hair wisped over the top of his head, and he let out a big yawn from his tiny mouth before dropping off to sleep.

Hattie cherished the moment, snuggling close to the baby and feeling his warm weight in her arms. She'd never have a babe of her own, but she'd been a part of bringing this precious child into the world yesterday. It was enough. It had to be.

❦

Logan waited for Hattie to come back from the Rucker place. He'd walked a ways up so they'd be able to talk in private, but he wasn't sure how well the meeting was going to go.

She didn't seem glad to see me. Why did she leave the second I got back, like she couldn't stand to be in the same room as me? Is she nursing the grievance that I left?

Did it hurt her so badly? Wouldn't that mean she cared for me, if she missed me that much? Will she let me make it up to her?

The questions flooded his mind as he held the ring, warming it in his hands while he waited for Hattie to walk down the road—hopefully into his arms. If felt as though he'd waited for months when he finally saw her coming along the path. She stopped for a moment when she caught sight of him, and something flickered across her face before she kept walking.

"I've been waiting for you, Hattie." Logan's voice sounded gruff to his own ears, but the words had a double meaning. He hadn't just waited for her today by the side of the road—he'd been waiting to love her for his entire life.

"I cain see that." Hattie didn't look at him, and she kept walking.

"Hey, hold up a minute!" He fell into step beside her. "There's something I need to talk with you about."

"Right now?"

"Yes. Now." He guided her over to a fallen log so they could sit down. "Why are you trying to get away from me, Hattie?"

"I. . ." She sighed. "Why don't you say what you have to say, Logan?"

"I know you don't understand why I left," he began.

"No, I don't," she stated flatly.

"And I can't tell you yet," Logan continued.

"I didn't ask you to."

"It's a matter of honor," he tried to explain. "I can't tell you until I've told the others first. I gave my word."

"And what of yore promise to me, Logan?" She spoke the question softly, but it demanded an answer. "I entrusted you with the holler while I was away."

"Hattie." He took her hands in his. "You have to believe me. I didn't leave *from* the holler. I left *for* the holler. I can see now that my leaving hurt you, Hattie." He looked into her eyes. "I'm sorry for that."

"You couldn't have waited one day?" The small whisper nearly broke his heart.

"No. It would have meant waiting for more than a week. I had to follow through with my responsibilities."

"Fine, Logan." She tried to stand up, but he held on tight.

"I came back to you, Hattie." Silently he begged for her to understand. "I love you. I want you to become my wife." He brought out the ring and tried to slide it onto her finger.

"No!" She pushed him away. "I cared for you. I trusted you to keep yore word to me, to take care of the others I love. Instead, you went hieing off to Louisville. I cain't give my hand and heart to a man who gallivants off whenever the notion takes him." She wiped furiously at her tears. "You spoke of responsibilities. I have many. Even if I did trust that you wouldn't take off and leave me, I cain't marry you and leave my people."

"Hattie!" He tried to stop her, but she ran off. He sank down onto the log.

How did I mess everything up so badly? How can she think I would willingly hurt her and abandon the people she loves? Should I explain myself, or is this Your answer, Lord? I can't wed a woman who doesn't trust me. I thought Hattie and I shared something special. Where do we go from here, Lord? I love her.

Hattie ran until she had no more breath and sank down underneath a white pine, sobs wracking her body.

He wants to marry me, and I said no! I love him, and still I said no! Lord, I cain't leave the holler. I know the work and purpose You've given me. But I ache, Jesus. I love him, but I cain't rely on him. He's not grown enough to truly understand responsibility. I cain't wed a boy with a wandering spirit and a charming smile. How soon would that smile fade and take him away forever—especially when he found out I'd bear him no children?

Father, I've done my level best to make peace and be content with what You give me. Why do You put temptation in my path? Why put this love in my heart if I cain't do anything about it? I yearn for a family, Lord. Why am I to be denied a husband? My first marriage held precious little love, and here a man is promising to care for me. And I love him, too. Why do I love the one man who will leave me or force me to leave the place You've given me? I don't understand, but I'm trying so hard to follow Yore will. I love him, but it cain never be. Why?

She whispered again in a broken sob that carried away on the wind, "Why?"

Chapter 22

So how'd it go?" Bryce asked later that night as they were heading back to the barn.

Worse than I ever could have imagined. Logan realized there was no possible way Bryce could know he'd proposed to Hattie—and been rejected.

"What?" He shook his head to clear it.

"Louisville? Jack Tarhill?" Bryce looked at him strangely. "You know, the whole trip. You took off for a walk right after you got back, so you haven't told me what happened."

"It went well." Logan managed a smile at the thought of telling the guys tomorrow. "Jack wants more checker sets and nativities. Bart will take the furs on an ongoing basis for an appreciable fee increase. I also got everything on the list so they could get started. Jack and Bart already paid me for the first installment."

"That's the best news I've heard all week." Bryce grinned. "Do we get to tell everybody tomorrow?"

Logan thought about how upset he'd made Hattie that evening. It'd be a good idea to give her some space and give them both time to think. He nodded at Bryce.

The next morning they set out to see Otis Nye. They found him squinting at a carved owl, which was squinting right back.

"If you're in the middle of a staring contest, I have to tell you, Otis, I don't think you're going to win." Bryce grinned as he said it.

"Listen up, whippersnapper," Otis growled. "I could out-stare you anytime, anyplace."

"I'll have to take you up on that someday." Bryce laughed. "But for now, Logan here came to talk business."

"Oh?" Otis raised one scraggly white eyebrow.

"How many of those checkerboards do you think you can make, Otis?"

"I'll be." A smile broke out across the old man's craggy face.

"This is your cut for the first two—they both already sold." Logan handed him a small bag.

Otis opened it with shaky hands, and his mouth dropped open in disbelief. He peered at Logan suspiciously.

"What are you tryin' to pull?" He pulled himself up and flung the bag back at Logan. "You tryin' to make me a charity case? Git out."

"No." Logan tossed the bag back. "Take that, divide it by two. That's how

222

much you get for every checkerboard that you make and Jack Tarhill sells. He's getting just as much profit as you are—more, in fact, since you put in all the time. He'll pay for the freight costs."

"Glory be." The old man turned the coins over in his blue-veined hands. "Thankee, Logan Chance. You, too, Bryce. You tell that Jack fella he jist has to tell me how many he needs."

After giving Otis his new whittling knife and a can of varnish, Logan and Bryce took their leave. They still had to visit the Pleasants and the Trevors. They came across Asa first.

"Mornin', Asa." Logan tried to sound happy in spite of his busted heart.

"Good to see you, Logan. Bryce." Asa gestured for them to come closer. "What's the word?" Cautious hope flickered in the man's eyes as Logan and Bryce grinned at him.

"Jack Tarhill's customers loved the nativities. He sold two in three days and had another woman come in asking after them." Logan handed him his money. "She paid in advance, so you've already got an order to fill. This is your share of the profits off the three sets."

"You wouldn't be pulling my leg, would you, boys?" Asa looked at the cash in shock.

"Nope." Logan clapped him on the back. "Jack wants to know how many you can make per month and still have them be of the same quality."

"I don't know." Asa shook his head in disbelief. "It were jist a hobby afore. He wants more? At this price?"

"That's right. Jack thinks they'll sell particularly well around Christmas, so he wants you to be ready to fill a big order by winter." Logan grinned. "He says that since you put in all the work for half the profit, he'll pay for the freight costs."

"By the way," Bryce added, "Otis Nye carves mighty fine checkerboards. Jack's put in an order for those, too." He handed Asa another whittling knife and can of varnish, just as they'd given to Otis. "We figure you two might keep each other company while you work sometime."

"Thankee." Asa still looked stunned. "I'll be shore to do that."

When they got to the Trevor place, Ted and Fred took one look at their grins and started whooping.

"Good news is a-comin'—I cain tell by the look on yore faces." Ted, Logan guessed, gave an excited jump.

"Like the cat with a saucer of cream," Fred agreed.

"You're right." Logan handed them their money and started going over the prices Bart Rumsford was willing to pay for the various pelts.

"No foolin'?" Their jaws hung open.

"No fooling," Bryce repeated, then handed them their package. "So we thought you could use a few more traps."

"You boys come on with us to put them out," they insisted.

In no rush to get back to the healers' place, Logan decided to go along. Bryce came, too. They made their way around the hills to the places where the twins promised they'd had the most success this time of year.

On their way back for something to eat, they heard someone yell. A single gunshot followed. Without a word, all four men raced in the direction of the noise. The closer they got, the more screams they heard.

Hattie scrubbed at a spot on her yellow dress, rattling the washboard. She welcomed the hard work—it gave her hands something to do and her head something to focus on besides Logan. He and Bryce had started off right after breakfast, during which Logan hadn't said but two words.

The strong fumes of the lye stung her eyes and nose. She sniffed and blinked back tears as she took the now-clean dress over to the rinsing water, but even without the lye, she had a hard time stopping the tears.

Is this the way it has to be now? We cain't even be at the same table? There'll be no more shared laughter or smiles so long as this keeps up—and even fewer onc' he's gone for good.

"Hattie!" Logan came charging up on an unfamiliar horse.

"Not now, Logan." She bent over the laundry and surreptitiously dried her eyes.

"Now, Hattie." Logan's tone brooked no argument. "Get your satchel while I saddle up Legs. Rooster stumbled into a bear trap and shot himself in the foot, trying to get free."

Hattie sprang into action, running to the storeroom and pulling down anything she thought she could possibly use. She grabbed the entire bolt of clean white gauze Lovejoy had sent, along with every cleanser and calming powder she could lay a hand to. Every yarb known to stop blood flow found its way into a bag.

She had tweezers and a magnifying glass in her satchel. The most she'd ever used them for was a splinter, but today they'd be needed for much more. Needles and strong thread lay at the ready. She grabbed clean bandages and her cloak and headed out the door. Logan already stood there with Legs. She tied her bags to the saddle, and he lifted her up. She refused to dwell on the warmth of his hands on her waist. Now wasn't the time to think of such things.

They galloped all the way to the Linden place, and Hattie could hear the yells for half a mile before they got there. A bloody makeshift stretcher lay outside the door. Hattie rushed past it to get inside.

Nessie was pressed against the far wall, her hands over her mouth as she watched her father fight Bryce and the Trevor boys. He shouted nonsense about how they all wanted to kill him. The moment Hattie drew near, she could detect the odor of moonshine underlying the smell of blood.

"He passed out while we carried him," Bryce grunted, trying to hold Rooster down. "But he came to not long ago and won't lie still. He's making the bleeding worse."

She looked at the blood-soaked sheets around Rooster's mangled leg and knew there wasn't a moment to lose. As quickly as she could, Hattie doused a rag with ether and held it against Rooster's nose and mouth. He looked at her with wild eyes and clawed at her arms before he passed out.

"Nessie, I need you to get some strong rope—as much of it as you cain find." Hattie rolled up her sleeves. "I'm going to need you boys to tie him down. Even unconscious, he'll jerk around while I try to staunch the bleeding and clean his wounds. I'll have to find and remove the bullet if it didn't pass clean through."

Hattie applied pressure to the leg to stop the bleeding. The bottom half of Rooster's right shin was shredded from the teeth of the trap and looked to be fractured in at least two places.

His foot was in slightly better shape. "Looks like the bullet shot straight through the side of his instep."

"Lucky shot iff'n ever there was one," Ted thought aloud.

"God was merciful," Logan murmured.

His opinion took Hattie by surprise. Most folks would think Rooster deserved this; Logan's compassion for a drunk made her glad of his help. A sick-bed ought to be a place of healing, not of judgment.

"Leg's busted up, Hattie," Logan observed.

"It's too swoll up to set. I'll have to tend the wounds for now. In a day or two I'll need to set and splint it." Hattie cleaned the wounds with water before applying a witch hazel wash. Then she brought out the needle to stitch up the deep gashes along his leg. He'd obviously tried to yank himself free of the trap.

Hours later she wrapped the leg in bandages and sat back. Rooster slept fitfully but couldn't move enough to hurt his leg. "Breathing looks fairly steady," Logan judged.

"Iff'n we cain keep the wounds from festerin' and set them bones, might be he gets through jist fine," she replied. She looked Logan in the eye before delivering her warning. "The real trouble will come when he wakes up."

Chapter 23

"Nessie," Hattie said, "you go tell Miz Willow what's happenin'. She's been at the Ruckers' today. And take yore nightdress. I want you to stay the night and holp Daisy with Miz Willow and Jamie." Hattie tried her best to keep Nessie away from the worst of Rooster's treatment. Logan suspected if the young woman stayed, Hattie would have another patient.

Logan took his cue from her. "Ted, Fred, you were a great help. I think we have things under control here now."

They looked to Hattie, who nodded her approval.

"We'll walk Nessie on o'er to Miz Willow," Ted said. They took their leave.

Hattie spent the next hours pouring water down Rooster's throat, though he mostly slept through the night. It must have been the combination of the moonshine he'd so obviously been drinking before the accident, the ether she'd used before looking at the wound, the intense pain he suffered, and the lady slipper root tea she trickled into his mouth. Whatever the reason, Rooster slept.

Hattie sat for a while in a straight-back chair, her knees drawn up to her chest as she watched Rooster fight off some unknown demon in his dreams. She closed her eyes. When she opened them again, Logan was looking at her.

"Go lie down, Hattie." He spoke softly so as not to wake Bryce. "I'm watching him. You need to sleep—you've done the best you can for Rooster. I'll wake you if anything changes."

Too tired to argue, Hattie nodded gratefully. "You done good tonight. I couldn't of done this without yore holp."

"We'll keep watch, Hattie. You sleep."

"You'll wake me?" she asked again.

"You can count on me."

～～～～～

Hattie collapsed onto the pallet and fell asleep immediately. Logan watched her. She seemed so peaceful, so fragile for the work she did. He and the Trevors had been all but certain the leg would have to be amputated, but she'd worked for hours to save it. Even now, tuckered out as she was, she somehow found the strength to get up every hour or so to check Rooster's bandages and pour some kind of tea down his throat. Logan guessed the tea was to help the man sleep.

"I cain't marry you and leave my people."

Her words from the night before echoed in his mind. She was right. He hadn't thought about what he was asking of her. How could he have imagined that the woman who cared so deeply about everyone around her—the woman he'd fallen in love with—would leave them without a healer?

Logan saw Rooster's eyelids flicker and went to wake Hattie up. When she first opened her eyes, the soft smile that spread across her face melted his heart. Then it faded. She sat up quickly.

"How is he?" She rushed over to the bed.

"I think he's coming around." Logan moved to stand at her side.

Hattie felt Rooster's forehead with her hand and frowned. "He's hot. I'll give him something for the fever along with the calming powder. The longer he sleeps, the better." She bustled over to the fire and started brewing the tea before returning to check Rooster's leg.

"How does it look?" Logan held his breath while he waited for the answer. The thought that Rooster might lose his leg was bad enough without the knowledge of how hard Hattie had worked to avoid that very thing.

"Like he tangled with a bear trap." Hattie began dabbing at the wounds with something. "It's bad, but so long as we keep infection away, he has a chance. The other problem is that I cain't splint it much beyond the knee, so although he cain't bend the leg, he cain still move around a bit. If the bones don't set to heal over the fractures, he'll never walk on it again, no matter what else I manage to do. I'll be able to apply a splint better in a few days, onc't the swellin' goes down, but for now I'll have to watch him."

"Bryce and I will help you," Logan offered. "Nessie will be back during the day."

"I know. But it's not jist his leg we'll be dealing with, Logan." She sounded as though she were girding for battle.

"Oh?"

"While he's healing, he cain't drink. He don't have the strength to fight the headaches and the vomiting after he's been drunk," she explained. "He has to keep down enough to holp him heal."

"He can't move, so he doesn't have much of a choice," Logan reasoned. Still, Rooster would be hurting badly for want of a drink. It wouldn't be a pretty sight.

"I've brung everything I cain to holp with him wanting likker." She gestured toward the bags lying around the room. "But you cain be shore he'll try to get up and get to it any way he cain—even if it means he'll never walk again. Moonshine's got that strong a hold on him. He'll need watchin' 'round the clock." She looked at him with tired eyes. "If he pulls through this, it'll have to be body and soul. It ain't jist his leg that needs healing, Logan."

"I'm here, Hattie." Logan could only hope she heard him with her heart and not just her ears. "I'm here."

❧⟨§⟩❧

The days melted into each other, each as difficult as the last. Hattie hardly stepped foot out of Rooster's cabin. She slept in snatches on Nessie's pallet while Logan and Bryce took turns watching Rooster. Some nights she couldn't sleep until she poured enough calming tea down Rooster's throat to make him sleep first.

He slipped in and out of consciousness, alternating between fevers and chills, his body sweating out the poisons he'd been guzzling far too long. He twisted and turned, yelled and cussed, begged and pleaded for a drink. He brought up almost every drop Hattie managed to get down into him.

Many times he shouted in his delirium, calling for people who'd long left this world or breaking into off-key snatches of songs. There was nothing she could do but keep pouring various medicines down his throat to help with the nausea, headache, fevers, and pain. Eventually she was able to splint his leg fully, the fear of swelling and renewed bleeding subsiding with time and treatment.

Through it all, Logan never left Hattie's side. Regardless of the blood, sweat, yells, and never-ending mess, he stuck with her.

"Rooster, no talking like that. Miz Hattie's a lady. Here, I'll help you." Time and again, Logan stepped in. He never once lost his temper—which stunned her. She still recalled his smoldering anger the first day he'd met Rooster. Now he showed firm resolve mixed with Christian mercy and abiding respect in dealing with the man.

Often Logan escorted Hattie to the door and gently nudged her outside when it came to basic or messy matters. "I'll take care of it, Hattie." He was her anchor in the storm, strong and protective, making sure she got enough sleep and food so she could continue.

I wouldn't have gotten this far with anybody else.

The realization of how much she needed Logan shook her to the core. She didn't have time to look at it too deeply, but Hattie knew that when all of this was over, she'd still have to face a future without Logan Chance.

Hattie amazed him. Through the entire week and more, she'd relentlessly fought to save Rooster Linden from himself. She'd held the man's hand as he cried for liquor, gave him calming tea when he swore and thrashed against his constraints, filling the air with words the likes of which Logan would never want any woman to hear. Hattie returned Rooster's curses with prayers.

She slept little, grabbing catnaps when Rooster wore himself out. Curls sprang free from Hattie's loosened braid to hang around a pale face. Dark circles beneath her eyes tattled about how weary she'd grown, yet her dignity and determination never waned. Logan had never seen a woman so beautiful.

Then, as suddenly as the gunshot had gone off and started the whole ordeal, the storm began to ebb. Rooster's eyes, no longer lit with the manic need for moonshine, darkened in pain. He stopped yelling, stopped trying to get to his still, and lay quiet for hours on end. Logan and Hattie couldn't tell whether he was lost in the pain or his thoughts—probably both.

"Go home, Hattie." Logan put his hands on her arms and looked into her eyes. They looked tired but carried the first flickering of victory.

She shook her head wordlessly.

"Listen to me," he demanded. "You've held off the infection, nursed him through the fevers, and took the abuse he rained upon you. That's all over now. You've splinted his leg, and he's no longer thrashing, so he won't hurt it further. Bryce will help me watch him through the afternoon and night. You need to go home and sleep."

"I. . ." She closed her eyes, thinking it over. Determined, she raised her chin before proclaiming her decision. "I'll be back come mornin' tomorra." Her face softened as she looked at him. "Thankee, Logan."

He bundled her up in her cloak, even though the sun shone outside, and had Nessie ride with her back to Miz Willow's house before she could change her mind.

So many people had worked alongside them. Nessie had come every day to bring more medicine, mop her father's brow, and help keep the cabin as clean as possible. Bryce stayed every night, holding Rooster down when he thrashed violently against his restraints, taking turns staying up at night, and caring for the animals in the barn. The Trevor twins came to help muck out the barn every morning. Since Rooster had stepped in one of their traps, they felt partially responsible.

Silk Trevor, Miz Willow, and Mary Pleasant took turns cooking and bringing by breakfast, dinner, and supper. They also carried out the towels and bandages every day, washed them, and brought them back to be dirtied again. The entire holler banded together once they heard what was happening and looked to Logan to tell them what they could do and how Rooster was progressing. Everyone prayed.

"Logan, is Rooster sleeping?" Bryce stuck his head through the doorway.

"Yep."

"Then we need you to come outside," Bryce ordered. "Asa has gathered together the men of the holler, and they say we have a decision to make."

What is going on now? Logan walked to the door and found a crowd waiting in the yard.

"Glad yore here, Logan." Asa stepped beside him and clapped him on the shoulder. "We're having a town vote, and you and yore brother have more than earned a say in the matter."

The men nodded and gave a general rumble of agreement before they all headed for the barn. Logan had an inkling of what this was all about.

"Here's the thing," Asa continued, once they were out of Rooster's earshot. "We don't hold with laying a hand to the property of another man, but this here is whatcha call a unique circumstance."

"Rooster coulda shot anybody," Edward Trevor growled.

"He's become a danger to the holler!" someone else shouted.

"So we're fixin' to dismantle the still." Asa opened the barn door and pointed to the far wall.

"Everybody in favor?"

Logan looked at Bryce as they both raised their hands.

"Aye!"

Chapter 24

Logan helped with the most rigorous part of the work, then needed to check on Rooster. When he stepped into the cabin, he found Rooster's eyes wide open.

"Hey, Rooster," Logan spoke softly, not certain how the man would react.

"Hey, Logan." He took a deep breath. "I've a favor to ask you, though I've no right."

Lord, please don't let him ask for moonshine. Not after all Hattie's gone through. Don't let him backslide. Please.

"What is it, Rooster?" Logan pulled a chair next to the bed and sat down.

"I been doin' a lot of thinkin'," Rooster began. A rueful smile stretched across his face. "Ain't been much else to do these days. Fact is, I need to git the thoughts outta my head and into the air—see iff'n my good intentions cain live in the world."

Can it be? Has Rooster decided to turn over a new leaf? Logan nodded his encouragement.

"So I need you to do two things. First is, untie me. Now don't go shakin' yore head already," Rooster pleaded. "Listen, I'm not goin' to try and git outta bed. I ain't gonna ask for a drink or even try to git one m'self. I jist want to sit up and talk, man to man. I ain't been upright for a long while, Logan."

Something in Rooster's eyes convinced Logan. He understood the deeper meaning behind the man's words. If there was even a chance that Rooster wanted to leave liquor and come back to God, Logan could do nothing less than listen and support him. He undid the knots holding Rooster down and helped him carefully slide up and lean back on a mound of blankets. Rooster kept his word and didn't try to get up.

"Thankee, Logan." Rooster took a deep breath. "Fer everything. I cain't remember much of this week, but I know it ain't been easy on either of us. I owe you more'n I cain say."

"You don't owe me a thing, Rooster." Logan looked into his eyes. "But you do owe it to yourself and Nessie and Hattie to take better care of yourself."

"I ken what you mean, son." Rooster closed his eyes. "I stepped off the path a long while ago and lost my way. I ain't been able to see straight in a good long while."

"I know." Logan took a deep breath and plunged ahead. "Isaiah tells us of men of God who 'are swallowed up of wine, they are out of the way through strong drink; they err in vision, they stumble in judgment.' "

"That's it, right there." Rooster bowed his head. "Moonshine. It'd be easy to lay the blame on the drink, but I allowed myself to let it destroy me."

"You aren't destroyed, Rooster. You're alive, and you haven't had a drop in over a week." Logan saw the need to encourage him. "Your leg is in a bad way, but Hattie has it on the mend. You have a chance to make things right."

"That's what I want to do." Rooster's eyes filled with the depth of his emotion. "I cain decide niver to touch the stuff agin, but I don't know how to make right what I already done."

"You can't change the past, Rooster," Logan told him. "But the good news is, you don't have to. Remember 1 John 1:9? 'If we confess our sins, he is faithful and just to forgive us our sins, and to cleanse us from all unrighteousness.' Sounds to me like you're confessing and want to make a change."

"I do." Rooster began to cry. "Lord, forgive me for what I done. Holp me not to do it agin. Holp me to make it right with the people I love."

Logan prayed as he held the old man, who cried away the years he'd drowned his soul with liquor. After a while, Rooster's sobs subsided, and his drained face shone with peace.

"You know, I'll need to take down m' still," he mused, sinking down onto the bed and closing his eyes.

"I'm glad you mentioned it." Logan grinned as Rooster began to snore.

⬥

Hattie woke up late the next morning to the smell of bacon frying. For the first time in more than a week, her eyes didn't feel as if a fistful of grit had blown in them. She stretched and got out of bed, pulling on her blue cotton dress. She needed to get back to Rooster.

"Oh, no you don't." Miz Willow's voice stopped her in her tracks. "You jist sit yore pretty little self down at that thar table and eat. Yore nothin' but skin an' bones."

Hattie obediently sat down and buttered a roll, suddenly realizing how hungry she was. She'd have to bring some of this back for Logan and Bryce.

"Things shore been changing 'round the holler since Logan left for Louisville." Miz Willow poured herself a cup of tea and lowered herself into the rocker.

Yep. He left without saying a word, come back with no explanation, and then proposed as though nothing had happened. How cain you expect that I'd deem him worthy of my trust anymore? I placed you and ev'rybody I love in his hands, and he let y'all slip through his fingers when he wanted to go off on another adventure. He acted like an overgrown boy.

Hattie pushed away her plate, her appetite gone.

"Otis Nye came by an' tole me all about it." Miz Willow's head bobbed up and down. "Now I ken why Logan couldn't tell us till after he talked to Otis, Asa, and the Trevor twins."

"What do you mean?" Hattie had no idea what her friend was going on about.

"You've been with him all week tending to Rooster, and it never came up?" Miz Willow stopped rocking. "Dearie, Logan went to Louisville on business. He done met up with an old friend and struck up a few deals. Otis has a standin' order for his fancy checker sets, and so does Asa for those nativities of his. Logan even found a new buyer for the pelts the Trevor boys trap—all at a very tidy profit."

Hattie couldn't say a word, but Miz Willow kept right on going.

"Every one of them families'll be farin' well now. Bryce says he reckons Logan can do the same for Daisy's lace, too. Ain't niver seen the like of what that buck's done for our holler."

Hattie got up and headed for the door. She needed to think all of this over. She mumbled a hasty good-bye to Miz Willow and waved to Daisy and Jamie, who were working in the vegetable garden. She walked as fast as she could until she came to the stream. She couldn't sit, so she paced.

He didn't abandon the holler, Hattie acknowledged ruefully. *He knew I'd be back in about a day, and Bryce was still there with Miz Willow. He knew thangs would be fine with them here. I jist felt like he'd left us behind because he wasn't home when I got back. He told me he'd had to go—that he'd done it for the holler. I didn't listen. I was too wrapped up in my own assumptions. He deserves better.*

Look at how hard he's worked to holp people around here. He's chopped enough wood to see me and Miz Willow through the winter. He went huntin' on account he knew he and Bryce et a lot of our meat. He spent time with the people of the holler and valued them for who they are and what they do, and then he took that and found a way to give them a better life. He stayed by me an' Rooster through thick and thin and showed respect to us both, even after I railed at him for his proposal.

He didn't leave us. Logan wouldn't leave me. I don't jist love him; I trust him. I had no call to say those awful things to him, and he turned the other cheek and holped me anyway. He deserves a woman who sees him for the man he is. Even though I know I was wrong, it cain never be. I still won't leave the holler, and even if he wanted to stay, I wouldn't tie him down. He should have children. We cain't ever be together, because I'm not good enough for him.

She gave herself some time to mourn her mistakes and accept that Logan would move on, then headed back to Rooster's cabin. When she got close enough to see it, she noticed Logan standing in the yard, watching her.

"Nessie's with him now. They have a few things to talk about." Logan met her halfway beneath the shade of a towering elm. "So do we."

"Yore right, Logan," Hattie looked into his intense blue eyes. "I owe you an apology. Miz Willow tole me what you done in Louisville. You tried to tell me you was lookin' after the people I care about, but I didn't listen. I misjudged you, and I'm sorry for that."

"You don't bear the blame alone, Hattie." He reached out and held her hands, sending a wave of heat through her arms. "I shouldn't have proposed until I could explain where I had been. You deserved to know everything before giving me an answer." His eyes searched hers. "Now you do. I still want you for my wife, Hattie." He raised a hand to cup her cheek. "I love you."

"I love you, too, Logan," she whispered, tears coursing down her cheeks and onto his hand. "And I know I cain trust you." She swallowed hard. "But I still cain't marry you."

"Why?" Logan demanded an answer, not budging an inch.

"I cain't go to Californy." She silently begged him to understand. "These are my people, and they need me, Logan."

"I know. Over the past months, they've become my people, too." His words sent a shiver of hope to her aching heart. "Asa, Otis, Fred, and Ted need me to follow through on the business agreements. The men of the holler came and said I'd earned a right to voice my opinion in a community vote about disassembling Rooster's still. Rooster himself cried in my arms and forsook liquor, coming back to Jesus. I can't leave them, Hattie, and I wouldn't ask you to, either."

"You mean. . ." She couldn't even voice the question.

"I want you to marry me, Hattie, and we'll stay here together." He drew her into her arms. "Say you'll love me forever."

"I cain't wed you." She pushed him away and wrapped her arms around herself to ward away the pain. "You deserve a woman who cain give you sons to carry on the Chance name. I cain't."

"Hattie." He put his arms around her once more and waited until she looked at him. "I already knew that. I want *you*. Having children isn't important to me. I have five brothers, four of whom are happily married and having babies about as fast as they can. The Chance name is well taken care of. As for me, I left Chance Ranch to find my place in the world." His arms tightened around her. "And I found it here, with you. Marry me, Hattie."

"Yes, Logan." She raised up on tiptoe to kiss him. "I love you, and I'll marry you."

"I love you, too." He smiled and spun her around. "And I've got a feeling that my adventure is just beginning."

Epilogue

Dear Gideon and Miriam, Titus and Alisa, Paul and Delilah, Daniel and Lovejoy, Obie and Eunice, Hezzy and Lois, Mike and Tempy, Pollywog and Ginny Mae, and all the kids,

Sorry, but just writing all of your names took up the entire first sheet of paper, so you'll have to move on to the second one! I didn't want to leave anybody out.

Actually, we didn't want to leave anybody out. The beautiful and all-around-wonderful Hattie Thales has agreed to marry me, Logan Chance, on the first day of fall. We know you won't make it out to the wedding, but you're in our hearts. We hope you're not mad we didn't send a telegram right away, but we figured that getting a message saying only, "Getting Hitched," would raise more questions than it was worth.

All this means I won't be coming back to Chance Ranch. We plan to visit sometime, but Salt Lick Holler has become my home. I've found my purpose and my place here. I love you all, but I won't even pretend that I don't know you're a little relieved to hear that I'm settling down.

The truth is, you're dead wrong. Hattie's the most exciting thing that's ever happened to me, and I'll have her all to myself (except for the rest of the holler) for the rest of my life. I've become a greedy man, and I don't aim to change. Lovejoy, Hattie says to tell you that I'm the most difficult package you've ever sent, but she wouldn't have it any other way. Neither would I.

Don't worry about us. I've become a businessman of sorts between here and Louisville. Bryce will tell you all about it when he comes home—which will be late fall now instead of late summer. He's promised to stay long enough to help me build a cabin for me and Hattie.

God has been good to me, and I pray He sheds as many blessings on you. You're all in our prayers.

Love,
Logan Chance and Hattie Thales-soon-to-be-Chance

P.S. Lovejoy, your father is doing very well. He's taken down his still and come back to the Lord. He prays that you're well and asks you to write. Bryce and I decided to give him the packhorse we didn't use to replace his old mule. He and Nessie have started getting the land ready to plant corn. It's been a beautiful season for all of our lives.

Chance of a Lifetime

by Kelly Eileen Hake

To my family and friends, who love and support me unconditionally. Thank you, guys!

Chapter 1

1874

Billows of soot filled the air, enveloping the yard. Daisy Thales put all her disappointment, hurt, and rage into the rug beater as she walloped the smoky taint of the fire from the clothes.

Whump for Peter, her first sweetheart and loving husband, who had died from pneumonia just months before their child came into the world.

Whump for everyone who looked at her palsied son in pity. Jamie's hands and legs weren't steady, but his heart more than made up for it. She would only have him for a short time—he wasn't strong enough to live past childhood.

Whump for their home in Hawk's Fall, Kentucky, which burned to the ground a fortnight ago, leaving them with only the clothes she couldn't wash until now, because they had nothing else to wear.

She and Jamie had made it through everything life hurled at them, and she'd make sure they kept on doing so. After Peter went to his eternal reward, she'd supported herself and her son by making delicate lace for fancy ladies. She had birthed Jamie alone in their house, the pains coming too quick to fetch help. When Jamie's little legs jerked and twitched, she'd taken him to the doctor three towns over and learned her son had palsy and likely wouldn't live past his first birthday without professional medical care. Her beautiful boy would be turning five come the fall. Every time she came up against a grief greater than she thought she could survive, Daisy had plowed on ahead and made a life for herself and the son who was her one joy.

And I'll do it again. Hattie took us in after the fire, but we cain't live off her and Widow Hendrick's generosity for long. It would be so easy to stay in the warm home with Hattie's healing knowledge to help Jamie sleep through the night. But we're nothing more than charity, no matter what Hattie says about me holping with the old healer.

Daisy straightened her shoulders before whipping the clothes off the line and carrying them over to the soapy wash water.

Owin' Hattie is one thing—she's kin. But I'm even beholden to those Chance men—complete strangers, mind. If it weren't for how Logan brung me that material to make new clothes, I couldn't have washed the old ones. We barely escaped that fire with the clothes on our backs.

She winced at the memories. Jamie had awakened her in the middle of the night, the hearth rug aflame and the fire greedily spreading to take away all they owned. She scooped him up and bolted for the door, not stopping until she was sure Jamie would be safe. Then she ran back for her lace-making basket, the only way she could eke out a living and take care of her son. She'd had the presence of mind to snatch Jamie's favorite blanket, as well. By the time she made it out, the roof was collapsing behind her. It was still hard to breathe sometimes on account of the smoke she'd taken in that night.

The fumes of the lye soap stung her eyes, and she let a few tears fall before taking the clothes and plunging them into the cool, fresh rinse water. She wrung them out, then pinned them to the clothesline to dry.

Almost good as new. Daisy nodded to herself. *And we will be, too.*

She finished the rest of the washing before going inside to start dinner. Hattie'd set out early in the morning to visit an ailing family and wouldn't be back before supper. The Chance brothers had been hard at work all day, so Daisy reckoned they'd have a hollow leg apiece to fill.

"Ma! 'Ook!" Jamie pushed his slate toward her, and she picked it up.

"That's wonderful, Jamie!" He'd copied his name from Miz Willow's spidery scrawl, and his big, wavering, loopy letters filled the slate. She handed it back to him. "Now practice it one more time."

Jamie's chalk rubbed slowly along the board while Daisy wondered whether or not to call Logan and Bryce to come in and wash up. She could still hear them sawing lumber outside while she sliced bread and put it on the table. She hastily put together a platter full of chicken sandwiches and cheese. She rang the dinner bell. That'd do. After dinner she'd start a hearty pot roast with potatoes and carrots for supper. And as a special treat, she'd bake a fresh apple pie.

Logan and Bryce deserved it for working so hard on the new addition to Willow Hendrick's house. The healer's home already had an extra room to store medicines and such, but with Hattie and Logan fixin' on marrying each other, they'd need a place of their own. Logan worked like a man with a fine reward waiting at the end of his labor, and his brother kept pace alongside him.

The two brothers walked into the cabin, and Daisy was once again struck by how much they could look so alike but be so different. Both were tall and well built, with blue eyes and brown hair. Logan, his easy smile and chin set like someone who usually got his way, stood a few inches shy of his older brother.

Daisy reckoned she'd pegged Logan Chance the first time she saw him—a good-natured, exuberant, polite young man who'd treat her sister-in-law well and give Hattie the love she deserved. Every person on earth wanted something, and Logan wanted Hattie, as well as to stay in Salt Lick Holler. By building this addition, he'd get both.

Bryce wasn't so easy to figure out. His broad shoulders and quiet manner announced to the world that he was a man who stood firm in his decisions. His smile, though much harder won than that of his brother, would break across his face like a lightning bolt and shine with an intensity that startled her. There was a calm in his deep blue eyes that made Daisy wonder what he knew that she didn't.

"Hey, buddy." Bryce's strong hands gently ruffled her son's pale blond hair.

"Hi, Byce." Jamie beamed up at the big man with all the adulation usually reserved for a boy's father. But Jamie had no father, so it would do him good to be around Logan and Bryce for a while.

If only Peter had lived, everything would be so different. . . .

Daisy pushed away the wistful thought. "If only" had to be about as useless an idea as ever existed. Stuck in the here and now, longing for the past only made each day that much harder.

⤜⟡⤛

Bryce straightened up and mopped his brow. He and Logan had come a long way on the addition to the main cabin, but it would still take a lot of work to complete.

It took so much less time back in California at Chance Ranch where Gideon, Daniel, Titus, and Paul were on hand to help me and Logan. Now that Logan's staying here in Salt Lick Holler, all six of us will never put our hands to the same project again.

And recently they'd worked on many projects like this one. The past five years had brought five brides—one for each of Bryce's brothers. Before Logan came to the holler and met Hattie, they'd acquired four sisters-in-law back at the ranch. Miriam, the missionary's daughter, came for her sister's children and got Gideon. Alyssa, maid turned heiress, popped up mysteriously to snare Titus. Delilah, the gambler's daughter, planted herself into Paul's heart. Meanwhile, the three McPherson brothers who'd courted her simultaneously were persuaded to write back home for brides. So Eunice, Lois, and Temperance had arrived to wed Obie, Hezzy, and Mike. Lovejoy, Tempy's older sister, shepherded them all to Reliable, won a hard-fought battle for the widower Daniel's love, becoming his second wife and stepmother to Polly and Ginny Mae.

Yep. Things had gotten pretty crowded and chaotic back home, and Bryce had noticed Logan itching for some adventure. When Bryce first suggested that Logan stretch his legs and see some of the world, he hadn't planned on tagging along. All the same, he somehow got hitched to Logan's wagon. The Chance vote approving Logan's trip came with the condition that Bryce accompany his younger brother, so the two ended up in Salt Lick Holler, a tiny community carved into the Appalachian Mountains. Bryce had suggested visiting Lovejoy's hometown, never suspecting that once it came time to return to California, he'd be leaving his closest brother behind.

The supper bell rang, so Bryce put away his tools and ambled into the cabin. *Something sure smells good.*

" 'Ook!" Jamie ordered, pushing a slate into Bryce's hand.

Bryce held it up in the light and saw a row of *J–a–m–i–e*s squiggling down the board in the painstaking and still shaky hand of a young boy. He nodded seriously and handed it back to Jamie before taking a seat.

"You're coming a long way, Jamie." Bryce wasn't one to scoop out handfuls of praise. He figured an honest assessment would go further than ebullience. Besides, Jamie deserved to be treated with the dignity befitting a man. Even if he was young, the boy had more inner strength than just about anyone Bryce had ever met. It looked like Jamie got that from his mama. She'd been through a lot of tough times—too many, to Bryce's way of thinking—but she still had a smile for her son and anyone else who needed encouragement. Bryce admired them both.

He sneaked a surreptitious glance at Daisy as she poured fresh milk into her son's cup. A petite woman, her generous curves and loving smile lent her an unconventional beauty—the beauty of a woman rather than the untested prettiness she undoubtedly possessed as a young girl. Her long, honey-colored hair hung past her waist. Not a single lock dared to break free. She braided her hair in an intricate pattern similar to the woven reins he used when training a horse. He wondered what she'd look like when it came unraveled, her hair shining in waves to frame her big brown eyes and the smattering of freckles across her sun-kissed nose.

She turned around, and a puzzled look crossed her face when he was too slow to hide his gaze. Bryce cleared his throat.

"Ahem. Could I have some of that?" He stuck out his empty cup. Never mind the fact that he didn't like milk—he drained the glass by the end of the meal, since she'd smiled so pretty when she filled it for him.

Miz Willow—Bryce had to keep reminding himself to call her that instead of Widow Hendrick, since Hattie'd told him that the older woman preferred those who lived in her home to call her by that name—chatted with Logan and Daisy, but he didn't see any reason to join in. Why speak up if he didn't have something to contribute? He mostly got by with *yes*, *nope*, or a good shrug. Sometimes he wished he had a little more to add and Logan a little less.

Bryce ate his sandwiches silently, listening to the others, and nodding his head occasionally as the conversation required. He noticed Jamie eyeing the sliced cheese. The little tyke was too polite to interrupt the adults to ask for some more. Bryce winked at Jamie as he pushed the plate close enough for him to choose a piece. The little boy's smile—so full of joy and gratitude—warmed Bryce's heart as he and Logan left and got back to work.

"Hand me more nails. I ran out," Logan directed from up the makeshift ladder, where he was hammering together the frame of the first wall.

Bryce, holding the base, rummaged through his pockets until he gathered a fistful, then offered them to his brother. He squinted as Logan pounded the nails in and joined the frame to the pre-existing wall of the cabin. Then Logan jumped down, and Bryce clambered up to make sure the lines were even—it was always best to double-check these sorts of things.

"We're fine." Bryce came back down and walked over to the pile of lumber. He picked out another piece of wood to saw down to a small piece. The tiny bar, when wedged and secured between the two bigger pieces forming the corner, would support the wall and make it stronger.

"Lumber pile's getting low," Logan observed.

"Yep." Bryce finished his sawing.

"We should go fill up the wagon with another load from the barn and bring it over." Logan shifted his weight from one foot to the other, eager to build Hattie their new home. "Are you done with that yet?"

"Yep." Bryce nodded his head and jumped back down beside his brother. "You know that getting something done quick and getting something done right don't always go together."

"Yeah," Logan grumbled and picked up the pace. "I can only take one thing slow at a time. The wedding's already waiting!"

Bryce grinned. He'd spoken his piece, and Logan had heard him. That would be good enough. They'd been working steadily since dinner, but now the sunlight was failing. After they moved this load, he and Logan would be done working on the cabin for today. One more week and it would be finished.

He saw Daisy come out of the house with a basket on her hip, walking over to the clothesline. The setting sun caught the fire in her hair, surrounding her face with a golden halo. Bryce drank in the sight. *She's the closest thing to an angel I'll ever see.*

Chapter 2

Today's your big day, Hattie!" Daisy gestured to the old wooden tub, which she'd already filled with warm water. "I've drawn you a bath." Jamie snoozed in the big bed.

"Thankee, Daisy." Hattie slid the screen in place and disappeared behind it, only the soft splash of water marking her presence.

"While yore in there, Miz Willow's taking some breakfast out to the barn for your groom and his brother." Daisy put the cinnamon rolls in the ash oven to keep warm. "Silk Trevor's already at the schoolhouse, making shore it's neat and tidy." Daisy didn't tell Hattie how Silk and the women of the community had gotten together to decorate the schoolhouse with flowers. A bride deserved to have a surprise on her wedding day.

"It's so kind of them!" Daisy could hear the smile in Hattie's voice.

"When yore finished in there, don't dawdle." Daisy forced herself to be strict. "We've still got lots to do this morning, and you haven't et so much as a single bite."

"Oh, I don't think I cain eat a bite," Hattie demurred. "I'm too nervous."

"Nonsense." Miz Willow came in and banged the door shut. "Yore a healer— you have to have a strong stomach. Comes with the job."

"You've been married once before," Daisy encouraged. "You know how the ceremony will go. He waits for you, Otis Nye escorts you to him, and then you both say, 'I do.'" The words carried her back to the happiest day in her life. Daisy had stood all in white, with flowers woven into her hair as she promised to love Peter for as long as they lived. . . .

Why did it have to be such a short time? We didn't even have a single full year together as man and wife.

No. I cain't think about that now. It's Hattie's day. She deserves to be happy, especially after how hard her first marriage to Peter's brother was. She never uttered a single word of complaint but waited on Horace hand and foot for precious little thanks.

"Let me do that for you." Daisy took the towel from Hattie's hands and sat her down by the fire so her hair would dry more quickly. Hattie had wisely donned her yellow dress instead of the green one she'd chosen to wear for the ceremony.

"You have such lovely color," Daisy murmured as she rubbed Hattie's hair, combing through it before toweling it again. The deep mahogany of her damp locks slowly gave way to burnished copper. "We've all decided you cain't wear it back in a braid on yore weddin' day," Daisy spoke firmly over Hattie's tiny squeak of dismay. "And none of those awful buns where yore head looks scraped back, neither."

"What are you going to do?" Hattie moved restlessly as Daisy gathered up a few locks and began to weave them in a pretty fishtail pattern.

"Yore jist gonna hafta trust me." Daisy finished the first plait, then made another of the same kind on the other side of Hattie's head, joining them together in the back with a pretty green ribbon. The joined braids were fitting for a bride, and they seemed almost to form a crown atop the rest of her hair, which hung in loose waves past her waist. Daisy coaxed a few wispy tendrils to curl alongside Hattie's face and let it be. "There. That'll do."

Hattie got up and headed for the mirror to inspect her new hairstyle. She peered at herself from a few angles and sighed in satisfaction.

"I don't know how you did it, Daisy, but you made me look almost young again!" Hattie rushed over and wrapped her in a hug. "Thankee!"

"You are young," Miz Willow piped up. Her face softened. "But I'll allow as how nice you look with the way Daisy done yore hair."

"Jamie, time to git dressed!" Daisy began laying out his new clothes.

"You should do yore hair jist like this," Hattie begged.

"It ain't fittin' for the matron of honor," Daisy protested. *Matron, and me practically the same age as the bride.*

"Yore not weaselin' out of this. Today is the last day for the Thales sisters to be all done up like each other." Hattie took Daisy's hands in hers. "I want you to share this with me, Daisy."

"I cain't say no to that." Daisy gave in before helping Jamie into his Sunday best.

"Good." Hattie went over to put on her wedding dress, a light grass green that set off her hair and creamy skin.

Daisy pulled Jamie's shirt on over his head and began to comb his hair, pretending to be completely engrossed in what she was doing as she heard Hattie's gasp.

"Daisy! When did you. . . ?" She fingered the delicate handmade lace collar adorning her wedding dress.

"It's what I do, darlin'!" Daisy smiled at the look on Hattie's face, glad she'd decided to give her one of the lacy collars she made to sell in fancy shops. "I'm jist glad you like it."

Jamie and I coulda used that money, but good friends are worth more'n gold, and Hattie's the best there is. She deserves to feel as beautiful as God made her, and I may not have much to my name right now, but I could give her this.

"It's beautiful, Daisy!" Hattie slipped into the dress and went over to show Miz Willow. "I don't know how you do it!" Her face changed as she looked into Daisy's eyes. "Thankee."

"Yore welcome, Hattie." Daisy squeezed her friend's hand. "I hope today is as special and full of love as yore marriage will be." *And as mine was.*

◦◦◦◦◦

"Hold still, Logan!" Bryce gritted, trying to make sense of Logan's necktie. "You're jumpier'n a frog."

"Sorry, Bryce." Logan looked anything but sorry. He had a grin as big as all get-out on his face. "I'm excited. Today I take Hattie to be my wife."

"I'm gaining another fine sister-in-law," Bryce agreed, taking the ends of his brother's tie once more. Between their efforts, they'd already crumpled the thing past all hope. Somehow Bryce managed to finally work it into a presentable shape.

"And Louisville for our honeymoon—have you seen how excited Hattie is about buying new books for the schoolhouse?" Logan buffed his boots one last time.

"Yep." Bryce ran a comb through his hair. "Who would've thought when I told you to visit Salt Lick Holler that you'd find yourself a bride—much less one who'd found a hidden box of money while cleaning out the loft for us?"

"Lovejoy's first husband must've been quite a clench fist to squirrel away seventy dollars and hide it up in the barn," Logan mused. "Sure was nice of her to give Miz Willow her old home and even better that she trusted me to spend the money on helping the holler."

"Just who she is," Bryce observed. Lovejoy Spencer had been Willow Hendrick's protégée and the main healer for Salt Lick Holler before coming to California with the new brides and had wound up finding a husband of her own in surly old Daniel. She'd worked wonders for their brother back at Chance Ranch and made a good mother to his children, Polly and Ginny Mae.

If it weren't for Lovejoy Spencer and the McPherson family, Bryce never would have suggested this trip. As it was, the whole thing had taken a lot of unexpected turns—like how the whole family insisted that Bryce go along. And now Logan was getting married and leaving Bryce behind at Salt Lick Holler while he took his honeymoon trip!

"Funny how things work out." Bryce shook his head.

"Are you sure you're okay with staying here until we get back?" Logan peered at him anxiously.

"Yep," Bryce hastened to reassure his brother. "Besides, I'll chop enough wood to last you through winter. You could use some more meat in the smoke-house, too, so I'll be hunting and fishing. I'll have plenty to keep me busy until you get back."

◦◦◦◦◦

A soft melody floated through the air as Hattie began to walk down the aisle. Bryce stood beside his brother and watched. The duties of the best man were few on the surface—stand by and encourage the groom—but deeper truth lay beneath. Today, for the last time, Bryce would be the closest friend to his brother, and for the first time, he would watch as someone else became the most important person in Logan's life.

Now Hattie would help him, love him, make a home with him, and share the days they were given—as it should be. A man should leave home and cleave to his wife. But Bryce didn't look forward to going back home. Chance Ranch wouldn't be the same without his younger brother, who always understood what Bryce couldn't find the words to say.

As Logan looked at his bride, Bryce watched him. His baby brother—the only one younger than Bryce—had grown up right before his eyes. His brother, the scapegrace who managed to find mischief and fun as though he had a compass for it, stood straight and tall, with the love in his heart shining from his face. Coming to Salt Lick Holler had made a man out of the boy, and Bryce had to admit that Hattie had a lot to do with it. She would be a good wife to him, and Logan would be a devoted husband for her.

They exchanged *I do*s, and Bryce snapped out of his reverie. That did it.

Six brothers, but with Logan hitched, I'm the last Chance bachelor.

Chapter 3

As the entire holler and some folks from neighboring Hawk's Fall sat down to enjoy the wedding feast, Daisy led Jamie to the far end of the tables in one long row for the occasion. She'd love to sit in the middle of the banquet across from Logan and Hattie, but Jamie needed as much space as she could give him. His jerky movements would distract and discomfort others if he sat in the midst of the goings-on. She took the very edge of the bench and lifted him next to her—she couldn't take the risk that he'd tumble off the end.

When Logan and Hattie took places across the table from her, she looked up in surprise. Customarily, the newlyweds sat at the center of the table, surrounded by well-wishers. As Bryce escorted Miz Willow over, getting the old healer situated, Daisy shot Hattie a questioning look.

"It's our wedding," Hattie murmured, positively glowing.

"We'll sit at the head of our table, with our closest loved ones," Logan finished. "No one will gainsay us."

"Hey, buddy." Bryce came and took the spot on Jamie's other side.

" 'Ey, Byce!" Jamie squirmed excitedly.

"Easy, there." Bryce reached out to steady Jamie when he leaned back a little too far.

Daisy shot him a grateful smile, but Bryce only gave her a brief nod before bowing his head for the prayer. She'd never before met a man of so few words. *What goes on in that quiet head of his? Mayhap without his brother around to talk for the pair of 'em, Bryce'll speak up, and I'll learn more about him. Any man Jamie spends so much time with is someone I need to get to know.*

Soon enough, nothing more than crumbs dusted the tables, and it was time to get things moving. Silk Trevor gave Daisy a decisive nod.

"I need to go holp Silk for a minute," Daisy leaned over and whispered to Miz Willow. "Would you mind Jamie for a while?"

"No problem." Bryce Chance stood up and swung Jamie in the air.

"I—" Daisy's heart caught in her throat as Jamie squealed with the fun of falling back down. She couldn't breathe for a few minutes even after Bryce caught him easily.

Doesn't the man realize Jamie's condition? Was Bryce so oblivious he didn't know Jamie needed special care?

One look at the delighted surprise on her baby boy's face and the words died on her lips. Bryce wasn't about to drop Jamie—she needed to stop overreacting.

Daisy took a deep breath and joined Silk, while Bryce carried Jamie and walked with Miz Willow to the circle that was forming.

Everybody gathered around Logan and Hattie to watch them open their wedding gifts. Daisy and Silk waited for the chatter to die down before handing the first package to the happy couple.

"Wait a minute!" Rooster Linden stood up. "I got summat to say. Firstly, my gift for the happy couple is up at my place. It's a new buckboard, only I ain't got a horse to pull it down here jist yet, on account of loanin' her to a friend in need." He grinned, then sobered. "Second, and more important, I want to say in front of everybody here how grateful I am to Hattie, Logan, and Bryce Chance. They saw me through a time when I had to fight my demons. I wouldn't have pulled through if it weren't for them. Yore fine folks, and I'm glad to have Logan stayin' in the holler. I'm shore I ain't the only one who feels that way." He paused while cheers erupted all around.

"Because of their holp and yore prayers, I've stopped drinkin' likker. I know I ain't the only man in this holler who owes you a 'thankee,' but it comes from the bottom of my heart. I wish you two a long and happy marriage!" With that, he sat back down, and the gift giving could truly begin. Logan ripped open the first package.

"Beautiful workmanship," he praised, running his hands over the graceful curves of hand-carved swan-neck towel pegs.

"I thought they'd look good on the wall of yore new home." Asa Pleasant spoke modestly but beamed at their pleasure.

"I expect so," Logan agreed.

Hattie opened the next gift, a full set of towels, embroidered by Silk Trevor.

"These're lovely, Silk!" She held up the corner of a wash-cloth and traced the delicate blue *C* adorning the corner.

"We'll be sure to hang them on our washstand," Logan planned aloud as he opened a bundle.

"That thar's an ole family recipe fer pickled pigs' feet." Her husband nowhere in sight, Bethilda Cleary spoke loudly as Hattie picked up a card from the baking dish. "Ain't nobody makes it better'n my daughters, Lily and Lark, but you cain't go wrong with that thar recipe." Having spoken her piece, Bethilda sat back down.

"Thankee, Bethilda." Hattie put the cookware to the side as Logan accepted another parcel.

"I hope you like it." Abigail Rucker shifted her new baby to her shoulder while her husband, Nate, the holler's hulking blacksmith, rubbed her back between her shoulder blades.

Logan unfurled a braided hearth rug in varying shades of blue cloth.

"When did you ever find the time to make this, Abby?" Hattie stroked the pretty rug.

"Bitty Nate here don't let me sleep much anyhow." Abby blushed with pleasure. "I started it as soon as y'all tole me 'bout yore engagement."

"So did I." Cantankerous old Otis Nye shuffled forward with a large object covered by an old sheet. He set it before the newlyweds and backed up, waiting for them to reveal what he'd made.

Logan gave the sheet a short tug. It slid to the ground, revealing a maple wedding chest.

"Ooh," Hattie breathed, reaching out to touch the flowers chiseled into the wood. Otis had carved blooming vines to encircle the smooth wooden sides of the chest.

"Figgured it were fittin' since yore our healer, Hattie." The old man spoke gruffly, but everyone knew he couldn't discount the time and care he'd put into his gift. "And Logan here's the one who's got me carvin' all the time now anyway."

"That's right." Logan walked over and clapped the old man on the back. "Jack Tarhill back in Louisville is gearing up for that next shipment of yours. He's very pleased with how things are working out with your and Asa's carving. Those checker sets and nativities sell very well."

"Of course they do!" Otis drew himself up and broke into a grin.

Hattie opened the next package, drawing out a beautiful blue and green wedding ring quilt.

"Miz Willow, you shouldn't have!" She fingered the thick fabric. "This belonged to yore ma."

"The good Lord didn't see fit to give me a child of my flesh." The old woman's eyes glistened. "But yore the daughter of my heart, Hattie. I figgured the time's come to pass it on."

Hattie handed Logan the quilt before rushing over to the old widow and enveloping her in a tight hug.

Ma gave me a quilt like that on Peter's and my weddin' day. Daisy blinked back tears of loss. *It burned in the fire, and now I don't have anything to remember her by.*

⌒⌘⌒

Women started to gather up the dishes left over from the feast. A lot of folks had a bit of a walk before they got back home, and the celebration had stretched through the afternoon. The time had come to get home to waiting chores.

Daisy slung Jamie on her hip and gathered the now-empty dishes she'd brought for the celebration. Miz Willow leaned on her cane as she hobbled on the path. Logan carried the swan-neck towel pegs and the hearth rug, while Hattie cradled their monogrammed linens. Bryce walked a bit behind, his arms full with the new wedding chest. He'd seen to it that the quilt rested inside.

After putting the bounty in Hattie and Logan's new home, Bryce retired to the barn loft where he and Logan had slept since arriving in Salt Lick Holler. He tossed his boots on Logan's empty pallet before bunking down.

At least I'll get a good night's sleep without Logan's yammering.

"Hope you have a fine time," Miz Willow called after them as Logan and Hattie departed for the train station early the next morning.

"Good-bye!" Daisy waved.

From her arms, Jamie clapped his hands and let out a slightly garbled "Bye!"

"See you in two weeks." Bryce supported Miz Willow's elbow out in the yard. It seemed only fitting to give the newlyweds a proper send-off.

Once the happy couple disappeared around the bend, Daisy and Jamie trailed into the house behind Miz Willow—probably to clean up after their hasty breakfast. Bryce headed for the barn. He grabbed the milking pail and set the three-legged stool beside the cow.

"Mornin', Starla." He gave her a pat on the rump before he set about the business at hand. When the pail was full, he went out to the well and drew up last night's cold milk to exchange for the fresh. Before he and Logan had arrived, this well was the only way Hattie and Miz Willow could draw water. Now that he and Logan had installed a new water pump and piping, the well could be used strictly to keep things fresh and cool. He picked it up and headed for the cabin.

"Here you go." He plunked the pail down on the table.

"Thankee, Bryce." Miz Willow made her way across the room. "I'm fixin' to do some baking today."

Bryce looked around. Daisy busily swiped a rag around the furniture, keeping everything spick-and-span. Jamie sat on his pallet, stacking blocks. Bryce hunkered down to look the boy in the eye.

"What do you say you come and help me gather eggs this morning, Jamie?"

"Ma?" he questioned his mother before answering.

Bryce saw Daisy hesitate and could practically hear the thoughts running through her mind. *What if the chickens scratch her son or, worse, peck him?* He hadn't missed the panicked look on her face the day before when he'd tossed Jamie into the air.

"I'll hold him," Bryce reassured her. "Jamie can help me hang on to the basket." It would do the little tyke good to do something other than play with blocks and study. Jamie's legs were twisted and jerky, but he had a lot more control over his hands and arms.

"All right," she assented with a slow nod. Jamie mimicked the motion, nodding eagerly and stretching up his arms.

Bryce scooped him up, handed the boy the egg basket, and tromped back to the barn. Jamie sat in the crook of his left arm, cradling the basket as Bryce opened the chicken coop.

"You have to be real quiet so you don't startle them," Bryce explained. "Then you reach under them, nice and gentle, to see if there's an egg." He spoke the instructions as he found the first egg. "Then we put it in the basket. Want to help with the next one?"

" 'Es." Jamie nodded somberly.

"Good." Bryce took the basket and looped it over his arm, then guided Jamie's hand into the next nest.

Jamie stroked the feathers of one of the birds. His touch was clumsy but gentle.

Bryce helped the little boy reach under the chicken and find the egg. "Feel that?"

" 'Es," he whispered excitedly, his little hand closing around the egg and tugging it free.

"Good job," Bryce praised as he steadied Jamie's arm so he could place the egg in the basket.

The job took far more time than usual, but Bryce enjoyed the look of wonder and excitement on the little boy's face. If something as simple as gathering eggs could make the lad feel included, Bryce would make sure to find other things the boy could do. He carried the child and eggs back into the house.

"We're all done." Bryce transferred Jamie to Daisy's arms, then set the eggs on the table. "Eleven of 'em."

"Did you have fun?" Daisy cuddled her son close.

"None boken," Jamie declared proudly.

"That's right. Jamie was a big help. The chickens like him."

"That's my little man!" At the grin on her son's face, Daisy broke into a matching smile.

When she turned the full force of that smile onto Bryce, he almost stepped back from the impact. Daisy's brown eyes positively shone with the joy she found in her son. Bryce always knew she was attractive, but when she glowed with love, Daisy became the most beautiful woman he'd ever seen.

Bryce headed for the door. "I've got some things to tend to." He winced at how abrupt he sounded, but it couldn't be helped. He'd hardly taken a step when he felt a soft hand on his arm.

"Thankee." Daisy smiled up at him with gratitude and happiness. The warmth of her smile and the heat of her palm on his arm sparked something in him.

"Welcome," Bryce responded gruffly before retreating to the safety of the barn, where he always knew what to do.

Lord, I can understand what to do with a horse or any other creature—how to put 'em at ease. So why am I at such a loss with the pretty little widow with her heartfelt smile?

Chapter 4

*I*f I didn't know any better, I'd think that man got flustered when I thanked him, Daisy mused as Bryce disappeared from view. *He's one of those men who likes to do for others but doesn't know how to handle the appreciation afterwards. It's sweet—jist like the way he treats Jamie. It's mighty nice of him to take an interest in my boy while he's here. Jamie'll never know his pa, but he cain relish bein' 'round a man like Bryce, even iff'n 'tis for but a brief time.*

Well, if he won't take an honest thankee I'll jist find another way to show my appreciation. Daisy thought for a moment before remembering the way Bryce tucked into the apple pie she'd made last month. *I reckon he's got a sweet tooth to match his nature. I'll whip up some pudding for dessert today. He oughta enjoy that. Besides, it's one of Jamie's favorites.*

With her mind made up, Daisy left Miz Willow teaching Jamie his letters and walked into Logan and Hattie's cabin. Her closest friend hadn't had the time to settle into the home her man made for her before being whisked off to Louisville. *By the time Hattie and Logan get back,* Daisy determined, *their cabin'll be all fixed up and ready to be a home.*

She rolled up her sleeves and set to work. The addition wasn't overly large, but it didn't need to be. The cooking would still be done in the main cabin, and Logan married Hattie knowing full well she couldn't bear any children. For the two of them, the cozy room would be a perfect fit.

A harp-backed washstand with a single drawer and small cupboard sat beneath a goodly sized window, where the sunlight would warm the wash water a bit. Another wall boasted a modest fireplace to heat the room. Logan's new desk butted up against the third wall, and a real, above-the-ground bed nestled up to the wall this room shared with the main cabin.

But the pile of wedding gifts lay in the corner, waiting to put the finishing touches on the home. Daisy walked over and found the swan-neck clothing pegs. *These should be hung by the hearth, with winter coming on. Jist not too close.* She shuddered at the memory of the fire before straightening her shoulders. She walked out to the barn to find a hammer and ran into Bryce.

"Howdy." The big man took a step back.

"Hello. I'm lookin' for a hammer and some nails." Daisy peered around the barn. "Any idea where I cain find 'em?"

Bryce nodded, walked to a far corner, and returned in a minute with the requested tools. He held them out to her wordlessly, and Daisy accepted them.

I cain't make him talk to me, she reasoned, *but maybe iff'n I speak first, he'll come 'round.*

"You and yore brother made a fine home for Hattie." Daisy smiled as she spoke. "I'm gonna fix it up a bit so it's ready when they get back."

"Needs a woman's touch," Bryce agreed.

" 'Zactly." Daisy breathed a sigh of relief that Bryce didn't actually seem to mind talking to her—he just needed to be drawn out a little. "Hattie'd have it done in a trice, but she's off to Louisville, so I figgured I'd put away the weddin' gifts and get 'em all set up."

"Mighty thoughtful of you." Bryce rubbed the back of his neck as if puzzling over something. "What're the hammer and nails for?"

"The swan-neck wall hooks need to be hung." Daisy laughed. "I cain only hope I get 'em up straight."

"I'll do it," Bryce offered. "I've just finished the mantelpiece and need to put it up anyway."

"Makes sense to me." Daisy passed the hammer back to him, pleased at the progress she'd made. Bryce wasn't much of a talker, but that was all right. He went out of his way to do nice things for the people she cared about, so Daisy didn't mind making the extra effort to put him at ease.

The rest of the morning passed quickly as Daisy and Bryce worked together inside the cabin. Neither spoke much. It was enough to be working alongside each other.

While he made tiny pencil marks on the wall, determining where to hang the pegs, she carefully folded the monogrammed towels and hung them across the top of the wooden washstand. The monogrammed *C* in the corner of each towel marched across the row, each one a little higher than the last.

"They don't have a mirror," she noted. She didn't realize she'd spoken aloud until Bryce stopped hammering.

"You think they need one?" Bryce's words could've been a question or just a flat statement.

"Of course!" Daisy decided to treat it as if it were a question. *Men!* "How else do you get yoreself ready for the day? What about yore hair?"

"Not that complicated." Bryce ran a hand through his wavy brown hair, mussing it up just enough to make Daisy itch to tug it back in place.

"Maybe not for you," she admitted, "but what about Hattie? Or," she added triumphantly, "Logan shaving?"

"We don't have a mirror out in the barn." Bryce rubbed his jaw with his big, strong hand. "We do it by feel."

Daisy's mouth went dry. *By the end of the day, Bryce's jaw boasted a dark shadow, making him look a little rugged—like he needed a good woman.* She couldn't think of a single thing that was fitting to say, so she just shrugged.

"Those hooks look wondrous fine!" He'd put four of them in a neat row by the hearth, and the other two were thoughtfully stationed beside the door.

Bryce jerked a thumb toward the latter. "I thought it'd be nice for when Hattie comes in after healing, to hang her cloak." He smirked. "And then there's one for Logan's hat."

"His and hers," Daisy mused. "Perfect."

⌘

Bryce got to work on the mantelpiece he and Logan had sanded together. With supportive legs along either side of the hearth to brace it, the subtle curves of the mantel wouldn't overpower the wall but would look like a natural part of the room.

While he worked, he watched Daisy from the corner of his eye. She bustled around contentedly, plumping a pillow here, then tucking in the edges of the wedding quilt she brought out of Hattie and Logan's new chest and put on the bed. He caught her trying to scooch the chest across the floor.

"Here." He picked the wooden chest up off the ground just as she was ready to give it another hefty push. A few flaxen tendrils of hair had escaped her fancy updo, and Bryce had a sudden picture of her brushing her hair, the golden locks spread over her shoulders. He decided to get that mirror she'd been talking about. Their eyes locked, and Bryce felt the breath hitch in his chest.

A sudden gust of air banged the door shut, breaking the moment. Daisy shook her head as though to clear it, then pointed to the far wall. "I was fixin' to put it at the foot of the bed."

Bryce tromped over and obligingly lowered the carved trunk in place. He stepped back to where he'd been working on the mantelpiece.

"Thankee, Bryce." Her words were so soft, he almost thought he imagined them.

And why wouldn't she be hesitant to thank you after the way you jackrabbited out of the house this morning? he scolded himself. *Say something this time!*

"Anytime." He forced a smile. "You could've just asked for help, Daisy." Her name tasted sweet as he spoke it.

"I would've gotten it there." Daisy's shoulders straightened, and she poked her chin out. "Women aren't helpless."

Now you've done it. You offended her. Bryce gave himself a mental kick. "I never thought you were helpless." He searched for the words. "You're a strong woman, supporting yourself and your son. I just meant you don't always have to do everything alone."

"You're right." She softened a bit and rewarded him with an apologetic smile.

Bryce grinned in return before turning back to the mantel. He finished up while she straightened the blue gingham curtains. He stepped back to survey their handiwork.

Everything stood in place, as it had when they'd started, but now it looked. . .nice. Inviting. She'd looped the curtains along the wooden bar to make them flutter prettily at the window. The chest looked at home at the foot of the bed, where the quilt fell in neat folds just shy of the floor.

"The mantelpiece fits real good," Daisy commented. "All the wood—the walls, the hooks, the furniture—it melds together nice." She stepped over to the chest and drew out the braided hearth rug. After she laid it out, she stepped back to see the effect. "Blue rug, blue curtains, blue embroidery on the towels—even blue in the quilt. All looks put together jist right, with a lot of love."

That was it exactly. She'd found a way to say what he'd been thinking. The colors and goodwill made the room pleasant. Everything in here fit, just like Hattie and Logan matched each other.

"Yep."

Bryce rolled over for the umpteenth time. He couldn't sleep. It was just too. . . quiet.

Now he understood what those fancy writers meant when they wrote about the "deafening silence." The lack of sound pushed in on him and stifled all thoughts of anything else.

The din of all the Chance children surrounded him back on the ranch, and here he'd had Logan's jabber—or snoring—to put up with. Even today when he'd worked with Daisy, she hummed under her breath.

He smiled at the memory of how she didn't follow any particular tune, just made the happy noise of busyness. He'd noticed she did the same thing in the evenings while she worked over her lace. Humming came as naturally to Daisy as buzzing came to bees. Same as smiling came to Jamie. Except for when the boy bent over his studies or something requiring his absolute focus, he expressed joy. No one came closer to being a breathing sunbeam than Jamie when that bright smile spread across his face and into the heart of its recipient.

Bryce rested his head on his hands, leaning back to stare at the sloping ceiling of the loft. The lad possessed an eager young mind. He thirsted to learn about the world around him and to help those he lived with.

The eggs are a good start, Bryce decided. *Tomorrow I'll see if I can't find something more to show him. Just because he can't walk doesn't mean he can't enjoy learning how to do other things.*

A thought seeped into his mind. *It might take some smooth talking, but when the time is right, I'm going to convince Jamie's pretty mama to let me teach him how to ride. It'll give the boy something to look forward to and a way to increase his strength. After all, tending to animals is the best way I know to work the muscles and the mind.*

Chapter 5

A few days later, Bryce woke up early. He tended to the cow, mucked out the stalls, and gathered the eggs. He and Jamie had made egg gathering into a sort of morning ritual, but today Bryce needed to have everything squared away before breakfast.

He gave the door a cautious tap rather than walking in unannounced.

"Come on in," Daisy's cheerful voice called.

He opened the door and sniffed appreciatively. Coffee cake—one of his favorite breakfasts, but not rib sticking enough for every day.

"You're up and about a little earlier this morning," Daisy observed, pouring him a cup of coffee.

"I've got business to tend to." Bryce took a long, appreciative drink. "I'm going out to Hawk's Fall to pick up Logan and Hattie's wedding present. I won't be back until tomorrow." He waited to see her reaction.

"I see." Her words didn't match her expression. She seemed a bit confused, a little lost.

Will she miss me? Bryce shrugged the thought away. "It won't be long, but I have to go. I'm borrowing the new wagon to haul it in—it's from the whole Chance family."

"It's big enough to need a wagon?" Daisy's deep brown eyes burned with curiosity, though she was too polite to come out and ask what the present was.

"Yep." Bryce wouldn't tell her anything more. Sooner or later she'd have to learn to ask for the things she wanted, even if it was just harmless information.

"Does Miz Willow know?" Daisy changed tack, and Bryce suddenly remembered that the elderly healer had spent the night with the Peasleys, where a baby's cough caused her some worry.

"I spoke with her about how I'd need to fetch the present when it came in," he assured her. "I trust you to pass on the message."

"Let me pack you some lunch before you go," Daisy offered.

"Thanks, but I've eaten more than enough of this wonderful cake to tide me over. I'll be spending the night with Abner McPherson, and he'll expect me to bring my appetite."

"Fair enough," Daisy conceded. "Have a safe trip, Bryce. Good-bye."

His ears all but perked up at the sound of his name on her lips. She didn't say it often, so when she did, it sounded special.

"I'll be back as soon as I can," Bryce promised, swiping one last bite of coffee cake before standing up. *I plan on sticking around for a while yet.*

❦

Out in the garden, Daisy plucked weeds as she sorted her thoughts.

"He's only going to be gone for two days—less, even," Daisy muttered to herself. "What am I doin' gettin' all het up about it? It's not like I have to be afeared of livin' without a man—it's all I've done for the past four and a half years. Me an' Jamie'll be jist fine, and I still have Miz Willow's company."

Daisy reached for a scraggly weed and plucked one of Miz Willow's yarbs out clear to the roots. She hastily replanted it and continued her musings.

What do I care iff'n Bryce Chance didn't want to tell me what he was goin' to fetch? It ain't like he's trying to be mysterious. He's just naturally tight-lipped. He's so quiet; I reckon I'll hardly even notice he's not around.

Daisy's thoughts ground to a halt as she acknowledged the falsehood of that last one. She sat back on her heels and rubbed the nape of her neck.

True, Bryce was quiet, but it was hard not to notice him. The man had a presence that seemed to command her respect. He didn't need words to make his opinion known—the way he stood or even shrugged spoke volumes.

Jamie'll miss him. Jamie always notices even when people simply aren't feeling their best. Bryce didn't wake him to let him know he won't be around for a couple days.

Jamie'd looked around for Bryce at breakfast and asked her, "When go holp Byce wit eggs?"

"Not for a coupla days, Jamie." Daisy couldn't read the look in her son's eyes. "Bryce has to be gone for a while, but he'll come back soon. He has to fetch something for Hattie and Logan."

After the initial surprise, Jamie had thought for a moment.

His "oh" came out so serious it near broke my heart. But what do I expect? Bryce doesn't owe me and Jamie anything. Shore, he's spending time with us now, but we all know it won't last. As soon as I've made enough lace, I can get us back to our land and rebuild a roof o'er our heads. It won't be as nice as the one before, but it'll do, and we won't be beholden to Hattie and Miz Willow no more.

It would take a long time—probably all through the winter months—to make enough lace. Logan would stay in the holler with his new bride, but Bryce hadn't made his plans to go back to California any kind of secret.

Yes, the more I think of it, the better this is. It'll get Jamie used to the idea of his friend leavin' for good. It's nice to have Bryce around, but we can't rely on him forever. She tugged hard on one particularly stubborn weed. *We don't need to. I can take care of us myself.*

The weed snapped from its roots, the sudden lack of resistance toppling Daisy backward. She scrambled up and stared at the scraggly mess of leaves.

"Stubborn thing," she muttered, shaking her head. "Don't you know when to let go, and when to hold on?"

"Hold it steady, right there," Daisy directed.

"Got 't!" Jamie's brow furrowed as he held the dustpan steady.

Daisy moved the pile of dirt from the wooden floor to the dustpan with one swift, short stroke. This was the only house she'd ever been in with real floorboards. She could sweep these, scrub them, keep them nice and clean for Jamie. That way, Jamie wouldn't get so dirty when he scooched around the house. It also gave him a steady surface to stack his blocks in complicated piles.

"Perfect!" Daisy lifted the dustpan victoriously, and Jamie clapped as she went outside to empty it. Popping back a moment later, she tickled his tummy. "Yore such a good helper, Jamie. Thankee."

"We good teeaa. . ." Jamie took a breath and tried the difficult word again. "Teeaamm."

I wonder where he heard that? Daisy passed her hands through his soft blond hair. "We do make a fine team."

"Byce say so." Jamie smiled up at her.

"Ah." *That explains it.*

"Do t'gether," Jamie recited carefully, "wurk dun better."

"Yore a big help. You do a lot for yore ma." Daisy waited for him to look at her. "Yore a good boy and a fine worker all by yoreself. Remember that, Jamie."

" 'Es, Ma." Her son nodded happily as Daisy sloshed some water onto the floor and they began to scrub.

They giggled and made zigzags and circles as they cleaned. Jamie liked to help clean, and this was one of his favorite things about Miz Willow's house. He could help with the floors without anybody carrying him.

Daisy handed him a dry rag and took one herself. She dried a swath through the middle of the cabin, while Jamie scooched around to help mop up the water. After they finished, Daisy helped him get ready for bed. It'd been a long day.

As she wove her needle through the intricate mesh of the netting she used to create fine filet lace, Daisy fumed. She'd always tried to let Jamie think he could do things as well as anybody else.

"Wurk dun better. . . ." The words echoed in her mind and rankled. Bryce had no call to tell her son the work he did alone wasn't good enough. Come to think of it, he'd said something like that to her the other day—about asking for help. Well, she didn't need Bryce's help, and she didn't want Jamie thinking he did, either. She and her son worked hard, loved each other, and made it through each day grateful for what they had. It might not be much, and they might not do things the way everybody else did, but her son was just as good as any other boy in the holler. And she wouldn't allow Bryce to let Jamie think otherwise.

When that Bryce Chance gets back, I'll have a little chat with him, Daisy decided. *We don't need him trying to change anything.*

"Yore fixin' to make a powerful change with this." The general store owner, Mr. Norton, thumped the big crate decisively.

"Yep," Bryce agreed, eyeing the crate with grave misgiving. It seemed a lot larger than he'd expected. Maybe they'd packed it in with a lot of stuff so it'd have safe shipping.

"Let's get 'er into yore wagon." Mr. Norton punctuated the order by narrowly missing the spittoon sitting outside the store. "Aw, now I'll hafta clean that."

Bryce doubted it. From the looks of that spittoon and the porch around it, Mr. Norton rarely cleaned it—but he missed often.

The enormous crate barely fit in the wagon, and even then, it took Bryce, Mr. Norton, and three other men who'd happened to see them struggling and lent a hand. Cast iron made for a heavy load.

"Thank you, gentlemen." Bryce slapped his hat back on his head before shaking their hands. He was set to go when he remembered something.

"Mr. Norton, would you mind bringin' out that mirror you already wrapped up?" He wondered what Daisy would say when he showed it to her. It was tangible proof that he'd listened. He'd probably get one of those glowing smiles of hers that made him feel warm clear down to his toes. He jumped onto the buckboard and flicked the reins. It was time to get back home.

Good thing I started out early this morning, Bryce reflected. The horses were having a rough go of it. *I understand why—the thing's heavier'n an ox stuck in a mudhole.*

He pulled the wagon over to the side of the road when he heard the unmistakable gurgle of a mountain stream. He unhitched the team and led them to the water, letting them drink their fill and cool off.

"There you go, girls. You've worked hard today, and we've still got a ways to go." Bryce spoke softly, patting the faithful mares' necks one after another. "I'll give you some sugar lumps later, after your rubdown. But first we've got to get back. Ready?"

Both horses nosed his palm one last time with velvety muzzles before giving soft whickers and turning around.

"Good girls." Bryce let them know how much he appreciated their hard work. Too many people expected animals to push, pull, and carry things for them without so much as a thank you. Some didn't even give them enough rest or food, either. Bryce shook his head at the thought. How could anyone look into the eyes of a horse and not know it deserved to be cared for in return for its loyalty and hard work? To Bryce's way of thinking, treating animals right just made good sense.

Refreshed by the break, the horses managed to trot a bit faster despite their heavy burden. Bryce came to the fork in the road just as the sun began to set. A few hundred yards farther, he pulled up to Miz Willow's barn.

CHANCE OF A LIFETIME

Bryce's stomach rumbled loudly as he unhitched the team. The horses deserved to be taken care of first—after all, they'd worked a lot harder today than he had! He'd just led them to their stalls when Daisy walked into the barn.

"Hello, Daisy." It was good to see her in her pretty blue dress. But something wasn't right. He noticed it in her gait—if she'd been a horse, he'd've figured she'd gotten a rock wedged in her shoe.

Chapter 6

Daisy walked toward Bryce stiffly, her arms crossed in front of her and her jaw set. To be sure, something had caused a hitch in her getalong.

"Bryce." Daisy didn't say another word until she stood in front of him.

He waited. No sense trying to find shelter until you knew which way the wind blew.

"We need to talk."

Uh-oh. Men never said that. Women did—and only when they were angry. Bryce knew from living on Chance Ranch with four sisters-in-law that if a woman said "We need to talk" it roughly translated to: "If I were a man, I'd've given you a shiner, but I'm more civilized than that, so I have to get the message across another way."

"All right." Bryce fought the urge to cross his own arms. The last thing he wanted to do was intimidate her. Whatever was on her mind, it was important to her, and that meant he needed to hear it.

"I know you're trying to be a friend to Jamie, and I appreciate it," she began.

There was a "but" lurking in there somewhere. Bryce waited it out.

"But. . ."

There it is. I knew it!

"I don't think I've been clear about the way I choose to raise my son." She paused to look at him expectantly.

He had no idea what she expected. Somewhere along the line, he'd managed to botch things up, but he hadn't a clue where. An uncomfortable silence filled the barn before Daisy let out an exasperated breath.

"I've tried my best to raise my son with the knowledge that he's as good as everybody else." She glared up at him, challenging him to disagree with her.

The lioness was protecting her cub. Daisy's eyes lit with an amber fire, glowing through in her indignation.

"He is just as good as everybody else," Bryce agreed readily. "Better than most, I'd say."

She visibly deflated. He'd stolen the wind from her sails. The anger left her eyes, leaving behind two empty pools of hurt. Bryce ached to hold her close. He'd caused her pain somehow, and he wanted to make it right.

"Then why did you tell Jamie he couldn't do things well enough by himself?"

"I never said that." Bryce felt as though he'd been punched in the gut.

"Yes, you did!" She blazed with anger once again. "You told him the work was done better if he did it with someone else!"

"Something's not right here. True, I tried to teach Jamie that working with someone isn't any cause for shame." The boy's ma already had an aversion to asking for help, but Bryce wanted Jamie to know it was all right.

"Work together is done better," Daisy chanted.

"Oh." Bryce finally understood. "Close, but not quite. I taught him that work is better when done together—it's more fun being part of a team. It makes the time go faster." A sudden thought chilled him to the bones. "I was so sure Jamie understood what I meant. Does he think I was saying he wasn't good enough?"

"No." Daisy practically shrank before his eyes. "I thought that's what you meant. Jamie said he and I were a good team when we swept the floor, and then he repeated that rhyme. . . . He swapped the words a little, but I'm the one who messed up the meaning." She bit her lip. "I'm so sorry, Bryce. I could hardly believe that you would think that, but my son. . ." Her voice trailed off.

"Is your priority." Bryce finished the sentence for her. "I understand you were protecting your own, Daisy. It was just a mix-up."

"Thanks, Bryce." She managed a tight smile. "I don't know how to make it up to you."

"I do." Bryce grinned. "What's for supper?"

<hr/>

How could I have been so foolish? Bryce Chance never gives anything to me and mine save kindness, and I repay him with accusation and suspicion. Daisy paced the floor as Miz Willow and Jamie slept, berating herself.

Do I trust him when he's never given me a reason not to? No, I jump to conclusions. Then do I ask him about it? Give him a chance to explain? No. I barge into his barn like a mother hen with my feathers ruffled, ready to peck him to death with my angry words. And after I've accused him of faults he doesn't possess, he understands. He forgives me and acts like I never spoke a rotten word to him.

He's a good and wise man, that Bryce Chance. Jamie's lucky to learn from him for however long he stays. I'm glad he's here. I jist wish I could say the same thing about myself. When I think of how I treated him, I could sink into the dirt like a worm.

"Tomorrow I'll do better," she resolved as she finally crawled into bed.

The next morning, Daisy awoke feeling better than she had in two days. Bryce was back, and better still, he hadn't insulted Jamie and never would.

Daisy jumped out of bed and hurried to get dressed. She'd make a huge mess of flapjacks to celebrate. It was going to be a wonderful day.

Bryce tapped on the door while she set the platter of food on the table. Miz Willow slid the comb through Jamie's hair one last time.

"Come on in," she called.

"Morning." Bryce stood for a second in the doorway as he always did, probably letting his eyes adjust. After the bright morning sunshine, the cabin seemed dim in comparison.

His broad shoulders filled the doorway, the sun catching his brown hair and giving it a rich glow. His image alongside Daisy's recollection of his kindness the night before made him seem larger than life as he stepped inside.

"Hi, Byce!" Jamie scooched urgently across the floor and flung his arms in the air.

Bryce didn't hesitate a second to scoop the little boy into his arms. "Mornin', Jamie."

"Mor'in'," Jamie repeated excitedly.

"Do you remember what I told you I'd bring back when I left?" Bryce leaned close and spoke in a loud whisper. Daisy heard every word.

So he had told Jamie he'd have to be gone for a short time. Jamie wasn't sad when she told him; he was remembering that Bryce had shared a secret with him.

Jamie glanced around the cabin at Daisy and Miz Willow before putting a finger to his lips.

"Not anymore, buddy." Bryce turned Jamie a bit so they both faced the women. "Now we get to tell them. We're going to be hauling in a. . ." Bryce nodded at Jamie to finish telling the surprise.

"Sofe!" Jamie threw his hands up in the air.

"That's right. A stove." Bryce set Jamie down at the table and sat beside him. "And not just any old stove. This one's for heating and for cooking."

"Glory be!" Miz Willow beamed at them. "The Chance family bought Hattie and Logan a kitchen range stove! What a surprise for when they get back."

"Wonderful!" Daisy exclaimed. Cooking would be a lot simpler with a stove, once she and Hattie learned to use it. "We'll have to move a few things. . . ."

"No, it's far too big to fit in Hattie and Logan's room." Bryce beamed. "Besides, the cooking is done in here anyway. Just makes sense."

Daisy couldn't stop smiling at that. It did make sense, and it made sure that everyone was included. A stove would mean a warmer winter for Miz Willow's rheumatiz and less chance for stray sparks. She'd sleep better knowing her son wouldn't face another fire.

After breakfast—Daisy noticed with satisfaction how Bryce happily polished off the last few flapjacks—she and Bryce went to open up the crate. Miz Willow had taken Jamie to visit with a few young children in the area.

"Shore is big," Daisy observed.

"I thought the same thing," Bryce admitted. "I hope it has a lot of packing straw inside for shipping."

"We'll see." Daisy grabbed one of the hammers to start prying off some nails.

"Wait a minute." Bryce stopped her.

"You want to start on the other side?" She craned her neck to get a better view.

"No. I want to show you something." Bryce handed her a flat package.

"It's for Hattie and Logan, but it was your idea." His smiled seemed a little shy. "Open it."

Daisy unwound the brown paper to uncover a framed mirror a little bigger than the one on Miz Willow's wall.

"You remembered!" She traced the wooden oval that was decorated with vines similar to those Otis Nye had carved on the wedding chest. "It matches the chest so well. Hattie will love it."

Bryce's grin filled her heart. He hadn't agreed that a mirror was strictly necessary, but he trusted her and was thoughtful enough to follow through. He surprised her at every turn.

"Let's go hang it above the washstand," he suggested.

She nodded, following him into the cabin. He pounded in a nail at the right height, and she reached up to hang it.

"Whoa." Bryce's hands covered hers as the frame slipped. The metal ring on the back of the frame hadn't caught on the nail.

He was so close, his arms reaching over her shoulders, his hands warm and rough on hers. Heat coursed through her. She hadn't been this close to a man since Peter died, and she had forgotten how safe and cherished it made her feel.

Why would she remember that now, with a man she already knew would leave soon? Bryce Chance was a good man, but surely he didn't feel anything for the plump widow with a four-year-old son. When Jamie was born, she'd become a mother. Why did Bryce remind her she was still a woman?

Daisy felt so soft against him, fresh and sweet like some kind of flower after the rain. Her hair brushed softly against his sleeve; her hands seemed so small and smooth beneath his.

Her surprise was reflected in the mirror. Daisy's golden locks and fair skin glowed next to his dark hair and sun-darkened skin. Her pink mouth opened in an *O* of surprise; her brown eyes looked deep and dreamy.

She made him feel big and strong, powerful to protect her against the world, and all he wanted was to hold her safe. He didn't realize he'd been holding his breath until Daisy slipped her hands from beneath his and moved away.

He stood for a moment, bereft, before sliding the mirror into place and clearing his throat. He stared into her eyes.

"Looks good to me." He didn't mean only the mirror, but Daisy didn't acknowledge what had passed between them.

"Jist right." She patted her hair. "Now let's go see about that stove." She led the way out the door, but Bryce didn't mind. Daisy was worth going after.

Chapter 7

Bryce hitched the horses to the wagon and had them pull the stove as close to the door as possible before tying the stove directly to the harness. It was the only way to get the box out of the wagon. Then he tackled trying to open it.

"There!" With a final heave of the crowbar, the front of the crate opened wide. Bryce stared at the stove, which took up almost the entire space inside the crate.

Whoever boxed it hadn't used a lot of packing straw; they hadn't needed to. The crate itself made a tight fit, with little chance the stove would slide around and become damaged.

"It's incredible!" Daisy walked around it, looking from every angle. "A wood-burning stove, a kitchen range top, and even an oven built right in!" She opened the oven door experimentally and peeked inside.

Bryce smiled at her excitement. The stove was a beauty all right, but he didn't see how he could move it. If it had come in pieces or could be disassembled, he'd have managed. As it was, the thing was fully constructed with the pieces welded together. It had already been difficult to ease it out of the wagon onto a haystack and down to the ground. Bryce didn't see how he could move it to the cabin.

"I'll go get the pie tins." Daisy rushed off before Bryce could ask her what she was talking about. She returned in a moment with four metal pie tins.

"Ready?" she asked expectantly, crouching beside one of the stove feet.

"For what?" Bryce hated to admit it, but he had no idea what she was doing.

"You lift up the edge, and I'll slide the pie tin under the leg. We do it four times; then we can slide the stove to the door." She blinked at him. "It's too heavy to lift."

"Right." Bryce hefted one corner of the stove. Pie tins weren't wheels. He had his doubts about this scheme.

Once the pie tins were in place, Daisy hopped around, pushing aside bits of wood to clear a path. When she gave the signal, Bryce got behind the stove and gave it a mighty heave, expecting the heavy thing to scarcely budge.

He just about ended up on the ground for his doubts as the thing slid a goodly distance.

"It works!" He couldn't hide his amazement. The metal pie tins made the stove slide smoothly across the hard-packed dirt. He'd never have thought of this in a million years.

"Of course it does," Daisy teased him with an amused grin. "So how about putting those pie tins to work?"

"Yes, ma'am." Bryce put his hands on the stove and slid it to the doorstep.

"We'll have to lift this monster to get it inside on the wooden floor," he mused. "I'll go in backwards and lift while you push it on the two back feet. It'll slide forward, and then I'll yank it inside."

"Sounds good."

Bryce backed into position, stepping inside and crouching to lift the bottom of the stove the requisite few inches. "Now!"

He pulled, Daisy pushed, and a resounding *cra—a—ack* rent the air as the stove lodged itself in the doorframe. Bryce let go, but the stove didn't move. He put his hands on the range and leaned over it to get a view from the outside.

"It's splintered the doorway," Daisy moaned, hovering close. She squinted and stepped back. "Mayhap if I try and yank it back—"

"Nothing doing," Bryce stated firmly. "If the weight of the thing itself won't tilt it, there's precious little you or I can do. The thing's about two inches too wide to get inside the building."

"What're we gonna do?"

"Stand back, Daisy," Bryce ordered. "I'm going to have to try and push it back out."

"All right, Bryce. Go ahead."

He gave the stove a quick shove, but the thing didn't budge. He put his weight into it, digging in with his feet and using all the force he could muster.

"I'm out of the way now," Daisy clarified.

Bryce couldn't help it. After three days of miscommunication, hefting, and transporting the stove. . .

"It's stuck," he admitted.

❧

"Stuck?" Daisy repeated dumbly. "Just how hard a push did I give that thing?" She walked up to the blocked doorway before venturing an opinion. "Mayhap if I wiggle it a little. . ." She grasped the edges and tried to move it from side to side, hoping to loosen the metal from where it jammed in the wooden doorframe.

She leaned back as Bryce leapfrogged over the stove and slid down the flat range to stand beside her. Together they looked at the very heavy problem.

"So. . .no new stove inside the cabin." Daisy spoke more to break the silence than to really contribute. This had her stumped.

"And no doorway at all," Bryce finished woefully.

"Miz Willow and Jamie will be back in a couple hours," Daisy fretted. "What are we going to do?"

"If we can't get the stove in," Bryce said, "we'll have to get the doorframe out. If you go to the far left corner of the barn, you'll find the toolbox. Bring that and an ax from the wall. I'll get back inside and start taking the door off its hinges to give us more work space."

Daisy watched as he carefully squeezed through the doorway, somehow managing not to bang his head on his way through. Then she hurried to the barn, found the tools, and brought them back.

Bryce had already popped the door off its hinges and leaned it against the far wall. She passed him the saw. He squinted at the frame and placed the saw a few inches above where the stove stuck out.

Daisy stepped back. The doorframe was made of three pieces; the two long ones connected by the short one at the top.

"Wait a minute! Why don't you try separating the door-jamb at the top? It's gonna be awful hard to saw hunks out of that frame."

"Hmm." Bryce stepped back and craned his neck upwards. "I see what you mean." He pulled over one of the benches. "Would you give me a hammer?"

She passed him one and watched as he pried loose the nails joining the wood together, then worked the top beam free. He clasped his hands around one of the sides and tugged.

Cre–e–eak. The wood protested ominously as Bryce tried to angle it a little. He hopped down from the bench.

"Easiest thing to do will be using a chisel to split the board longways, then pull it apart."

"All right." Daisy rummaged for a chisel and rubber mallet.

"The stove being jammed in already started a crack." Bryce ran his hand along the frame. "I'll continue it."

He was as good as his word. After expanding the crack, he asked for the crowbar and pried the wood apart.

"I'll take care of it from this side, Bryce." Daisy wielded the crowbar with precious little skill but more than enough determination. Soon she'd torn the last of the doorframe from around the stove.

"I think," Daisy panted, tossing the last fragment away, "this should be the first wood we burn."

Bryce's laughter rumbled over her, the deep sound sweeping away her frustration and making her see the humor in the situation. She started to laugh, too.

After they recovered, they managed to coax and shove the stove into the cabin. Daisy gathered the pie tins, and they pushed the cast-iron monster into place.

"Ah," Bryce drew out the appreciative sound, "the time and effort saved by modern technology."

Daisy was giggling again. They stood side by side, each with more splinters than they could count, surveying the ruined doorway.

"I won't be able to rebuild it tonight," Bryce assessed. "You, Jamie, and Miz Willow will have to sleep in Hattie and Logan's room tonight."

"Fine by me." Daisy stretched her aching arms. "Doesn't matter where I am. I'm shore I'll sleep jist fine."

Chapter 8

The next morning, after a quick breakfast of day-old bread and butter with milk, they all headed to the school building for church.

"Beautiful mornin'," Daisy remarked, toting Jamie on her hip.

"Yep." Bryce, his stride shortened so he wouldn't outpace her and Miz Willow, took in a deep, appreciative breath of the fresh mountain air. He held out his arms to take Jamie, giving her a much-needed rest.

"We cain fix the door tomorra. I aim to enjoy the day." Daisy hoped Bryce felt the same way. He might be used to hauling heavy loads—his broad shoulders and strong arms certainly attested to that—but she wasn't. That stove had been far too heavy, and she, for one, was glad to have a day of rest before tackling the broken doorframe.

"Right."

"Good thing we're goin' to the Lindens' for Sunday dinner." Miz Willow chuckled. "I don't know what I would've done iff'n Otis Nye, Rooster, and Nessie were expectin' to come to our place. No door to open for 'em, stove ain't ready to cook on, and it blocks my hearth! It'd be a fine sight to see me and Daisy rushin' around like that."

"True." Daisy gave a small laugh, but the rueful look on Bryce's face stopped her. "It's been a lot of work, but that's a mighty fine gift. I reckon having such a grand stove'll be more'n worth the wait. Bryce's been so clever in figgurin' out how to get the thang inside, the rest should jist fly by. Ev'rythang'll be up and runnin' afore Hattie and Logan get back."

Bryce's shoulders relaxed, and though he didn't smile outright, Daisy knew he understood her appreciation. He'd worked hard and deserved for it to be acknowledged.

In a few minutes they slid onto their bench and bowed their heads while Asa Pleasant, filling in for the circuit preacher, prayed.

"Lord, we ask to feel Your presence in this place as we gather together to worship You and strengthen our knowledge of all You are. Please bless this congregation and let it be a fruitful time. Amen."

Lord, please give me the strength I need to take care of Jamie. I have a lot of work ahead of me to provide for my son. Let me have the will and the determination to see it through. Holp me to figgur out what I need to do. Amen.

Daisy rose to her feet, cradling Jamie on her hip, as they began to sing the hymns. *Funny how I cain't hear Bryce's voice so much as feel it next to me. Like a cat purring. I know it's there, happy and reassuring, but it ain't like Asa's raspy voice up there.*

As they began a favorite folk song, Bryce's comforting rumble stopped. Daisy could tell he was listening hard, trying to catch the words:

> *"Enoch lived to be three hundred and sixty-five,*
> *And then the Lord came down and took him up to heaven alive. . . ."*

They moved through the other verses about Paul being freed from prison, Moses and the burning bush, Adam and Eve, each time coming back to the chorus:

> *"I saw, I saw the light from heaven*
> *Come shinin' all around.*
> *I saw the light come shining.*
> *I saw the light come down."*

By the third time they sang the refrain, Bryce joined in with them. Daisy smiled as the praise rolled out of him so low and deep it flowed under all the other voices. *His sangin' fits him—quiet and not showy but powerful strong.*

⚮

The next morning, Miz Willow took Jamie out to the garden for an outdoor lesson. Daisy had taken care of the herb garden, but the vegetable garden needed weeding.

Bryce brought out a yardstick and wrote down the dimensions for the doorframe. Then he and Daisy checked out the lumber left over from building Logan and Hattie's new home. After selecting three pieces of the right width, she and Bryce worked at sawing them to be the proper length. Bryce finished the first two before coming over and polishing off the one she hadn't gotten through.

"I don't know how you do it," Daisy marveled aloud. Bryce's shoulders rippled beneath his tan cambric shirt as he worked the saw.

"Practice," Bryce answered as he finished. "Lots and lots of it."

Next they needed to sand the wood smooth. Bryce handed her a piece of sandpaper, and they got to work.

Daisy took the rough paper and scrubbed at the lumber vigorously. She had enough splinters to last through the rest of the year.

"Easy." Bryce came up alongside her. He reached over and put his hand atop hers, leaning in and pulling back. "You don't have to attack it. Simple, straight strokes."

Daisy's arm tingled. She turned her head the slightest bit and barely refrained from burying her face in his chest. Bryce smelled so good, like sawdust and leather and strong soap.

He let go, and Daisy had to force herself to keep sanding. Suddenly, the afternoon felt cold. She hoped this project would be finished soon—she didn't know how much longer she could work alongside him and not push back that errant lock of wavy brown hair that teased his strong brow.

❦

As Bryce continued working, he noticed how rough the sandpaper was. He'd used it often in his life but never realized how coarse the paper felt beneath his fingertips. Daisy's hand had been so soft—had she noticed how rough his own palm was?

He shook away the pesky thoughts. He'd never met a woman any finer than Daisy Thales. She didn't demand he entertain her or even expect him to try to fill the air with meaningless chitchat. Daisy made him feel comfortable—except for when being near her made him ache to hold her closer.

And he couldn't. Strong though his attraction to her had grown, Bryce had noticed how Daisy made it more than clear she didn't need him. She'd already lost the man she loved, worked hard to build a life for herself and her son, and was trying to regain what the fire took from them. Daisy had made her plans, and he wasn't a part of them. When he left, it would be easier to quell his urge to take her in his arms, but now, while she filled the house and his mind, he struggled.

Lord, I know this is not the woman for me. She isn't interested in me and has no place for a new husband in her plans, much less one who would take her and her son from everything and everyone they love. My home is Chance Ranch, my place beside my family. Daisy works so hard to make a life for her and Jamie here. They've lost so much. I can't pursue her with the aim of making them leave behind the few things they have. I won't try to make her feel for me what I feel for her. Lord, please take away my longing and let me enjoy her and Jamie's friendship instead. Amen.

After a quick break for a hasty lunch of bread, cheese, and apples—with the stove not hooked up and still blocking the hearth, no cooking could be done—he and Daisy finished reconstructing the doorframe.

Daisy shut the door, then opened it again before passing judgment. "Perfect!"

"Snug, but it shouldn't stick." Bryce nodded. It would hold out drafts and danger, keeping Miz Willow—and Daisy and Jamie—warm and safe.

"I'll have the stove installed tomorrow morning," Bryce planned aloud. "We'll need to move it over near the table for tonight so it doesn't block the heat or the beds. Where are those pie tins?"

"Jist a minute." Daisy rummaged around on the shelves and pulled them down. After they'd slid the stove to the foot of the bed, she put her hands on her hips. "Seems to me I better get some supper going."

"I'm not going to argue with that." Bryce laughed. They'd worked hard for two days. A hearty meal would go a long way to renew his strength.

He left her bustling around the hearth and went to clear up the area where they'd prepared the lumber. He threw the scraps on the woodpile, which would need attention. He and Logan hadn't cut nearly enough to last the cabin through a long mountain winter, and that was before they'd put on the addition, which would need heat through the cold months, as well.

He gathered the sawdust and added it to the barrelful he and Logan had collected already. Sawdust was good for the stables—coated the floor and helped with the barn smell.

As he worked, the crisp crunch of fallen leaves beneath his boots caught his attention. Autumn, bringing with it bold colors of gold and red, had touched the holler. Soon the fall shades would take the place of all the green of summer. Bryce had to leave before winter; his time here was growing short.

Which meant he had to make the most of it. He fetched a rake from the barn and attacked the leaves, drawing them into a single pile.

Not big enough. Bryce had already cleared the way from the barn to the cabin, but the pile didn't yet suit his purpose. He went around the barn and on the other side of Hattie and Logan's room to gather more leaves. He corralled them into one huge pile—big as a small haystack—in the middle of the cleared area.

"Can I borrow Jamie here for a minute?" Bryce stuck his head through the doorway. "I need his opinion on something."

Jamie looked at his mama with the big brown eyes so like hers. Bryce saw Daisy hesitate, then smile.

"Of course." She gave her permission without asking Bryce what he wanted to do.

Good. She was learning to trust him. She needed to loosen the apron strings a little so Jamie could try more things.

"Why don't you come with us?" Bryce scooped the little boy into his arms and tromped back outside. He knew Daisy followed.

He stopped just outside the door and made a show of surveying the land. Jamie's big eyes looked around eagerly.

"Nope. Guess I must've left it a little farther away." Bryce turned past the side of the cabin and stopped again. He smiled as Jamie peered around excitedly. Daisy cast a quick look around, then, seeing nothing, sent Bryce a questioning glance.

"Hmm. . .I know I left it around here somewhere." Bryce made a show of looking around before turning the corner once again and letting out a triumphant "Ha!" He bounced Jamie a bit. "Now isn't that the biggest pile of leaves you ever saw in your life?" Bryce waited for the little boy's nod.

"Do you know what we do with leaf piles?"

Jamie shook his head.

"Well, I'd better show you!" Bryce held Jamie aloft. "Ready?"

Jamie barely nodded when Bryce tossed him high in the air, sending the shrieking boy toppling into the massive pile of leaves.

Chapter 9

J amie!" Daisy screamed as she ran to the pile of leaves. What if he'd hit his head or broken an arm? Her baby lay shrieking in fear and probably pain, or—

Laughter! Jamie rolled around in the huge pile, flailing his arms and twisting around to make the leaves crunch. As she knelt beside him in the pile—even under their weight, neither touched the hard ground—her son gathered handfuls of leaves and threw them up to shower around them.

"F–un!" Jamie giggled when he got back enough of his breath. He struggled to sit up on the shifting pile, then gave a few experimental bounces.

"Oh," Daisy gasped and gathered him close. Praise the Lord he wasn't hurt. She'd heard that piercing shriek and thought the worst.

"Go." Jamie wriggled out of her grasp and flopped back in the leaves.

Daisy drew a deep breath and stood up. She turned around to find Bryce regarding her with those deep blue eyes of his. She smoothed back her hair and walked up to him.

"You gave me a fright, Bryce Chance," she said, admitting what he already must know.

"I'd never hurt Jamie," he responded in a low voice, so the little boy wouldn't hear.

"I know," Daisy apologized in those two words. "I heard him shrieking like that, and I was afeared. . . ." Her voice trailed off as they both watched her son happily crunching leaves. "I've never heard him laugh like that."

Jamie smiled almost all the time, always ready with a giggle to lift her heart. But this spontaneous cry of joy, the adventurous yell of a little boy exploring the world, was new. For both of them.

She looked around. It was early in the season to have raked up so much foliage. Bryce had purposely gone all around the barn and house to make a pile big enough so Jamie would be safe. He'd thought up a way to give Jamie a new experience and make the little boy feel daring without danger. She'd never have thought of something like this.

"Thankee, Bryce." She remembered his apparent discomfort when thanked, only after the words were spoken. *I hope I didn't embarrass him again.*

"You're welcome." Bryce grinned at her, his easy acknowledgment warming her heart.

"Ag'n?" Jamie's eager question caught their attention.

"I don't know." Daisy surveyed the flattened and scattered pile doubtfully.

"Hold on, buddy." Bryce hauled Jamie out of the pile and deposited him in Daisy's arms. He grabbed the rake he'd probably used in the first place and busily set about reconstructing the pile. He reached for Jamie, and Daisy willingly gave him up.

"Wait." Bryce sat Jamie down where he could lean up against the wall. "I think something's missing."

Too late, Daisy realized what Bryce intended as he headed her way. She let out a flustered "Eek!" as his strong hands closed around her waist. She didn't have time to enjoy the sensation before she went sailing through the air and crunching through the leaves.

"Bryce Chance!" she blustered, struggling to extricate herself.

"Yes?" He stood over her, holding Jamie.

"This was supposed to be for Jamie." She tried to scowl but couldn't manage it in the face of her baby's delighted smile.

"You're right." Bryce jumped in beside her, sending Jamie crashing though the leaves and into her arms.

She laughed so hard her sides hurt, and Jamie giggled right along. Finally, she was able to stand up and move Jamie to the edge of the pile. She needed to go check on dinner. She was about to tell Bryce as much when he started climbing out of the flattened mess, but then she changed her mind.

"Your turn." She planted her hands on Bryce's broad shoulders and shoved until he toppled back.

Jamie's laughter rent the air once more as he scooched over and pushed more leaves on top of Bryce. Daisy couldn't remember the last time they'd had so much fun.

❧

"Whew," Bryce breathed as he leaned back and stretched. "I'm so full I couldn't eat another bite."

"I should hope not!" Daisy smiled to soften the words.

"Nothin' left even if yore stomach could hold it." Miz Willow looked at the empty dishes on the table.

The healer has a point, Daisy reflected. Bryce alone had packed away three biscuits slathered with butter, two bowls of stew, and almost half of her fresh-baked apple pie.

She watched as he gave his stomach a satisfied pat, only to have a wince crease his face.

"Too full, Bryce?" She knew he was startled by the look he gave her.

"Nah. Can't get enough of your fine cooking, ladies." Bryce held up his left hand. "Stubborn splinter." He massaged the area around the wound.

"Why didn't you say so?" Miz Willow straightened up and came back with tweezers and some witch hazel. She filled a bowl with warm water. "Put yore hand in that for a mite, and the wood'll swoll up so it cain be picked out. Daisy'll hafta do it." The old woman looked ruefully at her hands, so gnarled with years of work and late rheumatism.

Daisy cleared the table as Bryce obediently stuck his hand in the bowl. It didn't fit, so he stuck his palm into the water with his fingers rising up out of the bowl.

I hope I cain get it without hurtin' him, Daisy fretted. *I should, after all the time I done spent doin' fine needlework.*

The memory of his hands on her as he caught the mirror and later taught her to use sandpaper sent a shiver down her spine. Keeping steady while she felt the strength in his work-roughened palms would be far more difficult than embroidering lace.

After Miz Willow declared he'd soaked long enough, Daisy patted the area dry and looked at the splinter. The offending piece of wood, now plumped with water, made a dark, jagged path down Bryce's palm near his thumb. She slid her right hand beneath to hold it steady in the light before gingerly grabbing the edge of the wood with the tweezers. She held her breath as she tugged the splinter, having to work it to the sides a bit before it slid out. Blood filled the line made by the splinter as she cleansed the wound with witch hazel.

He didn't flinch or make a sound, even though it had been the biggest splinter Daisy had ever laid eyes on. *Must've hurt somethin' awful.*

∞⚬∞

He could hardly feel it. The second Daisy touched his hand, the pain lessened. When the trickle of blood stopped, Daisy released him.

"You're left-handed," Bryce spoke the realization aloud. She'd held his injured hand in her right and used the left to work the tweezers. How had he not noticed it before? Little wonder she'd had so much trouble with the saw—he'd had Daisy using her right hand.

"Yes. Always have been." Daisy gave the witch hazel back to Miz Willow.

"I never noticed before—I would've given you a different saw. Why didn't you tell me?"

"Didn't think it was important." She visibly bristled. "I don't need any extry help."

This is the way she lives her whole life. Not speaking up when she needs help, not trusting anyone else to care for her or her son properly. Does she even realize how thoroughly she cuts herself off from other people? She goes to church and teaches her son Bible verses, but Daisy relies only on herself. Who am I to point out her flaws when I'm not staying around anyway? Lord, she's been hurt and survived a lot of loss, but she still needs to lean on You.

∞⚬∞

It took the better part of the next day to get the stove set up and functioning properly. Bryce could hardly make heads or tails of the blurry, smudged instructions, so he ended up learning by trial and error.

Finally, Bryce stood back and surveyed his work. They'd put it in the original hearth cavity, but not all the way. The range and oven poked out for easy use. All in all, it hardly took up any more room than the original hearth, and it would work a lot better.

"Nice," Daisy said appreciatively.

"I hope so." Bryce scowled at the troublesome machine. "Two days to fetch and haul it back, one to destroy the doorway and get it inside. Another to repair the damage, and one more to set the contraption up. Five days of work." Bryce shook his head. "I was beginning to think it wouldn't be ready before Logan and Hattie got back!"

Daisy burst out laughing. The hearty, happy sound made Bryce smile in and of itself, but. . .

"What's so funny?"

"Oh!" Daisy gasped and pointed to the stove. "I was jist thinkin' now might not be the best time to point out how we left two pie tins under the back legs."

"No!" Bryce hunkered down and peered at the floor of the hearth. Sure enough, two pie tins lay beneath the stove legs, halfway into the recess of the hearth.

"I already put together the stovepipe and connected it to the flue." Bryce hung his head in frustration. "I can't lift it now."

"Cain't lift what now?" Miz Willow stood in the cabin doorway.

"The stove, Miz Willow." Daisy gestured to the far wall. "We left two pie tins under the back feet."

"Hunh." Miz Willow squinted at her shelves for a minute. "Well, I had three, and Hattie brung a pair when she moved in, so I reckon we don't need 'em."

"Praise be." Bryce stood up and brushed stove black off his hands. "It's done then."

"Good thing, too." Miz Willow turned back outside to resume her lesson with Jamie. "Logan and Hattie'll be back tomorra."

Chapter 10

Daisy didn't see Hattie or Logan until the next night. But when the newly married couple arrived, they were tired and decided to go straight to bed. Daisy and Bryce met them in the barn to help unload the wagon and settle in the horses.

"It's late, and we ate some jerky and biscuits on the ride here," Logan explained.

"It's good to be home." Hattie yawned, but despite being tuckered out, she glowed from the time spent with her new husband.

Daisy felt a surge of gratitude toward Logan Chance for seeing beyond her sister-in-law's barrenness to the worth of the woman herself. He'd made Hattie happier than Daisy had seen her since before Horace Thales passed on.

Now that Hattie's remarried, she's not a Thales anymore, Daisy realized. *I wonder if that means we aren't sisters-in-law no more. Not that it matters. Hattie will always be kin in my heart.*

"Daisy and I'll help you carry in your bags," Bryce offered, winking at Daisy.

Ignoring the flutter caused by that wink, Daisy nodded and gathered up the luggage and purchases the newlyweds had brought home.

When they got to the cabin, Bryce opened the door but hung back near Daisy to let the happy couple inside first. They wearily headed straight to their room, completely missing the fact that the new stove now dominated the hearth. Daisy and Bryce exchanged a shocked look. He held a finger up to his lips, and she nodded. It could wait.

The glow from the small fire Daisy had set in the hearth in the newlyweds' room bathed the finished place.

"Look, Logan!" Hattie turned around to take everything in, still holding a saddlebag clutched to her chest. "The quilt is on the bed, and they moved the carved trunk." She dropped the saddlebags onto Logan's desk and walked over to the washstand. "Daisy, you hung the curtains and our new towels! What's this?" Hattie traced the carving around the mirror. "It's beautiful!" She enveloped her friend in a warm hug.

"We thought it'd be a nice surprise." Daisy hugged her back.

"You put up the mantel." Logan ran his hands across it. "And hung the pegs." He turned to beam at Bryce and Daisy. "You two finished everything!"

"Not everything." Bryce shrugged off the praise, but Daisy could tell he was pleased with their reaction.

"We put things in order," Daisy agreed, "but it takes love to make a house a home."

"With Hattie by my side and good friends around us"—Logan put an arm around his wife and smiled at everyone—"I think we've got a good start."

The next morning, Hattie made her way into the cabin's main room to help prepare breakfast. After hugging Miz Willow and swooping down on Jamie for a quick kiss on the forehead, she turned to the hearth.

"Is that a. . ." Hattie couldn't find the words, her blue eyes wide as saucers as she approached the new stove.

Daisy watched in silence as Hattie looked it over from top to bottom, holding out her hands to capture the fire's warmth. She waited until Hattie opened the oven door and sent the smell of rising cinnamon rolls swirling through the cabin.

"The Chances had it shipped to Kentucky from clear across the country," Daisy explained. "Bryce fetched it and hauled it back here while you were gone."

"It's wonderful," Hattie breathed, her eyes shining. "It looks complicated, though. I hope it wasn't too much trouble."

Daisy couldn't hold back the laughter that welled up at Hattie's innocent statement.

"What's got you laughing so hard, Daisy?" Logan asked as he and Bryce came inside.

Daisy couldn't catch her breath enough to repeat Hattie's words.

"I don't know." Hattie shook her head in confusion. "I just told her I hoped they didn't have to go to too much trouble to bring in the new stove."

Daisy almost had the spurts of laughter under control when Bryce's deep chuckles made her lose her composure again. They were the only ones who knew just how funny it was.

"I don't get it." Logan shrugged and walked over to inspect the stove. "Hey, are those pie tins under there?"

Daisy and Bryce just shook their heads and laughed harder as Miz Willow took over.

"What of it? I cain't think of a better place for a pie tin than the hearth!"

"How was yore honeymoon, Hattie?" Daisy asked after the men had finished breakfast and gone off to do chores. She shifted Jamie to her other hip. He was getting big.

"Wonderful!" Hattie's one-word answer said it all. Logan treated her right, and she was happy with the life she'd chosen.

"Good." Daisy stopped as Hattie stooped to harvest some leaves for her medicine satchel. "Meet anyone interestin'?"

"Yes. Jack Tarhill is a real sharp businessman with a good eye for detail." Hattie stopped talking and looked Daisy in the eye. "He noticed the new lace collar on my green dress and asked where I'd purchased it."

"That's nice." Daisy enjoyed hearing that such an astute man would remark on the quality of her work.

"Daisy, I know you've been doing business with Mitch Flaggart for years, but Jack asked me to try and change yore mind." Hattie waited for a response.

"I've relied on Mitch since I was jist a girl and Mama traded her lace with him." The lessons on making lace were some of Daisy's fondest memories of her mother. She loved it when the two of them sat quietly, needles moving rhythmically as they created something beautiful.

"Yep. But he's getting on in years, Daisy." Hattie paused, and Daisy nodded to acknowledge it was harder for Mitch to make the trip to Hawk's Fall—and would be harder still to get to Salt Lick. "And the fact of the matter is, Jack reckons he cain get a fine price for yore work."

The figure Hattie quoted stopped Daisy in her tracks. *So much money. I cain't cipher, but even I cain tell the difference is impressive. I hate to leave Mitch in the lurch, but I have to do what's best for Jamie and me.*

"He knows I work collars and veils and table runners—not christening gowns or hoods?" Daisy had to make sure the market was right. *Filet Lacis,* while stunningly intricate, wasn't pliable enough to use for those things. Tatted lace worked well, but Daisy didn't know that method.

"I tole him as much," Hattie affirmed. "He says it's hard to find yore fancy handmade lace here in the States. Iff'n yore agreeable, he won't have to pay such hefty trading taxes, so you'll both come off well."

"That's good." Daisy nodded as much to herself as to Hattie and absent-mindedly stroked Jamie's hair.

"He said summat about how yore lace is different than even the stuff he ships over. Summat about it going the other way?" Hattie puzzled aloud.

"I do it backward on account of bein' left-handed." Daisy smiled. She'd practiced enough with Mama to do it with her right, but she worked so much faster using her left.

"He says as how that makes it more rare." Hattie smiled.

"I suppose it might be so, but plenty of other thangs are more precious," Daisy said. "Thangs like family and friends."

❧

"What've you decided to do about your share of Chance Ranch?" Bryce asked Logan as they mucked out the stalls later that morning. Each of the six brothers held equal stake, and Logan was owed his due even though he didn't plan to return.

"I telegraphed with Gideon and Paul while I was in Louisville," Logan admitted. "We're thinking the best thing to do is buy me out. I'll take a few of the horses and a few head of cattle. Whatever my share of land and other livestock amounts to, I'll take half the money value of what I'd get after taxes if we were selling it all outright."

"Only half?" Bryce echoed. "You're entitled to all of your portion, Logan."

"I know, but I'm not going to be around to work it. Besides, I'm the youngest, so we all know there was some time when I didn't pull enough weight for the equal split." Logan grinned happily. "Truth is, I've got the business started up right here, and Hattie and I won't hurt for money. We have land, friends, steady income, and purpose. She's the healer, keeps the bodies around here hale and hearty. I negotiate trades and keep their finances healthy. That's more'n enough for any man."

"I understand." Bryce thought of all the new Chance children. The next generation would be much bigger than the six brothers who started out at Chance Ranch. They'd decided long ago that, regardless of how many children each brother had, the land would be redivided equally among their progeny when the time came ripe. Every Chance son and daughter would hold equal stake once more. Logan wouldn't have any children, so it made sense to let his brothers buy him out.

"I can't believe I'll be going back without you." Bryce spoke gruffly, slapping his brother on the shoulder. "Things just won't be the same."

"When things stay the same," Logan mused, "it means you're not growing. I hope Chance Ranch keeps on growing. I know I can depend on you to take care of things."

When did my baby brother become so serious and grown-up? He's a man now with a wife and a business. Logan's found his place and his purpose. I always figured mine was Chance Ranch, but I thought the same for Logan and was wrong.

Bryce saw Daisy walking with Hattie across the yard. *Seeing Daisy tugs something in me, especially when I think of leaving and never seeing her or Jamie again. Could those be growing pains?*

"Pretty, isn't she?" Logan had followed his gaze.

"Absolutely," Bryce agreed so fervently that Logan looked at him askance.

"She is my wife, Bryce." A steely glint lit Logan's eye as he planted his feet a bit wider.

"And I'm happy for you." Bryce tried to calm Logan down. "But there's nothing more beautiful than seeing women playing with a child."

Logan looked again toward the women, where Daisy held a squirming Jamie as Hattie tickled him. "It's a fine sight." Logan relaxed as he said the words. "But all the same, I'm happy to have Hattie all to myself."

"So I noticed," Bryce teased his brother with a grin. *But I can't imagine Daisy without Jamie. He brings out the loving mother, the strong lioness, the laughing girl, and the gentle homemaker in her. Jamie's a great kid, and he makes Daisy a better woman.*

"How much wood did you get cut while we were gone?" Logan's question snapped Bryce back to their conversation.

"About that. . ." Bryce launched into a shortened version of how the stove monopolized their week. "Between moving and setting up the stove and repairing the doorframe, I didn't get so much as a full cord cut."

"So that's why you and Daisy couldn't stop laughing this morning," Logan reasoned with a big grin. "I can't believe one little stove made you go through all that hassle."

"Little?" Bryce drew himself to his full height and jabbed a finger at his brother's chest. "Why don't you go try to haul that thing around?"

"Sorry!" Logan put his hands in the air. "It is pretty big."

"And heavy," Bryce added. "Thing's made of solid cast iron all welded together."

"Hmm. I wondered how it managed to survive all you put it through!" Logan laughed and slapped his hand on his knee. "Come on, let's go get to work. Aside from the wood chopping, I've been thinking we need to build a second barn. If I'm going to transport those horses and cattle here from Chance Ranch, Miz Willow's barn can't hold them, and they won't survive the winter."

"Right." Bryce frowned at the thought of any domesticated animal left out to contend with the snowy chill of an Appalachian winter. "Any other work you want to get out of me?"

"I don't know." Logan pretended to give the matter serious thought. "Cabin, chopped wood for winter, impossible stove installation, new barn. Nope. That's it, but I'll let you know if I think of anything else!"

Chapter 11

*T*hunk. *Thunk. Clunk.* Bryce grinned at Jamie's efforts. The night before, Bryce had cranked the hand-held drill to force peg-sized holes through a small piece of wood. He filled the holes with pegs, only a single whack apiece, so they stuck up and needed to be driven in. Today he'd balanced the board on two bricks, sat Jamie down in front of it with a small wooden mallet, and showed him what to do.

The little boy had been banging with plenty of enthusiasm—if precious little accuracy—ever since. Jamie liked being outside, doing "man" work with them. The mallet clattered from his little hands to the opposite side of the makeshift worktable. Bryce put down the ax he'd been using to chop firewood and loped over to put the tool back in Jamie's hands.

"Tanks, Byce." The little boy beamed at him before holding the mallet with both hands and pummeling the wooden peg. The exercise was good to increase his arm strength and improve coordination.

"You're welcome, buddy." Bryce looked down. "You've already finished two of them? Good job, Jamie!"

"Fun." Jamie waved the mallet exuberantly before losing hold of it again.

"Hold on there." Bryce took the small tool. "I'll be right back." He made his way to the barn and grabbed the drill. The mallet's handle was small, so it didn't take long to make a hole through the end. Bryce grabbed some twine and headed back to Jamie.

"Here." He knotted the twine through the new hole, then looped the other end around Jamie's wrist. "Now you'll be able to get it whenever it jumps out of your hands. Mallets are tricky that way."

"Yes." Jamie nodded seriously. He dropped the wooden hammer over the side of the board, then pulled it back using the twine. "Wurks!" He beamed and began thunking at the pegs again. After a few clumsy swipes, he managed to knock one of the pegs farther in.

"Looks like you've got things under control," Bryce told him. "I'll leave you to it."

" 'Kay."

❦

"Boys drank that water faster'n fish." Hattie wiped her hands on a tea towel. "Working up quite a thirst out there."

"I'll bet." Daisy looked up from kneading bread dough. "Jamie all right? I

282

hope he ain't bothering 'em iff'n he gets bored."

"Happy as a raccoon with summat shiny." Hattie smiled. "Bryce drilled some holes and steadied in some pegs. Jamie's out there bangin' away with a tiny mallet."

"Oh?" Daisy hoped her son wouldn't come back from that little adventure with bruises dotting his hands. No, Bryce would watch over him. Jamie could have his fun and be fine. "That's nice." *I wonder how many times Bryce has had to pick up that mallet.*

"Works out well," Hattie said, answering Daisy's unspoken thought. "Bryce even drilled a hole in the mallet handle and tied some twine to it so Jamie can yank it back if it falls."

"That's clever of him. Right smart." Daisy dropped the dough back in a big bowl and covered it. "It's nice for Jamie to be out working with the men."

"Bryce doesn't say much, but he's a thoughtful one." Hattie slanted Daisy a look she couldn't decipher.

"He says plenty without running his mouth," Daisy defended. "A body cain't always rely on words."

"I know. It's why he's so good with the animals—he has a kind heart that speaks for itself." Hattie smiled. "He's taken an interest in Jamie. Logan would never have thought to do something like that peg board."

"Maybe not." Daisy smiled. "Logan's too busy holpin' grown folks."

"He does have a heart for the people of the holler." Hattie's love shone through her voice. "Bryce tends to the animals and the children. I noticed it at the sang when they first got here—children like bein' 'round him."

"Jamie shore does. He ain't had a man around afore." Daisy drew a deep breath. "It'll be hard on him when Bryce goes back to Californy."

"Maybe." Hattie shrugged. "I know Logan'll miss his brother greatly, and I've grown fond of Bryce."

"He grows on you." Daisy thought of how Bryce had quietly undertaken to spend time with her son and come up with ways for him to do things she'd never thought possible. "I didn't take much notice of him before yore wedding, but then, suddenlike, he's become a big part of Jamie's life."

"Jist Jamie's?" Hattie raised her eyebrows.

"All of us." That was the closest Daisy dared come to admitting how much she'd miss Bryce for her own sake, not just Jamie's.

"Seems to me a man don't go out of his way and befriend a child without good reason." Hattie looked meaningfully at Daisy. "From what I hear, betwixt sprucing up our cabin and takin' care of this wonderful stove, you two stuck together whilst Logan and me were off on our honeymoon."

"I. . ." Daisy started to deny it but quickly shut her mouth. He'd done a lot for her that she'd never asked. On those occasions when his hands closed over hers, a bolt of heat shot straight down her spine.

Cain it be that I didn't misinterpret the look in his eyes? Could a man like Bryce Chance—tall, strong, capable, and able to have any woman he wanted—possibly be interested in me? Shorely not.

"I see." Hattie found her answer in Daisy's silence. "What about you, Daisy? Could you find room in yore heart and family for a man like Bryce?"

Yes. The answer came so swiftly it shocked her. She closed her eyes to clear her thoughts. *But he's so different from Peter. How could I even think of caring for another man that way when the love of my life is gone forever?* Tears welled in her eyes.

"Don't talk nonsense, Hattie Thales—ahem, Hattie Chance." Daisy squared her shoulders and vigorously scrubbed the already-clean table. "Jist 'cause you have a happy second marriage, don't mean I'll get a chance."

"And here I was thinking that a certain Chance might be jist what you need." Hattie delivered that parting shot and sailed from the cabin.

"But yore wrong, Hattie," Daisy muttered even though no one was around to hear the words. "The last Chance is leavin' town. Soon."

◦◦◦◦◦

"A barn raisin'? At this time of year?" Hattie gave voice to the questions Daisy wouldn't ask. "What for? We've already got one!"

"I know," Logan placated. "But I'm taking my share of the ranch in part cash, part livestock, sweetheart. The milk cow's getting on in years, and the mule's come up lame. I aim to bring in a few head of cattle and some horses, but we don't have enough room in the barn as yet. They'll be arriving on the train's cattle car in two weeks. I've already arranged for the conductor to stop at the bend before Hawk's Fall so we can pick 'em up."

"We can't leave them outside with winter comin' on," Bryce added.

"Yore right." Daisy threw in her two cents. "We'll spread the word. Folks oughtta be glad to come and lend a hand, what with all Logan and Hattie done for 'em." Logan had come to the holler and used his affability to get to know folks personally. He found out who could carve and who could trap fine pelts, then went to Louisville to arrange selling it all. Daisy's lace would be the most recent addition, so she knew from experience just how grateful they all had cause to be.

"Holler's full of good people," Logan agreed. "Bryce and I've arranged for the lumber to come two days from now. Thick beams enough to build onto the existing structure. Between now and then, Bryce and I'll be carving a door outta the far wall so it'll all end up being one big barn."

"Yep." Bryce rocked back on his heels. "Going to get the word out. We'll be raisin' it next Saturday, if all goes well."

"Logan Chance, that's only four days from now!" Hattie shook her head in disbelief. "We have to get ready! You better hitch up the wagon. Daisy and I need to go to town to buy supplies. There'll be a lot of mouths to feed come Saturday, even if people bring vittles with them."

"No problem." Logan made his way toward the door. "That's why we told you early in the morning. We oughtta have plenty of time for a nice ride to the mercantile."

"Oh, no you don't." Daisy caught Bryce's arm as he followed Logan. "Hattie and I'll go. You and Logan have a lot of work ahead of you."

"What do you mean?" Bryce asked.

"Believe it or not"—Hattie bit back a grin—"we're gonna need those pie tins."

⚬⚬⚬

"Pie tins," Logan grumbled as he squeezed beside the stove. He was thinner than Bryce, so he had to contort himself into the hearth. "What on earth possessed you to use pie tins?"

"Daisy's idea." Bryce handed him the tools so Logan could start disassembling the stovepipe.

"Where'd she get a cotton-headed notion like that?" Logan demanded, clanking around.

"I don't know, but I'm mighty glad she did." Bryce jumped to Daisy's defense. "Just you wait until you try to move this thing. I never would've moved it more than a yard if it wasn't for her 'cotton-headed notion.' "

"All right, I didn't mean anything by it." Logan came as close to apologizing as anyone could expect. "But how'd you go and forget to take 'em off before you put it together?"

"Not sure." Bryce thought about how fast he'd worked to pull this whole thing off. He'd botched it so badly, he didn't want Daisy to think he was inept.

"Huh?" Logan craned his neck to stare at Bryce. "You must have been distracted by something."

"I don't know." Bryce wished his brother would quit staring at him and get back to work. "We tried so hard to get this thing together, it's not surprising we overlooked one tiny detail."

"We?" Logan kept right on staring.

"Daisy and me."

"Aahh." Logan raised his eyebrows. "Distracted by a woman. Makes sense to me."

"Hey, don't talk like that." Bryce started, surprised at his own anger. "Daisy wasn't in the way at all. I couldn't have gotten this thing up and running without her."

"I didn't mean she was in the way or messed up, Bryce." Logan grinned at his brother. "Sounds to me like it wasn't her fault at all. Just how much time have you two been spending together?"

"Daisy's an honorable woman," Bryce thundered.

"I know." Logan held up his hands in surrender. "But seems to me you've taken quite an interest in her son." He paused for a moment, but there had never been a time when Logan didn't speak the full weight of what was on his mind. "I think you've taken a liking to Jamie's mama."

"We've become friends," Bryce hedged.

"Just friends?"

"She's a beautiful woman with a fine boy." Bryce wouldn't come any closer to admitting his attraction. "Daisy's worked hard to build a life for herself and her son. I have a lot of respect for her."

"I see."

Bryce waited for Logan to say something else, but for once, his chatty brother worked in silence.

What does he see? Bryce wondered. *Since when does he let a subject drop without having the last word? Well, whatever it is he thinks he sees, he's wrong. Daisy doesn't need me, and I've got a life back in California. Doesn't mean we can't be civil to each other while I'm here. Logan's just twisted things in his mind.*

"Ouch!" Logan's head banged against the hearth wall.

"Well, what do you know?" Bryce teased. "That was a pretty loud clunk. Must be somethin' in there, after all."

Chapter 12

Pot roast?" Miz Willow sounded off.

"Warmin' in the oven," Daisy answered.

"Rabbit stew?" she demanded.

"Simmerin' on the range," Hattie responded.

"Mashed taters? Carrots?" Miz Willow peered at them.

"Taters keepin' warm on the stove next to the stew," Hattie said readily. "Carrots are already boiled and in with the pot roast."

"Bread? Corn bread? Biscuits?" The old woman read off her list.

"Four loaves, one pan, and two batches waitin' in the breadbox," Daisy ticked off.

"Another loaf in the hearth nook, up in the wall jist high enough so the stove doesn't block it, and another pan finishin' in the new oven," Hattie added.

"Coffee cake?" Miz Willow was obviously determined not to miss a thing. "Apple pies?"

"Two cakes covered on the table." Hattie pointed. "One pie coolin' on the windersill, and another bakin' in the old ash oven."

"Anything I missed?" Miz Willow looked around in satisfaction.

"We've got cool fresh milk and lots of coffee for drinkin'," Daisy mused. "We set out half a barrel of apples in the shade. Butter and honey are covered and on the table, along with preserves. The egg salad is keepin' cool in the well."

"And I'll have the cheese sliced and on a platter before you know it," Hattie finished.

"Well, ladies." Miz Willow beamed a gummy smile. "I'd say we're ready for the onslaught."

"Yes, ma'am!" Daisy and Hattie exclaimed in tandem before collapsing onto the benches. They'd stayed up through most of the night getting all the food ready for the barn raising, but it would be worth it.

Daisy closed her eyes for a moment before pulling herself up again. "I'd better go get Jamie. I hope he slept all right in the barn loft with Bryce." She turned to Hattie. "It was good of Logan to spend the night up there with them, making it a boys' night."

"Yes." Hattie smiled. "Almost makes me feel bad I didn't make him a special breakfast!"

"I think he'll live." Daisy cast a glance around the food-filled cabin and shared a laugh with the other women before heading out to the barn.

She tapped hesitantly on the door. What if they weren't up and dressed yet? She rubbed her eyes while waiting.

"Good morning!" Bryce flung open the door, striding out with Jamie in one arm and the eggs they'd gathered in the other.

"Morn'g!" Jamie echoed.

"Good to see you!" Daisy bit back a yawn and swung Jamie into her arms. "My!" She hefted him up and down until he giggled. "I think you've gone and grown since I saw you last."

"Uh-huh!" Jamie grinned before planting a kiss on her cheek.

"Did you have fun with yore sleepover?" Daisy directed the question to Bryce.

"Yep." Bryce nudged Jamie's shoulder. "After working all day and tucking in to dinner last night, we all just fell into our beds and slept."

"Sounds lovely." Daisy stifled another yawn. "He wouldn't have gotten much sleep in the cabin last night—we were making such a racket getting things ready."

"Oh?" Bryce's close scrutiny made Daisy want to scurry back inside to wash her face and brush her hair. "Didn't you get to sleep at all last night?" His concern showed in an uncharacteristic frown.

"A bit." Daisy lightened her tone and smiled. "We snatched a few minutes here and there in shifts. We made shore Miz Willow drifted off more often than she told us to let her."

"Well." Bryce smoothly took Jamie from her. "I'd say you should go catch a few minutes more. Folks won't be showing up for another hour or so. I'll watch Jamie, and I'm sure Miz Willow has things under control. Why don't you and Hattie go to her room and snooze for a bit? I'll knock on the door to wake you up when it's time."

"Thankee, Bryce." Too tired to turn down the generous offer, Daisy smiled at him.

As she and Hattie snuggled into bed for a quick nap, Daisy thought of how natural Bryce looked with Jamie in his arms. It was the last image she remembered before drifting off into a sleep too deep for dreams.

～⚬～

Knock, knock, knock. The pesky sound wouldn't let up, no matter how deeply Daisy burrowed into the pillows.

It cain't be time to rise yet! I jist shut my eyes!

"Daisy?" Bryce's questioning rumble caused her to open one eye.

Ooh. She swung her feet over the side of the bed and nudged Hattie. *Today's the barn raisin'. I wouldn't have had a wink of sleep iff'n it weren't for Bryce ordering me to sneak in a nap.*

"We're up!" Daisy called, reaching out for a deep stretch.

"All right." She heard him walk away.

"C'mon, Hattie." Daisy rubbed her friend's shoulder. "People are comin' for the barn raisin'."

"What?" Hattie sat bolt upright. "Oh! We'd better get goin'!" She scrambled out of bed and tossed Daisy the only other dress she owned. They quickly donned the fresh clothes and splashed their faces with cold water.

"Mercy." Daisy stared at her hair in horror. "Did I look like this before I went to fetch Jamie this mornin'?" she demanded of Hattie.

"Not quite," Hattie responded loyally, swiftly plaiting her hair into one long braid down her back. "But jist 'bout."

"How could you let me step foot outside lookin' a fright," Daisy wailed, hastily pulling the pins from her tresses.

"I look 'bout the same." A sly grin spread across Hattie's face. "Who're you tryin' to impress? Cain't be me, Miz Willow, Jamie, or Logan." She intentionally left out the only other person on the property that morning.

"Hobble yore mouth, Hattie!" Daisy raked her fingers through the worst of the snarls. "It ain't that I have anyone to impress. It's a matter of being ladylike!" *Though I don't want Bryce seein' me all disheveled.*

"Shore." Hattie drew out the word as she handed her friend the brush. "Well, whatever it is, you better hurry. I hear some folks startin' to arrive."

"No!" Daisy gasped, staring at her reflection in dismay. She finished brushing her hair and made a quick decision. She didn't have time to do anything but one long braid like Hattie's. *I cain get the snarls out, but how am I ever gonna get that man out of my hair?*

⤪⤨

Within a matter of minutes, the homestead went from empty to teeming with neighbors. Bryce stood alongside Logan and greeted everybody who pulled up, taking the horses over to the hitching posts they'd put up just for the day.

"Good to see you, Bryce." Asa Pleasant slapped him on the shoulder. "Glad to see you haven't left us just yet."

"I wouldn't miss this," Bryce answered. Asa was a good man—uncle—to Eunice and Lois, two of the MacPhersons' brides. But that was a story in and of itself. For now, Bryce was glad to see such a talented worker here to help raise the barn. Asa was one of the local carvers whose work Logan sold to a dealer in Louisville. Asa Pleasant's swan-neck wall hooks and hand-carved nativity sets were nothing less than works of art.

"Hey, Bryce!" Ted Trevor stood before him.

"Hello, Ted." Bryce looked around for Ted's twin brother. "Where's Fred?"

"He's around here somewhere." Ted shrugged. "Listen, we've whatcha call a minor disagreement you cain settle for us."

"Oh?" The comment piqued Bryce's interest.

"Most folks we've grown up with cain't tell the two of us apart, but you don't seem to have no trouble." Ted grinned. "I say it's 'cuz you noticed that I'm taller, but Fred is of the opinion that he's the handsome one. What's the reason?"

"Wait a minute!" Fred came dashing up alongside his brother. "You cain't ask him less'n we're both in front of him." He puffed out his chest, and Ted stood up as straight as he could and craned his neck. "All right. We're ready."

"Sorry, fellas," Bryce apologized. "But you're like two peas in a pod. Neither one is taller or shorter or more handsome."

"But I've only had my nose broke once!" Fred scowled at Bryce.

"Only on account of you bein' too lily-livered to climb that rockfall," Ted retorted.

"You mean havin' the good sense not to!" Fred shot back before they both looked at Bryce again. "So how cain you tell?"

"Fred has a scar on his right hand that you don't, Ted." Bryce watched both their faces crumple in identical disappointment. "But listen, I've got five brothers, and Logan's the one who looks least like me. People get us mixed up all the time back home. Don't mean a thing unless you let it."

"Right. So I'm the brave one," Ted crowed.

"And I'm the one with more sense than God gave a goat," Fred added. The two brothers shared a grin.

"Good enough." They spoke in tandem. "Thanks, Bryce!"

He watched as the two scampered off to get into some new mischief. The Trevor twins were three years younger than Logan, and Bryce had five on the pair of 'em. They were a rambunctious set but had their hearts in the right place.

"Bryce!" Ed Trevor, father to the twins, headed his way. "Jist the man I wanted to see!"

"How are you, Ed?" Bryce liked the good-natured hound-dog breeder.

"Wondered if you could see yore way clear to comin' down after church tomorrow. One of my older dogs whelped unexpected, and the litter came late, too. One of the dogs's a runt, too scrawny to make it through winter as is."

"I'll see what I can do, Ed." Depended on how strong the critter was. "What makes you think it'll be such a bad winter?"

"Spring came early this year, so the winter'll be rough. 'Sides, dogs' coats are comin' in extry thick. Gearin' up for the cold. God takes care of critters like that."

"Good thing we're getting this done today." Bryce spotted Otis Nye struggling to walk with his cane while carrying a sack. He quickly took the sack from the old man. "Where does this go?"

"To wherever yore puttin' the vittles." Otis thumped his cane for emphasis. "That's a ham."

"I'll take it to the kitchen for the women to decide where it goes," Bryce offered.

Otis nodded as he plunked himself down on a bench. "Good thing you and that brother of yourn didn't wait any longer for this barn. Gonna be a rough winter—I cain feel it in my bones. What're you waitin' for, boy?" Otis waved Bryce off. "Get goin'!"

Bryce pushed toward the cabin through what he thought of as a veritable herd of women. *No, wait a minute. I can't talk about women like that,* Bryce reminded himself, *even if they are all gathered in one nearly impenetrable mass, jabbering on and getting in my way. Would "flock" be any better? They do chatter and cluck like birds. No, I don't think they'd appreciate that, either.*

Bryce shook his head as he waded through the plumage—really, one of the women had droopy feathers on her hat that tickled his nose when he walked by. Women stumped him. If only all of them were as easy to be around as—

"Daisy!" He called her name as he saw her making her way into the cabin.

"Yes, Bryce?" She stopped. He loved to hear the sound of his name on her lips. She said it soft and careful, not short and clipped like so many others.

"Otis brought a ham." Bryce lifted the sack. "Where do you want me to put it?"

"I'll take it." Daisy reached out, and he slid it into her arms, his fingertips tingling as they brushed against hers.

Chapter 13

Daisy carried the sack inside, winding her way through the crush of people.

"I done brought you two roast chickens." Silk Trevor pointed to where she'd laid them out on the table. "Nice thang is, they cain be jist as good et cold."

"Thankee, Silk." Miz Willow rocked contentedly in her chair.

"We brung salad filled with vegetables we grew!" Young Lark Cleary plunked the bowl down.

"I cain't think on another thing we ain't got already," Hattie mused. "Look at that spread!"

"One more thing." Daisy grunted as she slid the bag onto the table bench. "Otis Nye sent this here ham."

"We'd best get to carvin' it then." Hattie handed Daisy a big, shiny new knife. "The barn raisin'll begin any minute now, and we don't want to miss it!"

I ain't so shore about that, Daisy disagreed. *The last time I attended a barn raisin', Peter worked alongside these men. His blond hair won't catch my eye in the crowd today. I won't have a man to take water to and smile with.* She bowed her head for a moment. *These women all around either don't know me or feel sorry for me. I cain't spend the day jabbering with them. I hate when Jamie and me don't have a place at big get-togethers. So many others don't know how to treat Jamie. When they talk at him like he's a baby, it cuts him deep. I know they don't understand that his mind's as sharp as this knife even though his words come out garbled, but that don't make it hurt any less.*

Daisy took a deep breath, relieved that the women had left the cabin. People would be pressing in on her, around her, all day. Normally that didn't get her goat, but since she didn't feel able to join in the conversation, it made her feel insignificant. *Invisible.* She'd rather be alone in the cabin working than with ten other women and just standing there with nothing to say or do.

"None of that now." Miz Willow's order cracked Daisy's thoughts.

"What? Am I doing this wrong?" She looked down at the platter of ham she hadn't been paying close enough attention to, but it seemed fine to her.

"Yore doin' somethin' wrong, child. But it ain't the ham." Miz Willow came close to stand beside her. "Yore cutting yoreself off from others before the day's begun."

"I'm not cutting myself off," Daisy denied. "I don't have to prove anything to these people. They all seem so nice, but I know what's under it." She squared her shoulders. "Jamie and me don't need their pity."

"That's jist what I mean," Miz Willow declared. "Yore rejecting the folk around here without even trying. You been cut off so long at Hawk's Fall, busy with Jamie, you ain't spent much time with others. You know a lot of these people. It ain't been five years since you moved from Salt Lick Holler with yore husband."

"Six." Daisy's voice cracked. *And nearly five of being alone. Taking the responsibility for a household and my son.*

"And now, here you are surrounded by good people. Are you talkin' to any of 'em?" Miz Willow demanded. "No. Yore retreating in silence while that attitude jist rolls outta you."

"What attitude? I'm simply minding my own business."

" 'Zactly. You mind yore own business and expect ev'rybody else to mind theirs." Miz Willow kept on. "So you tell yoreself how you and Jamie don't need folks' pity. How do you know they pity you? Do you pity yoreself?"

"No! I've worked hard for what Jamie and I got."

"Yore full of pride at yore own self-reliance, Daisy. You don't open yore heart and let people care about you." Miz Willow rested a hand on Daisy's shoulder. "We've all known loss, Daisy. We all need something."

"We lost our home, but we'll still make our way." Daisy spoke aloud the words she lived by. "We survive no matter what."

"Let me tell you somethin' I've learned from bein' around longer than yore pa cain remember." Miz Willow headed for the door. "Survivin' ain't livin'."

Bryce looked around. The Trevors, Pleasants, Peasleys, Ruckers, and Clearys had all shown up, along with some faces he recognized but couldn't put a name to.

"Looks like we're about to begin." Bryce found Logan, who was clanging a cowbell to get everybody's attention.

"All right. Looks like everybody made it." Logan surveyed the crowd with satisfaction. "I'd like to thank you all for comin' here today to help us raise this barn. I know it's a bit late in the year, but together we can get this done!" A few calls and whoops of agreement filled the air as he paused.

"We need the barn for the horses and cattle I'm having brought up. Now that I've decided to stay in Salt Lick Holler with my beautiful bride, Hattie." He stopped to blow Hattie a kiss. She blushed scarlet and motioned for him to continue.

"I'm fixing to set us up with my share of Chance Ranch. So it seems to me that you fine folks who're helping us out deserve something in return." While Logan paused to let that sink in, Bryce marveled at his brother's dramatic flair.

"We're asking the men to divide into teams. We're building on to the existing barn, so we'll have three walls. That means three teams. Bryce and I will make up one team—it's only fair we put up at least one of these walls! That means we need two more. When you have your teams together, Miz Willow will write your names down. First team to construct their wall wins the little mare." Logan pointed to the pretty brown pony tied to a post. The rest of the animals were grazing in makeshift corrals over the hill. The hastily made fences wouldn't hold them for too long, but they wouldn't have to after today.

Murmurs of surprise and excitement filled the air as people sought out friends to form teams.

"We've got a team right here, Logan!" Ed Trevor waved his hammer in the air. "Me, m' boys, and their uncle Asa." He turned to the crowd. "And we aim to win that pony!"

"Not if we have anything to say about it!" Nate Rucker called out the names of the men on his team.

"All right then. Otis Nye'll be our judge. Watch yourselves. He's got the keenest eyes in the holler." Logan set out the rules, listed the dimensions of the walls, and explained how the lumber had already been divided. "Everybody ready? Let's go!" The race was on. Bryce grabbed a bag of nails and strode up to Daisy.

"Our team's a bit short on manpower. How 'bout if you let Jamie here hold our tools for us so we can get to them real fast?

"Shore thang." Daisy set Jamie down on a small patch of grass just outside of the range of swinging lumber. She sat down next to him and arranged the drills, saws, hammers, and such in front of them where it would be easy for Bryce and Logan to see them. "Thanks, buddy." Bryce winked at Jamie and Daisy and ran to help Logan heft the lumber. They were already behind, but that didn't matter. He didn't aim to win this race.

I don't want the pony. Bryce glanced over at Daisy and Jamie. *I've got my eyes on a sweet little filly who's a much finer prize. Too bad she's so dead set on running the other way.*

<hr/>

"And the winner is. . . ," Otis Nye bellowed grandly, "team two! Ed, Ted, Fred, and Asa win the pony!"

"Yea!" Ted jumped in the air while Fred whooped. The rest of the men grumbled good-naturedly and threw a few overblown glowers toward the winners.

"That don't mean yore done, men!" Otis squawked. "Everybody get back to work!"

Ted and Fred joined Logan and Bryce, who lagged far behind, in part because it was just the two of them but also because they'd taken on the wall with the door, which made things more complicated. With the extra help, they began to catch up. The twins proved to be nimble climbers and swift workers as they poured all their considerable energy into the task at hand.

The scent of fresh sawdust coated the air as hammers rang and saws scraped.

Men yelled back and forth for whatever they happened to need at the moment. Occasional "ows" punctuated the rhythm of hard work. The women drifted around the work site with fresh water to drink and cool rags to mop overheated brows.

"Nails." Bryce took the small pouch from Jamie's hand and traded him an empty one. Daisy filled the small pouches so Jamie didn't ever touch the sharp points of the nails. "Thanks, buddy. We make a good team."

He rushed back to lift a heavy piece of timber with Logan. They'd nearly finished constructing the bents; now they'd need to raise the skeleton of the wall. He looped a strong rope around the topmost bar while Logan did the same. The twins were ready with the long, spiked stockades to brace the fledgling structure while Logan and Bryce pulled it upright.

His muscles strained at the weight. If this barn were any bigger, he and Logan couldn't have raised this wall even with the twins' assistance. Nate Rucker ambled over and grabbed an extra rope Bryce had thought to tie in case one gave way. With the help of the burly blacksmith, the frame rose far more quickly.

"Thanks, Nate." Bryce grinned at the enormous man, affectionately called "Li'l Nate" because his father, the blacksmith of the holler before him, was "Big Nate." Bryce had been in the holler for just a few days when Li'l Nate's wife, Abigail, bore him a son. Bitty Nate looked to be taking after his pa already.

"Any time," Nate grunted, holding tight while others rushed over to help secure the frame. Finally, they could let go.

Bryce gave a mighty stretch to work out the kinks. He took a few deep breaths, fanning himself with his hat.

"Have some water." Daisy's voice floated to his ears as she walked toward him.

"Much obliged." Bryce took the cool drink and downed it in three gulps. "Ah. That's better."

"I cain get some more," she offered. "Yore working terrible fast."

"I'm fine." He grinned at her. *She's been watching me.* The thought took his mind off his weary muscles.

"I wanted to thank you." Daisy leaned close enough that he could smell the fancy soap she used. "For includin' Jamie. It meant a lot that he got to holp the men instead of only watching."

"And help us he did. You, too. Having everything at the ready made things that much easier." Bryce slapped his hat back on his head and tipped the brim toward her. "I've got to get back to work. We've got to get the rafters up before dinner, and I'm mighty hungry."

"You always are!" Daisy's laugh followed him as he joined the other men.

❦

Daisy got some more water and brought it to Jamie. She tipped the cup to his lips. Usually he could do it, but today he'd already used a lot of his strength. She wiped his chin and cuddled him close.

She knew he was tired but didn't press him. He wouldn't doze off until after the rafters had been raised and he had a belly full of lunch. Daisy hummed softly as she ran her fingers through his soft blond hair, so like his father's.

She raised her head to see Miz Willow watching her. A surge of anger at the old woman's scolding welled up.

How dare she criticize the way I behave! Daisy stewed. *I know I'm beholden to her for her hospitality, but I don't intend for it to be permanent. Does sharing her home give her the right to berate me for nothing? I don't cut myself off from others. I've established a friendship with Bryce, haven't I?*

Only in spite of yourself. Daisy didn't like the niggling voice in the back of her mind, but the tiny seeds of guilt wouldn't rest. *You didn't reach out to Bryce until he was kind to Jamie. Even then, you accused him of cruelty not in his nature. If the friendship has grown, it is not due to yore tender care in nurturing it. Miz Willow said those things to open yore eyes, not to hurt you.*

Well, she did hurt me. And if she feels that I'm so difficult, it's all the better that I've taken Logan up on his offer to sell my lace. His deal puts far more money in my pocket. The more I save, the sooner I cain leave the old woman's charity, and me and Jamie cain get on with our lives.

I've wasted too much time already. After the fire, we spent two days searching the rubble before moving here. Sewing new clothes was necessary but cost me a lot of time, and holping with that behemoth of a stove ate up still more time. I need to focus on the important things. How am I going to put a roof over Jamie's head and food in his mouth? By making lace. That's how I should be spending my time. Her resolve strengthened, Daisy vowed to work more quickly.

While she'd been lost in thought, the men had finished putting up half of the rafters. The noontime hour had passed, so when the skeleton of the barn was up and ready, everyone would break for dinner.

"Mama's gonna go set out the food," Daisy told Jamie. "I want you to stay right here where I cain see you, okay?"

" 'Kay, Ma." He nodded, happy to be watching everything around him.

Daisy walked over to the cabin and began carrying out dish after covered dish. They hadn't set it all outside before now, so the sun wouldn't spoil the food and insects wouldn't swarm around the tables. Logan and Bryce had constructed two huge tables and numerous benches in preparation for the day.

Daisy, Hattie, Silk Trevor, and a few other women scurried back and forth while Miz Willow passed them dishes. Before long, the first table groaned beneath the weight of sliced ham, a pot roast, two chickens, rabbit stew, egg salad, vegetable salad, mashed potatoes, gravy, steamed carrots, and hunks of cheese. Baked goods filled the second table to bursting. Bread, rolls, biscuits, corn bread, pies, coffee cake, and cobbler spread in a tantalizing profusion.

Logan called for silence before blessing the meal.

"We're going to take a minute to thank the Lord for the food and friends gathered today.

"Lord, I thank You for each person here today. Every one of them has things they need to be attending to, but they've taken the time to come and help me and Hattie and Miz Willow build a bigger barn. Thank You for the food on the tables. We ask that You bless it so we have the strength to finish our work today. You've provided graciously for us, and we ask You to shed Your blessings on the people here today. In Your name. Amen."

The smell of savory meat mixed with the earthy fragrance of baked cinnamon as the men gathered around to fill their plates. Daisy couldn't remember ever seeing so much food, much less watching it all disappear so quickly. After the men hunkered down, their plates piled high with food, the women and children swarmed around the tables.

"Here, Jamie." Daisy returned to find Bryce sitting with her son. Jamie nibbled on a chicken leg while Bryce attacked a mound of mashed potatoes. Daisy sat down and put Jamie's plate in easy reach. "How're them taters, Bryce?"

"Good." Bryce barely stopped eating long enough to grunt his approval.

" 'Ood." Jamie nodded, waving his piece of chicken.

Daisy's heart twisted. *Jamie used to copycat me like that. Now he's apin' Bryce. Lord, why do I feel as though that's a loss? Bryce has become so important to my son, but he'll be gone all too soon. What am I to do?*

Chapter 14

I've put the axes and saws in the back of the wagon." Logan sauntered into the cabin two days later and tried to peek in the lunch basket the women had packed.

Daisy chuckled when Hattie swatted his hand away.

"I have the horses hitched." Bryce came in behind his brother. "What's the holdup? We've got to get going if we're going to chop enough before dark."

"Here you go." Daisy handed the basket to Bryce while Logan wolfed down a leftover biscuit.

"Thanks, Daisy." Bryce's rugged smile made it difficult for Daisy not to stare.

"Yore welcome." She stepped back. "A man needs plenty in his belly so's he cain get a lot done."

"Me man!" Jamie scooched over and jabbed his chest. "I go?"

No. Not a chance. Not even with two Chances. They'll be fellin' deadwood—ain't safe for any child, much less my son! Jist the thought of that two-man saw makes me wanna hold Jamie close and never let him go.

Daisy bit back the words, knowing how hurt Jamie would be if she explained it like that. She scrambled to concoct a reason to refuse.

"Of course you're a man," Logan proclaimed.

Oh no. He's going to say yes. Logan'll let Jamie tag along, and then summat terrible'll happen. Daisy chewed the inside of her lip. *A deadwood branch cain fall, a blade might be left unattended, a shift in the wind so a felled tree goes the wrong way. . . And I cain't think up an excuse to tell them all no. What do I do? I cain't let him go!*

She saw Bryce bending over to talk to Jamie. *No, Bryce! You've let Jamie do so many things already. I was wrong about the eggs and the leaves but not this. Don't take Jamie where he cain't be safe. You must have the sense to know this won't end well. Don't make me let loose the words that will shame my son afore you and yore brother.*

"Not today, buddy."

Thankee, Bryce. Daisy took a calming breath. *Jamie'll be safe. I was so worried.*

Bryce squatted down to look Jamie in the eye. "We need you to stay here and keep watch on things for us. We're chopping enough wood to fill the whole wagon before we bring it back. The pieces'll be so long." He spread his arms wide. "We'll have to make 'em smaller tomorrow. Then you'll be right there with us. Fair enough?"

More than fair. You found a way to protect my son and still make him part of the task.

298

" 'Kay." Jamie puffed out his chest. " 'Morra I holp."

"But today yore going to holp yore mama!" Daisy gathered him in her arms. "We've got lots of thangs to get done afore Logan and Bryce come back!" She smiled at Bryce, hoping he understood that she meant to thank him for protecting Jamie but not treating him like a baby. He was so good with her and Jamie. *Yep. Bryce Chance jist has a way of makin' a body feel special.*

Bryce pitched a forkful of hay into one of the new stalls. Logan was setting up tack.

"I think we should keep the cattle in the old half and the horses in the new," Bryce planned aloud.

"Makes sense to have the horses on hand," Logan agreed. "Seemed like everyone I talked with is preparing for a rough winter."

"Heard about Otis Nye's bones, did you?" Bryce grinned.

"And how spring came early." Logan grabbed a pitchfork and started spreading hay around. They'd transfer the animals the next day. "Ed Trevor mentioned something about the hounds having thick coats."

"I heard the same thing. That reminds me." Bryce leaned on his pitchfork. "After we get the animals settled in tomorrow morning, I need to go to the Trevor place. Has a runt no one's spoken for. All the others have homes lined up."

Logan shrugged. "If it's made it this long, I think it's got a good chance of growing."

"Not with winter coming on fast." Bryce shook his head. "He won't have enough meat on his bones to get through the cold."

"That's rough," Logan commiserated. "How did it happen that Ed got in such a late litter?"

"Happens sometimes." Bryce thought a moment. "Ed said something about her being one of his older breeders."

"What are you going to do with the pup?" Logan asked.

"I won't know until I see it. Might be it just needs some extra attention and some cow's milk to fatten it up. It's worked before. Ed has too many dogs to spend that much time on a runt. Maybe I can take it off his hands."

"Oh?"

Something about Logan's tone raised Bryce's hackles. "You got something to say?"

"How are you going to manage a pup on your five-day, cross-country train trek?" Logan drummed his fingers against one of the new walls.

"Might be a bit of a problem," Bryce admitted.

"You could stay through the winter." Logan got the words out in a rush.

"I've been away from the ranch for six months already. You want me to sleep out in the barn through a mountain winter?"

"I have it on good authority that this is a mighty fine barn! You could use the tack room so the smell won't get to you. We both know that the animals will put off enough heat to keep the place warm."

"For the sake of a little dog?" Bryce shook his head. "You can feed the thing without me."

"I was thinking you might have other reasons to stay." Logan waggled his brows. "I saw you eating lunch with Daisy the other day. She's a fine woman."

"Yes, she is." Bryce set to work again and avoided his brother's piercing gaze. "But that doesn't amount to a hill o' beans. She's dead set on rebuilding the home and life she and her son lost. Even if I stayed the winter, I would eventually go back to Chance Ranch. Daisy's already lost too much to give up anything more."

"I see you've given this some thought, but did you think about all she stands to gain? You two seem to enjoy each other's company, and you get on well with Jamie."

"He's a great kid." Bryce chewed the inside of his cheek. "But I can't leave Chance Ranch shorthanded this winter to pursue a woman who has other plans."

"Are you so sure she wouldn't give up those plans?"

"She's a good friend, Logan, but she's a mother first," Bryce tried to explain. "Jamie's welfare is the only thing she's interested in."

"So how come she smiles at you like that and brings you water and makes sure we have something for dessert every night, if it's not because she likes you and noticed your sweet tooth?"

"She's a thoughtful woman." Bryce tried not to let Logan's words sink in. False hopes never made a man anything but wrong.

"Hattie's of the opinion that Daisy's thinking, all right." Logan paused meaningfully. "On you."

"You talked to Hattie about this?" Bryce practically bellowed the words.

"She brought up how much time Daisy spent with you while we were gone," Logan said casually, "and we've both kept an eye on the pair of you. Hattie thinks you two have something, and I agree."

Could that be true? Is Daisy interested in me the way I'm attracted to her? There were those times when we touched—she seemed flustered. Could there be room enough in her heart for a new husband? I care for Jamie a great deal, and I'd treat him as my own son. Would Daisy be willing to come with me to California?

"I can see the questions rolling about in your head, Bryce." Logan stared at him long and hard. "Are you willing to give up a winter to find the answers?"

༺⚬⚬ৡ

Daisy looked up as Bryce entered the cabin. The determined set of his jaw as he strode across the room sent a chill down her spine. She rested her lacework in her lap and waited. Whatever it was he had to say, it must be important. Could something be wrong with the new barn? Then he stopped in front of her.

"Daisy Thales, I've made a decision." The intensity of his gaze stirred something deep within her.

"What is it, Bryce?"

"I'm staying through the winter."

What? No! How am I going to guard my heart against this man iff'n I cain't be shore he's leavin'? We'll be snowbound more often than not. He'll be here every time I turn around. What would make him change his mind? Why is he telling me and not Miz Willow and Hattie? What is he waiting for me to say?

Her breath caught at a possible answer. *He. . .he wouldn't be staying for me? Yes, I'm attracted to him—but does he feel the same way? About me? Plump, plain me with a son by another man? Only one way to find out.*

"What made you change yore mind?" She tried to keep her voice steady and light but failed miserably.

"You." He stepped forward and took her hand in his. Heat coursed through her fingers. "My mind's made up; I plan to court you, Daisy."

"Me?" The word came out as a squeak. She shook her head in disbelief, and his grip tightened as though he wouldn't let go.

"Don't say anything now. It's beginning stages yet, but I figured you deserved fair warning." He gave her palm a final squeeze. "Good night."

Daisy watched, dumbfounded, as he left. She stared down at her hand, still tingling from the warmth of his. She leaned back before she registered Hattie and Miz Willow staring avidly. *At least Jamie's already fast asleep!*

She opened her mouth, realized she had no idea what to say, and cleared her throat instead. *I cain't believe it. I got no choice but to believe it. I don't even have time to work it through in my head 'cuz the man didn't have the sense God gave a flea. He tromped in, made his declaration in front of Miz Willow and Hattie, and took off. What am I supposed to say?*

"Well?" Hattie prompted, leaning forward in anticipation.

"Well, what?" Daisy picked up a piece of lacework to keep her hands busy.

"Put that stitchin' down, missy," Miz Willow ordered. "You've got some thinking to do, and yore gonna need some wise counsel."

I ain't ready for counsel, Daisy rebelled. *I don't know what to say! How cain you not see that?*

"Daisy?" Hattie caught her attention. "Do you not have any thoughts on what Bryce jist said?"

"I've got too many," Daisy moaned, burying her face in her hands. "And not a-one of 'em makes a lick of sense!"

"Then let's make sense out of it," Hattie declared firmly. "Now, puttin' aside the fact that Bryce surprised you, we have to remember that it's what he said that's important. Not the time or way he chose to say it."

"He could've spoke to me in private," Daisy muttered. *At least then I'd have my wits about me before I had to talk it over.*

"That probably would've been best," Miz Willow agreed. Her blue eyes crinkled with amusement. "But then Hattie and I would've been left out of the fun!"

"Never you mind 'bout that." Hattie swatted away Miz Willow's entertained cackle. "We ain't gonna tell anybody yore business, Daisy. What's important is whether or not yore interested in that buck." She eyed Daisy shrewdly. "I think you are, but yore the only one as knows for shore."

"I—I might," Daisy admitted. "But he's so different from Peter."

"As well he should be." Miz Willow resumed rocking. "Iff'n he was too much like yore first husband, you'd be comparin' 'em all the time. Bryce is his own man. If you want him, you want him for who he is, not who he cain't never be."

Daisy nodded slowly. Peter would always be her first love, but that was the way he was frozen in her thoughts. She'd married at fifteen, been widowed a scant year later. Peter had never even seen his eighteenth year. How could she ever compare her childhood sweetheart with a strong, steady man like Bryce?

"Could you love him?" Hattie got to the heart of the matter. "If not, then nothin' else need be considered."

"I'm not shore." Daisy bit her lip. *Could I spend the rest of my life with Bryce Chance?*

"But yore not willing to say no," Miz Willow observed. "There's something in that. For what it's worth, I say let Bryce Chance court you. He's a strong man dedicated to the Lord. Comes from good stock, takes you to be more'n jist a pretty face, and he's good with little Jamie."

"I'll sleep on it," Daisy decided. It was all she could commit to at this point.

"You need to pray on it." Hattie walked over and wrapped her in a hug. "Give it to God."

Give it to God. Hattie's words echoed in Daisy's mind later that night as she tried vainly to sleep. *I've been on my own for so long. How cain I give up somethin' this important?*

Chapter 15

Bryce stared at the ceiling, unable to sleep. *What made me go in there and burst out with a declaration like that? I should've waited for a better time. No, how would I have known it was a better time? I had something to say. Best to be out with it.*

He recalled the expressions on Daisy's face: surprise, followed by a kind of heat deep within her eyes, only to be extinguished by confusion. *But not disgust or outrage. She feels something, but neither one of us knows what it is yet. I hope that by declaring my interest, I've made it easier for her to trust me. What do I do now? Wait for her response?*

Bryce shook his head in frustration. He'd put himself out there, and she could leave him twisting in the wind for as long as she needed to. Why did it all have to be so difficult?

Lord, I've prayed about my feelings for Daisy. I've thought long and hard about what to do. When Logan passed on the word that she might return my interest, I took it as a sign that I should go after what I wanted. What I still want. You know the desire in my heart. If it is a mistake, if this is not the path You want me to take, let Daisy tell me soon enough for me to leave before winter. I know she's spent the past five years standing on her own, but You and I both know she doesn't have to. Whether or not You intend for her to be my wife, I ask that You work in her heart and remind her that she's never alone. You are always with us. In Your holy name. Amen.

Having cast his cares upon the Lord, Bryce finally closed his eyes. Whatever the outcome of his decision tonight, he was sure he'd need to be well rested to face what lay ahead.

❧

He awoke the next morning refreshed. After milking the cows—there were two dairy cows now in the extended barn—he headed for the cabin. He knocked lightly at the door, waiting for the go-ahead to step inside.

"Come on in." Miz Willow's voice came through the door, slightly muffled.

Bryce entered and set the milk on the table. Daisy stood before the stove, her back to him. It wasn't the welcome he'd hoped for, but he'd known Daisy might refuse him. Still, he took a deep breath before greeting her.

"Good morning, Daisy." He stepped close, lingering beside her a moment before picking up Jamie.

"Mornin'," Daisy spoke softly, but he heard it.

"Jamie and I'll go gather eggs. We'll be back soon." He left, only realizing when he got to the barn that he'd left the basket inside. He improvised, grabbing a spare bucket from the wall.

"Wun," Jamie counted, placing the first egg carefully in the bucket. "Two." He reached in as far as he could. "Tree!"

"That's right!" Bryce affirmed. "Three. Now you've got one more. Do you remember what number that is?"

"Umm. . ." Jamie scrunched his face in concentration.

"How old are you, Jamie?" Bryce shifted the egg pail to hang on the arm holding the boy. He held up his left hand and splayed four fingers. "This many, right?"

"Yes." Jamie nodded and reached out to tap the fingers. "Wun, two, tree. . ." He paused and looked at the last digit in consternation.

Bryce waited. If Jamie couldn't remember, he'd admit it. Sometimes all it took was an extra minute, so no sense rushing it. Jamie was a smart kid.

"Four!" Jamie burst out the number in excitement. "Four eggs, me four." He pointed to himself proudly.

"Exactly!" That was enough for today. The boy could count to ten, but there was no sense pushing it. As Jamie's hands grew less steady, Bryce helped him gather the rest of the eggs.

They carried the eggs back inside. Logan and Hattie were up and moving around. Suddenly, the cabin seemed too crowded. Bryce tried to catch Daisy's attention, but she kept busy until they sat down for breakfast. As Logan said grace, Bryce silently offered a prayer of his own.

Father, forgive me my impatience. Perhaps she needs time to think it over. I'm asking her to consider me as a husband, to decide whether she could move to California if the answer is yes. That's a lot to expect her to answer after one night's thought and prayer. But, Lord, I don't want to wait. Just seeing her and not knowing if this is as close as we can ever be is tearing me up. Give me patience and forbearance, Lord. Amen.

~~~

Daisy waited until Hattie and Miz Willow were checking their stock of yarbs and medicines for winter, then crouched down beside Jamie.

"Yore doin' real good with yore letters, Jamie. Mama wants you to keep practicing for a while. I'll be back in a little bit, understand?"

"Mm-hmm."

Daisy planted a quick kiss atop his golden head and slipped out of the cabin. She'd hardly taken three steps when Miz Willow's voice stopped her.

"C'mere and give an ole woman some of yore time," the healer instructed as she hobbled out of the house and took a seat on the porch.

Stifling a groan, Daisy sat down next to her.

"Now I know I ain't the person yore fixin' to talk with," Miz Willow began, "and I riled you the last time we spoke in private."

Daisy sat silently, not denying her words, but refusing to let Miz Willow know how angry she'd been.

"But I seen you all mornin' thinkin' so hard it's a wonder you got anythin' done." The old woman held up her gnarled hands. "Not that I'm sayin' yore not a fine worker. Truth is, you've been a big holp 'round here, and I should have thanked you afore now."

"Yore kind enough to let me and my son stay in yore home." Daisy softened. "It's the least I cain do to see after a few chores."

"You've a good heart, Daisy Thales." Miz Willow tapped her cane on the porch. "I'd never say otherwise. But it's yore hard head we need to talk about." Daisy's back stiffened at the words, but the old woman plowed on ahead. "Try as I might, I cain't walk in yore shoes, Daisy. Bryce Chance is, as I said afore, a strong man of God, a fine provider, and a man who knows you better'n any other and wants to take care of you and yore son. I tried to wrap my mind around it, but I jist cain't seem to find the hitch. What're you caught on that I don't see?"

Miz Willow's voice had become tender, and she reached out to put an age-spotted hand atop Daisy's. The healer was trying to understand, and maybe voicing her fears would help Daisy allay them.

"First, it came as such a surprise, I couldn't see straight." Daisy tried to explain. "I've already married and lost the only man I ever loved. I didn't plan on loving another. Doesn't it disrespect Peter's memory?"

"I don't think so." Miz Willow shook her head. "Yore not lookin' to replace yore childhood sweetheart, Daisy. You didn't set out to nab a husband. God put a fine man in yore path, and it does no discredit to Peter to find a husband for yoreself and a pa for young Jamie. The Bible even talks about how young widows should remarry.

"First Timothy, chapter 5, talks all about honorin' widows," Miz Willow added. " 'I will therefore that the younger women marry, bear children. . . .' "

"That holps a bit," Daisy admitted, breathing a little easier. "But that's jist part of it. I don't know if I cain love another man as a husband, and I don't want to encourage Bryce without cause."

"Sounds to me like yore putting the cart afore the mule, Daisy. He's taken a liking to you and yore boy. Yore not averse to him. He ain't popped the question yet, only said he wants to court you. Courtin's all 'bout findin' out whether or not you suit."

"Mayhap that's true. It's so different from afore. Peter and I growed up together, had a friendship that deepened and turned to love. It all came so natural." Daisy looked down at her hands. "Now it seems so forced. It's all up in the air with so many questions and no answers, and ev'rybody around is privy to the whole thing. What if he stays, and it don't work out? What will people think?"

"Why are you worried 'bout what goes on in the minds of others? Fretting 'bout yore standin' with others 'stead of wanting to foller God's will for yore life is a sure sign summat's sore wrong in yore heart and soul." Miz Willow stood up. "Would you rather not take the path God has put before you, not open yoreself to the chance of love, for the sake of avoiding a few gossips? If so, you don't deserve a man like Bryce Chance." She turned to go back inside. "Think on it, Daisy. Be shore you have the right reasons behind yore decision."

Cain't she see that's 'zactly what I'm tryin' to do? Talking with her don't make this any easier. The only person I should be talkin' this over with is Bryce. I don't know what I'll say, but we'll have to come to some sort of decision.

She hurried to the barn and eased the door open, checking to see if Bryce was tending to one of the animals as he did so often. Not seeing him, she made her way farther back, to the older half of the barn.

"He's not here." Logan's voice made her jump.

"You gave me a fright!" Daisy put a hand over her heart.

"Didn't mean to." Logan put down an empty water bucket beside a full trough and leaned against a post. "But like I said, Bryce isn't here."

"Oh?" Daisy tried to sound nonchalant but could see from the grin on Logan's face that she had failed abysmally.

"Yep." Logan finally took pity on her and broke the silence. "He went up to the Trevor place. He might not be back until suppertime. Something about an underweight pup."

"I see." *No, I don't! He laid all that on me last night and takes off the next morning? How am I supposed to sort out my feelings iff'n Bryce ain't even around?*

There it was. The answer she'd been looking for all night. Truth of the matter was, she did bear feelings for Bryce. Affection that could grow to love. But he had to be around for her to find out. *I want him to stay through the winter.* The knowledge both frightened and exhilarated her. *I'm not ready to promise anything, but I'm willing to give it a try.*

"Thanks, Logan." She smiled at him and started to leave.

"Wait a minute." Logan walked beside her. "Is there a message you want me to pass on?"

"Nope." Daisy determined she'd talk to Bryce before anyone else. "I'll see you both at supper."

Logan looked at her as though trying to figure out what her decision would be, but Daisy didn't so much as lift an eyebrow. As she left the barn, she thought about the difference between the two brothers. Logan used words to understand and be understood. *Bryce would've knowed my answer just by looking at my face.*

❦

"She's got spunk." Bryce laughed as the wriggly puppy burrowed a cold, wet nose into his neck. The ropy tail waved wildly, beating the air, Bryce's arms, and anything else within reach.

"Likes you," Ed noted. "Done everything I cain think on, but she's still a bitty li'l thang. Cain't sell her, that's for shore." He looked at the furry black-and-tan pup. "I make a habit of not keepin' the dogs inside. Coddles 'em too much, and then they're not as good for tracking. But this one might not have enough weight to make it through the winter."

"She needs fattening up. I'd give her cow's milk—as much as she'll take. I'd rest easier if I knew she had a warm place to sleep." Bryce pulled the puppy from where it was climbing onto his shoulder. "Plenty of energy."

"I've got two late litters this year to look after, and I'm behind on getting m' winter firewood." Ed sighed. "I cain't be givin' this one special treatment, and no one chose the runt. Iff'n you want her, she's yores."

Bryce looked down at the small bundle of fur currently burying her black nose in the bend of his arm before sniffing her way over to nuzzle at his buttons.

"I've got to go feed the breeders." Ed shoved his hands in his pockets. "Get to know her. I don't want you to take her and regret it later. I'll be back in a bit."

"Sounds good." Bryce cradled the pup in both palms and brought her to eye level. Her tail thumped as she craned her neck to poke his chin with an inquisitive snout. "Snuffly little thing, aren't ya?"

She's bitty now, and even after I get some more weight on her, she'll never be as big as her brothers and sisters. Ed's right—she won't make the best hunting dog. Definitely has the nose for it, though.

Bryce cradled her close, and she buried her face in his chest. He ran his fingertip between her floppy ears.

Friendly mite. She'd make a good companion—affectionate now, she'll be protective once she's bigger. Every boy should have a dog, and this one's tiny enough for Jamie to hold now. They can grow a bit together, and she'll look after him when she's older. Jamie likes to feel things with his hands, and this pup is soft and warm and cuddly. She won't mind that he's a little clumsy. It'd do Jamie good to have something to look after. Make him feel important and capable.

Daisy might not like it at first, but she'll melt when she sees the smile on Jamie's face while he plays with his dog. I'll help him look after the pup while she's small. She won't need a lot of looking after when she's older—food and water. Jamie'll give this pup all the attention she needs, and she'll love him right back. Dogs are loyal creatures.

Bryce saw Ed coming back and gave the pup a reassuring pat. It didn't seem right that no one wanted her. He just couldn't bring himself to leave her behind. "I'll look after her, Ed. What's her name?"

"I don't know. I try not to name 'em, since their owners like to do that. Then they cain't get confused iff'n I train 'em under a different name and not come when they're called." Ed thought a moment. "Since no one paid for her, she don't have a name. Reckon it's up to you. What'd you like to call her?"

Bryce looked down. Having tuckered herself out, she snuggled in his arms, pink tongue lolling out as she snoozed. She was a cute little thing. Her small black nose twitched in her sleep, and he could think of only one name that would do.

"Nosey."

Chapter 16

Daisy stared at the apple pie in dismay, its black edges and smoky scent declared it burned beyond redemption. She fanned a tea towel to wave the last few wisps of smoke out the door. She'd need to clean out the new oven.

I must've put too much wood in the stove and got the oven hotter'n it should be. I'm right glad Miz Willow and Hattie are at the Ruckers so they don't see this. I cain't believe we managed all the victuals for the barn raisin' with nary a single problem, and now I done ruint the dessert I made to tell Bryce I'm glad he's staying. I ain't got time to make another!

"Well, Jamie," she sighed aloud, even though Jamie was napping, "that plan went up in smoke."

"What went up in smoke?" Bryce sniffed the singed air as he walked into the cabin.

No! Daisy couldn't let loose the howl that rose in her chest. *Yore not supposed to see me like this—hair all flyaway, face flushed from the stove, spots all over my apron...and a burned apple pie on the windersill.* She took a deep breath, realizing Bryce waited for her to say something.

"I baked you an apple pie, but it came out more burnt than anything I'd ask a body to et." She flapped the towel toward the window, as much to point at the tart as to vent some of her frustration. "I made the new stove oven too hot."

"Looks fine to me." Bryce picked up the still-warm tin, set it on the table, and grabbed a fork.

"What're you doin'?" Daisy protested as he plunged the fork into the middle of the charred dessert.

"The edges are. . ." Bryce took another bite and swallowed before continuing. "Crispy. That I'll grant you. But it's not ruined. The middle's wonderful." He speared a spiced apple slice and held it to her lips. "Taste."

"I—" She didn't get a word out before he slipped the bite into her mouth.

"Got a speck here." Bryce's finger brushed her lip tenderly. Warmth spread through her.

"See?" Bryce kept on eating. "Delicious."

That shore was. Daisy resisted the urge to touch where his fingertip had brushed her mouth. "You didn't have to do that."

"I know." Bryce held her gaze steadily. "I wanted to." Tension spread between them, tight and warm, before he lightened his tone. "Burnt offerings pleased God, and now I know why." He polished off the rest of the pie, leaving behind only the black edges.

Daisy shook her head and smiled at him, reaching for the tin. It'd have to be scrubbed. He gently caught her wrist.

"Leave it." He rose to his feet and started for the door, not loosening his hold. "I want to show you something."

"What?" Daisy glanced back at Jamie, still asleep on the bed.

"It's a surprise." He released her hand. "I'll bring it to you if you'd be more comfortable."

"I'll go." His consideration immediately made her relax. Besides, she'd been wanting to talk with him in private. Jamie would be fine, and this way she and Bryce could figure a few things out without her son overhearing the conversation. She followed Bryce out to the barn, and he led her to the tack room.

"Hold out your hands, Daisy," he instructed. "Now close your eyes."

Daisy did as he said, resisting the urge to peek through her lashes as he put something small and soft in her palms. Something cold and wet snuffled her hand, and she would have dropped it had Bryce not cupped her hands in his.

"Open 'em."

She looked down. "Oh!" She cradled the tiniest puppy she'd ever seen. Daisy lifted it up to get a better look, and the pup bumped her nose with its. She giggled as the pup nosed its way over her face, the soft fur tickling her skin.

Although mostly black, tan markings decorated the fur around its eyes, paws, and the tip of its tail, which wagged enthusiastically.

"I cain't recollect the last time I saw such a cute critter," Daisy marveled. When Bryce stepped back, she cuddled the puppy close. It immediately poked at her stomach with its nose, snuffling excitedly. "Curious li'l thang."

"I've named her Nosey." Bryce reached out and stroked the soft black fur.

"Fits her." Daisy laughed. *But why are you showing her to me? Is she a gift?* There was no denying the little pup had winning ways, but the last thing Daisy needed was another mouth to feed.

"Yep." Bryce waited for her to look up from the furry bundle before speaking again. "She's a runt, and Ed Trevor doesn't have the time to look after her like she needs. I'll be feeding her cow's milk so she bulks up for the winter."

"I'm glad. She's too friendly and precious not to be loved." Daisy smiled her approval. *And how wonderful it is that you care enough to bring her home.* "You've got a fine heart, Bryce Chance." *Do you understand what I'm saying?*

"Every boy needs a dog." He looked her in the eye, then said, "I was hoping. . .Jamie could help me with her." Bryce asked her more than one question with that statement.

"He'd like that," Daisy answered, pausing for a moment before adding softly, "and so would I."

"Thank you, Daisy." A grin split across his face. "So you're all right with me staying?"

"Yes, Bryce." She nodded but became serious. "But I want to make a few things clear."

"I'm listening." Bryce reached for the puppy and leaned forward to catch her words.

"I'm not committing to anything jist yet. I don't know iff'n this whole thang'll work out, but I want to try."

"That's all I'm asking for, Daisy. A chance to spend more time with you and Jamie to see where it leads."

His words lifted a load off her shoulders.

"Then we're agreed. Yore staying but no promises." Daisy had to make sure she wasn't misleading him.

"Yep. And I want you to know that I care for Jamie in his own right, not only because he's your son." Bryce alleviated a concern Daisy had left unspoken. "I'm courting you with an eye to becoming part of a family, not just a husband."

Daisy didn't say another word, but her eyes shone with relief. Bryce knew she wouldn't have agreed to step out with him unless she already knew he'd care for Jamie, but he wanted her to hear the words and know how deeply he meant it.

"I've got to go wake Jamie, else he won't sleep through the night." Daisy passed Nosey back to him.

"Why don't we let Nosey wake him?" Bryce suggested, keeping apace with her. "That cold nose of hers would make a fine wake-up call."

"Sounds like fun."

They tiptoed into the cabin and snuck up near the bed. Bryce reached out and deposited the dog beside the sleeping boy, then watched and waited. Sure enough, Nosey stood up, placed one dainty paw on Jamie's chest, and buried her wet nose under his chin.

"Huh?" Jamie looked up at them with bleary eyes before tilting his head and seeing what had woken him up. "Puppy!" He sat up straight and scooped the puppy into his arms. She thumped her tail so fast it became a blur while she covered his face with doggy kisses. Jamie giggled. "Mine?" he asked excitedly.

Bryce looked at Daisy. She sent him a brief nod, and they answered together. "Yours."

They watched the little boy play with the puppy, who sniffed him, the pillow, the blankets—anything and everything around her.

I understand, Nosey. Bryce couldn't stop grinning if his life depended on it. *I'm testing the air, too. If we play our cards right, we'll both have a new family.* He glanced at the window as a sudden cloud cast the sun in shadow. *I hope it's a long winter.*

"I et too much." Daisy leaned back on the tattered quilt and put her hand on her stomach. The sun shone down on the folks gathered for the Harvest Games and Picnic.

"Me, too." Bryce stretched out beside her on the grass. "I couldn't fit in another bite."

"So you don't want the pie I brought you?" Logan flopped down, passing Hattie a piece of apple pie that Daisy had baked for the day before tackling a wedge of his own.

"Aw. . .my favorite." Bryce looked longingly at the dessert before him.

Even Daisy's mouth watered at the tantalizing aroma of apples and cinnamon. *At least this one turned out right. The last one I baked all but burnt to a crisp, and Bryce et it anyhow.*

"Maybe one small bite. . ." Bryce jabbed his fork into the treat and chewed the first bite. "Mmm. Nope. I need another taste." He closed his eyes as he savored the next bite. "I can tell Daisy baked this." He opened his eyes, held her gaze, and lowered his voice. "It tastes like cinnamon, sugar, and sweetness."

"Oh?" Daisy tried to be nonchalant but felt the blush beginning anyway. She nabbed his fork. "Guess I'd better try some of that myself then!" Together they polished off the rest.

"Now I really can't get up." Bryce groaned, but it didn't look to Daisy like he planned on moving anytime soon.

"Come on, folks!" Asa Pleasant called for everyone's attention. "It's time for a little friendly competition! Everyone who wants to compete in the sack race, get over here and grab a tater sack."

"I always win this one." Logan sprang up from the ground and held out his hand to Hattie. "Want to try to beat me?"

"Sometimes I want to beat you, all right." Hattie laughed as she said the words. "But not at this. You go on ahead." She waved him on.

"Bryce?" Logan issued a one-word challenge.

"Not after that pie," Bryce refused. "I'll join you in a bit."

"Suit yourself." Logan rushed across the eating area to grab a potato sack.

Daisy's heart clenched at the longing in Jamie's eyes as the other contestants lined up. Some things were stark reminders of what he'd never be able to do. *Maybe we should've brought Nosey along, after all. Leastways then Jamie'd have something to play with while the other children run around.*

"Buddy, I want to ask you something." Bryce distracted them both. "I'm going to need a partner for the wheelbarrow race. What'dya say?"

I want Jamie to feel like a part of the fun, but the wheelbarrow race? Where you hold the person's legs and make them walk on their hands? Jamie has much better control over his hands and arms than his legs, but they still jerk around some. Iff'n he spasms and falls. . .

"See, what you have to do is sit inside the wheelbarrow and tell me to swerve left or right to avoid the logs." Bryce's explanation wasn't what she expected.

"You'll have to have sharp eyes, but I know I can count on you. First team across the finish line wins some peppermint sticks."

" 'Es!" Jamie's excited nod made Daisy wish she could think of ways to make him feel as included.

"Let's go tell 'em we want to be one of the teams." Bryce picked Jamie up and threw Daisy a wink before tromping over to talk to Rooster Linden.

"Now maybe it ain't my place to tell you this, but you should know." Hattie leaned close to whisper in Daisy's ear. "Bryce arranged this wheelbarrow race special. He's not jist a good, smart man. He's a thoughtful one. I know he won't never tell you what he done, so I'm tellin' it for him."

Daisy sat for a moment, speechless. *Why didn't Bryce tell me hisself? I'm right glad he done this. How am I s'pposed to let him court me when he keeps secrets about how wonderful he is?*

"Bryce told me he aims to win." Hattie grinned. "Betwixt you and me, I hope they do. Logan's gotten too puffed up for his own good. Brags he'll win every race he enters. I caught him hopping 'round the barn t'other day, practicing for the three-legged race."

"Well then." Daisy smiled mischievously. "What say we level the playing field?"

312

Chapter 17

L et's have a quick review. Hold out your left arm. Good. Right? Excellent."
Bryce patted Jamie on the back. "Now you say it."

" 'Eft, rite," Jamie recited, holding out the named arm.

"We're up." Bryce set Jamie down in the wheelbarrow, facing forward. "Are you ready to win?"

"Yeah!" Jamie gripped the sides of the wheelbarrow and leaned forward to have a better view of the grass.

"On yore marks. Get set. . ." Rooster roared, "Go!"

Bryce, tensed and ready, took off like a shot.

" 'Eft!" Jamie shouted, and Bryce quickly maneuvered around the block of wood.

"Rite!" Jamie directed. "Rite ag'n!"

Bryce kept pushing, running hard and angling the wheelbarrow tightly. He spotted the Trevor twins out of the corner of his eye, gaining.

" 'Eft, Byce!" Jamie screeched. "No mor! Go!"

Bryce saw Daisy waiting at the finish line, jumping up and down and clapping her hands. He managed a final burst of speed. *For Daisy and Jamie!* He sailed over the finish line.

"We win!" Jamie yelled, flailing his arms joyfully as his mama ran over.

"I saw, Jamie!" Daisy scooped him up and swung him in the air. "You were so fast to see those blocks! I'm proud of you!"

Bryce felt as though he'd grown about ten inches taller, seeing Jamie flushed with victory and Daisy beaming with pride. He drank in the sight of them.

After Rooster and Asa presented Jamie with his peppermint stick prize, the whole holler walked by to congratulate him on his sharp eyes. To Bryce's way of thinking, the day was complete.

But it seemed that Daisy had other plans. When Logan grabbed Bryce for the three-legged race, she and Hattie followed over to the racing field.

"What do you think you're doing?" Logan demanded as Hattie tied herself and Daisy together at the ankle.

"We're joinin' the race. What's it look like?" Daisy calmly slipped her arm around Hattie's waist to steady herself.

"Oh-ho," Logan guffawed. "Well, if you wanted a close view of me and Bryce winning, you could've waited at the finish line."

Bryce tried to elbow Logan in the ribs to get him to shut his mouth, but he just bumped Logan's arm.

"We'll see about that," Hattie shot back, her eyes alight with challenge as everybody lined up.

On "Go!" Bryce took off for the second time that day. He and Logan loped across the field, but Logan's shorter legs made Bryce abbreviate his stride. "Come on! They're gettin' ahead!" he whispered, doggedly dragging Logan along with him.

"It's not my fault we're lopsided!" Logan huffed.

Hattie and Daisy thumped across the field right past Bryce and Logan. *How can they be so graceful? Look at them go!* Bryce watched with a mixture of admiration and disbelief as the women half-walked, half-hopped to victory.

After he disentangled himself from Logan, he went to congratulate them. Seeing Daisy, face flushed from exertion, eyes sparkling with laughter, made Bryce grin. *I'd gladly lose this race if I can win her in the long run.*

⁓⦿⁓

"Bryce?" Logan's voice carried across the barn.

"Up here!" Bryce used the worn ribbon to mark the passage he'd barely finished reading, then closed the Bible. He heard Logan's heavy boots on the loft's ladder before he saw his brother.

"Did I interrupt your devotions?" Logan looked at the Bible at his brother's side.

"It's a good place to stop."

"Good. Listen, I've got to go to Louisville in about two weeks and deliver a big shipment before the weather turns bad." Logan jerked a thumb toward the covered window, where very little sunlight strained through. "Train leaves on a Monday afternoon, and I was wondering whether you wanted to come with me."

Hmm. If I stay, I'll see Daisy more often before the snow comes. If I go, I can take care of a few things. I don't like how Daisy wears Hattie's old cloak. She's sewing Jamie a new winter coat, but he should have some warm gloves, too. Besides, I need runners for a sled. That way Jamie won't have to scooch around in the snow and catch cold.

"Sounds good. There's some stuff I need to pick up. You think this is the last trip you'll make this year?" Bryce wondered whether he'd have a chance to buy everyone Christmas gifts.

"I don't know." Logan scratched his jaw. "I know snowstorms up here make winter traveling difficult, to say the least. All the same, I'd like to get back once more before Christmas. It'd give Daisy time to make more lace, Otis could turn out a few more checker sets, and Asa could carve more nativity sets—Jack says they're sure to be in demand for Christmas. It's a good time of year for selling, and I want to see everybody make the best of it."

"So long as you don't put yourself at risk to make a few more dollars," Bryce warned. "I don't want to see you set out with a full load of merchandise when you can't see ten feet in front of you."

"I wouldn't do that." Logan instinctively looked toward the cabin, although all he could see was the walls of the barn. Bryce knew he was thinking about Hattie. "I don't want to be stuck away from my wife."

"She's good for you," Bryce stated. "You've made a fine choice, Logan."

"Don't I know it!" Logan shot him a grin. "Seems like you're following in my footsteps. I heard tell that Daisy's glad you're staying."

"Mm." Bryce shrugged, knowing his brother was fishing for answers.

"If you're going to clam up, I'm not taking you to Louisville," Logan prodded. "Especially after you slept practically the whole way to Salt Lick Holler when we left Chance Ranch!"

Bryce threw back his head and laughed. "I wondered how long it would be before your patience ran out, Logan. I have to say, it took longer than it used to."

"Stop trying to get my goat and spill it." Logan punched him on the arm.

"I'm staying to court Daisy. She knows it, and she's agreeable." Bryce folded his arms across his chest. "We're taking things slow, seeing how it works out. No pressure and no promises." *Yet.*

❧

"Did we ferget anything?" Miz Willow fretted from the back of the buckboard a week later. The day's corn shucking would keep them all busy.

"Nope." Bryce turned from hoisting Jamie onto the buckboard and spanned his hands on Daisy's waist. "I've got everything I need."

Daisy could feel the heat spread from her cheeks to the tips of her ears as he lifted her up beside her son. She expected him to go around and take the reins, but instead he jumped in the back and sat next to her. Logan lifted Hattie to sit with him on the seat. She caught Logan sending Bryce a wink, and Daisy knew Bryce and Logan had planned it this way.

They think they're so doggone clever. I see straight through it, but I'll play along. Hattie knows what they're up to, same as me. It's almost endearing.

What're folks gonna think when they see us like this? It's so strange having a man sitting this close, knowing we're courting. Takes me back to when I was a young gal out on hayrides. Bryce is offerin' me a fresh start, and I want to see where the road leads.

The trip to the Trevor place went by fast, and before Daisy knew it, they'd arrived at the corn shucking. Today they'd get through the Trevor harvest, and Asa Pleasant was bringing his over by the wagonload. With everybody in the holler showing up, the work should be done by the end of the day—leaving enough time for a nice lunch and a few friendly games.

"Everybody settle in!" Asa and Ed had already set up the working area. Piles of corn sat ready around every seat. Daisy sat Jamie with the other young children, where he could help, but stayed close. Bryce took the seat next to her, making her the recipient of several scowls from unwed young ladies.

"You all know the rules. Shuck fast and well, and we'll finish real quick. Find a red ear and you get to kiss anyone of yore choosin'." Ed whispered something

in Asa's ear, and Asa held up his hands. "Wait a minute. It seems as though las
time around we had a few folks not abidin' by the spirit of the rule. No kissir
yore kin anymore, lessen 'tis yore husband or wife. Now get shuckin'!"

No! Daisy briefly closed her eyes. *Iff'n I cain't give Jamie a kiss on the forehea
I'll be in a real fix. This here's whatcha call an impossible situation. Lord, please don
let me find a red ear!*

She worked rapidly, tearing the green leaves off the cobs and pulling awa
the fine corn silk. People chitchatted back and forth as they worked, and Dais
was glad Bryce didn't require a lot of conversation. They kept shucking in com
panionable silence for a good hour or so before someone found the first red ea

"I got one!" One of the Trevor twins waved a red cob in the air, and everyon
stopped to watch.

"All right, son." Ed slapped him on the back. "Who's the lucky lady?"

Daisy watched Ted as he swaggered around the circle importantly befor
stopping. As the young man looked at Nessie, Daisy could've sworn she saw bot
of them flush. Nessie had already been married once. Her husband ran off on he
and after he'd been gone almost two years, she'd received word that he'd died.

*Interesting. So one of the Trevor twins fancies Nessie. She's a good gal; she deserv
to have a second husband after what she went through with the first. I wonder, sin
he'd run off so long ago, should Nessie have to observe a year's mourning? He'd alread
been missing longer'n that, after all.*

Daisy kept her thoughts to herself. Truth to tell, it wasn't any of her busi
ness. She didn't like the idea of folks speculating about her and Bryce, though sh
knew it was unavoidable. *Hopefully we cain keep it casual-like for a while yet.*

Lost in her thoughts, Daisy hadn't realized how quiet it'd gotten. She looke
down at the ear of corn she'd shucked out of pure habit. The contrary thin
glowed red, and she was the last one to notice.

Oh no! What do I do? I ain't s'posed to kiss Jamie. I cain't kiss Bryce! He stare
at her steadily, and Daisy felt like a fool. *Why not? We're courtin' now. So what
folks jabber on about it?*

She held the red ear up in the air before turning to Bryce. Daisy gave him
small smile and leaned in to kiss his cheek. Even though he'd shaved that morn
ing, a slight shadow rasped against her lips, making them tingle at the contac
Up this close, she could smell the faintly spicy scent of his aftershave. She close
her eyes and breathed in his closeness before drawing away.

Bryce looked at her, smiling only enough to show that he was pleased. T
everyone watching, he seemed glad to have been chosen but not ruffled by it. Bu
Daisy saw a different story in his gaze. Those blue eyes gleamed with the grin h
wouldn't show off, filling the moment with fire and promise.

A few catcalls and some applause sounded out as they always did, but Dais
didn't mind at all. *Let them think what they will. I care for Bryce, and he cares for m
It wasn't a public spectacle, jist a show of affection.*

With the most nerve-racking challenge of the day behind her, Daisy relaxed. The trees wore shades of gold and auburn as the autumn sun shone down upon them. Jamie's movements, alongside those of the other young children, didn't appear too jerky. They all struggled to shuck a few ears of corn, uncovering more giggles than anything else.

"I done got one!" Lily Cleary waved a red ear in the air, chin lifted in triumph. Daisy watched with interest. Lily had been no more'n a child when Daisy moved to Hawk's Fall. Was there a young gentleman she had her eye on? As the girl purposely made her way around the circle, Daisy thought she knew who it was.

I wonder which twin Lily fancies. Shore hope it's the one as didn't kiss Nessie. It's always nice when things work out like—

Daisy felt her jaw drop as Lily stopped in front of Bryce.

What?

Chapter 18

Not me. Not me. Not me. Please keep walking, Lily. Bryce resisted the urge to lean back and howl in frustration as Lily Cleary, no doubt egged on by her mother, put her hands on his shoulders, leaning close for a kiss—a kiss on the lips that lasted far, far too long in Bryce's estimation. When Lily let go, Bryce wiped the back of his neck, wishing he could wipe his mouth. Then he snuck a glance at Daisy.

He'd seen her eyes widen in shock when Lily stopped in front of him, but now her face was blank. *Should I be relieved that she's not upset or disappointed? It would help things if Lily would go back to her mama, so I could think about how to fix this.* Bryce looked at Daisy to see if her expression had changed. *Nope. But wait. Something about the set of her jaw. . .*

Daisy's clenching her teeth! She's not unaffected by Lily's ploy. Bryce bit back a grin. He'd rather ease a little pang of jealousy than try to create emotion where none resided. He remembered her tentative kiss, Daisy's soft lips lightly grazing his cheek. *She kissed me, and she's not happy that Lily did, too.*

Well, don't you worry, sweetheart. Bryce tried to send the message without speaking. He didn't want to embarrass her. *There's only one woman I'm staying in Salt Lick Holler for.* Something in his face must've reassured her, because her jaw loosened, and she gave him a barely perceptible nod. *Then we understand each other. It's a good start.*

The day passed, the piles of unshucked corn growing smaller while the corncribs strained to hold their bounty. Everybody took a leisurely lunch before getting back to the work at hand. A plentiful harvest this year meant that the fun and games would be postponed.

A short while later, Otis Nye stood up. "Got to stretch these ole legs of mine," he muttered. "Rheumatiz."

Bryce didn't pay him much mind until cheers erupted from the crowd. He looked up to find out what all the fuss was about.

Otis Nye straightened up from bussing Miz Willow's cheek. He wore a self-satisfied grin on his craggy face as he walked back to his seat and reached for another ear of corn.

Miz Willow blushed scarlet, eyes wide in surprise. She lifted her hand to touch her cheek before she realized everybody was watching. "What's so inter-estin'? Get back to work." She grabbed more corn and got to shucking. For the rest of the afternoon, everyone snuck glances at wily old Otis Nye, but he stayed put as the day wore on.

"I gots another one!" Lily Cleary crowed, looking straight at Bryce.

Oh, no you don't, Bryce glowered. *Don't even think about trying that again. No matter how much your mama pushes you toward me, it won't do any good. I've already found a woman.*

"Lily Cleary, you set back down this minute." Miz Willow's voice cracked through the circle with the force of a whip. "I done saw yore mama pass you that there corn. Shame on the both of you."

"Cain't get anything past Miz Willow!" someone called out.

"How cain you say such a thang, Willomena?" Bethilda Cleary puffed up like a riled peahen.

"I cain say it 'cuz I seen it." Miz Willow didn't give an inch, and Bryce's affection for the old woman grew. *She's a fine woman, that Willomena Hendrick.*

"Don't get all het up, Bethilda." Ed Trevor intervened with a jaunty step. "Fair's fair. It's yore corn, and you do the kissin'."

A sour look crossed Bethilda Cleary's face as she sought out her husband.

"Good to see you, darlin'!" Ed Cleary waggled his brows at his wife as she stood on tiptoe. He swiftly turned his head so her demure peck on the cheek became a full-blown buss on the lips.

"Ed!" Bethilda blushed scarlet and scurried back to her daughters, but she no longer wore a frown. It was obvious that she cared more for her husband than she liked to let on. Ed's mischief had relieved the tension in the air and gotten a chuckle at his wife's foibles.

Bryce laughed along with everyone else but started working double-time. The day was almost over, and he had a goal to reach. *Come on, one of these things has to be red. . . .*

~※~

"I've decided not to go to Louisville, Logan," Bryce announced a week later.

"Why not, Bryce?"

"Bad timing. If I go to Louisville with you," Bryce reasoned, "I'll be missing the last days before snowfall."

"That's right." A knowing look passed across Logan's face. "I should've guessed you'd want to be here with Daisy."

"And Jamie."

"How's that little wagon coming along? Nate Rucker make those wheels like he promised?"

"Yep. He slipped them to me at the corn shucking. I'll have it finished this afternoon." Bryce paused. "We'll take it with us to the church social."

"Good idea. Jamie's on the scrawny side for a boy his age, but he's still almost five. He's getting too big for the women to be carrying him around."

"It should be a good solution for now." Bryce pulled a scrap of foolscap from his pocket. "But when the snow comes, the wagon won't work. I'm planning on making a sled for him. Since I'm not going to Louisville, I'll need to have you pick up a few things." He handed the paper to his brother.

"Runners, rope, wood glue. . .makes sense. I'll see what I can do." Logan squinted at the list. "What's all this other stuff for?"

"Daisy's making Jamie a winter coat, but he'll need gloves, since he uses his hands to get around the cabin. Daisy doesn't have winter clothing, so I want you to get her a ready-made heavy cloak and a wool dress—somethin' fancy, like with stripes."

"I don't know anything about dresses." Logan shook his head.

"Come on, Logan. I had Hattie write down Daisy's size so the clerk can help you. The cloak can be simple—light brown, like a newborn fawn, oughtta do it."

Bryce watched Logan frown and shake his head some more. *Time for a new approach.* "Listen, Logan. We can rope, ride, herd cattle, mend fences, judge horseflesh, shoot straight, work with our hands, play a mean game of horse-shoes—are you tryin' to tell me you can't buy one little old dress?"

"Of course I can." Logan jutted out his chin and stalked out of the barn. "But I don't have to like it."

Bryce chuckled and went back to the tack room. He whistled as he fitted the wagon handle to its boxy frame. He'd made it small enough so it wouldn't be unwieldy but large enough so Jamie wouldn't outgrow it anytime soon. Tightening a few pieces, he heard light footsteps.

Without enough time to fling a covering over the wagon, Bryce barreled out of the tack room, all but running straight into Daisy.

"Bryce!" She took a step back to steady herself. "What's the rush?"

"Uh. . ." Bryce cleared his throat. "I was on my way to see if you wanted to go for a walk during Jamie's nap." He cringed at the fib. Truth was, he did want to ask her that very thing but hadn't planned to go for a few more minutes, at least.

"That's mighty nice of you." Daisy's smile tugged at his heart. "I was jist goin' to ask if you wanted to go for a ride."

"Sounds good," Bryce agreed, then panicked when she stepped toward the tack room. "But a walk sounds better." He snagged her arm.

"It's been a long time since I rode around the hills, Bryce." Her quiet plea melted him. "Soon it'll be winter, and then I cain't."

"All right. I'll go get the saddles. Why don't you. . ." He paused, unable to think of anything.

"I'll get a few sugar lumps for the horses." Daisy slid past him into the tack room and stopped short at the sight of the wagon. "What's that?"

"A wagon I made for Jamie." Bryce hastened to explain why he hadn't wanted her to see it. "It's not quite finished yet."

"It's. . ." Daisy ran her fingertips along the side of the wagon, reaching out to pick up the handle. She gave an experimental tug, and it rolled forward. Bryce held his breath, waiting for her pronouncement. "Wonderful."

"I'm glad you like it."

"Yore so thoughtful!" Daisy turned and gave him a hug. "Jamie will love this, and I'll have an easier time takin' him around. Thankee, Bryce."

She looked up at him, her brown eyes glowing with gratitude. Her lips hovered so close. . . .

"You're—" Bryce groaned and closed the distance between them, holding her against him as he touched his lips to hers. *Gentle, soft. . .*

After they both drew away, Bryce touched his forehead to hers. "Wonderful."

Chapter 19

Daisy shoveled ashes from the stove belly into the ash pail.

Wonderful. She touched her lips, reliving Bryce's kiss. Had it only been two weeks since he decided to stay? How quickly she'd come to see him as more than a friend. He was so strong, gentle, tender, rough. . .*Bryce.*

The puppy's cold nose bumped against her elbow insistently, causing her to scatter a few ashes onto the floor. "Nosey!" Daisy put down the shovel and cuddled the animal close.

The tiny pup served as yet another reminder of how thoughtfully Bryce attended to the needs of her son. Daisy rubbed Nosey's silky fur once more before setting her down. The pup immediately scrabbled toward Jamie, nails clicking on the hardwood floors.

" 'Ook!" Jamie held up his slate for her inspection. There, in the big, loopy letters of her son's hand, rested one word. *L-o-v-e.*

"Oh, Jamie!" Daisy knelt down and pulled him into a hug. "That's some mighty fine work. It does yore mama's heart good to see you so smart."

" 'Ove you," Jamie crooned, giving her an awkward pat on the shoulder.

"I love you, too, baby." Daisy drew away so Jamie could keep working. As Nosey stuck her snout on the slate, giving it a wet imprint of approval, Daisy smiled. *Jamie and I love each other. And Bryce loves us both.*

"Hello in there!" Bryce's voice called from the yard.

"Yes, Bryce?" Daisy flung open the door.

"Can Jamie and Nosey come out to play?" His voice sang with mischief and fun.

"Jist a minute!" Daisy waited for Jamie to get a firm hold on the puppy before carrying them both outside.

"Hi, Byce!" Jamie positively sparkled whenever they spent time together.

"Hey, buddy. Got something for you."

"Wut?"

"This!" Bryce whipped the cover off the wagon he'd made just for her son.

"Wow!" Jamie wiggled with excitement, and Nosey let out a few celebratory yaps.

"What say your mama and I take you and Nosey for a ride?" Bryce suggested, wheeling the wagon closer.

"Pease?" Jamie looked at her with wide eyes.

"Of course!" Daisy laughed and deposited him in his wagon. He still clutched

Nosey, who kept very busy snuffling the sides of the wagon.

Bryce nestled a blanket in the bottom so Jamie would be more comfortable and steady. *He's so good at adapting things to make others feel comfortable.*

Bryce pulled the wagon smoothly along the path while Daisy walked alongside. Jamie squealed with glee when Bryce began making wiggly zigzags. They didn't go too far—just enough to know that the arrangement would work.

Seems to me that with Bryce around, a lot of things are better'n afore. Mayhap the wagon isn't the only thing that will work between us.

⁓⦿⁓

"Now let me see. . . ." Bryce rubbed his jaw and stared at the wagon. With Logan gone to Louisville, he had the time to take Jamie fishing before it got too cold. "I've got Jamie—you've got Nosey?"

" 'Es!" Jamie held up the wiggly pooch before tucking her back in his lap. Nosey fared well with Jamie's attention and the cow's milk Bryce kept feeding her.

"I've got the poles and tackle box. You have that lunch basket your ma packed?"

Jamie nodded and patted the basket. It rested in front of him in the wagon.

"Sounds like we're ready to go catch some supper!" Bryce took hold of the wagon handle with his free hand and set off. "The fish know the weather's changing, so we should have no trouble coaxing a few onto the line."

Jamie played with Nosey as Bryce pulled the wagon along the dirt road. He stopped when he spotted a shady patch of moist earth. He turned the wagon onto the grass, where it jounced along more roughly.

"Whee!" Jamie held on tight but looked around in confusion when Bryce stopped. " 'Ish?"

"Before we catch fish, we'll need bait." Bryce lifted the youngster out of the wagon and sat him down. He pulled out his pocketknife and dug up some of the dark dirt. "I need your help. We have to dig around until we find worms!"

"Mess." Jamie looked at the dirt longingly.

"This is man's work. Your mama knows we'll get a little dirty." Bryce scooped some of the dirt into Jamie's fingers and unearthed a pink worm. He grabbed it and dropped it into the jar he'd brought along. "See? Now let's get a bunch more."

Jamie didn't need to be told twice. The small boy burrowed into the earth with gusto, scattering dirt everywhere. Nosey watched for a minute before joining in, her front paws scrabbling to widen the hole. The little boy held up his filthy fist, eyes shining in glee. "Got't!"

"Good one." Bryce held out the jar, and Jamie dropped in a fat earthworm.

It didn't take long for Bryce to judge they had enough. He picked up Jamie, turned him upside down, and gave him a few light bounces. The lad giggled as specks of dirt rained to the ground. Nosey gave herself an emphatic shake, starting at her nose and wiggling all the way down.

"Let's go to the stream." Bryce got them both situated in the wagon—Jamie insisted on holding the jar of worms—and made their way to the fishing hole. Bryce splashed Jamie's hands with water before they shared a picnic lunch of egg-salad sandwiches and coleslaw. Then it was time to get down to business.

"Eeww!" Jamie shrieked, fascinated as Bryce laced the first worm onto his hook.

"Here." Bryce cast the line into the water and handed the small, lightweight pole to Jamie. "Hold it tight, and let me know when you get a bite."

"How I know?" Jamie stared at the pole blankly.

"It'll move." Bryce reached out and gave the line a gentle tug. "Like that. Then you tell me, and we'll haul in your fish. Remember, you have to be as quiet as you can."

" 'Kay!" His little brow furrowed as he concentrated on the task at hand.

Bryce baited his own hook, then hunkered down beside Jamie. The little boy couldn't really hold the pole steady, but he did a good job trying. They sat in silence, listening to the rippling water and the whisper of the wind through the long grasses at the water's edge. Birdcalls rarely disturbed the quiet, since most of them had flown south already.

"Byce!" Jamie gripped his pole tightly, trying to steady the wobble.

It took Bryce a moment to decide if it was Jamie shaking or a fish on the line. Bryce scooped Jamie up and put his hands over the little boy's to steady them. The line danced in the water. He immediately started walking back, drawing the line from the water until a fair-sized fish flopped on the bank. Bryce pulled it farther from the water so it wouldn't slide back.

Nosey trailed the slippery fish from the water's edge, backing away when its tail hit her in the muzzle. The little dog looked up at Bryce and Jamie, wagging her tail as though to say, "We did it!"

"Would you look at that?" Bryce sat Jamie down before sliding the hook from the fish's mouth. "First fish of the day. Way to go, buddy!" He handed it to Jamie and pushed the water pail closer. "Go ahead and put it in the bucket of water."

Jamie dropped his catch into the pail, beaming with pride. "Ag'n?" he asked hopefully.

Bryce nodded and handed him the pole, ready with a worm dangling from the hook. "We've got a whole pail to fill. Let's get to it so we've got enough for supper when we go back home."

⁓⁓⁓

Winter came in a flurry of snow and ice, blanketing the ground in a single night. Daisy woke up to see her own breath and rushed to put more wood on the stove. She dressed Jamie in the flannel long underwear she'd scarce finished for him, layering his pants and shirt atop so he'd keep warm. His woolen winter coat hung ready on the hook by the door iff'n she took him outside at all.

Don't see no reason to risk it. Jamie gets along jist fine even though he cain't use his legs, but in the snow he'll get drenched and icy cold so quick. His wagon won't pull him through snowdrifts. Iff'n he catches cold, Jamie ain't strong enough to fight it off like most boys.

Daisy shredded the potatoes, pushing the knife into the roots hard as she thought about how frail her son's health could be. *It'll grow into pneumonia, and I'll lose him. Best keep him inside. Bryce'll still take him to the barn to visit the animals, and Jamie has Nosey in here. It'll have to do.*

The fried potatoes and coffee steamed on the stove when Logan and Hattie walked through the adjoining door and said good morning to Miz Willow, who didn't look up from reading her morning devotions. Bryce fetched Jamie to gather the eggs, then brought the basket back full. Hattie helped Daisy scramble them up with chunks of ham.

"First snow of the winter!" Logan grinned as he downed his breakfast.

"Beautiful out there," Hattie agreed. "Snow turns the world into soft white curves, like givin' it a clean coat of whitewash, only better."

"I can't wait. Fresh-fallen snow has so many possibilities." Bryce turned to Jamie. "You have your long underwear on, buddy?"

"Yep!" Jamie pulled on the neck of his shirt to show Bryce the red flannel beneath.

Now why would Bryce ask a question like that? He's not planning on taking Jamie out in the snow!

Alarmed, Daisy stared at Bryce.

"Snow angels are a must," he said, going right on with his planning. "Maybe a snowman, too."

"Not today, fellers." Daisy rose and cleared the empty platters.

"Why not?" Logan demanded.

"I haven't made Jamie his gloves yet, so he cain't go out in the snow." *There. That's a solid reason. It'll even take me awhile to make the gloves. Iff'n I stretch it out, I might not have 'em done afore blizzarding season. Then he'll hardly use 'em a'tall.*

"That reminds me." Bryce fumbled in his pockets and pulled out a pair of small blue woolen gloves with a matching scarf. "Seems as though I missed your birthday, Jamie. Just a month before we met." Bryce shook his head. "I had to do something to fix that!"

Daisy drew a deep breath as he fit the gloves onto Jamie's tiny hands before wrapping the scarf around his neck. Her son held his hands out in front of him and wiggled his fingers gleefully. The gloves Logan had picked up for him in Louisville fit perfectly.

"Ready!"

"What about yore lessuns?" she burst out, desperate to keep Jamie out of the cold.

"It's the first snowfall, Daisy!" Logan pushed aside her protest like it was nothing more than a pesky gnat.

"But Jamie don't have a second pair of flannels," Daisy protested. "Iff'n those get soaked through, he'll get cold."

"We'll have warm towels waiting in the oven to dry him off before he changes," Bryce reassured her as he helped Jamie into his coat and put on his own, too. "And I'm sure you'll have some hot tea waiting, too. It'll be fine."

With that, he whisked her son out into the snow, the door banging shut behind them.

"I said no! Why won't they let me raise Jamie as I see fit?" Daisy paced around the cabin. "He cain't catch cold. It's too dangerous!"

"I know." Hattie began fixing some tea. "But I'll have those towels warm, and we'll get him some tea. He's bundled up out there, too. I reckon a boy's got to play in the snow sometime, Daisy. Might as well be now."

No, it shouldn't.

Chapter 20

This way." Logan lay down in a fresh drift of powder and spread his outstretched arms and legs open and shut. "That's how you make a snow angel!"

Bryce put Jamie down and grabbed his shoes to move his legs in the proper motion. The boy waved his arms up and down in imitation of Logan. Bryce lifted him back up so he could survey his handiwork.

"Ange's!" Jamie pointed excitedly at the impression he'd made in the white blanket covering the earth.

"And a very fine one it is, too," Bryce assessed. He put Jamie down in his wagon. Sure, it wouldn't roll through the drifts, but it was a dry place for Jamie to sit down. Hattie had spoken with him about Jamie's health. He wasn't strong enough to handle a cold like most kids. It'd turn to pneumonia and take his life. Bryce needed to be extra careful.

All the same, it did no good protecting Jamie's life if no one let him live it. The boy deserved to enjoy all the wonder of childhood. Bryce intended to give him all the laughter and adventure possible during the time they had.

"We're going to teach you how to make snowballs." Bryce put a lump of the soft ice in Jamie's hand, took one for himself, and demonstrated how to mold it into a round ball.

"Once you're done, put it down and start a pile. Keep making more." Bryce, Logan, and Jamie all worked to make dozens of snowballs.

"I've got an idea." Logan started carrying some and putting them in a heap beside the cabin door.

"What are you up to?" Bryce had a funny feeling it involved getting Hattie and Daisy to play in the snow.

"You'll see." Logan came back and hunched on Jamie's other side. "Hattie! Daisy! Grab your cloaks and come out here for a minute!"

The door opened, and Hattie stepped outside in her pink-hooded cover. "What is it?"

"Snowball fight!" Logan lobbed one at her shoulder.

"No fair! We're unarmed!" Daisy glowered at Bryce.

"Snowbaws!" Jamie pitched one, but it fell short with a soft thud.

"To your left, ladies!" Bryce waited for them to throw the first volley before reciprocating. Then the fight was on.

He held Jamie's hand and helped him swing his arm, showing him when to

327

release the snowball so it would go farther. The little boy learned quickly, hitting Hattie and Daisy more times than Bryce thought possible. Their carefully created supply of ammunition dwindled rapidly.

"That's it. We're out." Bryce stood up. He heard the whoosh too late to duck and ended up with a collar full of melting snow. "Who did that?"

"Me!" Daisy stood like a warrior, framed in the doorway she'd built with him. Her cheeks glowed a pretty pink, a smile stretched across her rosy lips, and she gripped one last snowball in her left hand.

"We surrender! We've got nothing left!" Logan put his hands up.

"Nothing doin'!" Hattie swiped Daisy's final snowball to toss at her husband. It smashed into his chest, and Logan sank to his knees.

"Brought down by my own wife!" he moaned. "Right in the heart!"

"Quit yore bellyachin'!" Miz Willow shook her cane at them. "You called the girls out for a snowball fight and came off the worse for it. You got nobody to blame 'cept yoreselves. Come inside and warm up afore you catch your death out here."

Daisy stayed outside after Hattie and Logan tromped into the cabin, waiting for Bryce to hand over Jamie. As Bryce saw her cuddle her son, burrowing her face into his hair, he felt warm despite the cold. He, Daisy, and Jamie would make a good family. All he had to do was bide his time until Daisy realized the same thing.

⁓⁓⁓

"Daisy," Miz Willow began as she laid down the pad of paper with numbers scrawled across it. "You know you don't have to do this. We got plenty of room here."

"Don't get me wrong, Miz Willow. Yore place is mighty fine, and I cain't tell you how much I 'preciate yore hospitality." Daisy searched for the words. "But Hawk's Fall. . .Peter bought that land when we first wed. It's home to Jamie an' me."

"Darlin', I know it was. But that house is gone forever." Miz Willow's observation tore at Daisy's heart. "Even iff'n you could scrimp enough to rebuild, it wouldn't be what holds yore memories."

"I ken that. But the land is all we got left now." Daisy drew a deep breath. "So I need for us to keep on goin'." *Logan, Jamie, and Bryce won't stay out in the barn for'ver, and Hattie'll be back from the Pleasant place soon.* She managed a tight smile as Miz Willow picked up the paper and pen once more. "You got how much per piece? Now we need to figgur out how many veils, runners, and collars you cain make per year."

"It takes a powerful long time to make lace, so. . ." Daisy thought long and hard before she gave the answer.

Miz Willow's pen scratched across the paper as she laboriously added it all up. "How much did Logan tell you the lumber would run? Hearth bricks? The workers?" The old woman frowned at the numbers she wrote. "You take into account all the thangs you'll need? Furniture, pots, pans, stock of dry goods, blankets, hearth rug, buckets, hay for yore mule, and such?"

"Not yet." Daisy lifted her chin in determination. "We'll get by on whatever's left after food and clothes for Jamie an' me." She rattled off still more numbers Logan had helped her figure out.

"That's it, Daisy." Miz Willow sucked in a sharp breath. "You only got but two dollars left. Ain't nearly enough to outfit a home, even iff'n you manage to make as much lace as you say you cain this winter."

Daisy's throat closed. *It's not enough. I cain't possibly make any more lace than that, and even with the extry money from Logan's trade deal, it won't suffice. Why? I work so hard. It should be sufficient to provide for Jamie and me. I've always managed afore. I'll think of somethin'.*

"Iff'n I swaller m' pride an' ask Logan and the men 'round here to help me out"—Daisy shut her eyes at the thought of asking for charity—"so's I don't pay for the work, would it be enough?" *It has to be.*

Miz Willow squinted at the pad. "I don't reckon it would, Daisy. Even if the men of the community pitch in like they should and build the house and even yore furniture for you, you'll jist have enough left to buy wood for next winter and keep yore mule in hay. Yore still missin' blankets, pots, pans, and such like."

"I'll work harder," Daisy spoke quickly, desperately. "How 'bout iff'n I make two more collars this winter?" *I'll work into the nights. Somehow, I'll get it done.*

"Not quite." Miz Willow shook her white locks. "It'd almost be enough, but yore forgettin' how you an' Jamie need winter thangs. Yore already makin' him a coat, but that's jist a start."

"I don't need anythin'. I got Hattie's ole cloak. I'll get by." Daisy straightened her shoulders with resolve.

"What about candles?" Miz Willow pressed her. "And Nosey?"

I cain't ask Jamie to give up his pup. She sleeps curled up aside him at night, follows him durin' the day. Daisy buried her head in her hands and willed herself not to give in to the sobs rising in her throat. *No matter how hard I work, I cain't do it. There's not enough time to take care of Jamie and make enough lace to rebuild our home.*

Her chest hitched, then tightened. Daisy's breath grew ragged. Panic welled inside her. *I cain't provide for my son.* She took in quick, shallow breaths, not getting enough air.

"Here." Miz Willow thrust a cup of tea in her hands. "The steam oughtta holp you breathe. I'll go get some eucalyptus oil." She rushed to the storeroom and back, dotting something beneath Daisy's nose. "Take slow, deep breaths now, else yore gonna faint." Miz Willow squeezed her hand. "And you might as well let out them tears. They've been a long time comin'."

The wail rose from the bottom of her soul as Daisy gave in. Hot tears rushed down her face, her shoulders shaking with the intensity of her sobs. Miz Willow held her as she cried for Peter, for Jamie, for the loss of their home, for knowing she couldn't keep everything together no matter how hard she tried. When there was nothing left inside her, she straightened up and used the third handkerchief Miz Willow passed to her.

"What am I gonna do?"

"First thang is to calm down, now that you've let it all out." Miz Willow briskly took the cooled tea from the table. "Then take a moment to realize yore already done with the hardest part."

"What?" To Daisy's way of thinking, the hardest part lay ahead.

"You admitted you need holp. That's somethin' you've been avoidin' for a far sight too long."

Mayhap, Daisy admitted. *But now I have to ask for the holp I need.*

"So now that yore facin' the facts, I figgur you've got two paths you cain take." Miz Willow pinned her with a no-nonsense gaze. "You an' Jamie are more'n welcome in this house. Yore son brightens my day, and yore a bigger holp 'round here than you know."

"Thankee, Miz Willow." Daisy swallowed the lump of pride lodged in her throat. "It's a good place to raise Jamie."

"Yore welcome, Daisy. I ain't jist returnin' the customary response to than-kee, neither. I want you to listen and pay me heed. You and Jamie are welcome here. Yore wanted and loved, and all of us know how hard you work. You'll still be providin' for yore son, jist under this roof where you cain holp me, too. Understand?"

"Yes, ma'am." Daisy's heart softened toward the old woman. *She's a good woman and teaches Jamie useful thangs, too. Truth of the matter is, Jamie's gettin' big-ger, but no better at carin' for hisself. I need more holp with him, and having Hattie and Miz Willow around puts me more at ease on account of them bein' healers. The wood floor is nice for Jamie, too. We cain have a good life here.*

"Now that we've got that settled, I'm going to put a fly in the ointment." Miz Willow's rocker began to creak rhythmically. "Seems to me yore overlook-ing Bryce. He's dead set on marryin' you. You've encouraged his courtin'. How cain you be so set on rebuildin' in Hawk's Fall iff'n yore givin' any thought to marryin' agin?"

"It's early stages yet." Daisy bristled. "I cain't see into the future, and I got to be ready."

"Say you two do marry up. His ranch is out in Californy. Have you given any thought to movin' out there?"

"I'd be lyin' iff'n I tole you the thought hadn't crossed my mind," Daisy admitted.

I cain't imagine leavin' these hills. My whole life's fit into the valleys and peaks. The cricks and crags of this land hold memories and reminders. A woman follows her man—that's why I left Salt Lick for Hawk's Fall. But it's only half-a-day's ride. Californy's clear cross the country.

"Are you willin' to pack up Jamie and leave?" Miz Willow prodded further. "Otherwise, you should tell Bryce now."

"Iff'n he offers for my hand, and I accept, it'll be with the intention of going where he leads." Daisy spoke the words aloud for the first time. "Even if it is all the way to Californy."

"Good." Miz Willow stopped rocking to lean forward. "Lovejoy writes that it's a fine place. You'll have four sisters-in-law and lots of nieces and nephews for Jamie to play with. Weather over there'll be easier on him, too. Logan's sitting pretty from his share of the ranch, and Bryce'll be jist as well off. The Chance men are good workers. He'll take care of you and Jamie so's you needn't fret no more."

"That ain't any type of reason to enter into marriage. I don't aim to wed Bryce so's he'll put a roof o'er my head," Daisy denied firmly. *Iff'n we wed, it'll be for love—'cuz we don't want to part. We'll become a family together—not a burden Bryce has to work to maintain.*

"Jamie's my responsibility. I cain't rely on Bryce to provide for us."

Chapter 21

Bryce froze at the certainty in Daisy's tone. He'd just left Jamie in the barn to towel off some of the dried mud from Nosey's fur, meaning to ask the women if they needed him to get anything from the smokehouse for supper.

"I cain't rely on Bryce to provide for us." The words knocked the air from his chest, and he exhaled sharply. Bryce stepped away from the cabin, unwilling to hear any more.

Jesus, help me! No matter how I twist the words, I can't make anything good out of them. She said outright that she can't rely on me to provide for her and Jamie. How can she think I won't provide for them? She knows about Chance Ranch. Daisy's seen me build rooms, barns, wagons. She has to know I'm more than capable of taking care of my own. There's only one thing those words can mean. I've done everything I can think of to show her that I'll take good care of her and her son. What more can I do?

Bryce trudged through the snow until trickles of water ran into his boots. He stopped pacing and shook his head to clear his thoughts.

Can it be money? Does Daisy think I'm destitute? I sleep in the barn because this isn't my home. I haven't showered her with courting gifts because I didn't want to raise her hackles. She hates thinking she's charity, and I wouldn't make her feel low for the world. So how do I tell Daisy I'm more than solvent? It's not exactly the type of thing you mention in conversation.

Bryce began pacing again.

Words won't do it. If I'm going to show her I am a good provider, I'll have to think of something else. I'll go to Louisville with Logan this last time before Christmas and buy up anything and everything I think she and Jamie would want. If she doesn't think of it as charity but as tokens of affection, it won't affront her. I'll prove that I'm financially stable.

Having determined a course of action, Bryce stomped back to the barn, shaking snow off his boots.

Lord, thank You for letting me overhear Daisy's concerns. Now that I know she's worried about finances, I can put those fears to rest. I don't know how she got the idea that Chance Ranch isn't prosperous and I might not be able to provide for her and Jamie, but it's a mistake I can set right. When I'm done, she won't have a doubt in her mind that I will be a good provider for our family.

❧

"Good thing the snow's light today," Daisy observed, trudging through the slush with Hattie.

"Otis Nye's place ain't far, but we couldn't make it the past few days on account of the snowstorm. His rheumatiz acts up somethin' dreadful in the cold. He'll be needin' more devil's claw tea." Hattie pulled her cloak tight against the frosty air, and Daisy followed suit.

"That cloak shore do look nice on you, Daisy." Her motion must've drawn Hattie's eye. " 'Twas good of Bryce to think of it."

"I never felt wool so soft." Daisy stroked the fawn-colored fabric. "It don't set right the way Bryce done give me this cloak and Jamie his scarf and gloves, while I ain't done nothin' in return."

"Don't be a goose, Daisy," Hattie harrumphed. "They's courtin' gifts. Fine choices, too."

"Bryce is good about findin' out our needs and fillin' 'em," Daisy had to admit. "It shore is nice to have a man pay me mind like that."

"Well, you pay attention right back. Don't think I haven't noticed how many apple pies and such you've been bakin', Daisy Thales!"

"Cookin's the only thang I cain do right now to repay his kindness. Courtin's betwixt two people, and I ain't 'bout to let him do all the givin'."

"We all know you ain't like that, Daisy." Hattie shot her a disgruntled look. "That winter coat you sewed for Bryce is dreadful fine."

"I ain't quite finished with the linin'." Daisy wanted the gift to be perfect. "It'll be ready for Christmas."

"I cain't believe he's made it through all this time with jist that one light coat." Hattie shook her head in wonder. "Mayhap 'tisn't my place to go runnin' my mouth, but Bryce shorely has gone outta his way to court you."

"I don't think there's any way left for him to show me how serious he is." Daisy paused. "Makes me feel. . ." *Beholden*. She pushed away the negative thought. Bryce made her feel so much more than that. *Wanted. Taken care of.* "Special."

"I hope so. A man don't stay through one of these winters sleeping in the barn unless he's dead set on gettin' his woman," Hattie observed. "Good reminder that money ain't ev'rything. It's God who provides for us in ev'ry way." She shook her head. "I cain't believe Bryce thought to buy you a cloak and plumb fergot to get one for hisself. Shows 'zactly where his mind is."

Yes. His mind is set on me and Jamie, and my heart's yearning for Bryce to return. He's been gone to Louisville less'n a week, and I miss him. When he gets home, I know this'll be a Christmas to remember.

~~~~~

"You think this'll fit her?" Bryce held up a green-striped wool dress.

"I dunno." Logan eyed him thoughtfully. "Put it up against yourself so I can see if it'll be too long or not. Daisy's a lot shorter'n you are."

Bryce gave a resigned sigh and held the ruffled collar under his chin. The end of the dress barely brushed his knees. "What's the verdict?"

Logan couldn't keep a straight face. "Makes you look almost dainty!" He let loose a few hearty guffaws.

Bryce rolled his eyes and handed the dress to the shopkeeper, along with Hattie's measurements of Daisy. "Will this fit?"

The man took out a measuring tape and busily checked the length and other dimensions. "Like a glove."

"Wrap it up," Bryce ordered. "Wait a minute. Do you have gloves?" He ignored Logan's loud groan as he surveyed a selection of ladies' hand wear, picking out a daytime pair of blinding white cotton before a heavy winter pair of black wool.

He laid the gloves in his palm, remembering the feel of Daisy's hand in his, so tiny and delicate. "These'll do." He passed them to the clerk.

"Is there something else you're looking for, sir?"

"What would you suggest in the way of robes?" Bryce had thought long and hard before figuring out what to get for Hattie and Miz Willow.

"A robe?" Logan echoed. "Don't you think you're going a little far, Bryce?"

"Nope. I'm getting one each for Hattie, Miz Willow, and Daisy. Folks come knocking on their door at all hours of the night, so they need dressing gowns. If I get one for each of them, no one will be affronted."

"That's a good idea," Logan murmured enviously. He started prowling around the shop, looking with renewed interest at the wares lining the shelves.

"These velvet dressing gowns are popular." The young clerk led him over to a display. "Any color in particular?"

"Purple for Miz Willow, pink for Hattie," Bryce decided. He fingered a deep forest green robe with white flowers embroidered on the edges. "This one for Daisy."

"These, too." Bryce pointed to a set of tortoiseshell hair combs lying in a case. Their gleaming brown color would make Daisy's honey curls shine even brighter. *I'll give these to her as soon as we get back to Salt Lick Holler. The other things can wait a few days for Christmas.*

"Very good, sir." The clerk's smile grew broader with each item he rang up.

Bryce eyed the growing pile, not yet satisfied. *There must be something else I can think of to get her. I have to prove that I've got the wherewithal to care for her and her son. Too much is riding on this to let it be, but what am I forgetting?*

"If I might be so bold," the clerk suggested, "we have a lovely selection of shawls to your left."

Bryce inched closer, picking out a cream-colored shawl whose delicate color and weave put him in mind of Daisy's lace. "I'll take this, too."

"An excellent choice." The clerk carefully folded the shawl and laid it atop Bryce's large pile of items.

Almost. Is there anything she'd really like? Something special that wouldn't do for any woman but just for Daisy?

334

"Do you carry things for women's toilettes?" Bryce knew he'd mispronounced the last word, but the shopkeeper nodded and showed him to the far corner. Bryce looked over the vanity sets, recalling how strongly Daisy felt that a woman should have a looking glass in her home. When he flipped over one of the handheld mirrors, he found a single daisy etched into the silver plating on the back. *Perfect.*

"It belongs to a set, sir." The clerk industriously laid out a matching brush, comb, and some other strange implement.

"What's this?" Bryce picked the thing up to scrutinize it.

"A nail buffer. I'm certain your wife would like it." The clerk lifted the silver buffer from its tray as he explained.

"She's not my wife," Bryce corrected. "Yet."

Daisy slid another batch of cinnamon rolls into the oven before tending to her hair. She slipped the tresses from their nightly braid and combed through the entire mass before pinning back half of her hair and letting the rest fall free. For the finishing touch, she slid the beautiful tortoiseshell hair combs in place.

"Jist right." Miz Willow nodded her approval at Bryce's homecoming gift.

He'd taken her aside right after he and Logan got back to push a small bundle in her hands. "I missed you," he'd whispered in a husky voice that made her heart sing.

"I missed you, too." Daisy had kissed him on the cheek before opening the bundle and finding the dainty hair combs. "You didn't need to do this!"

He'd laid her head on his shoulder, holding her close to his heart. "I wanted to."

So on Christmas morning, three days later, she wore them for the first time. Mistletoe and holly decorated the cabin in celebration of the Savior's birth. Boughs crackled in the stove, sending the woodsy scent of pine to mingle with the cinnamon and yeast of the rolls. The cabin smelled of cherished memories and surprises yet to come.

After a hearty breakfast, they got ready to leave for church.

"Here, Daisy." Bryce held out her cloak for her. "Beautiful." He reached out to touch one of the combs, running his fingers through her hair.

"They are." Daisy smiled.

"I didn't mean the combs." Bryce's compliment made her heart thump faster as they made their way to the Christmas service.

Chapter 22

Heart full to bursting, Daisy sang the familiar Christmas hymns fervently. *"Oh, come, all ye faithful, joyful and triumphant. . . ."*

I feel joyful and triumphant. Today, long ago, Christ came into the world to save us all. Here and now, I'm surrounded by the people I love. What more could I want?

They transitioned into her favorite carol. *"Silent night, holy night. All is calm, all is bright. . . ."*

Everything is calm, soothed by love that makes the world shine bright. I've done it. Jamie and me got through the fire and hard times, and now I cain make shore he's taken care of. I've got it all under control.

The circuit preacher cleared his throat from the makeshift pulpit.

"Today, on the birthday of our Savior, I'm planning to deviate from the normal Christmas service. Instead of reading the Gospel's account of Christ's birth, it's on my heart to focus on what Jesus meant to accomplish by the mortal life He took on."

What? Well, I s'pose it's all right. We cain read it together at home. I wonder what he's drivin' at?

"We're coming to the end of the year of our Lord 1874, and as another year has passed, I want each of you to think back on how you've spent your days. I'll give you a moment to think on it."

Losing a house, working hard to care for Jamie, and finding a home and mayhap even true love. Daisy couldn't help but be satisfied with her answer.

"If you're honest, you'll realize you thought of a lot of things you're proud of, and maybe a few you aren't so proud of." The preacher paused to let his words sink in. "Now don't raise your hands. This isn't between anybody but you and the Lord. How many of you thought of works you'd done?"

Of course I did. Daisy shifted restlessly. *Jamie and me's been through a lot this year, and it's taken a lot of work and determination to get through it.*

"How many of you thought about how you'd grown in your faith?" The preacher pressed on. "How you've been blessed in your walk with the Lord?"

No. I reckon I've been a mite busy of late.

"Have you been relying on yourselves and the things you do to get by, or have you put your faith in the providing hand of the Lord?"

I've been working. Iff'n it were jist me, I'd have the luxury of doin' thangs different.

336

"Well, today, on Christmas morn, I want to remind each and every person here why Christ came to earth. To save you and me and everyone who loves Him. No matter how busy we are, how much we do with the time we're given on this earth, we can't save ourselves."

A pang shot through Daisy's chest.

"We are saved through faith alone." The preacher's voice grew stronger. "Second Timothy 1:9 reminds us that Christ is He 'who hath saved us, and called us with an holy calling, not according to our works, but according to his own purpose and grace.'" The preacher laid down his Bible and faced them.

"We cannot take with us the things we work for here. We are saved through faith in the Lord Jesus Christ, who is the one and only way, truth, and life. Remember that as you go today. Put the Lord first and give Him your all. He already did as much for each of us."

Conviction surged in Daisy's breast. *I ain't been leaning on the Lord as much as I should, but I'll remember to do better in the future. I ain't even prayed about my feelings for Bryce! I've been trying to control my life when it ain't my own. I gave it to Jesus long ago, and I need to do a better job of trusting Him with it.*

Lord, I'm sorry for turning away from You. I been caught up in works and pride instead of love and faith. Thank You for all the blessings You give me—Jamie and Bryce foremost among them. Lord, I've fallen for Bryce Chance. Iff'n it be Yore will that he take me to wife, I'd be a happy woman. I leave it in Yore hands, and wait in faith for Yore will to be done. Amen.

❧

"Good sermon," Bryce commented as they made their way back home for Christmas dinner.

"Yes." Daisy's tone made him look at her. Consternation warred with relief as she spoke again. "Made me realize I been tryin' too hard to control everything in me and Jamie's lives instead of leanin' on my Lord. Somethin' that weren't pleasant to see, but I needed to face it."

"Good." Bryce smiled at her. "God made you a strong woman, Daisy, but He didn't make you to go through life alone. He's at your side every step of the way, even when you don't let Him carry some of your burden for you."

"I know." Her eyes shone with joy. "He sent you."

Bryce kissed her on the cheek. As his lips grazed her soft skin, he whispered a prayer of thanks.

Lord, that's the closest she's come to admitting she returns my feelings. Please let today show her I'm an able provider and put her fears to rest. Thank You for working in her heart so she knows she doesn't have to be strong alone.

As they gathered around the table, Bryce read Luke 2, telling of the Savior's birth: "'And, lo, the angel of the Lord. . . said unto them, Fear not: for, behold, I bring you good tidings of great joy, which shall be to all people. For unto you is born this day in the city of David a Saviour, which is Christ the Lord. And this shall be a sign unto you; Ye shall find the babe wrapped in swaddling clothes, lying in a manger.'"

The words washed over him, comforting and familiar while filling him with awe. *God gave up all His power to come to earth as a mortal child. He lived, loved, and taught the people around Him before allowing Himself to be sacrificed for us. Jesus Christ, Son of God, gave Himself to save us from our sins.*

"Lord," Logan prayed when Bryce finished the passage, "we thank You this day for coming to earth long ago as a child, living as a man, and dying for our sins. Your birth was a miracle; Your sacrifice amazes us. Having taken our sins upon Yourself, You rose again to create a place for us beside You in heaven. We thank You for all You've done for us. Amen."

As they ate the meal, Bryce drank in the love surrounding him. They came together to celebrate the Lord, and in doing so celebrated the life He'd given them. When the last dish was cleared away, they brought out the gifts, sharing with one another all Christ had given them.

Bryce watched in anticipation as everyone opened their packages.

"This is wonderful, Hattie! Thank you!" Miz Willow held up a box of fancy paper stationery. "I'll use it when we write to Lovejoy and our family at Chance Ranch."

Bryce didn't miss the sly look the old woman sent him. *Yes, Miz Willow. If I have my way, you'll be writing to Daisy and Jamie, too.*

"Look at this!" Hattie pulled on her pink dressing gown as Miz Willow opened hers. "Thankee, Bryce!"

"Thought they could come in handy," he explained.

"They should, what with folks droppin' by at all hours for the healer." Miz Willow patted the purple velvet with satisfaction. "Nice and cozy, too."

"Oh!" Daisy drew out her green dressing gown, touching the little white flowers embroidered on the collar. "How pretty!"

"Those flowers put me in mind o' daisies," Hattie praised. "What a clever gift!"

"Thankee, Bryce." Daisy's happy smile made him feel about ten feet tall.

"You're welcome, Daisy." He took the package she passed him.

"This is from me and Jamie."

"A coat!" Bryce put it on immediately. "I've been needing one of these. Now I'm glad I didn't pick one up. This is the finest coat I ever put on!" He rubbed his hand on his wool sleeve. "Nice and warm."

"I made it myself." Daisy beamed at his appreciation.

"'Ook!" Jamie lifted the pair of long underwear Daisy'd sewn him. "For sno'!"

"That's right." Daisy rumpled her son's hair affectionately. "So you have some after you play in the snow."

"Here, buddy." Bryce handed Jamie two packages, one after another.

Jamie attacked the paper, ripping it haphazardly until he uncovered a spinning top. "What is't?" He held up the toy and gave it a curious glance.

"A top." Bryce reached for it and set it on the ground. "This is how you use it." He gave the top a spin, and the brightly painted toy whirled around the floor. Nosey followed the whirling thing until it tipped over, then nudged it back to Jamie.

"Wow!" Jamie picked it up. "T'anks!"

"Go on and open the other one," Bryce urged. He grinned at Daisy as Jamie unearthed a miniature cowboy hat just like the ones he and Logan wore.

Jamie plunked it on his head. "See?" He craned his neck toward Daisy, who smiled.

"You look jist like a cowboy, Jamie."

Bryce nodded at her words. That was the whole idea. Every boy who lived on a ranch needed a cowboy hat.

❦

"Oh, Bryce." Daisy stared at the vanity set nestled in tissue paper. *How did he know I always wanted a vanity set? This one's so pretty, too. Brush, comb, mirror.* She gasped as she picked up the mirror and spotted the etching on the back. She traced the shape of a daisy with her fingertips. "It's perfect." She looked at Bryce. "Where did you ever find this?"

"Sometimes it's worth the search to find something special."

He thinks I'm special and I deserve special things. Bryce's words put a lump in her throat. *Lord, he's already given me so much.*

"This is beautiful, Daisy!" Hattie held up the long, thin piece of lace Daisy'd woven to serve as a bookmark.

"I'm glad you like it." She smiled.

"I'll use mine in my Bible." Miz Willow admired hers. "Such a fine piece of work. Little touches of beauty to enrich the heart."

Logan had gotten matching flannel nightgowns—one for his wife and one apiece for Miz Willow and Daisy. He and Hattie also gave Jamie a warm flannel nightshirt.

I have so much to be thankful for.

As the day wore on, Daisy's smile began to fade. *Is it possible to have too much to be thankful for?* Piles of presents from Bryce surrounded her. In addition to the vanity set and velvet dressing gown, she'd received no less than two pairs of gloves, a delicate cream-colored shawl, and a store-bought wool dress with green piping. She'd never owned any store-bought clothing before the cloak Bryce had given her at the beginning of the winter.

Jamie sat beside her on his brand-new beginner saddle, cowboy hat perched atop his head slightly askew as he bent over to spin his top. So many expensive things. Suddenly, Daisy remembered the combs in her hair, and the gloves and scarf Bryce had already gotten Jamie.

It's too much! I'd never be able to buy half of all this if I worked my fingers to the bones for years! Why did Bryce get so carried away? How can I let him know how I feel without angering him? He meant well, but Jamie and I aren't charity! The coat I made him seems so paltry now, and he's still wearing it as though it's the grandest thing he's ever received.

Daisy got up and busied herself with picking up bits of brown paper and twine, putting them in a bucket to burn later. Needing a moment to herself, she decided to tote Jamie's saddle to the barn.

"I'll take that." Bryce smoothly slid the saddle from her arms and walked beside her.

Daisy didn't say a word, her thoughts all a jumble.

Bryce hung the saddle on the rail beside his own and turned to her. "Something wrong? I'll be careful teaching Jamie to ride."

"It's not that—" Daisy broke off.

"What is it?" He stepped closer to rub her shoulders.

"Stop it." She backed away. "Why did you get all those thangs for us, Bryce?"

"Didn't you like them?" Consternation painted his face.

"Of course. They're all wonderful thangs, Bryce," she hastened to reassure him. "But they're so much."

"I want to give you everything in the world, Daisy." He tried to draw close again, but she put out her palm.

"We ain't charity, Bryce." Tears of frustration filled her eyes.

"I never thought you were." He held her hand, brushing his thumb across her palm. "Truth is, I want something in return." His eyes burned with meaning, sending a blaze of heat running up her spine.

"You don't buy love, Bryce." He dropped her hand like it was a hot potato, but she had to make him understand. "I never wanted yore money."

Chapter 23

Bryce stared at the woman he'd come to love so desperately, trying to understand what it was she wanted from him. *If you didn't have qualms about finances, then what—*

The only other possible explanation hit him like a punch in the gut. *She meant she can't rely on me. Won't trust me to take care of her and her son. Daisy's grown so used to making her own decisions that she won't give up control for the compromise of marriage.*

He realized Daisy was staring at him, waiting for him to explain why he'd showered her and Jamie with tokens of his love.

What do I say to her? How can I tell her what I overheard and ask her to explain? How can I not?

Bryce decided to lay it all on the line. "On the day Logan and I took Jamie sledding for the first time, I came back a little before the others." His throat grew hoarse as he told her. "I heard what you said to Miz Willow."

He watched as Daisy began turning bright pink with embarrassment.

❧

What, 'zactly, did he hear? Daisy frantically tried to remember the conversation. *Did he hear me and Miz Willow talkin' 'bout movin' to Californy? Is he angry that we even dared presume such a thang? Did he think I was trying to take advantage of his wealth?* Her heart constricted. Best to approach this with caution.

"A woman has to think about these things," she hedged. Bryce's eyes darkened further, and she swallowed. *Why cain't I say the right thang jist this once?*

"So there's no other explanation?" His voice sounded toneless, muted, and flat.

"We're courting seriously now, Bryce," Daisy begged him to understand. "It's a lot to consider. I have to think about Jamie."

"I see." A muscle in his jaw ticked. "And what did I ever do to lead you to think that?"

Oh no. He doesn't want to take me and Jamie back to Californy. It's his home. It's where he planned on going anyway, but we never talked about it. I jist assumed that's what he had in mind when he said he was goin' to court me. Her spine stiffened. *If I got that wrong, what else have I missed?*

"You said you were staying to court me." Daisy planted her hands on her hips. "You promised you'd treat Jamie as if he were yore own. What was I supposed to think?"

"That I don't make promises I can't keep." Bryce's eyes snapped blue fire at her.

"So that's why we never talked about it?" Daisy fumed. *He weren't makin' any promises on account of him not wanting to take us back to Chance Ranch. Why? Is he ashamed of us?* A chill shot down her spine. *Is he ashamed of Jamie? Is that why he don't want us to meet his kin?*

"I thought you knew!" Bryce growled. "You're a smart woman, Daisy Thales. How could you think for even a moment that I would propose marriage to a woman with a son without—"

"Without what, Bryce?" she interrupted. "Without making shore you wouldn't have to be ashamed of us in front of yore kin?" Daisy blinked back tears for the second time that day. "How could I have been so foolish? You bought all those thangs to fancy me up because I'm too plain and not book learned. You don't think me and Jamie are good enough to take to Californy!" She whirled around.

She didn't make it through the door before he grabbed her arm, forcing her to stop and face him.

"Let me go!"

"No!" he roared, pulling her closer. "Don't you understand that I've done everything I have so I wouldn't have to ever let you go?"

The anger and passion throbbing in his voice made Daisy stop trying to get away.

"What makes you think I could ever be ashamed of you? You're an amazing woman. I've pursued you every way I could think of so you'd be my wife." Bryce stopped shouting and looked at her in sorrow and disappointment. "How could you believe I'd be ashamed of you or Jamie? What? Because he can't use his legs? It doesn't matter to me, Daisy. I love Jamie like my own son."

"Then why are you so mad that Miz Willow and me talked about me and Jamie moving to Californy?" Her voice came out sounding small and sad, but she couldn't do anything about it.

Lord, I'm so confused. I hurt. Please holp me.

"What?" Bryce's brow knit in confusion. "I heard you say something else." He took a deep breath as though about to repeat something painful. "You told Miz Willow you couldn't rely on me to provide for you and Jamie."

"I never—" Daisy broke off as she recalled the very end of that conversation. "No. I didn't mean them words. You—"

"Heard them." Bryce stated flatly, cutting her off. "I thought you meant you weren't sure I had the money."

That's why he bought all those thangs—he was tryin' to prove he was a good provider! Daisy felt the faint stirrings of hope.

"Bryce, I know you're a good provider and a fine man. I seen you work with my own two eyes!"

"And now I know you don't 'want my money.'" Bryce's eyes glinted in pain. "I know that you weren't talking about how you thought I didn't have the means to support you."

"No! I never thought that at all!" Daisy argued excitedly.

"So you meant you couldn't trust me." Bryce shook his head. "If you don't believe me when I tell you I want to take care of you and Jamie," Bryce kept speaking as he pushed past her, "then there's nothing left to say."

Bryce stopped in midstep as Daisy grabbed him by the back of the collar.

"Yore not goin' another step till I've had my say." Her fury all but steamed out of her as he turned around.

"Fine." He crossed his arms in front of his chest and waited. *But we both know there's nothing you can tell me that'll change the problem.* His heart ached. *You're still not willing to share your life. Daisy, you won't even give control over to the Lord. So long as you rely on yourself, we're not spiritually suited. It's over.*

"You cain't jist catch the tail end of a conversation and assume you know all there is to know." Daisy put her fisted hands on her hips and stared up at him. "For yore information, Miz Willow had said summat about how well-off you and Logan was, and how you'd take care of me and Jamie. What you heard me say was the end of my response."

Bryce listened closely as Daisy gave a deep sigh. "I tole her that a roof ain't no reason to marry up. Iff'n we got married, it would be for love and nothin' else. Jamie's my responsibility, and I wouldn't marry you to ease my load."

Bryce took a moment to realize what she meant. *She doesn't want me for my money. It's not that she doesn't trust me. She just wanted to enter into the courtship with a pure heart so love could grow. How could I have been so wrong?*

"Daisy!" He enveloped her in his arms and clung tight. "I misunderstood."

"It's all right." She wiped her teary eyes. "Yore not the only one guilty of that."

"I thought you were still relying on yourself for everything, not giving control to God."

"I meant what I said this mornin', Bryce," Daisy spoke earnestly. "I've been wrapped up in my own works, and that cain't stand. Now I'm willing to trust in God's will."

"That's a big step." Bryce stroked her hair.

"And even though we misunderstood one another, I trust you, Bryce. I know I cain rely on you."

Bryce tipped her chin up and gave her a kiss. "Then I can't think of anything that could stand between us."

Bryce hoisted Jamie up into the saddle, then looped a length of rope around the boy and secured the other end to the pommel. "This'll help keep you on her back," he explained. "Now hold onto the pommel—this knobby thing on your saddle—with both hands while I adjust your stirrups."

Winter's snowstorms hadn't abated, so they'd only go up and down the barn a few times. Perfect for Jamie's first riding lesson.

"Now take your right hand and grab the reins," Bryce instructed, making certain Jamie had a good grip on both the reins and the pommel. "When you want to go forward, flick this up and down, leaning forward just a little. When you need to stop, you pull back. Remember to be gentle so you don't hurt your mount." Bryce went to the horse's head and took hold of the halter to guide her. "Ready?"

"Ready!" Jamie leaned forward and shook the reins. The horse took a few steps forward, ambling slowly.

Bryce watched Jamie hold on tight as the horse swayed side to side while moving straight ahead. "You're doing fine, buddy," Bryce called. "This is what we call a walk. When you've had some more practice, and we have you outside where there's enough room, we'll move up to a trot."

"What t'ot?" Jamie asked, yanking back the reins as they came to the end of the barn.

"Gentle, remember?" Bryce gave a quick reminder on how to pull to a stop without hurting the horse. "A trot is a fast walk. You know how you're shifting a little from side to side as you go forward?" He waited for Jamie's nod to continue the lesson. "When you go faster, in a trot, you'll go up and down a bit, too."

"Oh." Jamie nodded solemnly. The little boy concentrated hard as they went up and down the barn a few more times.

Bryce waited until after they'd seen to the horse and gotten it settled back in its stall. Then he brought up the subject he'd been biding his time for.

"Jamie?"

"Yep?"

"You know that I like your ma, right?"

"She 'ike you, too." Jamie nodded, eyes big.

"And we both like you." Bryce tickled Jamie's tummy, making the little boy squeal with laughter.

"I live in California," Bryce continued. "I was wondering if you and your ma might go back with me."

"Cal'fa?" Jamie struggled with the state name. "Wher'?"

"A long ways away. That's why I want you and your ma to come with me," Bryce explained. "It's the only way I'll see you anymore."

"Don' go," Jamie instructed. "Stay."

"I have to go back. My family and my home are out there. If you and your mama were there, too, I wouldn't be missing anything. We'd all be together, and you could meet my nieces and nephews. Some of them are about your age, so you could play together."

Jamie frowned as he pondered this. "Wiwwo?"

"Miz Willow would stay here," Bryce answered honestly.

"Oh." Jamie scrunched up his face. "Why me an' Ma go?"

"I want your permission to ask your mama to marry me. She'd be my wife, nd then you'd be my son. I'd be your second pa." Bryce held his breath and aited for the answer. He wanted to have Jamie's agreement before he proposed Daisy. They were supposed to become a family.

"Pa?" Jamie's eyes lit up, and his face broke into a grin.

"So I can ask your mama to marry me, and we can all go to California?" ryce asked.

" 'Es!"

"Good, because I need your help."

❧

Where's Bryce?" Daisy kept looking at the door every few minutes. "He was nly going to put away the sled."

"Jamie and I'll go check up on him." Logan stood up importantly, picked amie up, and tromped out the door.

When Logan and Jamie didn't come back, either, Hattie and Daisy put on heir cloaks to see what was going on.

"Jamie!" Daisy called. "Bryce?"

"Over here!" She and Hattie walked around the barn, following the voice.

"Stay right there!" Logan ordered.

"What's—" Daisy's words were cut off by a mighty *whoosh* as a sled came ying down the snowbank, stopping less than two feet from where she stood.

"Hi!" Jamie, all bundled up in his scarf and cowboy hat, waved his arms from here he sat, sandwiched in front of Bryce on the biggest sled Daisy had ever lapped eyes on.

"We've got a good team going here." Bryce grinned at her. "But I think we've ot room for one more."

"I'm not getting on that thing!" Daisy refused. "No matter how much room s on it!"

"Well, not until we get it to the top of the hill, at least." Bryce handed Jamie her. "Meet me at the top."

Left with no choice, Daisy trudged up the snowy hill. "Bryce, I. . ." The ords died in her throat as she looked around her.

"Surprise!" Jamie clapped excitedly as Daisy walked over to the sight be-ore her.

A blue tablecloth covered an old tree stump. Bryce stood beside it, taking er hand and helping her step over the roots. He helped her sit down, Jamie esting on her lap.

"What are you up to, Bryce Chance?" she asked.

"We're waiting for a friend." Bryce pointed over to where Nosey trundled hrough the snow, determined to reach Jamie. When the dog, no longer a tiny uppy, reached them, Bryce picked her up.

"Nosey has something for you." He held the growing puppy up, and whe Daisy reached out to pet the animal, she noticed a piece of twine tied aroun Nosey's neck.

"What's this?" She fingered the thick string. Nosey didn't need a collar, sin she hardly ever left Jamie's side.

"Pull it in and find out," Bryce prompted. Daisy grabbed the long end of th string and began pulling.

And pulling, and pulling. Jamie giggled with glee as she brought up mo and more twine. *What have they got on the end of this thang?*

Daisy gasped as she caught sight of the sparkling ring. Nosey snuffled he hand in wet encouragement as Daisy grabbed it.

"Daisy." Bryce dropped to one knee, still holding Nosey under one arn "We've got quite a little group here. I've spoken with Jamie man-to-man an gotten his blessing to ask you something." He reached for her left hand, lookin deep into her eyes. "Will you be my wife and make us a family?"

Daisy could only nod while Bryce slid the engagement band onto her finge "Yes!" She finally managed. She stood up, and Bryce gathered her and Jamie int his warm embrace. *I might not stay in Salt Lick Holler*, Daisy knew, *but I've four my home.*

⁂

"Got a surprise for you two back at the cabin," Logan announced a few minut later as he rocked back and forth on the balls of his feet.

"Oh?" Bryce wondered what his brother'd done this time.

"When you told me how you'd be proposing, I made a few arrangements my own." Logan grimaced as Hattie elbowed him in the ribs. "*We* made a fe arrangements."

They all marched back to the cabin, Daisy shooting Bryce quizzical looks.

"I have no idea what they've planned." Bryce squeezed her hand.

"Preacher Jacobs!" Daisy's gasp told Bryce what was afoot. Logan and Hatt had made arrangements for the preacher to stop by while he was still in town.

"Are you ready for this, Daisy?" Bryce cupped her face in his palms. "We ca wait if you want."

"Why wait?" Daisy's eyes sparkled up at him. "I love you and want to b yore wife."

His heart soared at her decision. "Let's be wed now then."

"Not quite yet." Miz Willow shooed Hattie and Daisy into the adjoinin room. "You have to give the bride a moment to ready herself."

Bryce waited with Logan, Jamie, and the preacher.

"What's taking so long?" Logan paced around the cabin impatiently. An stranger would've thought he was the one getting married.

"Hold still," Bryce ordered. "Daisy's worth the wait." *Always has been.*

She stepped out of the room in her green-striped wool dress, one of he elicate lace collars framing her face. She wore the gloves and hair combs he'd iven her, too. Bryce swelled with pride at the sight of her.

He scarcely heard the words spoken by the preacher, although he knew the ows by heart. When the time came for him to pledge his love, his voice sounded ruff to his own ears.

"With this ring, I thee wed." Daisy sounded ethereal, like sunshine dancing n the grass.

"I now pronounce you man and wife," the preacher intoned grandly. "You 1ay—"

Bryce kissed his bride.

⟿⟾

Good-bye, dearie." Miz Willow gave Jamie and Daisy one final hug. The snow ad cleared enough for them to travel back to Chance Ranch.

" 'Bye!" Jamie chirped. He patted his cowboy hat more firmly in place. 'Bye!"

Hattie stood on tiptoe to give Bryce a farewell hug. "I know you'll take good are of them," she whispered to him. "Give my love to Lovejoy."

"I'll be sure to," Bryce pledged. He turned as Logan slapped him on the back.

"Can't believe you're going." Bryce's younger brother shook his head. "Tell verybody I miss them, but I'm happy." Logan stopped to smile at Hattie. Thanks for coming to Salt Lick with me, Bryce." Logan gave him a quick nod efore almost cracking Bryce's back in a big bear hug. "Be happy."

"I will." Bryce smiled at Daisy and Jamie. "I will." After their final good-yes, they boarded the train and leaned out the windows to wave as Hawk's Fall, ogan, Hattie, and Miz Willow faded out of sight.

"I'm going to miss them." Daisy sniffed.

"I know." Bryce slung an arm around her shoulder and rubbed her arm. "Me, oo. But you're going to have a whole army of people waiting to meet you back t Chance Ranch."

"That reminds me." Daisy nestled Jamie into the seat next to her. "I still on't know their names."

"Well, I'll run through them with you. You won't be able to call my brothers y name until you've been around them awhile. We all look a lot alike." Bryce ubbed his jaw.

"No, you don't," Daisy said loyally. "I could tell you and Logan apart the first me I met you."

"I appreciate that I caught your eye right off the bat," Bryce teased, "but it von't be so easy when there are five Chance brothers around. I had to come clear o Kentucky to catch your eye."

"You'll always hold my attention, no matter how many relations are on that anch of yores." Daisy laid a hand on his chest. "I've already got me the Chance f a lifetime."

KELLY EILEEN HAKE

Kelly is the daughter of Cathy Marie Hake, and she lives in southern Californi Kelly Eileen is pursuing an English degree to share her passions with a ne generation.

A Letter to Our Readers

Dear Readers:

In order that we might better contribute to your reading enjoyment, we would appreciate your taking a few minutes to respond to the following questions. When completed, please return to the following: Fiction Editor, Barbour Publishing, Inc., P.O. Box 719, Uhrichsville, OH 44683.

1. Did you enjoy reading *Kentucky Chances*?
   ❑ Very much—I would like to see more books like this.
   ❑ Moderately—I would have enjoyed it more if _____

   _____

   _____

2. What influenced your decision to purchase this book?
   (Check those that apply.)
   ❑ Cover   ❑ Back cover copy   ❑ Title   ❑ Price
   ❑ Friends   ❑ Publicity   ❑ Other

3. Which story was your favorite?
   ❑ *Last Chance*   ❑ *Chance of a Lifetime*
   ❑ *Chance Adventure*

4. Please check your age range:
   ❑ Under 18   ❑ 18–24   ❑ 25–34
   ❑ 35–45   ❑ 46–55   ❑ Over 55

5. How many hours per week do you read? _____

Name _____

Occupation _____

Address _____

City_____ State _____ Zip _____

E-mail_____

If you enjoyed

Kentucky CHANCES

then read:

California CHANCES

*Three Brothers Play
the Role of Protector
as Romance Develops*

One Chance in a Million by Cathy Marie Hake
Second Chance by Tracey Bateman
Taking a Chance by Kelly Eileen Hake

If you enjoyed

Kentucky CHANCES

then read:

SAN DIEGO

Four Sun-Kissed Romances

Love Is Patient by Cathy Marie Hake
Love Is Kind by Joyce Livingston
Love Worth Finding by Cathy Marie Hake
Love Worth Keeping by Joyce Livingston